The Light Between Us

Nick Farrant

For my grandfather, Craig Cartwright. I did what you told me and just kept writing.

CONTENTS

ACKNOWLEDGEMENTS

No author writes a book alone, and this one is no exception. A big thank you to the friends and family who endured endless tirades about UFOs, writer's angst, and my otherwise paranoid ramblings. A special thank you to my mother, Jan, who is and will always be my favorite beta reader. Another big thanks to my editor Barbara Nessinger, who helped mold this story into a shape I can be proud of. Matthew Revert, who created the cover art for this book. And a final thanks to you, the reader, who took a chance on a strange little story about UFOs, telepaths, and love.

Love most of all.

1

LAST NIGHT ON MOUNT OLYMPUS

I lay in my crib and listened to the high mountain wind buffet against the rough wooden walls of the cabin and the muted arguments of my parents in the next room. I couldn't hear their words – wouldn't have made a difference if I could, as I couldn't yet speak. But I could read their emotions, like pulsing waves of midnight black water, washing over me, into me.

Daddy was torn. Love warred bitterly with obligation inside his heart. Inside my Mommy, love had burst aflame into rage, then to obduracy. I felt their emotions collide into each other, fight, grow louder and more out of control, all while the hard whispers in the next room evolved into grumbling shouts of frustration. And beneath it all was fear. A fear so deep and intense it felt like tar flowing down my throat, choking me.

I squeezed my eyes shut, trying to shut out the sensations but not knowing how. The storm of their conflict left me disoriented, filled my head with painful thoughts too large for me to understand. I began to thrash, then to cry, a ringing pain growing in my head with each barbed word they flung at each other. Eventually, their shouts turned to screams, someone hit something, the dull smack of flesh against wood.

I wanted Mommy and Daddy to stop. I wanted my Mommy to come and hold me, feed me and make the bad feelings go away. So I screamed, louder and louder, pushing every note until my little lungs burned and the coppery taste of blood flecked the back of my tongue. Then, suddenly, I opened my eyes and they were there.

Mommy looked down at me, her wide, mud brown eyes hidden behind a curtain of blonde hair. She had a narrow, hawkish face and a long neck, like a stork. Daddy, by comparison, was slighter, narrower across the shoulders, with short wavy black hair and eyes just like mine, a deep, unnatural blue.

Mommy picked me up, tucked me into the crook of her arm, and said something to Daddy, who slipped from the room. Then she was talking to me, holding me up to her eye level, her voice soft and loving. Her words were meaningless, but I could read her intention.

She loved me. She was going to keep me safe. Things would be very scary, very soon.

She took me from the nursery, and everything began to happen very fast. Images seared into the darkest corner of my mind as a series of snapshots. My daddy in the kitchen, shoving mason jars full of preserves into a bag. My Mommy clutching me as we slipped out into the rain. Hiding behind the outhouses while we waited for a patrol of sentries to pass, skittering by on their strange, elongated limbs. An old, rusted sedan, hidden beneath a tarp. The sound of the engine rumbling to life. Then my Mommy's scream, her face contorted in panic as she pointed towards the rearview mirror. The image of a dozen pairs of glowing eyes, chasing our car down the one road off Mount Olympus.

More screaming, shouting. I started to wail again and my Mommy pressed me to her breast. The car jerked and skidded along slick mountain roads, my terrified heartbeat joined my mother's like the bellowing of some great drum. Daddy touched the side of his head, looking pained, and said something to my Mommy before the car screeched to a stop. Suddenly Mommy was shouting at him, slapping at his shoulder with tears in her eyes. Then, I felt it too.

A hand clasped down over my mind. I felt someone pulling me open, peering inside at the strange little dreams of infants. Then, I heard a voice that spoke not in words but in meaning, a sudden understanding.

Turn back. End this foolishness and come home. She isn't worth it.

The words were meant for Daddy, and they came with images: of Daddy and me sitting at the dinner table beside granddaddy, all smiling and laughing.

I will find you, the message said. And then you will be sorry.

Then, an image of Mommy, hanging from a tree with black holes where her eyes had been.

Daddy recoiled, then looked at Mommy. He whispered something to her, then kissed her forehead. She shook her head, sobbing, clinging to his shirt. He pulled away all the same. Then, he looked at me, eyes swimming with love and a fierce determination. He said something to me that felt like goodbye and I wailed, reaching for him with stubby little fingers.

Daddy, Daddy no, don't go, no.

He reached to me and stroked the top of my head, smiling sadly. Then, he sent me a thought, one filled with warmth, love and a pain that rattled my heart.

I love you. I'm sorry. Please, forget me.

I felt his hand inside my mind, encircling my thoughts, squeezing them into a cage. In an instant I could no longer feel his emotions, couldn't sense the raw animal hunger in those who chased us. My mind had become a black box where it had once been a window. I screamed, thrashing in my mother's arms, suffocated.

Then he was gone, jumping from the driver's side seat and running back up the road the way we had come. A moment later, I was jammed into the car seat in the back, Mommy got behind the wheel, and we were moving again. Facing the rear window, I watched the shadowy figure of my daddy running up the road, towards the glittering sea of blue eyes that soon enveloped him.

We made it off the mountain, off the dirt roads and onto ones made from smooth asphalt. I watched the rhythmic waves of passing highway lights wash

2

over me. Soon, my throat hoarse, I stopped crying. Soon, I slept. And when I woke, I had done exactly what Daddy told me to do and forgotten him entirely.

2

THE LITTLE RED HOUSE ON STRAWBERRY LANE

1 - Jacob

"Dude, just eat the goddamn carrots," I muttered, wiping orange sludge from my face. Wendy slapped her little fists against the table attached to her highchair, splattering more pureed baby goop across the walls and the front of my shirt.

"You have to make the train noise," Hannah said from the other room. "She likes the train, not the plane."

"You are supposed to be napping," I called, scooping another heap of mashed carrot onto a spoon. "I got this handled."

Hannah appeared in the doorway to our little kitchen, her large eyes catching the light from the window and sparkling like pale sapphires. She was still in her gardening clothes, a pair of mud-stained capris and a tank top made from one of my old Metallica shirts.

"I would sleep better if our little monster ate something," she sniffed the air. "Is that the carrot?"

I nodded. "Yeah, she usually loves the carrot."

"She did last week," Hannah walked past me and reached into the pantry, scanning the row of miniature jars until she found what she was looking for. Then, she plucked the carrot goop from my hand and replaced it with one of apple goop. "Now, it's apples. She doesn't hate the strawberry-pear one, but she usually gets sick of it halfway through. And don't even try with the pumpkin, she'll go on the war path."

"We living in fear of our own child now?" I unscrewed the cap and spooned out a heaping pile of mush.

Hannah snorted in amusement. "Only if we know what's good for us."

I waved the spoonful tantalizingly before Wendy's nose, who watched it with all the rapt attention of a cat watching a bird. "Is this what you want, princess?" I cooed, "Come on, open wide."

Yet Wendy's lips remained firmly shut.

"Choo choo," Hannah coached, leaning against the counter, jar still in hand, idly scooping out small bits of pureed carrot with her finger.

I sighed, feeling only slightly ridiculous as I waved the spoon through the air, making chugging sounds. "Here comes the train, choo choo." This time Wendy opened her mouth wide and clamped down on the spoon, leaving only one small chunk of apple that escaped her lips and rolled down her pudgy little face. Then she reached out towards the jar with both hands, grabbing at the empty air.

"See," Hannah teased, "was that so hard?"

"Nah," I said, scooping out another tiny mouthful and repeating the process. "Only thing it hurt was my pride."

I felt her hands creep over my shoulder, idly working at the dense knots she found there. "Don't worry, tough guy. I won't tell anyone."

"Damn straight. Gotta keep my cred."

"For sure, how else are we going to keep this family safe with all the street gangs in the area. The Rascal Gang claimed turf over at the Piggly Wiggly. I had to duck into frozen foods to escape getting my ass beat."

"Want me to go over there, set 'em straight?" The Rascal Gang was our nickname for the trio of widows who cruised around town on motorized scooters. They seemed to have the opinion that the sidewalks belonged to them. Best I could tell, there wasn't a soul in Victor's Point who hadn't experienced at least one mildly bruised shin from their "road" rage.

"Don't be a fool," she said, voice thick with mock horror as she ran her fingers over my scalp. "They would eat you alive and send us the bones when they were done."

I managed to get another bite into Wendy's mouth. "Good point. Guess we will just have to keep living in fear."

"Board the windows."

"Lock the doors."

"And don't let the Avon Ladies in."

Once feeding time concluded, Hannah put Wendy down for a nap and then, luring me one come hither finger at a time, invited me to take a shower with her. After it was done, and we were scrubbed pink, I carried her to the bedroom where our bodies found each other in the gloom of our cluttered bedroom.

After, we lay side by side, covered in a thin veneer of sweat and listening to bird song outside the window. It wasn't long until I noticed Hannah was snoring, her short black hair draped over her eyes. I rolled onto my hip and watched the slow rise and fall of her chest. How the hell had I ever gotten this lucky?

I was an OK-looking guy by Viking standards. Tall, broad, with a bald head and a full red beard that had sprung into existence the moment I turned fourteen. However, I had a thuggish face, my square nose mushed down from ten too many beatings, my lips bearing thin white scars where they had been split. Evidence of a life of violence that would never go away, no matter how well I played homemaker.

Hannah, by contrast, was like a living painting. One of those old ones where the women have skin like alabaster, eyes like gemstones, and the artist has some incomprehensible Italian name. Eyes too big, smiles too gentle, with the grace of birds. Hooking up with me was, as one of her former friends had said, "like an angel slumming it with an ogre."

I let Hannah sleep, slipping from bed and searching the hamper for a clean-ish pair of jeans. Wendy had only been two months old when we settled in Victor's Point. Since moving in, she hadn't slept more than an hour a night. She would nap just fine during the day, sometimes all day, but the moment the sun dipped beneath the horizon she came alive. For the first two weeks, neither of us slept a wink, taking turns rocking her, feeding her, changing her, and exhausting every clever little trick the internet had to provide short of drugging her. Eventually, I nearly nodded off at work in the middle of giving a trucker a new tattoo of his girlfriend's tits.

After that, we came to an agreement. Hannah would sleep during the day, whenever she could, while I would stuff a couple of ear plugs in and try to sleep at night. My job was the only lifeline we had. If I lost it, we would have no choice but to sell the house we had sunk our life savings into and move back to some roach-infested trailer in Echo City.

I padded down the hall, thinking that I might take a crack at fixing the wobbly porch railing. Hannah had been asking me to do it for weeks, but I had been pulling extra hours at Astrological and this was my first full day off since I could remember. I collected my toolbox from the spare bedroom, empty save for the few boxes of stuff we had managed to grab before fleeing town.

Our home was one of the oldest in Victor's Point and had been left empty for three years before we showed up. Back then the house had been painted a bright red, which had now faded to a mottled pink that was engaged in the slow process of peeling away from the siding, like a massive lizard molting in the sun. The yard was a mess as well, filled with tangling roots and thorny weeds. Only the flower beds had been wrestled into some semblance of order, now planted with a riot of different colored flowers and long rows of vegetables. That was Hannah's domain. Mine was supposed to be fixing up the inside, a job I was growing more and more sure I was ill-prepared for.

My grandfather had been a carpenter and while I hadn't followed in his footsteps, I knew a little and figured I could learn what I didn't know off YouTube. The basic idea had been to fix the place up, flip the house, and then use the profits to move to Portland, Seattle, or any of those trendy, new age cities where young couples could begin building their lives in earnest. I could work at some hipster tattoo shop, and Hannah would get a job at a botanical garden, or a greenhouse. It was the life I had promised her when I dropped to my knee in a glass-strewn parking lot and begged her to be my wife. The promise we talked about for hours each night, laying side by side and picturing the future. A promise that had been put on indefinite delay the moment the pregnancy test came back positive.

"Those places will still be there when we can afford it," Hannah had said, stroking her still flat belly. "For now, everything is for the baby."

"Are you disappointed?" I asked her.

"No," she answered without pause, smiling wide, a slash of white teeth in the dark bedroom. "A house is a house. Here, there, we'll make paradise where we find it." I believed her. That night though, as I tried and failed to sleep, I felt her slip from the bed into the bathroom. There I heard her sniffling softly as she mourned the death of a pleasant dream.

Back in the present, I made my way outside, summer heat prickling my skin. I opened the music app on my phone, selected a playlist. As the first wail of an electric guitar shredded out of the speaker, I nodded approvingly and set to work on the railing, tightening screws and hunting out rotten pillars, losing myself to the work and riding the waves of a rare, good, day and hoping to keep the party going.

Soon enough, though, my own muttered curse words joined the mix every time a water-rotted board dissolved in my hands, or the head of a rusted screw broke off under my clumsy ministrations. Eventually I found myself trying to dislodge a corner support post, first prying at it with a crowbar, then pushing and eventually kicking it when the stubborn bastard wouldn't give.

I was so absorbed that I didn't hear the approach of the stranger until his shadow fell over me, blotting out the July heat.

"Hey, hey." It was a man's voice, friendly and oddly high-pitched. "Working on some home improvement?"

I stood a little too suddenly, rising a full foot and a half taller than the man, unconsciously white knuckling the hammer in my hand.

The man looked like Elmer Fudd. He was older, just a few strands of wiry white hair stuck to the sides of his polished dome, as if they'd been glued there. He wore a faded red flannel shirt, the buttons pulled taut where they stretched over the girth of his belly. It was his smile, though, that I noticed first. Big and open, like a kid's.

"Whoa!" he said, holding his hands up in mock surrender. "Don't shoot, just a neighbor coming to say hello."

I glanced at the road and noticed an old Ford pickup parked on the dirt path that ran the course between the town's crumbling downtown and the more reclusive homes farther up in the hills. It was an old diesel chugger from the 50's, yet looked practically new, its bright red hood gleaming. How the hell had I not heard the damn thing rumble up the road? And that smile. Too open, too happy. Nobody was that happy. It had to be a trick, the old paranoid pit fighter inside me insisted. Unconsciously I gripped the hammer tighter before I caught myself and took two even breaths just like Hannah taught me. Serenity in, rage out. This wasn't Echo City, and I wasn't that guy anymore.

He's just a friendly neighbor, I told myself. No sooner had the thought entered my head when I felt a wave of calm sweep over me.

"Sorry," I replied sheepishly, hooking the hammer into my belt and approaching him, holding out my hand. "We haven't had many visitors, caught me with my pants down."

7

His smile returned, a Santa Claus twinkle in his eye. When he shook my hand, his skin was hot to the touch, like he'd just crawled out of a bath. "Big guy like you, I wouldn't think you have much to worry about."

"Big guy, bigger worries," I said, one of my grandfather's old jokes. "And you are?"

The stranger looked momentarily aghast. "Oh, where are my damn manners. Name is Friend, Gaylord Friend."

I blinked at him, sure that nobody on earth had ever had the audacity to name their child Gay Friend. "I'm Jacob Riley," I said, suppressing the snickering of my inner thirteen-year-old. "You live around here?"

"Yes sir, yes sir. Got a little retirement cabin up in the hills. Eighteen acres of peace and quiet, just as the Lord intended. Forgive me for prying, but I was just heading to town, and I saw you on the porch out here and thought I should do my neighborly duty. Did you know old Nancy?"

It took me a moment to place the name – Nancy Bowland, the librarian who had owned the house before us. "No, she passed before we moved in. My wife and I are from Echo City. We've only been here a few months." And before that, ten months in a never-ending carousel of cheap motels and uncomfortable nights sleeping in parking lots.

Mr. Friend tucked his thumbs into the pockets of his jeans. "That's south of here, right? I think I drove through it a while back. Don't remember much beyond a whole lot of corn."

"That's because there ain't much more than corn, meth, and soybeans."

Mr. Friend nodded. "Why here?" he asked. "Feel free to tell me to buzz off, but there ain't much reason to move to Victor's Point these days, since the mines closed up."

"Just had to get away," I said immediately. "Start fresh, you know how it goes."

"Fleeing the in-laws or just the law?"

"Neither. We're fleeing the corn," I lied.

Mr. Friend barked out a laugh like a cannon shot. It was an infectious sound; I couldn't help but chuckle. "Well then, allow me to personally congratulate you on your emancipation. Now," he said, eyeing the banister, "it's been a bit since I've swung a hammer, but this looks like a job meant for two. Need a hand?"

I looked down at the railing which looked worse now than when I had begun, half of it sagging and threatening to fall off the porch entirely. "Oh, all I can get."

Friend, already unbuttoning his cuffs and rolling up his sleeves, chuckled, "Well then ask and you shall receive. Just don't go asking me to lift anything bigger than a breadbox. Got a back more twisted than a politician's conscience."

With Mr. Friend's help, the railing was intact and stable as stone by the time Hannah and Wendy woke. Mr. Friend was no carpenter, but he had built his own cabin and, in his own words claimed to 'dabble a little.' His 'dabbling' proved to be far superior to my YouTube education and soon enough, the work took on the tone of a lesson as he walked me through each step, a broad smile breaking over his face every time I managed to get it right. We sipped cold beers and listened to classic rock, speaking little.

When the job was done, my earlier suspicions about the man had been laid to rest and I began to dare think I had made a friend. He stood, dabbing his brow with a handkerchief and smiling appraisingly at our work. "The good grace of a job well done. You're strong as a bear. Remind me to get your help next time I need to chop firewood."

"I'd be happy to," I offered my hand again. "Thank you for the help. I think I would have been sunk if you hadn't shown up."

He shook my hand. "On the wings of providence, the good Lord delivered me where I was needed." Inside, Wendy let out her opening shot in today's war on night, a low cry that soon turned into a bellowing scream. "And that, I believe, is my cue."

"Sure you don't want to hang around? I'm sure Hannah would be happy to meet you."

He waved me off. "I got to get home to the grandkids. They get downright ferocious when dinner is late. Don't you worry," he said as he turned and started the march towards his truck, "a good neighbor is a treasure, and you don't throw away treasure. I'm sure I'll be by again."

I waved as he went, then watched as his truck rumbled to life and sped off on the long dirt road in front of our house, headed up into the hills. After he was gone, I lingered a moment longer, eyeing the distant peaks of the Appalachian Mountains, rounded and weathered like the molars of giants, wondering which one Friend called home. Above one, the tallest in sight from our porch, the first star of evening blazed in the plum-colored sky. And as I looked at it, the strangest sensation came over me. As if, on some level, I felt it looking back.

Hannah called from inside and the feeling passed. I went to her, falling into the familiar motions of diaper-changes, feedings, and the ironclad promises that held it all together.

2

Astrological was one of the few actual storefronts left in what used to be downtown. The tiny tattoo parlor was nestled between the only pharmacy in Victor's Point and the Showtime Movie Theater, a small two-screen affair which, by the looks of it, went out of business at some point in the past three decades and had been left to rot. The marquee still had a few letters clinging to it, the rest having fallen or been stolen at some point, leaving only the message: "Going Bank- End- Goodbye."

The first time I saw the shop, answering Tracy Newland's ad in the *Victor's Point Journal*, I thought it had shut down, too. Two front windows, one cracked, flanked a rusted steel door that squealed on its hinges when opened. The interior was only marginally better, the white and black checkered tile floor kept clean save for where dust collected in the corners. At one time, it had been a barber shop. Hell, it still almost looked like one, as Tracy had elected to re-use the old barber's chairs for her clients. Two of them were still bolted to the floor where they had been since 1952, sitting alongside a more modern massage table that I had goaded her into buying secondhand.

"About damn time you showed up," Tracy griped as I entered, just as she had every day I had worked in the past two months. It didn't matter that I was ten minutes early. I think it was her way of keeping me on my toes. Or maybe she just thought I should live for the shop like she did.

Tracy was a four-pack-a-day kind of gal, who cut her teeth throwing bricks at cops back in the 70s. Now in her late sixties, she still dressed like the punk she was at heart, wearing her favorite denim vest, covered in anti-government patches and cartoon skeletons. She kept her turquoise-dyed hair cut short, her ears were even gauged out further than I had ever dared. It was her tattoos, though, that caught everyone's eye. One arm bore the massive image of Christ on the cross, his face twisted with anguish, a Roman centurion's spear in his side. The other arm was filled with cackling devils in a hundred shades of red, a black-winged angel looming over them with eyes like burning coals.

"Shift doesn't start for," I checked my watch, "thirteen minutes. But if you would like, I can clock in early and start to work on all these customers." Besides the two of us, the place was empty. Usually was. Every day or so we would get a couple locals, usually teens, but business wasn't exactly steady.

She narrowed her eyes at me. "You know, you aren't a funny man."

"Guess I'll have to get by on my looks." I moved past her towards my station and began to unpack my kit.

She snorted, "Ugly *and* stupid, why the hell did I hire you?"

"I'm cheap," I answered, and that was true. I had been inking skin since I was thirteen when my older brother, Hank, shoved a tattoo needle into my hands and told me he wanted a big smiley sun on his back. What he got looked more like a sad beach ball and gave him a nasty infection. What I got was an obsession. I read every back issue of *Inked* I could get my hands on, perused artist portfolios online, and spent days on YouTube learning from "the masters." The summer of my fifteenth birthday, I spent three straight months prowling the streets of Echo City in search of soda cans and discarded scrap steel until I had enough cash to buy a second-hand tattoo gun off Craigslist. I practiced on pig skin from the butcher, and then later my brother's friends. Soon enough, I was better than most of the guys in any of our local tattoo parlors and built my own little collection of customers. Sadly, tattooing meth heads in a trailer park isn't the kind of experience you put on a resume, which was how Tracy justified paying me as an apprentice.

I finished setting up my station, going through the usual movements of my own little ritual, ending as I always did, eyes closed, breathing deep, finding my center.

"You ever seen a UFO?"

I opened my eyes to see Tracy was still staring at me, the question so unexpected it scattered my calm like wind through a cloud of gnats.

"I'm sorry, what?"

Tracy rolled her eyes. "A UFO. You know, flying saucers, little green men, all that. You ever seen one?"

I leveled a steady stare at her, searching her eyes for the telltale signs of someone strung out on powerful psychedelics, but she met my gaze just fine, eyes sober and withering as always. "Uhhh, no? I don't think so. Why?"

"I have." There was a casualness to the way she said it, as if it was the most normal thing in the world. "Summer after high school me and some friends got in a car and headed west. Camped out in the Badlands. Third night there, we're laying on the ground, looking up at the stars, when I notice one of them is wiggling." She held up her pointer finger and wiggled it from side to side. "Then it starts moving, zipping around so goddamn fast."

"You sure it wasn't a plane, or a satellite?"

She glared and shook her head. "You think I'm stupid?" Then, not giving me a chance to answer, she continued, "It was moving too fast, turning too sharp for any of that. Eventually it went sailing over the hills and vanished. Was the damnedest thing."

"Ok," I said slowly, still confused. "What brings this up?"

She reached behind her and slid a thin newspaper off the counter, passing it to me. It was the *Victor's Point Journal*, this week's issue, the front page showing a red-faced man wearing a Budweiser baseball cap and pointing to the sky. The headline, written in bold across the top of the page, read, "Westvale Knows What He Saw!" I scanned the article. According to the author, last night a Victor's Point man named Herbert Westvale was out touring his property when he noticed a mysterious light hovering in the sky that seemed to follow him wherever he went. His dogs noticed it too and acted "real strange," barking and crying at the sight of it and apparently pissing themselves. Westvale, thinking it was a drone, went and got his rifle. Looking at the object through the scope, he reported that it was not a drone but in fact "a miniature sun." The object then zipped up into the sky and took off before he could shoot.

No other witnesses, no physical damage, just the kind of tall tale bullshit that qualified as front-page news in a town of 200. "Some local farmer got drunk and tried to shoot at an airplane, so what?"

She snatched the paper from my hand, "So what? Don't you think it's at least a little interesting?"

"Not really. Do you?"

She shrugged, eyeing the paper. "My son Carl is obsessed. Says we should watch for more sightings around here. He said they come in waves sometimes."

"I'll make sure to keep my blurriest camera on me," I said dryly, turning my attention back to my preparations.

Tracy scowled but let the issue drop. Instead, she began to ask me about Wendy, Hannah, and our house. Within the hour, a young couple came in to get matching tattoos and I lost myself to the comfortable buzzing of the needle in my hand.

I took my lunch at Ernie's, the only local diner left in town. The rest had gone with the majority of the population when the mines started closing back in the eighties. The east side of Main Street was still populated, with a half a dozen little churches and clusters of homes, but the west was where the Goldfield Mining Company had built the small, one bedroom miner's cottages that had become home to over twelve hundred workers. When the company left, the houses were left to rot, ancient for sale signs still stuck in the front of a few weed-choked lawns.

There was some fast food to be had, most of it inside the massive Super Center Truck-Stop a mile outside town, but as Hannah said, I had an obligation to prolong my life for her and Wendy. So, despite the urge to go grab a Whopper, I instead picked at a Cobb salad and queued up a podcast about the history of grunge metal.

I couldn't focus, the podcaster's voices drifting over me in an indigestible wash as I pushed bits of hardboiled egg around on my plate. Unbidden, I found myself thinking of the article Tracy had shoved into my hands that morning. It troubled me, and even more frustrating, I couldn't place why. I had heard of UFO sightings, aliens, all of that. I couldn't avoid it with some of the more psychedelic crowds I used to run with. But I'd never taken it seriously, never had time to while scrambling to survive. Did Tracy really believe all that bullshit? Did anyone?

It was just a crazy ass story, brought on by too much liquor, exhaustion, or both. Despite my best efforts, I couldn't hold onto my focus or my appetite. Eventually I gave up, turning off the podcast and pushing the plate away, intending to spend the rest of my lunch break trying to walk the feeling off.

The moment I pulled the ear buds out, I realized I wasn't the only one thinking of the article. Three men sat at the diner's counter, speaking loudly.

"I've known Herb for fifteen goddamn years," one man, an older guy with a Yosemite Sam mustache and salt colored hair said. "And he ain't no liar. If he says he saw a UFO, then he saw a damn UFO."

"Bullshit," one of the others said. He was a younger man, twenty at the most, in a sweat-stained muscle shirt, and was currently speaking through the syrup drenched waffle in his mouth. "Even if he did see something, and I'm not even sure he did, he has no idea what it was."

"Could be ball lightning," the third of the trio, a fantastically fat man in faded coveralls, said. "I heard about it on one of those Discovery Channel shows."

"Or it could be a comet. It could be he was drunk and saw an airplane. Or," the younger man said, tapping the counter with his index finger, "my money is on a drone. Shit, Herb even said that's what he thought it was at first."

"A drone?" Yosemite Sam said, as if the word were a particularly tough piece of gristle.

"It's the government," the younger guy said. "I've read all about it online. All this UFO stuff is a false flag. Get us used to mysterious crafts in the sky so they can spy on us. Figure out who the real patriots are. I'm not saying there aren't any aliens, but if they are involved, it's just because we stole their tech after that crash in Roswell. They're using it to control us, get going with that whole New World Order thing Bush, Jr. was talking about. Eventually they're going to fake an invasion to get everyone to drop the borders and bow to the throne."

The fat man nodded slowly, though without comprehension, uttering a noncommittal, "Huh."

Yosemite Sam shook his head. "Boy, that has to be the single dumbest thing that has ever fallen out of your mouth."

"How the fuck would you know?" the younger guy said, a lance of anger punctuating his question. "I'd bet a thousand dollars that it's true. And when that day comes, anyone who doesn't play ball is going to get the Auschwitz treatment. That's what FEMA is for. Round us all up into their special camps."

Yosemite took a slow, even breath. "So you mean to tell me that the government designed, funded, tested, and built a miniature flying sun? That they figured out how to do things the best fighter jets in the world can't do? And they took all that money, all that technology, and they used it to see if Herb Fucking Westvale would serve the New World Order? Yeah, I think between the two, little green men are more likely."

The younger man's face dropped and watching him, I saw a glimpse of myself. The tightening of the fists, the hateful reddening of the face, rage burning just under the surface. "It's all part of the cover-up!"

"Bill Goddamn Clinton couldn't cover up a blowjob, and he was the President. You really think anyone in Washington could keep a lid on something like that?" Yosemite was reaching for his wallet, clearly done with the conversation.

"You're just a fucking sheep," the younger man said, pure vitriol in his voice. Then, seeming to notice that he had drawn the stares of everyone in the diner, the younger man stood abruptly. "Fuck you," then, to the fat man, "and fuck you, too, Larry!"

He stormed out, fists clenched at his sides in a posture I knew well. He was going to go find a reason to hurt someone. Part of me, the old part, had half a mind to follow him, give him exactly what he wanted.

Yosemite turned on his stool and addressed the diner, "Sorry about that folks," he said, voice low and rumbling, but pleasant, summer thunder. "Danny's a good boy, but a bit soft in the head."

That earned a few snickers from the diners, most of whom were slowly drifting back to their own meals or conversations, the show concluded. I started reaching for my own wallet, needing that walk now more than ever, when I noticed that Yosemite's eyes were now fixed on me.

He made his way to my table in a slow, even, gait. "You must be Jacob Riley," he said, nodding to the seat opposite me in the booth. "This spot taken?" Then, before I could reply, he slid into the seat.

"I am," I said, confused. "How did you…"

He held out a hand. "Name is Quinn. Sheriff Montgomery Quinn, but most people around here just call me Quinn. I heard you and your wife moved into the old place up on Strawberry. Been hoping we'd cross paths, eventually. Figured if there was a face in town I didn't know, it had to be yours."

The moment the word Sherriff left his mouth, I had to resist the old urge to book it. I remained glued where I sat, keeping my breathing even. I took his hand and gave it a polite shake. "It's nice to meet you. Surprised it took so long."

"Yeah, well, for a small town, it sure does keep me busy," then, nodding to my hand, still clasped in his, the thick white scars on my knuckles practically glowing under the diner's fluorescent lights, said, "You a fighter?"

"Amateur MMA," I said immediately. *Very* amateur. "When I was younger, and a bit more stupid."

He nodded approvingly, releasing my hand and leaning back. "Big guy like you must have done well. I sure as shit wouldn't want to fight you."

"I did alright," I flashed him a tight smile. "That Danny kid is going to hurt someone," I said, looking to shift focus off me. "I've seen the look."

Sherriff Quinn nodded; he too had come to the same conclusion. "Don't worry about Danny. Usually, he works it out himself. If he don't, I'll set him straight tonight when I get home."

"He's your…"

"Yeah," Quinn said sheepishly, leaning back, looking off towards the door Danny had stormed out of. "That's my boy, little shit stain ain't he? But I'm more interested in you. You and your wife getting along alright? Anyone giving you trouble up there?"

"No trouble. Everyone has been really nice; though, if I'm being honest, we haven't gotten around much. New baby and all." Since moving in a little over two months ago, we had hardly left the house save for my work at Astrological or the weekly grocery runs, neither of which involved much socializing.

He nodded, stroking at the edges of his mustache. "You don't have many neighbors up there," he said matter-of-factly. "Used to be, half the town lived up in the hills. You met Old George? Or the Hagars?"

I shook my head, "Can't say I have. Met a guy named Gaylord Friend, but that's it."

Quinn ran his tongue over leathery lips. "Name doesn't ring a bell. He lives up in the hills?"

"That's what he said," summoning up Friend's words from the day before: "Eighteen acres of peace and quiet."

Quinn thought for a moment longer, then shrugged. "Must be just beyond the edge of my jurisdiction. These hills are old, lots of little communities out there." Then, noticing that the fat man at the counter was starting to reach for his wallet, the sheriff got to his feet and passed me a card. "You folks stay safe. You and your wife have any trouble, you call me right away, and if you can't get me, call Deputy Hanson. If the station isn't picking up, try the numbers on the back, they're direct lines. Tell you the truth, fact we still got anyone living up there never sat right with me. Takes too long to get to you folks, should the need arise."

"Doesn't seem like there is much trouble to get into around here," I said, relieved to be free of the encounter.

Quinn smirked and pointed up, a sparkle of mischief in his eyes. "Oh, I don't know, I hear there are Martians about."

3

That night Hannah and I sat down over a meal of black bean burgers and salad, while Wendy enjoyed a jar of butternut squash baby mush given to her one spoonful at a time. As Hannah worked, alternating bites of her own meal with feeding Wendy hers, she told me all about the trials and tribulations of her vegetable garden, effectively banishing the nagging thoughts of space men and local sheriffs that had hounded my afternoon.

As usual, I understood the basics. Most of her crop was doing well, some plants struggling. There was some kind of mite that was working through the herb garden which had thus far resisted her genocidal efforts, and she thought the high acidity of our soil may have something to do with it. Past that I was lost in her talk of soil types, growth patterns, and types of vermin she supposedly kept at bay with the long rings of marigolds she had planted encircling the back yard. As I had for the past fifteen years, I nodded and smiled, asking questions where I could, enjoying the vivid life in her pale blue eyes.

"I figure this harvest is going to get canned just for us. But next spring, I'll go even bigger. Half the yard, at least, maybe more. Enough to take some down to the farmer's market in town, maybe make some extra cash for our city fund."

The city fund was a mostly empty mason jar we kept hidden in the bedroom closet, part rainy day fund, part reminder not to settle. Currently it had two hundred and fourteen dollars in it, barely pocket change compared to what we'd need. "Someone has got to," I said. "I'm fairly sure Tracy is going to keep me as an apprentice till the day she drops dead."

"You know, we could arrange that," Hannah said playfully, one eyebrow arched. "Never let it be said that I'm not willing to commit manslaughter for our family."

"I think that would classify as first-degree murder, seeing as you're planning it."

She shrugged. "Not if I hit her with my car and, ya know, lie."

I laughed, opened my mouth to reply, when I was cut off by a sudden knocking at the front door – three hard raps.

We traded a glance, our faces mirrors of confusion. "Who the hell is that?" I asked, already standing to go check.

"No clue," she said.

"Probably just the Girl Scouts," I said.

"At 7:00pm on the side of a mountain?" Hannah called, also standing but not following, instead maneuvering herself between Wendy and the front hall.

I paused when I reached the door and stole a quick glance through the peephole. There was nobody, just the front porch, the newly repaired railing, and the dark yard beyond. I opened the door and leaned out, checking the spaces on either side of the door and finding them just as empty.

"Who is it?" Hannah called after me.

I stepped out onto the porch. "Hello?" I called. No answer, just the wind rustling the trees as it flowed down the mountain. I shrugged and went back inside, locking the door behind me as I went.

"Nobody there," I said. "Probably just some kids."

Hannah let out a breath. "Why the hell would kids come all the way out here to play Ding Dong Ditch?"

"Technically this was Knock Knock Ditch," I corrected.

She set a hand on Wendy's shoulder, the other absently stroking the peach fuzz atop her head. "Very funny, but still. Why would they come all the way out here?"

"Who knows? Maybe they like to mess with the newbies. Got to imagine there isn't much to do around here for a kid."

Hannah stared at the door, then sighed and shook her head. "You're right, it's just-"

Another series of raps came at the door, this time louder, more urgent. Hannah and I traded a look, coming to an understanding without a word. She scooped Wendy from her highchair and made for one of the back bedrooms while I returned to the front door.

I disengaged the deadbolt and threw the door open, muscles tight, head on a swivel, ready to scare the holy hell out of whatever kid was out there. Again, the porch was empty, the only sound the wind and the trees. Somewhere off in the dark an owl let out a lonely hoot.

I ventured out onto the porch. "Hello?" I called into the dark a second time, straining my ears for the sound of a snapping branch or a child's snickering. I turned to head back inside when there came another knocking sound, this time from the woods beyond, as if someone was rapping against a tree. I took a step towards the sound, squinting.

"Hey," I called into the dark.

Another series of knocks sounded in reply and I took a step off the porch. When I paused, the knocking began again. A hard nugget of fear nestled in my stomach. Were they trying to lead me into the woods?

"Whoever is out there, get the fuck off our proper..."

Hannah's scream from inside hit me like a bolt of electricity.

"Jacob!" she shouted, "Jacob in here!"

I left the front door open in my haste as I crashed through the dining room, down the hall, and into the nursery where I found Hannah, her back pressed to the wall, face pale, pointing at the window.

"Someone was looking in," she said, eyes alight with terror. "He ran around the back!"

With no thought, moving on pure adrenaline, I sprinted from the room, hammered through the kitchen and out the back door. The yard beyond Hannah's garden was a weedy nightmare of tangled roots and stones that soon gave way to a dense, piney tree line. I circled the house to the nursery window, guiding myself by the bright silver light of the full moon.

The area just beyond the window was empty, but someone had been there, the grass and weeds stamped down just beneath the window, as if someone had waited there, watching. Somewhere in the woods behind me a branch snapped, then another, heading deeper. I wanted to chase, to find the fucker and put the fear of the devil himself in them, but thankfully, Hannah caught my eye first.

She appeared on the other side of the window, sliding it open. "Do you see anyone?"

I shook my head, heart still hammering in my throat. "I heard someone running off up the hill."

She followed my gaze into the darkened wood, then shuddered. "Come inside," she whispered. "You're right, it's probably some kids."

"Just one second," I said, noticing something amidst the weeds below the window. "Get me a flashlight."

Hannah vanished from the window, reappearing a moment later with a cheap keychain flashlight. I shone the weak beam down, crouching to get a better look. It was a footprint, or half of one anyway, set in the dirt. It was odd – long and skinny, and flat bottomed. No ridges like you would see from a tennis shoe or boot, but no toe imprints either. I pointed the light into the darkness the direction the branch snapping had come from, saw nothing.

"Some crazy asshole is running around out there in moccasins," I concluded, standing and looking back in at Hannah and Wendy.

Hannah was looking at me, concern and confusion on her face. Wendy sat on her hip, blinking at me with wet lips and wide doleful eyes. And behind them, in the doorway to the bedroom, the silhouette of a man stood against the hall light, watching them. The front door, I realized with cold horror. I had left the front door open.

"Get the fuck away from them!" I shouted, lunging towards the open window. Hannah yelped, and Wendy unleashed a peal of hysterical shrieking. Hannah turned, saw the figure, and joined the screaming, backing away, holding Wendy to her side as if to shield her, while I grabbed each side of the window frame and pulled myself through. Hot pain lanced down my leg and something wet began to soak into my sock, but I could barely feel it.

As I tumbled through the window, the figure retreated, soft footfalls like the patter of bare feet retreating down the hall.

"Jacob!" Hannah shouted after me as I rose and sprinted after them, down the hall and around the corner, hands held out to throttle the first neck I found. I burst out the open front door onto the porch. Somewhere off in the dark, branches snapped, leaves crunched as someone made a quick getaway. My mind was abuzz, rage slamming up against confusion. How had they gotten into the tree line already? That was at least fifty yards from the front door, no way had they been that far ahead of me.

I wanted to scream after them, to dare them to come back, to list every one of their bones I was going to break, but when I tried, the anger choked my throat. I stood on the porch, breathing rough until Hannah appeared, still clutching a distraught Wendy to her side.

"Are they gone?" she whispered.

I didn't respond, instead leading her inside and bolting the door behind us. I leaned heavily against the door and closed my eyes, drawing in a deep breath, rage out, serenity in, just like Hannah taught me. As I was about to take my second breath, Hannah gasped and I opened my eyes to see her standing in the entryway to the kitchen, her face the color of snow. I went to her, saw what she saw.

Our dining room table, a thick oak antique that had been here when we got the house, had been flipped onto its top. The chairs as well. Our dinners had been carefully set on the floor beside it.

"Who would do this?" Hannah whispered.

I wished I had an answer.

We searched the house top to bottom, Hannah with me every step, armed with a kitchen knife. Then, when we found no hidden intruders, we searched again. Only then did I let Hannah see to the four-inch gash I had managed to open in my leg during my dive through the window, snagged on a loose nail in the frame. While she squirted on antibacterial cream, I called the Sherriff's station and then, when I only got a busy signal, Sherriff Quinn's personal number.

"Quinn?" I said as soon as he picked up, "It's Jacob Riley."

There was a moment's pause. "Jacob," he said. "Didn't expect you to be calling quite so soon."

"Someone just…" I paused. Just what? Invaded our home? Played a prank? "Someone is fucking with us," I concluded. "They came into our home, scared the shit out of all of us."

There was another pause while someone else spoke, the sound too muffled to make out. Then Quinn came back. "Stay put," he said, "I'm heading up there now."

Fifteen minutes later the red and blue lights of Sherriff Quinn's brown and black patrol car announced his arrival. I met Sherriff Quinn on the porch and was introduced to the young Deputy Hanson. My first thought seeing the black-haired magazine model mounting my front steps was that there was no way he was a real cop. Deputy Hanson looked like the police officers you saw in prime-time procedural television shows, where paperwork is done off screen, and everyone had straight backs, fit bodies, and clear skin. He had a deep tan, perfect white teeth, and a pair of green eyes that looked like they nearly glowed in the dark.

"Jacob," Quinn said conversationally. "This is Deputy Brandon Hanson, he's going to be helping us out tonight."

Hanson held his hand out to me, and I took it. "Real nice to meet you, Mr. Riley," he said affably, voice low and pleasant.

"Same to you," I said, trying and likely failing to hide my nervousness at the sight of the cop car and those shiny badges.

Quinn, meanwhile, had turned his attention to Hannah, who stood in the shadows of the doorway, Wendy clutched to one hip. "And you must be Hannah Riley?" Quinn said.

"I must be," Hannah said. She held out her hand, and Quinn shook it before nodding to Wendy.

"Who's this?" he asked.

"This is Wendy," Hannah said. "Say hello, Wendy."

Wendy let out a low wet babble and Quinn smirked, crouching to her level. "Nice to meet you Ms. Riley," he said. Wendy looked at the sheriff then and giggled, a bright smile spreading over her face as she reached out and gave Quinn's Yosemite Sam mustache a tug. Quinn laughed, Hannah laughed, Hanson gave a chuckle, and the tension in the air seemed to evaporate a bit.

Quinn stood, turning to face me. "Well, heard you folks had some trouble tonight. Why don't you walk us through what happened."

I told them everything, walking them through the kitchen where the table and dishes still lay, then into the nursery, then outside. Deputy Hanson took care to photograph the half a footprint left beneath Wendy's nursery window. Then, at Quinn's request, we did it again, walking through every step of the encounter while he nodded thoughtfully, only asking a few questions here and there.

"Well, you got a head scratcher on your hands, that's for sure," Quinn said once we had finished the story for the second time. We stood on the porch while he smoked, twisting the filter off a cigarette and pocketing it before lighting up.

"Any idea who could have done it? At first I thought it was kids messing with us, but the guy I saw in the hall was too big for a kid. Almost as tall as me."

"Ain't kids," Quinn agreed. "The shadow you saw aside, I can't imagine any kid could flip that table like that, not without making a hell of a racket." Deputy Hanson had helped me right our kitchen, both of us puffing and straining to maneuver the awkward, two-hundred-pound slab of oak. Even still, we gouged the kitchen tile when we set it down.

"I think there was more than one," I said. "Like I told you, I heard someone running off to the north. Couldn't have been whoever came inside."

Quinn nodded in agreement but said nothing, instead turning towards the road, and the darkened tree line beyond it, the moonlight touching the high branches but never penetrating the gloom beneath. "Been a lot of weirdness tonight," he said. "Lots of calls, though I won't lie, Mr. Riley, yours troubles me the most. Like I told you earlier, these hills are old, and there are some folks out there who don't take to living in the real world with the rest of us. Some of them are, if you'll pardon my French, fucking nuts. This place sat abandoned for what, two years?"

"Three," I corrected.

He took a puff off his cigarette and let the silver smoke roll out his mouth slowly. When he spoke his voice had a distant quality, almost dreamlike. "Mind if I tell you something a bit frightening, Mr. Riley?"

I almost laughed in his face. "Someone just snuck into my home and nearly got to my wife and child. I don't think a scary story is going to top that."

Quinn nodded thoughtfully. "About eight years ago, I was deputy under Sherriff Coleman. That winter, we got hit with a hell of a blizzard, total whiteout, phone lines down, power knocked out in half the town. Around midnight we start getting calls on the CB from a guy named Richard Townsend. He wasn't a local, he was a stock guy or something, built himself a mini-mansion up there somewhere." He gestured up the road, giving a dismissive shake of the head. "He called it a vacation home. What dumb bastard wants to vacation here?"

"Peace and quiet, I guess," I responded, thinking of Gaylord Friend.

"Calls started coming in around midnight, Townsend saying someone was prowling around his house, trying to get in. Said he caught them trying to wiggle up the window to his kid's nursery, little guy named Sammy, about the same age as your daughter. Cars couldn't make it up the hills, even our trucks, so I got a few guys and borrowed some snowmobiles, and headed up there. Took about an hour but," he shook his head, "we were too late. Found the front door open. Found Townsend and his wife in the front hall, stone dead. What we didn't find was the kid. Best we can tell, whoever killed the Townsends must have taken Sammy, just walked off into the storm with him. We found some tracks near the house, but all that wind wiped away whatever trail they left."

"Jesus," I whispered, "So you think this is the same people?"

"I can't say that, but I can say that I am concerned. I don't have the manpower to park someone outside your house, and the chances of us tracking them down in there," he gestured towards the wood, "are about as good a doe's chances in a tiger pit. And even if it ain't the same people, there are no shortage of weird stories coming down out of those hills. Missing hikers, children seen walking the slopes wearing rags. Hell, we even got ourselves a couple Bigfoot sightings, if you care to believe."

"So what do we do?" I asked.

Quinn stabbed his cigarette out on the porch railing and turned to face me. "Be alert. Keep your doors and windows locked. In fact, I'd suggest beefing up security if you can. Some new deadbolts, for one. And if you don't have a gun, I suggest you remedy that situation. The moment you smell trouble, you give me a call and take your family into the bathroom, or somewhere without windows. Best case, it'll take us about ten minutes to get someone up here. Just hold tight till help arrives, all right?"

Other people might have been outraged, demanded better assurances, promises of security. But in my experience, cops meant busted doors and months of lean times while my father dried out in whatever hole they stuck him in. Just the fact that Quinn was treating us like people was a big step up in my world. "I can do that," I said, privately doubting I would have to. If whoever it was stepped foot near Wendy or Hannah again, I would twist their fucking head off like a Barbie doll.

As if sensing my thoughts, Quinn caught me by the shoulder, pulled me around to face him. He was a head shorter than me, yet his weathered gaze made me feel small all the same. "I mean it, Jacob. Call us the moment trouble hits. I'm guessing you're someone who's probably used to taking care of things yourself, and I'm asking you not to this time. Your family needs a father more than it needs a hero."

I didn't notice it then – must have been the exhaustion of the day finally catching up with me. But there was something in what he said and his nervous glance towards the woods. He said call the moment trouble hit, not IF it hit.

I must believe he knew what was coming, even then.

4

The next day, on my lunch break, I went to Ripley Sport Supply, a weathered brick box on the edge of town. I had the vague notion that I would find a handgun, something easy to hide but with good stopping power, just like the .45s my dad's friends used to wave around the poker table in the living room of our doublewide trailer. David Ripley, a leather bag of a man who had run the place since 1953, informed me that "handguns are for shooting people, not for sport, so I don't deal with them. You want a man-killer, you drive down to Bellow Ridge."

I wandered a bit, eyeing the price tags on the rifles and shotguns, a growing unease mounting in my gut. I had grown up around guns, seen the damage they could do firsthand. My own father, the last night I'd seen him, had gotten piss drunk at his weekly poker game and, after losing one hand too many, blew a new skylight through Uncle Brad's head. That was the night I learned that none of the men my father played with were really my uncles, and that blood is one of the hardest things to shampoo out of carpet.

Towards the back I found the sale rack, mostly second-hand cannons. Thinking I'd do our bank account a kindness, I started hunting for a bargain and found an old Remington break action, two barrels, two shells, simple as could be. I hoisted the gun, felt the solid, lethal weight of the stock. I shouldered it, thinking of the intruder I had seen silhouetted against the hall light, imagined what it would feel like to pull the trigger, to feel the kick, and smell the stench of blood blasted into a fine mist. Then, I thought of Hannah, and lowered the gun.

She wouldn't like this; it broke the deal we had made at a gas station McDonalds during our final exodus from Echo City.

"This is a new start for us, both of us," she said, reaching past her half-eaten Egg McMuffin and giving my hand a squeeze. "I need you to promise me that you'll give this a chance. No more fighting."

I smiled at her. What a fucking spectacle I must have been, teeth bloody, both lips split, right eye swollen shut, and knuckles bandaged. "I promise," I said.

"I mean it," she pressed, "not even an argument if you can help it. And no weapons in the house. I won't put our baby at risk."

At the time, Wendy was a dream. Just a few clumps of cells growing inside Hannah. "I promise," I repeated, giving her hand a soft squeeze in return. "I'm not that guy anymore. No weapons," I smiled and gave my arms a flex, "except these guns."

She smiled, rolled her eyes, and it was like sun rose in my chest. I thought right then that I'd make any promise I had to, and mean it, if it meant keeping her in my life.

I set the gun back down on the rack, stared at it. What was more important, keeping my promise or keeping my family safe?

Then I thought of Wendy — small, defenseless. Thought of watching someone sprinting into the woods with her in their arms, snatched right out of the crib.

I put the gun on our lone credit card and walked out of the shop guiltily clutching the long box to my side.

I stashed the shotgun in the truck along with a box of slugs and spent the better part of the afternoon tattooing Mickey Mouse smoking a blunt on the calf of a local shithead named Emery Larch who, near as I could tell, labored under the delusion that Victor's Point was the ideal place to launch his rap career. By the time I was done, there was an hour left in my shift — just enough time to clean up my station and set the needles for the following day. Only before I could begin, Tracy tapped me on the shoulder.

"Hey, I need you to do me a solid. You got to close up for me tonight."

"I can't," I said immediately, thinking of the shotgun in the truck, the fight I would inevitably be returning home to once Hannah found out. "Got some trouble at home I need to deal with."

"Tough shit," Tracy snapped, hands perched on her hips and smoke grey eyes boring into me. "I have a family…situation. Just one night, all you need to do is stay an extra few minutes to lock up and take the trash out. I need this, and you need this job. Please?"

She was being polite but I knew a threat when I heard one. My first instinct was to tell her that no, I didn't need this job, that I was a better artist than anyone else in town and that I was the only competent help she could hope to have. But then I thought of Wendy's diapers, our failing AC unit, and the thousand other little expenses that kept us trapped in that little house on Strawberry Lane.

"Fine," I said, "but I got to call Hannah."

"Well get to it, I've got to get moving," she said, grabbing for her bag and her keys.

I went into the storage room to make the call. It was barely a closet, just enough room to walk in between old metal racks loaded with ink pots and spare needles.

Hannah picked up on the first ring. "When are you coming home?" She sounded tense, almost pained.

"Is everything all right?" I asked.

"No. Yes. I don't know," she took a heavy breath. "I met a neighbor, and it was pretty weird and…" she trailed off for a moment, the only sound the distant wails of our daughter. "It's just weird here, Jacob," she whispered. "I keep checking all the locks, and everything seems fine, but I keep jumping at shadows. I keep waiting for someone to try and get inside. And I don't know — my head is just really fuzzy."

"Did you get any sleep?"

She didn't respond, just breathed. A sliver of dread wound down my spine as I imagined her, clutching her cell phone to her chest and staring wide-eyed as a crazed man of the forest tapped on the kitchen window.

"Hannah, babe? Are you there? Is someone trying to get in?"

"No," she said, "it's just…when are you coming home?"

"Tracy asked me to close tonight, but I'll be quick. Coming to you in no time."

"Ok," she whispered, then she repeated it, sounding stronger. Then she took in a deep breath and let it out slow, "I love you."

"I love you too," I said back, then she hung up.

I stared at the phone, the disquiet that had ridden my shoulders all day now screaming. If anyone ever cared to measure, I think I set the speed cleaning record that night, locking the door a full forty minutes before closing and out the door only a minute past ten. I hustled towards the truck, hands shoved in my pockets, already flying up the mountain road in my mind. I had my hand on the door latch when the sound of voices drew my attention.

This late, the only light on the street came from a few sputtering sodium lights which cast a jaundiced yellow glow over the cracked sidewalk. Scanning the gloom, I spotted the source of the sounds. On the other side of the street, tucked in the shadow beneath the bakery's awning, Quinn's kid, Danny, was talking with someone else who I couldn't make out. Danny was standing straight backed, arms rigid at his sides, eyes wide like he'd taken a gut punch.

The other figure had a hand on Danny's shoulder and seemed to be the one talking, a low, confident voice that sounded oddly familiar. As I watched, the shadowy other leaned in close and whispered something in Danny's ear.

All the hair on the back of my neck stood on end. Something was wrong here. Danny looked like he was about to piss himself. I told myself it was none of my business, to just go home, not make waves, yet I found myself backing away from the truck and crossing the street.

"Hey, it's Danny, right?" I called, holding out my hand as if I'd just come to meet the locals.

It was too dark to make out the other's face, but I saw his head turn towards me. Then he whispered something else in Danny's ear and suddenly pushed the younger man out from under the awning. Danny stumbled off the curb, then pitched forward, knees crumbling beneath him. I ran the last few steps, trying to get to him before his face met the hard ground, but I was too slow. Danny's head bounced off the asphalt, and he let out a startled cry.

I ran to his side, knelt, and tried to pull him to his feet. "Hey, you," I called to the other man, "get his other side…" I stopped short, scanning the street to either side of me. The other figure was gone, melted away into the shadows beyond the streetlights. I turned my attention back to Danny, hoisting him up onto his feet.

"Hey, pal, you alright?" I asked, trying to meet his eyes as his head rolled around atop his neck, like he was drugged. I should call Quinn, I thought, get an ambulance out here. Clearly Danny was on something.

As I reached for my cell phone, though, Danny's head suddenly snapped up, eyes soft and dreamy. "What the fuck are you doing?" he asked. "I'm not a fucking queer, man, let me go."

I released him and, while he was unsteady, he stayed upright this time. "You all right? Was that guy bothering you?"

Danny narrowed his eyes, looked past me up the empty street. "What guy?" he asked.

"The guy you were just talking to. I just saw you."

"You think I'm gay?" he asked, slurring words. "You think I'm like, what, out here meeting some guy to suck his dick, you think that's what's happening?"

This was quickly going south. I shook my head, backed up a step, "Hey man, just thought you could use some help. I'll just be going …"

Danny's punch caught me square in my left eye, and my vision went white.

"Fuck you!" he howled, face suddenly baboon red, veins bulging out of his neck. "You think I'm some big fucking homo, don't you!? Don't think I haven't seen you hiding out around here. Skulking around, gobbling cock, you motherfucker."

Rage like napalm burned through my veins, and my fists unconsciously clenched and raised. I needed to exit the situation, before things got bad. Two breaths, just like Hannah taught me, serenity in, rage out, serenity in, rage – . And then Danny was coming at me again, swinging wildly for my head.

I managed to snare him by the wrist and pull him around into a choke hold on reflex, my forearm pressed firmly against his throat. "Easy," I ordered as he thrashed in my arms. "Nobody thinks anything, man. Calm down, everything is fine."

He thrashed, then kicked and finally, relented, falling limp in my arms.

"There," I said. "Everything is ok. No need for us to fight."

"I'm ok," he whispered. Then, finding his legs, he stood straighter. "I'm ok, sorry, I'm ok, I'm so sorry."

I released him, taking a cautious step back. "What are you on? I might be able to help, but I got to know what you took."

Danny turned to look at me, a strange, bemused smile growing across his face as once again his entire demeanor changed. When he spoke this time, there was no slur, no soft edge on his words. "I'll take your life," he said. "Then, I'm going to fuck your wife, and shove your baby in a wood chip – "

I hit him. I hit him really fucking hard.

Danny's head snapped back and he hit the road with a heavy thud. He tried to rise and I pressed a boot into his chest, pinning him.

"Not another word," I said, an old familiar fury raging inside me. "You don't say one fucking thing about my family, do you understand?"

He looked up at me and the sharp, lethal intent was gone from his face, replaced again with the peaceful expression of a dreamer. "Yeah, OK man," he wheezed. "I'm just – what's going on?"

I waited a moment, confirmed the fight had well and truly left him, then removed my boot. "Want to tell me what the fuck that was about? Who was the guy you were talking to?"

Danny shook his head, "What man? I've haven't seen anyone out here all night, you fucking freak."

I left Danny sitting confused in the street and called Quinn the second I got in my truck, thinking it would be better if Quinn heard about the incident from me first. I told him what happened through gritted teeth, careful to keep my own anger from showing. I left out the bit about the miraculous disappearing shadow man and Danny's strange accusations, but left in the threat he'd made on my family.

"Sorry, Quinn. Kid didn't give me much choice."

Quinn, sounding ten years older than he had the previous night, just grumbled. "No worries. This isn't the first time. Don't worry too much about the threat, the kid is just hot air. I'll scoop him up."

I drove in silence the rest of the way home, eyeing the shotgun sitting across the back seat, trying to calm down. Only with each mile I drove, the anger grew, fed by the familiar scent of blood on my knuckles. Two miles from the house I pulled over, got out, and breathed deep the pine scented air. I pressed my head against the cool exterior of the truck door, and waited until the rage became small enough to shove back into the bottle from whence it came.

I might have been there five minutes, maybe longer, when what I assumed was a car passed by with its brights on, the light pushing past my eyelids and bringing me back to myself.

However, when I opened my eyes, the road was empty save for me and my truck. Just another oddity in week of oddities. I briefly wondered if the flash had been inside my head, a stroke maybe, but I was too tired to wonder. I steadied myself, climbed inside, and made for home.

3

INTERLUDE

Hypnotic Regression Therapy Session #1
Subject: Jacob Riley
Administered by: Dr. James Lorenz

Dr. Lorenz: Can you hear me, Jacob?
Jacob: Yes.
Dr. Lorenz: Where are you right now?
Jacob: I'm in my living room.
Dr. Lorenz: Good. Now I want you to take me to the party, your last night in Echo City. Can you do that?
Jacob: …
Dr. Lorenz: Does that upset you?
Jacob: No. Yes. We don't like to talk about it.
Hannah: It's all right, Jacob. I'm here. We can talk about it.
Jacob: This recording won't be made public, correct?
Dr. Lorenz: Not if you don't want it to. Take a deep breath. I want you to take us back there. 126 Newport Circle.
Jacob: I… I'm with Doug. We're at Doug Bow's trailer, in the bathroom. We're doing coke, Doug also smoked some crystal, but I don't want any. He is telling me about the girl he brought tonight, Lindsay.

"She's a Jesus Bride," Doug said, the acrid smoke drifting out between his lips, "so she only takes it up the ass." He sat on the edge of the bathtub, which was half filled with garbage and a few inches of scummy yellow water. He had a rat's nest of greasy black hair, and a narrow face that held more wrinkles than it ought to at his age.

I grunted, focused on parsing out what little was left of our coke stash into thin lines on the lid of the toilet tank.

"But you know what I say," Doug continued, waggling his eyebrows, "every hole's a goal. She's a total freak. Real daddy-issues type. I figure I got a month to fuck her before she gets bored with slumming it." When I didn't respond again, he nudged me in the shoulder. "What about you, still fucking Rabbit?"

I grunted again, staring at the lines of white powder, the words of a murmured promise echoing through my head. I thought of Hannah, and the secret child that was growing inside her. I thought of the intensity in her eyes when she made me swear we'd leave Echo City, that I'd stop the drugs and start building the life I'd always promised her. And I would, I told myself. Just after I cleared up one little loose end.

I pressed my face to the toilet lid and inhaled. Acid dripping down the back of my throat, lightning in my veins. I stood up, gave my head a shake.

"Don't get me wrong, Rabbit is all right," Doug continued, "a bit too boy-bodied. Girl could use some hips or at the very least some tits. You fucking her must look like a Catholic grizzly bear mounting an altar boy."

"Why don't you worry about your own dick and leave me to mine?" I grumbled.

Doug laughed, "So it does speak!"

Doug was one of my oldest, and worst, friends. He grew up three trailers down from the Riley home until his seventeenth birthday when his dad was sent up to the Supermax for ten years, and his mom ran off with his kid sister and a gas station clerk. He spent a year crashing on various couches, ours being just another on the circuit, before he got his own place. Growing up, we had been close to hooligans, the sort of kids you see lingering outside the 7/11 most days of the week – bored, angry, and looking for someone to mess with. But once he got that place on Newport Circle, he promoted himself from go-nowhere kid to major-fuckup adult. It started with coke, then came party pills and finally, meth. If I was ever going to point at any one person who got me into that mess of a life, other than myself, it was Doug Bow. Always smiling, always quick with a joke, and quicker to drag his friends into his own bad habits.

He waved the meth pipe at me, the burning garbage smell turning my stomach. "You sure you don't want to mix it up? Coke and Crystal is a cool combo, man. Like you're fire trapped in ice."

"No," I said immediately. "Get that shit out of my face."

"Touchy," Doug said, retracting the pipe. "I'm just trying to make sure you have a good time."

"That's not why I'm here," I said. That seemed to sober him up a little, a reminder of the violence that stood poised on the horizon. He cast a nervous glance at the door, as if an inch of plywood would protect us.

"You really think he's going to show up tonight?"

"He will," I said, leaning down to the toilet lid, inhaling.

"I don't know man, after what happened last time, maybe he said enough was enough. Guy got his ass beat."

"He'll be here," I said, as sure as I was that the sun would rise come morning. Adam Letchie never could leave good enough alone. He had been making a big stink for a week now how he was going to come and gut my ass on account of a humiliating beating I had given him the last time we met. He might have started with some boasts to his friends, the kind of half-hearted promises uttered to ease his bruised ego, but word got out. Now most people we knew had heard of his promised vengeance and waited with bated breath for the next chapter in our sad little saga, which had been going for the better part of a decade, ever since a fist fight in the high school cafeteria. All this left Adam in a tough spot. Come at me again, he was likely to end up in the hospital. Don't, he loses all the respect he thought he had. For a guy like Adam, it was no choice at all.

"Well Jesus, I hope not. If he does show up, just make sure it doesn't get too crazy. Last thing I need is the cops crawling up my chocolate starfish, all right?"

Before I could reply, there was a rapid knock on the bathroom door. "Hey, Jacob?" a girl called. "Rabbit is here. She seems *pissed.*"

At first, I didn't think I had heard right. Rabbit should have been safely home. I didn't think she even knew I was here. I opened the door a crack, met eyes with the wide doe eyes of the woman on the other side, her breath stinking of menthol and Miller Lite. I thought I recognized her, one of Doug's regular crowd. "She's out front," she said before I could ask. "Won't come inside. Like I said, she seems really mad."

I shared a glance with Doug, mumbling a combination of prayers and half-grumbled curse words as I exited the bathroom and made my way through the living room, stepping over crushed beer cans and mounds of fast-food wrappers. I wiped my nose and upper lip clean, trying to force my thoughts to clear, to become as sober as she expected me to be.

It took me a moment to spot her as I exited the front door onto the trailer's sagging porch. Hannah, aka 'Rabbit' stood on the opposite side of the road, wearing one of my old Pantera hoodies, so large on her it looked like a dress. Her arms were crossed, the excess sleeve dangling at her sides, like she was a little kid. However, there was nothing childish in the open rage glowing in her eyes.

She remained still as I approached; my heart turned to cold lead in my chest. My mind raced, too fast, reaching for the words I needed, the ones that would put a neat bow on why I was here. Only they never arrived, my mind going blank as I reached her and my tongue sitting still and dumb in my mouth.

She slapped me on the chest, then she did it again, and again, rapid fire blows as the stony judgment on her face cracked, melted into pain. "You promised!" she said. "You promised me, goddammit! Less than ten fucking hours ago, Jacob, less than a fucking day."

"I had to," I said lamely. "Adam isn't going to drop this, he – "

"I don't care!" she was shouting now, face red, eyes wet. "It's always something!"

As always, I wanted to be her rock, cool and steady, but the coke was hammering in my blood, and my rage sparked to match hers. "What the hell do you want me to do!?" I shouted. "I can't just cut out my old life. It won't stop assholes like Adam from coming at me. You want me to just lay down and take it?"

"I don't want you involved at all!"

"Well, I am! I can't change that, I can't just end it. I've hurt people, Rabbit, you get that? People who don't give a shit that I don't want to be involved anymore." Behind me, I could hear Doug's front door open, followed by the low tittering of observers.

Hannah glanced behind me, shaking her head and jabbing a finger their direction. "It's not just Adam," she said, lowering her volume, effectively hardening her rage into something cold and deadly.

Behind us, a half dozen of Doug's regular party crowd now stood huddled on the rotten porch, averting their eyes, as if they all suddenly decided to take a smoke break at the same time. In the center stood Doug, his new squeeze pressed tight to his side. Lindsay was a head taller than Doug, with a long thin neck and a shock of straw-blond hair, cut into a jagged pixie. She leaned on Doug, her eyes hazed over, a distant smile on her face.

"It's them," Hannah continued. "Your friends are the ones who want you here. They are the ones who get you wrapped up in all this bullshit. You don't need them, Jacob. We don't need them."

My head was spinning, heart still hammering too fast, rage and guilt churning to a toxic stew in my gut. "Well maybe you don't need me," I shot back, regretting the words before they even left my lips. She recoiled, as if she'd been slapped. But I couldn't stop, the traitorous words flying out of my mouth as if rumbling up from some deep cavern inside me. "Let's face it, Hannah. You have been trying to change me for over ten goddamn years. Well, maybe I don't change. Maybe this is right where I belong. If you don't like it, then maybe you're the one who doesn't belong here."

Her face twisted with pain, open and raw. This was it, I realized. The moment I threw away the one good thing I had. The moment I dove into the life Doug advertised, became another of the crowd, just shuffling from calamity to calamity in search of my own self-conclusion.

She opened her mouth to say something, to speak the final words that would end it all, when a flung rock smashed into the side of her face. Hannah's head snapped back and she yelped, the impact sending her to the ground. I whirled, sure that someone on the porch had thrown it, sure that I was about to fucking massacre the entire party.

Instead, I saw Adam Letchie.

Adam was a thick man, with a large keg belly and two rolling chins, both covered with a few days of curly stubble. His right eye was still swollen and purple and he was favoring his right leg, leftovers from our fight a week prior, which had been retaliation for Adam stealing fifty bucks from Doug, which was retribution for something else, and on and on, like water over a prayer wheel.

Something was different about tonight though. It was his face. No smile, no projected confidence, just a cold hard anger in his muddy eyes. He raised his hand and threw another stone. I tried to duck, failed, instead taking the rock across my brow, splitting the skin and sending a cascade of stinging blood into my right eye.

"Jacob, don't ..." Hannah was screaming. But Jacob was no longer home. Just the red, just the rage.

"I hit your bitch, Riley," Adam said.

With a roar I ran at him, intent on knocking him down, needing to bash his teeth in and hurt him so badly that everyone would know deep in their bones that Hannah was off limits. When I got close, he threw a quick jab, catching me in the jaw, but it wasn't enough to stop my momentum as we crashed together. We hit the ground, rolling, flailing fists at each other. He hammered my sides, his hands like cannonballs, and while I would struggle to breathe deep for a month afterwards, in the moment I barely felt the cracked rib and bruised kidney. I rolled him, pushing him onto his back and threw fists into his gut, chest, and shoulder. Finally I elbowed him hard across the face, splitting the thin skin on his forehead.

Adam wheezed, hands scrambling for my face. He pressed a thumb into my eye, my vision going white, but the pain was a distant cry beneath the sea of anger, its waves crashing over me, into me, hollowing me out. I punched him in the face over and over again. As bones popped and skin split, the same thought echoed through my brain like a drumbeat: *He hurt my Hannah.*

Then, slender hands were wrapped around my arm, pulling me, a sweet voice coaxing in my ear. "Stop," Hannah whispered. "Jacob, stop, it's over. You won, it's over. Two breaths in, remember? Two breaths in?"

I looked at her, saw the fear there, then looked down at Adam. His face was swollen and slick with blood, his nose was split down the middle and mashed down to hamburger paste. "This is done," I said, sucking in wind. Two breaths in, two out. Serenity in, rage out. "We're done. You ever come near me or her again, I'll kill you. But leave me alone, I'll leave you alone, all right?"

Adam muttered something wet and unintelligible, but the fight seemed to have left him. I let Hannah bring me to my feet, then turn me around. Her eyes swam with hurt and fear. I wanted to wrap her in my arms, to say I was sorry, to make any promise I needed to keep her in my life. I touched her cheek, my sticky fingers leaving bloody blotches on her skin. Then she looked past me and screamed.

I spun, expecting to see one of Adam's friends charging out from the dark. But there was nobody else. In retrospect, that was likely part of the plan. Adam wouldn't want any of his buddies going down for what was about to happen. Adam had managed to rise to a knee; in his hands a small, black, revolver.

"You fucking fuck," Adam spat at me, the words thick and bubbling through the blood in his mouth, almost intelligible. "You fucking, bastard fuck!"

I shoved Hannah behind me, waiting for the blast, hoping my body was thick enough to stop the bullet. On the porch people were screaming, scrambling to go inside, all except Doug and his squeeze who stood transfixed, eyes hazy and only beginning to fill with alarm.

"You think I'd keep eating your shit?" Adam said, rising to his feet, legs shaking. "You think you can humiliate me, you giant fucking fuck!?"

I held up my hands. "Adam," I said evenly, "just let everyone else go back inside. This is just between us, you don't need – "

He took a step forward and screamed, blood and spittle misting the ground before him. "Don't you fucking tell me what I need to do!" This was it, I prepared for the impact, the heavy pain that would pull me down into the deep dark, into the silence at the bottom of all things.

A rock, the same one that had struck Hannah, went whizzing by my shoulder, and hit Adam in his already broken nose. The gun went off, and the ground exploded at my feet. I didn't wait for him to take a second shot.

When I reached Adam I grabbed him by the wrist, trying to wrestle the gun away, while Hannah hovered near the periphery, a second rock clutched in her hand. We tangled, muscles taut, no sounds save for soft grunts as our weights shifted and locked. I spun him and the gun went off, then it went off again, two bullets whizzing out of sight. I grunted, then twisted Adam's wrist toward his own body, the bones grinding and snapping. He screamed, then the gun went off a fourth and final time.

Adam jerked, the anger bleeding from his face, turning to shock, to pain. He stumbled back, the gun clattering to the ground between us. He pressed a hand to his chest, feeling the edges of the hole that had been blown into him. He let out a sound, somewhere between a gasp and a whimper.

Then, he died. No fanfare, no final words, just a short drop to the dirt road and a pool of spreading blood.

Hannah appeared at my side; hand clamped over her mouth to stifle a scream.

"Is he?"

"Yeah," I said.

Then we heard it, a choked sob breaking into a low moan. At first I thought Adam was alive, still suffering a sucking chest wound, but the sound was coming from the porch. Doug was on his knees, his shirt soaked with blood, a clump of blond hair sitting on his shoulder as if it had taken root and grown there.

Cradled in his lap lay the girl, Lindsay. Her face was nearly gone, just a raw wound of broken teeth and one green eye, exposed to the open air, staring sightlessly into the night. I looked at Adam's corpse, then the gun, remembering the shots that had gone off during our struggle. It seemed that one of them had found a home after all.

"Oh shit," Doug said, shaking his head, tears flowing down his face. "Don't be dead, please don't be dead."

Hannah was the one to approach first, sliding past me, up the stairs, silent as a ghost as she crouched next to the dead girl. She pressed two fingers to the girl's neck, then confirmed what we all already knew with a small nod.

Doug's wail joined the chorus of approaching police sirens. One of the neighbors had called the cops.

"We're fucked, man," he said, stroking what was left of Lindsay's scalp, "we're dead. We're all dead."

Hannah studied him, then looked down at the dead girl. "Who is she?" she asked, her voice thin, breathless.

"Her name was Lindsay," Doug said, shaking his head, almost hysterical now. "Lindsay Porter. She's the sheriff's kid, man!"

The sudden terror in Hannah's eyes mirrored my own. There wasn't a citizen alive in our corner of Echo City that hadn't been harassed by the cops, most of whom saw the sprawling network of trailer parks and strip malls as a Hellmouth that only birthed delinquents and psychopaths. The sheriff, Porter, was the worst of them, and had been trying to find a reason to put me away ever since he arrested my Dad. Hannah gave Doug one last pitying look, then rose, took me by the hand and started pulling me away from the trailer.

"What are …" I began and she held up a hand to silence me.

"Listen," she hissed, pointing a finger toward the dark sky. The sirens were closer, lots of them. "The sheriff already hates your guts. We got to leave town, now."

"But I didn't shoot her. Adam brought the gun, he's the one who …"

"And he's dead," Hannah responded. "Porter won't have anyone else to punish but you, and he will. You know he will."

I stared at her, struck with a perverse pang of love. I had yelled at her, broken my promise, and brought her into a maelstrom of violence and death. If she wanted, she could have vanished into the night, cut ties with me, with this night, with the thousand jagged edges that littered the ground around our relationship like glass. Yet here she was, at my side, trying to pull me to safety, still thinking of us as an us.

Behind us, Doug let out another choked wail as he plucked the bit of scalp off his shoulder and, gingerly, tried to set it back in place atop Lindsay's exposed skull cap.

"What about him?" I whispered.

She continued to pull me, leading into the dark between two trailers, towards the distant tree line that separated the bad part of town from the good. She remained silent for a moment, then shrugged, voice surprisingly cool. "He made his bed. Let him lay in it."

"Where are we going?" I asked, but she didn't reply, trudging doggedly ahead, hand squeezing mine so tight my fingers went numb.

I wanted to tell her that Porter might kill Doug. We could just explain it all away, pin everything on Adam. Sure, Porter may come for me, but by then Hannah would be safe. She could go back to school and finish her last year; leave me and build the life she deserved while I drowned in the filth I'd been raised in.

But I didn't. I suppose that even then, shock and adrenaline warring inside me, I knew that love ran deeper than reason, or even loyalty to a friend.

We left town that night, slipping down a midnight-black county road, my truck headlights barely illuminating a dozen yards before us. And then…

Dr. Lorenz: And then?
Jacob: …
Dr. Lorenz: You moved around a lot? Stayed mostly in motels, is that right?
Jacob: Yes.
Dr. Lorenz: You got married in Vegas, correct?
Jacob: Yes.
Dr. Lorenz: And then…then you came here?
Jacob: Yes.
Dr. Lorenz: Why?
Jacob: …
Dr. Lorenz: Jacob? Why did you come to Victor's Point?
Jacob: …
Dr. Lorenz: Jacob?

4

FLOWER CHILD

1 - Hannah

After the sheriff had left, Jacob and I went room by room and locked every window and every door. Then, before bed, Jacob checked them again, stalking through the house, his fists clenched at his sides until he slid into bed next to me. I took his fists into my hands and kneaded them open one at a time. Soon enough, the air filled with familiar pillow talk, both of us seemingly desperate to discuss anything other than what had just happened. Eventually, Jacob slept.

I thought I might, too. Wendy had cried for hours after the incident, and despite her usual nocturnal nature, she had slipped into a noiseless sleep the second I set her down in the crib. I dared to hope that I might do the same. It had been months since Jacob and I had slept a full night in the same bed.

But sleep eluded me. I laid in our bed, my back pressed against Jacob's chest, eyes fixed on the window, waiting for our visitor to creep up from beneath the sill. I imagined long thin fingers sliding under the frame, inching it upwards, the lock popping open as if to invite them in. I imagined waking to find Jacob dead, his arms stiff with rigor mortis and ensnaring me like a cage of flesh, trapping me, forcing me to listen as my baby died of dehydration only ten feet away. Worst, I imagined simply waking to find Wendy gone, spirited off into the night like children in the fairy tales of old, a bundle of birch bark and twigs left in her place.

Eventually, my racing mind drove me to my feet. I slid from the bed. I checked Wendy, her fist pressed to her mouth in slumber. I reached down to touch her, to remind myself that she was here and she was whole, but I knew all too well that a touch could spoil whatever spell kept her asleep. So I just held my hand over her, felt the gentle warmth of her body, and the small puffs of her breath. She had her father's ears, and if the fluff atop her head was any indication, his red hair. My eyes, though. And the shape of my face, my brow line. Yet, there were other parts of her I didn't recognize. The slope of her neck as it connected to her shoulders, her chin, her lips. Those seemed to be entirely her own as if, by some strange alchemy, Jacob and I had created something more than its constituent parts.

I left her to sleep and slipped into the darkened house, avoiding each creaky board in the hall with practiced steps. I checked the locks in each room, wiggling every window in its frame to make sure. Yet the feeling of disquiet didn't fade. Staring out into the absolute dark of the forest, I couldn't help but feel like a diver stuck inside a shark cage, cowering behind the illusion of safety while great fanged shadows prowled the waters beyond.

I tried to read, sitting in one of our thrift store recliners, the arms patched with duct tape. The book was among the stack I had gotten from the resale bin at the supermarket on one of my few visits to town, some steamy thriller about a lady cop who struggles to solve a murder and figure out which bad boy ex-mobster she wants to sleep with. Within minutes I found myself rereading the same paragraph over and over, eyes forever flicking towards the darkened window, sure that any moment a face would appear. I gave up and turned on the TV. Stretched across the couch, I half-watched a late-night marathon of *The Fresh Prince of Bel-Air*. After an hour, sleep found me there.

Usually my dreams are terrible, especially since that last night in Echo City, where the consequences of Jacob's lifestyle were finally laid bare before me. I dreamed of girls with pixie cuts, their faces vanishing into a red mist. I dreamed of bloodied fists, the sound of bones breaking, of sirens forever approaching.

That night, though, I dreamed of lights. In my dream I woke, startled to see the sun had already risen outside.

"Jacob?" I called, but there was no answer. Thinking that he had overslept his alarm, I rose, intending to run down the hall and shake him awake before he got into trouble with Tracy, when I noticed that the light was all wrong. Too bright, too pale, and only coming in through the large bay window that ran along the living room's northern wall.

I felt no alarm, only a gentle curiosity that drew me closer. Strange as it may sound, The Light seemed somehow familiar, like greeting an old friend. A soft warmth crept over me where it touched, pushing beneath my skin, until I glowed as if I'd swallowed the moon.

"Be not afraid," a voice whispered, seeming to come from inside my own head. *"You are just beginning to wake up."*

The Light swept up my arms and into my chest. My thoughts went quiet, my body breaking apart into light. I *became* it, one mote in an endless sea where time was but a word and death a frame of reference. Inside me, I felt doors opening – revealing cobwebbed rooms long forgotten, the dust on their floors swirling with the wind of new life.

The next thing I knew, Jacob was standing above me, gently shaking my shoulder.

"Hannah? Babe? I'm taking off," he said.

I blinked, the world coming back to me bit by bit. I was still on the couch, my body intact.

"No," I groaned, grabbing him by the hem of his shirt on reflex. "Stay."

He let out a soft laugh, wiping a few stray hairs off my forehead. "Rough night?"

"No," I said again, blinking sleep from my eyes and hoisting myself to a sitting position. To my great surprise I felt mostly OK, despite spending half the night awake. "Not terrible, actually."

"Good," he said, and with a glance at his watch, winced. "I've got to get moving if I'm going to make it on time. Wendy is still asleep, I just checked. You can catch a few more hours, if you want."

Wiping sleep from my eyes I looked up at him, reached for his beard, pulled him towards me. Jacob's body felt like stone against mine, his lips the only soft part of him and, as always, I inwardly delighted that they belonged to me alone. "I'm awake," I said, sounding anything but. "Go, say hi to Tracy for me."

"I will. Call me if anything else weird happens. I mean it, you see a funny looking squirrel, I want to know."

"Yes, sir," I said with a mock salute.

A few more words, the customary exchange of 'I love you,' and he was gone. I sat there on the couch, staring blankly at the television, trying to will myself to get up, to not waste this rare chance to be awake with the sun. It had been days since I had found time to tend to my garden, and that had been in the middle of the night, working by the dim light of an LED lantern and tripping over every rock. The prospect of working with the warm sun on my skin was enticing, but something kept me glued in place.

What an odd dream. I remembered The Light, the shine of my skin, the voice that sounded like it was coming from both within and without. I tried to hold onto these pieces, to push them into a pattern that made sense, but the longer I thought about it the more the memories drifted through my fingers like sand, leaving nothing but a few granules stuck to my palms.

Foggy-headed, I finally rose and made my way to the bedroom. Ten minutes later, now dressed in shorts and a tank top, I checked on Wendy, still asleep. Then, I made my way out to the garden. When we bought the house, I'd been delighted to find that the previous owner had maintained a large vegetable garden, a square of rich dark earth enclosed in a chicken wire fence. After some serious de-weeding, and the addition of a few planter boxes, I had made it my own. I planted rows of tomatoes, sweet potatoes, peas, and beans of a dozen shades. My real pride, though, were my pumpkins, currently just a tangle of riotous vines that ran along one entire wall of the garden. When the pumpkins themselves arrived, I would encase them in plastic molds that forced them to grow into outlandish shapes, my favorite being the leering skull and the Frankenstein face. I had been wanting to experiment with molds for years and had never enjoyed a space of my own to do it. I thought once they were grown, I might take them to the farmer's market in town, just in time for Halloween.

I set to work, carefully moving down each row and plucking small sprouts and weeds, trimming dead leaves, the familiar movements soothing the last shreds of anxiety that had had been nagging at me ever since the home invasion. Then, I noticed that one of my tomato plants had been trampled, the stalk broken, leaves ground into the mud. I looked to the rows on either side and noticed that other plants had been trampled as well, making a clear path straight across the garden box. At first, I thought it might have been a deer but if so, why hadn't it eaten anything, and how did it get past the fencing? I traced the path across the garden to where I found a single footprint, set deep into the mud beside my eggplants. It was long and thin, and entirely smooth. Just like the one Jacob had found beneath the bedroom window.

I wasn't afraid, the sun and open air banishing the terror for now. Instead, I was curious. I slipped my phone from my pocket and snapped a quick photo, wishing I had plaster on hand to make an impression. I could take it down to town and show it off, just like the crazy Bigfoot hunters on TV. I considered calling Sheriff Quinn – maybe this was a trail that could be followed. Before I could make good on that thought, I noticed the woman at the fence for the first time, only a few feet from me, and I screamed.

The woman jumped, startled, and held up her hands in surrender. "Whoa, whoa, whoa, I come in peace!"

She was tall and willowy, with a pointed chin, board-straight blond hair, and a narrow face that reminded me of a horse. Coupled with her kaleidoscopic sundress and the tangle of wooden beads that hung from her wrists, she looked like a flower child fresh out of Woodstock. "Sorry to startle you," she said, hands still raised. "Just out for a walk and thought I'd introduce myself to the neighbors."

I took a steadying breath and rose to my feet, noticing the bright yellow bicycle sitting parked on the grass behind her, a small basket on its front containing an old, beat up, boom box. "It's all right," I replied. "I just didn't hear you coming."

"I'm Astra."

"Hannah,"

"You guys just move in? Haven't seen you around before."

"Uh- a few months ago," I said, assessing her cautiously. She was a good two heads taller than me, and willowy though not without some muscle. The woman seemed harmless in broad daylight but hadn't Jacob said the person he saw behind me was tall and thin? What if she was one of the intruders? What if she was here for Wendy just like Sheriff Quinn had warned?

The woman watched me for a moment, as if waiting for me to continue. When I didn't, she grew flustered. "I'm sorry, I'm a shit head. Here you are minding your own business and I come butting in. Sorry, I'll leave you to it."

"Wait," I blurted out, a flush borne of embarrassment creeping up my neck. "I'm sorry. I'm just being paranoid. We had someone break into our house last night and I guess I'm a little on edge."

The woman's smile was bright, perfect white teeth lined up like headstones in a military cemetery. Then, seeming to spot the trail of crushed plants that cut a path through my garden, she asked, "Did the intruders do that?"

"I think so. The sheriff thinks it was teenagers."

"He's probably right," she said offhandedly. "I'd offer to help but I've got a black thumb. Can't keep a damn thing alive longer than a week. Mind if I hang around a minute?"

Part of me wanted to tell her no and send her on her way. But my apprehension was slowly easing, replaced with interest. I loved Jacob, but this was the longest conversation I'd had with another adult that wasn't him in over a month. A friendly chat would be good, a potential friend better. Lord knew none of my old circle from Echo City were calling these days. I shoved my paranoia into a dark pit at the back of my mind. "Sure. If you aren't in a hurry."

"I'm never in a hurry," she said.

Soon enough we were both on our knees in the garden, her dress hiked up and fanned around her, uncaring of the dirt and mud soaking into the fabric. She watched, rapt, as I trimmed damaged stalks, the steady snip of the garden shears a soft percussion to our conversation. I expected her to ask about the home invasion but, to my relief, she didn't. Not immediately.

"So, what is Hannah Riley all about?" she asked. "Other than gardening."

"I read, I change diapers, and I plant," I told her as I gestured to the garden. "I prefer to think of this as research," I said. "I completed three years of a botany program. Just a few classes short of my bachelors."

She snorted, delicately lifting the leaf of one of my tomato plants to view the small fruit growing beneath. "Better than I did. Ran away from home just after high school, bounced around the country for a few years, did too many drugs, screwed the wrong people – the usual sad sack story."

"Why did you run away?" I asked, and then winced, sure I had overstepped. But Astra didn't seem to mind.

"The usual reasons," she said, voice cool and even, eyes not leaving the tomato. "My Mom died when I was little. Stepmom treated me like a parasite, Dad let her. Eventually I met a sweet talker who promised to take me away from my life of degradation and treat me like the queen I was," she scoffed. "That lasted about three weeks, and by then I was cut loose. Eventually I joined up with a pretty cool group of people up in the hills, kind of post-modern hippies, real commune life. It isn't bad, just a little cramped sometimes. What about you?"

"What about me?"

"Well, you got a husband? What's he like? Been ages since I've talked *boys*."

"Not much to tell," I said slowly, a small part of me still quietly insisting that I shut the hell up.

"How'd you meet?" she pressed.

I didn't want to say, knew that that story often bled seamlessly into others. Stories that still could land Jacob behind bars if they somehow traveled far enough. But then before I knew it I was speaking all the same, as if the words had been drawn out by some strange gravity radiating from the woman's pale blue eyes. "My husband and I met when we were kids. He saved me. My friends and I were swimming at the community pool and we were competing to see who could hold their breath the longest, only it was super crowded that day. Some asshole kicked me in the head while they were thrashing about. Next thing I knew, some red headed delinquent I didn't know was pulling me out."

"Awww, that's sweet. Right out of a story book."

"Yeah," I said with a roll of the eyes, "maybe if it was written by Harold

Schechter. Jacob was… well, he was from the bad part of town. I wasn't. I didn't think I'd ever see him again, but a couple days later I stepped out of my house and he was in the front drive. He said that he just wanted to check on me, brought flowers. Dad hated his guts, though. Said he was a criminal, and to be fair, he was."

"Got a thing for bad boys?"

"No, I have a thing for Jacob," I said, crouching down before my most finicky bean plant. "We did the whole Romeo and Juliet thing. He'd sneak to my side of town; I'd find reasons to go to his. At first we had help – most of my friends thought the whole thing was terribly romantic, right up until they found out how poor he was. Hit a few rocky points when my parents found out and kept me on a short leash for six months. Couldn't call him, couldn't write. We were, geez, sixteen? I figured by the time I was free he would have moved on to someone else. God knows he could have."

"But he didn't?" Astra asked, her hands now still, bright blue eyes still fixed on me with unerring focus.

"No, he never did. Even when we broke up a few times, I don't think he ever so much as looked at someone else."

"That you know," Astra said, pointedly. "In my experience, guys don't advertise when they've been fucking around."

I just shook my head. "No, not Jacob."

He broke *other* promises. A flash, a memory, the gun going off, Lindsay Porter's head caved in like a rotten pumpkin.

Astra studied me for another moment, then shrugged, her gaze returning to the plant before her. "That why you guys are in hiding out here?" she asked the question casually, without judgment.

Still, my heart nearly exploded in my chest. "What makes you think we are in hiding?" I asked, trying to keep my voice steady and conversational.

Astra rolled her eyes again. "Come on. Good girl ditches college, runs off with her criminal boyfriend, and where do they go? Victor's Point?" She gestured all around. "Nothing out here but a town that hasn't figured out it's dead yet, and a bunch of crazies up in the hills. Not exactly a place you come to unless you're looking to drop off the map."

I knew what I should do at that point. Lie. Tell her that she's wrong, maybe that this particular patch of earth was of botanical interest? Or that we had family in town who got us the place cheap? Maybe I was tired, because right then I decided that not only did I like Astra, but that I was in desperate need of a friend. Besides, a voice whispered somewhere just below conscious thought, *it isn't like you'd be telling her anything she doesn't already know.* I took a deep breath. "It's kind of a long story."

Astra looked up at me, a sly smile on her face. "I got nowhere to be."

I decided I needed a drink first. I led her back to the house. Lemonades in hand, we sat out on a pair of battered deck chairs, our conversation low in fear of waking the baby. I started with Sheriff Porter.

"Porter was this mean old bastard; he'd been sheriff since I was a little kid. He hated Jacob. He hated everyone from the trailer parks. I think if he could have gotten away with it, he would have burned them all down. Maybe the whole southern half of Echo. Jacob had a few run ins with him, and he wasn't exactly gentle when he busted Jacob for vandalism, loitering … you know, kids' stuff. That changed when Jacob had his first big growth spurt. Next time Porter went after him, Jacob lost his temper and socked him in the eye. He spent some time in juvie for that, and the second he was free Porter was on his ass. Mine, too, for that matter. He kept talking to my parents, telling them that I was going to end up a prostitute if I kept hanging around the *undesirables*."

As I spoke, Astra had been digging around in her bag, from which she now produced a joint. She lit it without comment, the pungent smoke tickling my nostrils. She held the joint out to me and, though I can't say why, I took it. I had only smoked once, when some of Jacob's friends insinuated that I "couldn't hang," and my memory of the experience was decidedly negative, filled with hacking coughs and a deep nausea. Maybe it was the stress of the previous night, or my need for Astra to like me, but I didn't even think about it. I took a small drag off the joint, inhaled, held my breath, just as I'd seen Jacob do a hundred times in our old life.

The burn was there, though not as bad as I remembered. I cooled it with a gulp of lemonade and passed the joint back, trying to look like I'd done this before. Astra took it without comment, eyes forward, waiting for me to continue.

I took a deep breath. "We weren't careful. I got pregnant. After that, I made Jacob promise that he would leave all the bullshit behind. No more stealing, no more drugs, no more fighting. Took him about twenty hours to break two out of three of those promises. Some real bad shit happened." The world was shifting now, becoming more vibrant, as if the sun was creeping inside everything. *What* was in that joint?

"What happened?" Astra asked, voice soft.

Some small part of me resisted, screaming at me to focus. This was not a story to share, but one you took to your grave, and yet the words came out all the same. I told her about the last night in Echo City, Lindsay Porter, Adam Letchie, and our frenzied flight from town. I told her about the desperate calls from my parents, who thought I'd been kidnapped. I told her about the months spent drifting from small town to small town, staying in cheap motels, working odd jobs for cash. I told her about giving birth in a rural hospital in Wisconsin. I told her about our decision to try and settle in a place we could afford, and work towards a dream of distant cities. And then, for reasons I cannot understand, I told her about the night before, and the strange intruders who had briefly terrorized our household. Everything except the dream. The entire time, the joint continued to move between us, the silver smoke hanging around my thoughts, chemical lubrication dragging out the words I swore to myself I would never share.

When it was done she nodded, wide-eyed. "Wow. That's one hell of a story." She leaned back and took a drag, not exhaling but just letting the smoke roll out between her lips. "So you think that Porter guy went off the reservation?"

I nodded. "Jacob still can't get in touch with Doug. We heard Porter hauled him off, and says Doug's in prison, but we can't find anything about a trial online. Jacob thinks Porter did something to him."

"Does he know you were even there? You sure he wasn't the one snooping around here last night?"

"We don't know," I said. "But there were plenty of other people at that party. I'm sure one of them talked. Our hope is that by now he's given up looking for us."

Astra passed the joint back. "I don't know, man. If I thought someone was the reason my kid got killed, I'd end the whole fucking world to find them."

I took a hit, but this one tasted different. Acrid, like something chemical. My thoughts were growing hazier by the moment, and the light was changing. It grew brighter and somehow more solid, shafts of sunlight crystalizing into strange fractal patterns, throwing a spray of colors across the yard. "You have kids?" I asked.

Inside, Wendy began to cry. Astra looked back towards the house, then at me. "Yeah, a couple. But we can talk about that later. Sounds like you got your own little monster to deal with."

I nodded as I tried to stand, but my feet kept sinking into the ground. The trees began to bleed together, like paint swirling around on a wet pallet, mixing and merging into a dizzying portrait of color and sound. "Wha – what was in that joint?" I whispered.

Astra looked down at the smoldering nub in her hand. "Oh shit," she said, laughing. "Sorry, I should have warned you. It's my own herbal blend. Bit of marijuana, bit of mugwort, and a dash of DMT right there at the bottom. I like it how it eases you into the trip."

My heart started to hammer, the sound no longer inside me but all around. Astra's face swelled larger and larger until it stretched from one horizon to the next, each sapphire eye like the entrance to an infinite hallway of stars. A smile split across her face. "You've never done this before, have you?" she asked, voice booming like a god's.

"No," was all I could moan. Wendy's crying vibrated the air around me and seemed to come from the house, the forest, my bones. I tried to stand again; my baby needed me. But my legs felt like rubber and I collapsed, sweating, into the seat.

Astra laughed again. "Don't worry, babe. You just sit right there and enjoy the ride. Auntie Astra is here to help."

Then, I was lost. I fell into her left eye, falling past stars and swirling nebula, past planets, and suns, and great fields of tumbling stone caught in a forever waltz around the belt of a purple planet. Everything became fractal, reflections in a broken mirror repeating over and over again.

Images swam by in the cosmos of fractured light. Astra bouncing Wendy on her lap, singing a song in a language I couldn't comprehend. Jacob with his fists bloody, guiltily glancing at a package in the back seat of his truck. A man with a bushy beard and a double chin standing before a bonfire while stars danced above him. A face made from impossible shapes, smiling at me, seeing me, looking within me. I had no body, no reason, my thoughts protean, forever shifting, but above it all, love. A deep love that seemed to blanket me, wrap around me, perfect and whole and without complication.

Astra's face appeared again, but warped, the eyes set up too high and far apart, lips gone into a thin white line. "Just relax," she whispered. "I won't let anything bad happen."

I don't remember what happened next save for scraps. A color I can't name. A sound like the gears of a machine the size of the universe. The chattering language of the ones who maintain it. Then, I was back in my living room, lying on the couch, slick with sweat, and aching in my bones.

As I sat up, I noticed the sticky note that had been left on the arm of the couch. The handwriting was lacy, the ink red.

'Changed Wendy. Got her to eat. Had to jet, but this was fun. Call me if you want to hang out again. – XOXO, Astra'

I know I should have been alarmed that I had left a stranger alone in our house, with our baby, especially after last night. Though at the moment, I couldn't summon up much emotion at all. I felt like I'd been hollowed out and stuffed with cotton. I stood and lethargically wandered to the bedroom, to Wendy's crib.

There she was, our little miracle. She smiled up at me, one pudgy hand wrapped around the neck of a stuffed goose that Jacob had gotten her. In her other hand she held a bundle of sticks, crudely lashed together with twine into the rough shape of a man. That was new, likely a gift from "Auntie Astra."

"Hey, baby," I whispered. She giggled up at me. I checked the rest of the house, Wendy in my arms every step of the way. Nothing was missing, nothing broken. Astra had even washed the spoon she'd used to feed Wendy.

I sat back down on the couch and stared at her note. Had I just made a friend, or a mistake? Both seemed likely. And yet, I trusted her, and that trust seemed a natural thing.

We watched TV while I jangled plastic keys for Wendy. By the time the cotton had fully cleared from my head, dark had begun to descend. The moment the light began to shift, the fear returned with it, and Wendy started to cry. I found myself no longer watching the television but staring out the windows, moving silently from room to room and checking the locks. Then, obeying some sense that something was terribly wrong, I checked them again. We looked in closets, under beds, and with each reveal my dread grew, sure that eventually I would open a door to find we were not alone. Whatever presence I was feeling, we never did find anyone. We sat back on the couch, watching the gloom deepen as Wendy's wails grew with the persistent intensity of a tornado siren.

That was when Jacob called.

2

By the time Jacob's truck slid into the driveway, I was in the kitchen with Wendy, heating boxed lasagna, one eye on the window, the other on the dark doorway that led into the hall and the rest of the house beyond.

I watched Jacob climb out of the car, his massive body a shifting boulder in the dark. He got something from the back seat, climbed the steps and I ran to the front door, conscious of every inch of the dark hall as I ran through it. I threw my arms around his neck the moment he was inside, pressing my face to his chest, breathing deep. The hard stone of fear that had been sitting heavy in my stomach softened a little. I craned my head up to kiss him, but the look on his face gave me pause.

He was salt white, his muddy brown eyes wide, mouth set into a firm line.

"What happened?" I asked, cupping his face.

"We need to talk," he said.

"Oh, God," I whispered, a thousand possibilities running through my mind, none of them good. "Porter?"

"No," he said, shifting the long box he held under his arm, "but we need to talk."

We went to the kitchen, where he sank down into a chair, looking gaunt.

When he didn't immediately begin explaining himself, I sat down opposite him and drew one of his hands into mine, noticing that two of his knuckles were split.

"I hurt someone. Danny, Quinn's kid," he finally said. "I already called Quinn. He seems madder at Danny than me but – I'm sorry, Rabbit. I don't know what happened. It was like I didn't have a choice. Moment he said he was going to come after you and Wendy, I just lost it." Hearing him call me Rabbit was strange. The nickname had come from his friends back in Echo City, started as some joke about a moose fucking a rabbit. At the time I had taken it, made it my name, an alter ego to don every time I snuck across the woods into the trailer parks. Rabbit was tougher and meaner than I, and I thought she, and the nickname, died the same night as Adam and Lindsay.

"Tell me everything," I insisted. "From the beginning."

And so, he did. When he was done, I sat back, turning over the story in my mind, pangs of betrayal and hurt echoing through me. It wasn't fair, I knew that. From the sound of it, this Danny kid had instigated the whole affair. Yet, no matter how rationally I thought it through, the sight of his split knuckles hurt. As if the violence we had fled in Echo City had followed us here.

"Rabbit? You OK?" he asked, and I realized I hadn't spoken for at least thirty seconds.

"Yeah," I whispered, and started to cry.

Jacob frowned then stood and moved to my side, kneeling next to me. "I'm sorry," he whispered, voice like sandpaper. "I'm so goddamn sorry. I don't want to be like this."

I shook my head, hating myself for crying. "Don't be sorry," I said, shaking my head, eyes shut. "I would have done the same thing, I just —" I stopped speaking as my eyes fell on the box for the first time, the one that Jacob had retrieved from the truck and which now leaned against the wall beside his chair. "What is that?" I asked.

He glanced at it, then back at me, somehow losing even more color in the process. "After last night, Quinn said we should — well, with what happened last night, I just — "

"Jacob," I said, pain suddenly bursting into anger. "Is that a gun?"

He sighed, stood and grabbed the box, then opened it to reveal the weathered stock of a shotgun. "I'm sorry. I just want to keep you safe. You and Wendy. Quinn thinks there could be some really bad people up in those hills and I couldn't stand to think of someone carrying you or Wendy off."

I nodded slowly, "And you, what? Didn't think I deserved to be part of that decision? Or were you planning to hide it from me?"

"Dammit, I — " He took in two breaths, steadying himself. "I'm not hiding it. I brought it right in. I know we said no guns, but if someone busts in here, I need to know that we can defend ourselves."

I wasn't really hearing him anymore. I was staring at the box, but seeing something else: Gary Letchie's shirt stuck to the hole in his chest, and Lindsay Porter's exposed skull. "That isn't the fucking point," I shouted, standing, forcing my eyes to meet his, wiping furious tears off my face. "Goddammit, Jacob, you promised!"

"I'm trying!" he shouted back. "Fuck, Hannah, do you realize how dangerous last night was? Someone was here, in our house, and who the fuck knows how many of them were here. They could have hurt you, or Wendy, and I can't let that happen!"

"Well, maybe we should just leave then!"

"And what!? Spend another ten months living in the truck? God knows we can't sell this place, nobody else is dumb enough to buy it!"

I let out a small grumbling of frustration. I wanted to slap him. "You should have talked to me! You and me, in this together, remember? That was our deal. No fighting, no guns," no drugs either, but I'd already broken that edict, a fact I was still trying to wrap my head around. "We're supposed to be in this together. Sometimes I feel like you think I'm some porcelain doll. Don't forget, I'm the one who got *you* out of Echo City, not the other way around."

"Hannah, I – "

"No! I need more than excuses, Jacob. I need you to think before you – "

"Please don't leave me," Jacob said, the exhaustion suddenly lifted from his voice.

I looked at him, startled. We had been together, in one way or another, for almost twenty years. The idea of either of us dumping the other at this point seemed as improbable as one of us deciding to give up oxygen.

"Do you really think I'd leave you?" I whispered.

He looked confused, his voice hoarse again, "What? Hannah, I-"

"After the fights? The drugs? After Echo City, you really think I'd leave you *now?!*"

"I've been waiting for you to leave for ten years," I heard him say. And yet, his lips never moved. He just stared at me, eyes wide with concern, mouth sealed shut. I ripped my hands away from him and stood, knocking my chair to the ground, heart hammering in my throat.

"Hannah? What's going on? I never said anything about you leaving me," he said.

"But you- I heard you. You..." I trailed off, unable to give voice to the impossibility happening before my eyes.

The emotional hammer of everything that had happened that day came crashing down on me. Meeting Astra, the drugging, the paranoia, and now this. I tried to speak but the words mushed together into the moan of a terrified animal.

Jacob coaxed me to the living room, then onto the couch. He turned on the television and finished making the lasagna. We didn't speak as we ate, both instead pretending to watch some shitty ghost-hunting show about former electricians turned paranormal investigators.

When it was done, and the plates had been put in the sink, he wrapped his arms around me and waited in pensive silence until I could find my words again. I spoke softly into his chest.

"I've had a very strange day," I said.

"So, tell me about it."

And I did. I told him about Astra, about the laced joint, the paranoia, and finally, the words I'd thought I heard him say.

He listened, nodding along at a few points, saying nothing until I was done, eyes now dry and irritated, throat hoarse.

"You sure she said it was DMT?" he asked once I was done.

I nodded, that was my last clear memory before the trip had taken me.

He nodded, one hand absently rubbing my back, his eyes set on a blank stretch of wall above the TV.

"DMT is a hell of a hallucinogen," he said slowly. "And I'm guessing there was more than mugwort in that joint. Who knows how it all interacts. You're likely still tripping."

"It didn't feel like that tonight," I said. "It was like you were talking in my head."

"It's the drug," he repeated, firmly. Then, sucking in a deep breath, he turned his eyes on me. "Trust me on this. I've got experience in this department. Doug and I used to mix different pills – get the right combo and you'll roll for days."

I looked up into his eyes, wanting the comfort he provided, needing it, but there was something in his look I didn't like. His voice was soft, at ease, but there was a tension in his posture that radiated down his neck and across his shoulders. Maybe it was just the stress of the last few days, and his fight with Danny, but on some level, I knew that wasn't it. He was thinking, planning.

"Don't go," I said.

He looked at me, startled. "What?"

"Don't go looking for Astra's hippie commune or whatever it is," I said. "I know you want to, and it will just bring trouble."

"She drugged you," he said. "I can't just let that go."

"I took the joint," I said softly. "I didn't ask what was in it. I guess I broke our promise, too. Besides, until reality melted, it was kind of nice to make a friend." It *had* been nice and, while I couldn't yet admit it to Jacob, the trip wasn't all bad either until it ended.

"Don't tell me you're still going to hang out with this woman."

"I don't know," I said slowly. "I don't think she meant any harm, she's just a ditz."

"Or, she could be one of the people who tried to break in last night."

"I don't think so. She was alone with Wendy for over an hour. She fed her, put her to bed. I don't think she means any harm."

"But – "

I silenced him with a finger, feeling that it was somehow terribly important that I didn't give ground on this topic. "Jacob, I can't keep sitting in this house alone all day. I love you, I love Wendy, but I haven't had a friend of my own in over a year. I'll be careful, just … let me deal with this one on my own, OK? Trust me, I'll set her straight. No more drugs."

He looked down at me, jaw shifting slowly from side to side, the only sound his grinding teeth. "All right," he whispered. I took his hand in mine and held it. "Are we good?" he asked.

"Yeah, we're good."

Street fights, unwanted guns, and unexpected drugging aside, we were still good.

Sometimes I thought the whole universe could burn, and we would remain, two binary stars circling each other in the forever dark.

3

Two days passed without incident. Jacob went to work while I slept. He slept while I cared for Wendy – the old routine. I almost convinced myself that it had all been a fluke, and that our night of terror had been a singular event. Just some stupid local kids who learned their lesson when Jacob chased them off into the woods. Even the strange telepathy incident had yet to repeat itself, seemingly proving that Jacob was right, and it had all been in my head. Still, when each night fell, I found myself drifting from room to room again, checking the locks.

Three days after I met Astra, Jacob had the day off. He woke me around noon, dressed in his least tattered pair of jeans and a plum button-up that I had gotten him for Christmas several years prior. He had worn the shirt all of three times, and up until today, always at my insistence.

"Hey, hey, pretty lady," he whispered in my ear, kissing a smile onto my face. "Want to go on a date?"

He drove us out of Victor's Point, down through the foothills, the road winding past rivers and through tunnels. The nearest town was Gainsburg, thirty miles to the south and while hardly a metropolis, it had more than the lone greasy spoon diner that Victor's Point had to offer.

We got lunch at a sandwich shop called McGullie's. He had the chicken salad, I got a steak hoagie smothered in onions, both accompanied by heaping helpings of kettle chips. And for Wendy, a jar of pear paste that largely got smeared on the shop's lone highchair. As we ate, we talked about nothing, which is to say the idle banter that only comes through intense familiarity.

Once, when I was sixteen, I had become convinced that this kind of talk spelled the death of a relationship. It meant there were no more personal anecdotes to share, no more professions of love that hadn't been said before. There were, it seemed, no more words left to say to each other. That was one of the times Jacob and I had broken up; though to be more accurate, I dumped him. That lasted all of a week before I called him and met him in the woods around midnight. It had been November, and terribly cold, but neither of us had minded. We walked, hand in hand, talking about nothing at all. That was when I understood that there are two kinds of romantic love.

The first comes when love begins – it's like a supernova, its brilliance growing by the day, each moment together revealing new facets of the person to love. It burns hot and, most of the time, dies just as quickly. The second kind of love comes after, once the star has cooled, all the fire drawn back inward or ejected into the void of space. This love is calmer, a steady rock on which to stand. At that point, the spoken words themselves ceased to matter. The sound of the other person's voice was all you needed to be aware that you were loved and would never be alone.

After lunch, he took me to a park where, under the watch of century old oaks, we walked arm in arm, Wendy's stroller pushed before us. Wendy's head was on a swivel, turning to each new sound and sight, a look of consternation on her pudgy little face.

"What do you suppose she thinks about?" I asked.

Jacob looked down at her, a faint smile tracing his scarred lips. "Probably just a lot of internal screaming. New is scary, and everything is new to her."

"Nah," I said, proudly running a hand over the top of Wendy's scalp, "our girl is a warrior. Like her Dad."

Jacob snorted. "Just hope to god she doesn't end up following my path too closely. We can't afford the legal fees."

A pair of late afternoon joggers passed us on the trail, a young couple, fit in matching jogging suits. We waved to them, they waved back as they passed. I turned to watch them go, then looked up at the golden sunlight that snuck through the canopy of green above.

"It's nice here," I said softly, thinking of our home back in Victor's Point, and the darkness that had settled into it. Then, I was struck with a thought I couldn't dismiss. "Why didn't we move here?"

"Hmm?"

"Gainsburg," I gestured around us. "Public parks, multiple restaurants, probably more than one tattoo parlor. So why didn't we move here?"

Jacob furrowed his brow. "I think we tried," he said. "Remember, the apartment we looked at wouldn't take us? Something about my credit score."

"I think that was Iron Hill," I said. "Actually, I know it was." The apartment complex had had a giant hunk of iron ore out front, and the local high school's mascot was a miner. I remembered passing it when we rolled through town in our search for a place to settle.

"Maybe," Jacob said, scratching his beard. He shrugged, "Probably couldn't afford it then. That whole period is kind of a wash for me. Besides, this place is too on the map. We wanted someplace remote, in case Porter is actually looking for us, remember?"

To my surprise, I didn't remember. I was sure we had talked about it, weighed the options, decided to find some nowhere town up in the hills. However, the more I thought about it, the less I could place *when* we had discussed it. While the odds were I had simply forgotten, I couldn't shake the feeling that I was missing something.

I must have been making a face, because Jacob leaned over and kissed me on the forehead. "Hey, what's going on in that head, Rabbit?"

I smiled up at him and pushed the thought to the back of my mind. The day was bright, Jacob was with me, and we had the whole evening together ahead of us. My own faulty memory, no doubt complicated by my recent foray into psychedelics, could wait to be decoded another day.

"I love you," I said, delighted to see the smile spread across his face.

In response he kissed me, pulling me close in his tattooed arms. My thoughts scattered, my worries turned to ash, and for one moment everything was right in the world.

We took the long way home, avoiding the highway in favor of the winding mountain roads that approached Victor's Point from the south. Wendy, true to fashion, was slumbering in her car seat, no doubt gathering strength for her nightly tirade. I sat in the passenger seat, bare feet poking out of the open window, cruising to the low thrums of a bass guitar and a heavy drumbeat, one of Jacob's metal albums with the volume turned way down. In the distance, the high peak of Mount Olympus marked our destination.

Not nearly the tallest mountain in the Appalachian range, it was nonetheless the tallest in sight, its top rounded like the hip of a sleeping woman and covered in dense pine forest. By the time the lights of Victor's Point became visible, stuck in the shadow of Olympus, the sun had sunk behind the mountains and the sky had turned the color of a bruised peach. The road was dirt, and pitted from years of rain with little maintenance, the truck bouncing along, perpetually threatening to wake the baby. I kept reaching back to check on her, to soothe her, hoping to keep her cries at bay until we got home. So, when the woman appeared in the road, Jacob saw her first.

"What the fuck!" he suddenly erupted, slamming on the brakes. The truck hit a nasty pothole in the road, bouncing the entire frame hard enough to lift me off my seat. Wendy opened her eyes, looked directly at me and started to scream. The truck fishtailed and pitched to the left as Jacob wrestled with the wheel and screeched to a stop.

"What's going on – " I started to ask, then I saw her, too and the words turned to dust in my mouth.

A woman was standing bolt upright in the middle of the road, arms splayed to her sides, her entire naked body stretched like one taut muscle. Her head was tilted back, her mouth open in a silent scream, the whites of her milk saucer eyes glowing under the headlights. At first, I thought she was covered in mud. When I realized the truth, I let out a small gasp.

She was slick with blood, so thick it had congealed into wet lumps across her body, the thickest a river running from her throat to the gore matted bush of her pubis. A line of crude stitches, black and thick, held together a half-healed, crescent shaped wound across her belly. We both stared, mouths gaping, the only sound Wendy's hysterical screams.

The woman's head began to thrash from side to side. Then, her entire body followed suit and began to convulse, her stomach sucking in and out rapidly, her arms twitching and shuddering as if dancing on marionette strings.

"Holy shit," I heard myself say.

The woman dropped her head and looked at us, looked at me. She screamed, a full-throated howl, bloody spittle flecking her cheeks, and then she was running directly at us.

Jacob threw the truck into reverse and slammed on the gas, but was too slow. The woman, moving faster than should have been possible with her belly wound, scrambled atop the front of the truck, her hands pressed flat against the windshield, leaving streaks of clotted gore. Wendy's cries hit their peak and the woman shivered, then let out a hysterical sob.

"Jessie! Jessie, baby! Mommy is here!" she shouted.

Jacob kept on the gas, jerking the wheel from side to side in an attempt to knock her loose. To my horror, she held firm and then, moving an inch at a time to keep her balance, began to creep across the hood towards the passenger side window. I reached for the crank and began to hurriedly roll the window up, making it halfway before she managed to hook an arm around and through the half-closed opening.

Sticky fingers grabbed a fistful of my hair and yanked, bouncing my head off the glass, the pain a bright flash in my vision. Jacob slammed on the brakes and began to struggle with his seatbelt. I reached up, slapped at her fingers, and raked my nails along her arm. The woman slid off the truck, reached through the window with her other hand and caught me around the wrist, violently pulling my arm out the window as if intending to carry me off.

"Jessie!" she continued screaming, craning her head to look at Wendy. "Jessie! Hold on! I'm coming, Mommy is coming!"

Thinking fast, I swung the car door open as hard as I could, slamming it into the woman and sending her tumbling to the dirt, a fistful of my black hair still clutched in her hand. She howled in pain, clutching her crudely stitched belly, which was now bleeding freely.

Jacob approached the woman, having finally extracted himself from the truck. I got out as well, intending to tackle the woman if she took so much as another step towards Wendy.

"Hey," Jacob called to her, his face white, hands shaking. "Miss, what the fuck was that? Do you need an ambulance?"

The woman didn't respond other than to moan again, mumbling one word over and over again. "Jessie, Jessie, Jessie."

Jacob and I traded a worried glance. "She's hurt," I said. "We need to get her to a hospital."

"Or to a priest," Jacob said, tentatively taking another step closer to the woman. "I am going to try and help you, all right? You're delirious."

The woman's only response was to waggle her head from side to side, her eyes hazy and distant. That changed the moment Jacob touched her. As he reached down and gently took her by shoulder, she shrieked and clawed his face with hooked fingers. He let out a shout and stumbled back, a long scratch now running down his left cheek.

Then, she was crawling on all fours right at me, her limbs moving in a strange, herky-jerky dance. I backed towards the car, ready to throw myself back into the cab, but she was faster. The next thing I knew, she was on top of me, grabbing my face between her palms and opening her mouth wide to reveal two rows of jagged, rotten teeth. She lunged, as if to bite at my throat. I threw my hands up and instead her teeth found purchase in the meat on the underside of my forearm. Hot blood burst from the wound and ran down her chin.

I was screaming, thrashing, bucking in a desperate bid to dislodge her, but her thighs had locked around my abdomen and her jaw had begun to saw side to side, sending black dots of agony dancing in front of my eyes. Then, very suddenly, I was seeing something else.

I saw a cage, lined with filth and dirty straw. I saw a pair of inky black eyes hanging over me, something pushing inside me, violating me. I heard screaming but I wasn't sure if it was my own or the woman's or if there was any distinction anymore because I could feel her confusion and rage, and the pain that ran like an undercurrent through it all.

"Jessie!" I found myself screaming, "Jessie! Mommy is here! Jessie!"

Then, Jacob was there, grabbing the woman under the arms and ripping her off me, all four of her limbs clawing at the open air. He slammed her back down on the ground, face first. Then, he did it again, lifting her clear up and slamming her back down, bouncing her skull off the road. The fight left her and she lay in a heap, crying softly. Jacob planted a boot on her back and, breathing heavily, looked at me.

"Are you all right?"

Was I? I took stock. The bite wound was deep and bled freely, but nothing was broken and I could still wiggle all my fingers. "I think so," I said, voice shaky.

"Grab the bungie cords from my toolbox," he instructed, and numbly clutching my wounded arm to my chest, I hoisted myself into the truck bed and rooted through the large black toolbox Jacob had bolted to the truck bed. Just as I turned to climb back down, cords in hand, a wash of white light hit my face. The moment I saw it a thought sprang to mind, though it would be days before I considered how strange it was. *Oh, hello again.*

"Jacob…" I said softly.

"A little busy here!" he called back.

I slid from the truck and went to him, pressed the cords into his hand and then gently took hold of his face and turned it towards the source of the light.

"What are you – oh!"

A ball of luminous white light, like a miniature sun, hovered a hundred yards above the road. It was about the size of the truck, and bright – so bright it hurt to look at. Strangest of all was the odd liquid nature of The Light. It fell from its center in water-like streams, splashing across the ground where it touched, and dissolving into a fine mist that soon faded away.

Inexplicably, the woman sighed happily. "Jessie," she whispered. "I'm coming, sweetie."

The Light pulsed once, then, just as miraculously as it had arrived, it vanished as if it'd never been there at all.

"Oh my god," I whispered. "Did you see that? Please tell me you saw that!"

"I saw," Jacob said, voice terse. He looked down and suddenly recoiled.

The woman's head was turned to the sky, eyes open, mouth curved into a gentle smile, but there was nobody home in those eyes.

She was dead.

Quinn arrived with Deputy Hanson in tow half an hour later.

During the wait, we barely spoke. We just sat side by side in the cab of the truck, staring at the corpse spotlighted by the glow of our headlights. Trying not to think of the vision, or the odd light, I busied myself calming Wendy and bandaging my arm best I could, tearing strips off an old car blanket and wrapping it tight around the bite. The skin nearest the wound had already turned a livid red and, thinking of the woman's filthy jagged teeth, the word infection was never far from my mind. All the while I kept glancing up, watching the stars that emerged in the evening sky, waiting for that familiar thing I could not name.

When Quinn and Hanson arrived, they did so without lights or sirens – just a lone battered police cruiser, its headlights dim and yellow.

"About goddamn time," Jacob grumbled, climbing out of the car to wave them down. The cruiser came to a stop and both men climbed out, their eyes first going to Jacob, and then to the corpse. Quinn let out a long whistle and approached the dead woman.

"Sorry for the delay, folks," he said, sounding exhausted. "It's been – " he sighed, "well, it's been a hell of a few days and we're short staffed. This the woman who assaulted you?"

Jacob looked mad enough to scream, glaring at Quinn, but keeping the anger out of his voice. "Yes," he said, taking a steadying breath. "Crazy bitch jumped on our car, tried to get at Wendy. I had to wrestle her to the ground but…" he trailed off, at a loss for words.

"Uh huh," Quinn said.

"That how she ended up dead?" Hanson asked.

Jacob looked down at the corpse then let out a breath, shaking his head. "I don't know. She was alive one minute then I looked down and she wasn't moving anymore."

"Either of you hurt?" Quinn asked.

I stepped out of the truck and approached, clutching my wounded arm to my chest. "She bit me," I said. "I think the bleeding has stopped but I wouldn't say no to some gauze."

Quinn nodded and gestured to Hanson who ran back to their patrol car, returning a moment later with a red bag marked "Emergency."

"Deputy Hanson will do his best to patch you up. Both our EMTs are out on calls, so if you need anything more than a pressure bandage, we'll have to take you to the hospital in Gainsburg."

The thought of the hospital sent a pang of anxiety through my stomach. We couldn't afford that. We were still buried under the bills from Wendy's birth.

"A bandage should be fine," I said. "It's not deep."

Quinn frowned, looking from me to the woman, then turned to Jacob. "Why don't you step over here and tell me everything that happened." He led Jacob a few steps away, their conversation low, just out of earshot.

Hanson helped me to the back of the truck and as I sat on the tailgate, gingerly peeled my makeshift bandage off, wincing once he got sight of the wound.

"Yikes. This is deeper than it looks. You'll want stitches, otherwise this thing will scar up like a motherfucker." He winced and flashed a boyish smile my way. "Pardon my French."

"No fucking problem," I said.

The deputy started to work on my arm, washing out each of the tooth marks with hydrogen peroxide, then applying a smear of antibacterial cream to the wounds. Then came a roll of gauze.

"Long night?" I asked, just wanting to fill the silence.

"Long week," he said with a sigh. "Not that I need to tell you folks."

"Wouldn't think you would have a ton of trouble around here," I said, looking towards the woman. "Any idea who she was?"

He looked at the corpse, a look of annoyance flickering over his face, then vanishing as fast as it had appeared. "No, but I'm guessing she belongs to the mountain folk. We get someone like her wandering into town or turning up dead every few years. We'll try to ID her, but they aren't too big on birth certificates or public records, so my guess is Ms. Monster has a date with a government funded cremation." He finished wrapping my wound then stepped back to assess his work.

"Apologies if you think I'm being crass. Half the town is chasing balls of light, and the other half thinks the first half is crazy. We just came from breaking up the third fist fight that's broken out tonight alone. I swear there is something in the water."

The image of the miniature sun flashed in my mind and my mouth went dry. "Balls of light?" I asked, trying to keep my voice neutral.

He nodded, chuckling, "Yeah. You would think people would be past the whole UFO thing by this point, but all it takes is an airplane with a spotlight to turn people into a pack of panicked assholes."

I wanted to tell him that he was wrong to doubt them. That the ball of light I had seen could not have been a plane. It made no noise, and it didn't move. But the subtle derision in his voice stayed me. If I spoke, I would be just another crazy in a long night of them and I was too tired to force the issue.

Apparently satisfied with his work, he closed his kit. "It should heal up just fine, but keep an eye on it. Human mouths are petri dishes." He glanced at the woman. "Some worse than others. If it starts getting infected, you're going to need a real doctor."

"Thank you, officer."

"Please, call me Brandon." He paused, glancing over his shoulder back towards Jacob. "Mrs. Riley, do you mind if I ask a weird question?"

I snorted. "Call me Hannah. And I'm not sure how it could be weirder than what just happened."

"Well, do we know each other from somewhere? I keep looking at you and I could swear we've met."

I paused, studied his face. "I don't think so. I'd never even been to this state before we moved here. I must just have one of those faces."

He shrugged and flashed a sly grin. "No worries. Like I said, it was just a feeling."

I don't remember what we talked about after that, some pleasantries offered with a tight smile, most likely. I don't even remember them telling us to leave while they dealt with the corpse. All I remember is riding home in the passenger seat, one hand wrapped tightly in Jacob's, my eyes glued to the starry sky above.

4

By morning I had a mild fever, and a deep ache that ran through my forearm into my fingertips. Before he left for work, Jacob made an attempt to convince me to go to the hospital, but I begged him off.

"It's just a little infection," I told him. "Give me a few days. If it gets any worse, I'll let you take me. I promise."

Eventually he agreed, reluctantly leaving me in a shaky pool of my own sweat. I had been up most of the night with Wendy, and had felt fine until we both fell asleep around five in the morning. When I woke two hours later, my skin was slick with sweat and the burning in my arm had escalated from an ache to a full burn. Peeling away the bandages, a sour smell filled the room.

The skin around the spots where the woman's teeth had punctured my arm had begun to turn a mottled grey, and a few leaked bloody pus. I slathered more antibacterial cream into the wounds, hoping that it wasn't as bad as it looked.

I rewrapped it, then did my best to pass the morning in fitful sleep. When I woke around noon, I knew I might be in trouble. The burn had crept up into my elbow and had begun to move into my bicep. The veins closest to the bandage had darkened, giving my arm the appearance of shattered glass. Blood poisoning – had to be.

I felt no great alarm, just a deep well of despair opening beneath me. I needed to call Jacob, needed to bring him home, get me to a hospital. He would lose out on a day's pay, not to mention whatever the hospital charged; it would set us back months. I delayed as long as I could before I reached for my phone but it wasn't in my pocket. I sat up, looked at the side tables, the coffee table, all bare save for a couple of Jacob's tattoo portfolios. I settled back down on the couch, trying to remember the last place I had seen the damn thing, when I must have fallen asleep again.

Everything got hazier from there. I remember shaking terribly, my very bones feeling like they were about to vibrate out of my skin. I remember the sound of someone knocking on our door, and Wendy. She started to cry at some point. I tried to get up, but the moment I moved a lance of pain shot through my arm, so intense I screamed and fell from the couch.

I laid there for a long time, staring at my bandaged arm as pus began to leak through the wrapping. I wondered what the hell had been in that woman's mouth, and how it could spread so fast. I wondered if I was going to die in the name of financial stubbornness. My mind slipped, colors bled together, the pain now a distant wildfire scorching the horizon.

Other noises. The back door opening, the soft tsk-tsk of a disappointed mother, maybe my mother. Yes, I could see her now, with her dark hair piled high and her plump body looming over me, her eyes narrowed somewhere between love and disapproval. Then she was gone. Someone was talking to Wendy, the child's cries dying off. Someone in the kitchen. Someone placing a wet rag on my head.

Then my mother, standing above me, her bright eyes burning like blue stars. "Went and messed around with a crazy lady, didn't ya?" she said. Her voice was all wrong – too young, too chipper.

The woman knelt closer and I saw it wasn't my mother at all. She had blond hair, a narrow horsey face. Astra. She stroked my brow with a damp cloth. Then, she sang. I didn't recognize any of the words but the tune was soft, etheric, almost like bird song put to words. I closed my eyes and let Astra's voice trickle in. My pain eased, the shaking becoming a mere tremor as she lifted my arm and carefully unwrapped it.

"Oh, sweetie," she whispered. "You're in a real bad way. That filthy breeder almost got you."

She used another rag to clean my arm then smeared something on it. The smell was strange, woodsy and floral but somehow spicy at the same time, and it burned. I let out a small moan, opening my eyes. She was hunched over me, a deific smile on her face, as she pushed small clumps of gray ointment into each of my wounds.

Don't move, she whispered, though her mouth did not move. *It's all right. I will never let anything bad happen to you.*

"Who are you?" I whispered.

I'm you, her voice said inside my head. *Just a few years down the road. When you wake up, call me. You know how.*

She pressed something new into one of my wounds. My vision flashed red. Then darkness was all about.

I dreamed of The Light again. It was pouring through the windows of the house, casting harsh shadows up the walls. As before, I stood at the window, bathing in it, watching with immense pleasure as the light leaked through the pores of my skin and pushed through my veins, filling me with warmth.

"Be not afraid," a voice said to me.

I laughed. How could I be scared? The Light loved me, I was sure of that. I could feel it as an awesome wave, wrapping around me, cradling me.

"What is there to fear?" I asked.

The response was not a word, but a shadow. It started as a dark splotch on the wall beside me and spread like crude oil leaking into the ground. The shadow swelled, grew arms, legs, a long thin body and a high crowned head. Then, a spark of fear alighting in my chest, the shadow swung its oblong head towards me.

"What is it?" I whispered, staring at the shadow, knowing it was staring back.

"That which remains."

The shadow reached for me and I could feel its malice, and a need so deep it had become hate. I froze, my heart hammering, the perfect light pulling back from me as the shadow reached out a hand. Fingers in my mind, cold probes peeling through my memories. It was in my head! Oh god, I could feel it.

"No," I screamed. "No, leave me alone!" I tried to back away, to run, but my legs suddenly stiffened and, to my horror, began to turn to stone.

The shadow pulled against the wall on which it was cast, as if trying to break free.

"Lacie," a voice whispered darkly in my mind. It wasn't the same voice as The Light. No love, only harsh contempt. *"It's time to come home."*

"Go away," I shouted, still unable to move. The shadow stretched, its dark fingers only inches from my face when I finally managed to scream.

The Light returned. It crashed over me, and the shadow howled, a sound like warping steel. It shrank away, became a mote of darkness on the wall.

"Seek and find," The Light said.

"I don't understand!"

"Seek," the voice repeated, *"and find."*

"What am I looking for?"

"You are our instrument."

5

I woke just past 5 pm. The sunlight outside had begun to shift towards gold. I sat up, surprised to find myself in bed. Peering around the gloomy bedroom, I spotted Wendy in her crib, upright and alert, fiddling with something in her pudgy little fingers.

I got all the way to my feet before I realized the pain was gone. I sat, lifted my arm. It had been re-bandaged. Unwrapping it, I prepared for pus, for black veins, and a frenzied flight to the hospital.

The infection was gone. The bite mark was still there, a dozen narrow punctures arranged in a crescent, but they were all scabbed over, little more than scratches now. Had it all been a hallucination? The bandage proved otherwise. It was rough linen, not like anything you'd buy at a pharmacy and while I couldn't be sure, I didn't think we had anything made of the same fabric in the house.

Moving to Wendy's crib, the last of my doubts evaporated. She was playing with the same stick man that Astra had left on her previous visit, a smiley face now painted on its head in yellow nail polish.

I took the doll from Wendy, handing her a stuffed dinosaur that Jacob had gotten her in exchange. I studied the doll, turning it over in my hands, as if hoping it would somehow provide answers and explain what the hell had just happened. Its crude face revealed no answers, just a vague sense of discomfort. Questions littered my head. Who the hell just lets themselves into someone else's house? And, most importantly, what exactly had Astra done to my arm to heal it so quickly?

I glanced at Wendy. "Do you have anything you want to explain?"

She cooed at me, then giggled, shaking the stuffed dinosaur by its neck.

Auntie

The word entered my head, so loud and clear that for a moment I thought there was someone else in the room. I whirled, searching, then looked back at Wendy as her eyes met mine with a curious stare.

"Did you just…?"

Wendy only babbled in response. I let out a breath. "No, of course you didn't."

I left the doll sitting atop the dresser and ventured out into the rest of the house, dimly hoping to find Astra sitting in the living room so she could explain what the hell she had done. I found my old bandages, bloody and caked in dried pus, lying in the kitchen trash can, along with a small clay pot, no larger than a baseball. It looked handmade and was empty save for a few smears of some dark grey cream, the same stuff she'd put on my wound. I sniffed it, then ground a bit of it between my fingers, trying and failing to discern what it might be made of. Plant material, most certainly, but the scent was very odd.

I checked the living room. My sweat-soaked pillow was there, along with another of Astra's sticky notes left on the arm of the couch.

'Glad I swung by when I did. You were in a bad way. Keep it wrapped for a few days, but you should be fine. Grandpa's secret herbal remedy. – XOXO, Astra.'

I read the note, sat, then read it again, turning over my two encounters with Astra in my mind. Thus far, she had proven twice that she was not a threat. She had taken care of Wendy, fixed my arm, and maybe even saved my life. Saved our bank account for sure. But all the windows and doors were locked. Jacob made sure of it each day before he left, so how had she gotten in? And what was that she had said about the crazy woman being a breeder? Had she even said that, or had I hallucinated it?

I thought of the dream, and The Light hovering over the road, and our midnight invaders. Were there connections among it all? The Light above the road might have been the one from my dream. What was the shadow on the wall? How could I find The Light again? Or was I drawing connections where there were none? Which, inevitably, led to the question I'd been avoiding ever since I first thought I heard Jacob speak without speaking. Was I insane? The more I pondered, the more elusive the answers seemed.

Growing frustrated, I stood and made my way back to Wendy's crib, and scooped her into my arms.

"What do you think?" I asked, staring into her big blue eyes. "Is Mommy losing her mind?" Wendy giggled, reached up, and gave my nose a squeeze. "I'll take that as a no."

I looked past her, spotted the crude stick doll sitting atop the dresser, the beginning of an idea forming in my mind. The dreams might just be dreams, and I had no clue how I was supposed to find the thing I had seen above the road. But Astra was real. She had left enough physical evidence behind to prove that. And, if I wasn't hallucinating, I had heard her voice in my head. Whatever was happening to me, she had to be part of it.

So, bouncing Wendy on my lap, I fired up my old laptop, decorated with flower stickers and a 'Save the Forest' bumper sticker, and went looking for Astra.

I spent the next three hours parked there, Wendy sitting upright on the couch beside me, fiddling with her plastic keys and occasionally staring wide eyed at my screen. In all that time, I had found precisely nothing. There were a dozen Astras in the state, but based off their social media, none of them were the same woman, leading me to wonder if Astra was even her real name. If that was the case, my task was truly hopeless. Her name was the one concrete thing I knew about her save that she lived with some nebulous hippie commune somewhere in the nearby mountains. I checked property records in the area but, save for a few cabin plots, the hills were devoid of settlement as far as the county was concerned. Wherever she lived, it was off the grid.

I didn't hear Jacob enter over the sound of my ear buds, which were currently blasting the Best of Bowie, but I felt his heavy hands fall on my shoulders and start to knead out the knot that had formed in my neck. I groaned, pressing back into him, craning my head back to see him.

He smiled down at me, though the smile didn't reach his eyes. "Feeling better?" he asked.

"Much," I said, noticing the deep worry lines that framed his face. "What's wrong?" I asked, pulling my ear buds out.

He arched an eyebrow at me. "Who said something was wrong?"

"I did," I said, then patted the couch beside me. "Sit?"

He sighed, but came to my call, lifting Wendy and setting her down on his lap as he settled in beside me. He spent a moment greeting her, letting her tug at his fingers.

I leaned against Jacob, eyes on Wendy, ears trained for the steady beat of his heart. "So," I said, "is everything OK?"

Jacob looked at me, then at Wendy, his smile faltering. "Yeah," he said unconvincingly. "I mean, as good as it can be. I'm just a little on edge, I guess. Keep thinking about that woman last night. Can't stop wondering if I really did kill her."

"With those wounds, she was probably already near dead. Besides, I think The Light is what finished her. Did you see the way she was looking at it?"

He blinked at me. "What?"

"The thing above the road? I know you saw it." He looked at me as if I'd slapped him, confusion furrowing his brow for a moment before giving his beard a ponderous scratch.

"Yeah, I guess you're right." He shrugged. "Any idea what you want for dinner?"

"Jacob," I sat up, turned to face him. "You remember The Light, right?"

"I remember," he said dismissively.

"Well," I pressed, "shouldn't we, I don't know, talk about it?"

"I'm not sure what there is to talk about. We saw a light, it shouldn't have been there, and then it was gone."

"What do think it was?"

"Who knows? Probably an optical illusion, or a passing plane, or swamp gas or something. It was gone too fast to tell."

I shook my head. "No, it wasn't a plane. The light was all wrong, it was like liquid. Didn't you see it?"

Jacob's expression turned worrisome, his eyes searching my face, mouth drawn into a tight line. "Liquid? I saw a big bright ball, but that's all." He reached out and pushed a stray lock of hair off my forehead. At the same moment, I heard his voice, this time not coming from his mouth but rumbling inside my head. *She's probably in shock. Oh God, I hope she isn't losing it.*

I pushed his hand away, "I'm not crazy."

He blinked and tensed. "Hannah, babe, I never said – "

"But you thought it," I blurted out, trying not to feel as hurt as I felt. I

63

couldn't blame him for thinking I'd gone off my gourd when I still wasn't sure I was sane either.

"I did not," he said, shaking his head. "I don't think you're crazy."

At least I hope not, he added mentally.

No doubt about it, I *had* heard that. Not with my ears, but heard it all the same. This was real, it had to be, because if it wasn't then I needed a bucketful of antipsychotics.

I took a deep breath. "Jacob," I said slowly, trying to force his eyes to meet mine. "I need you to listen because what I'm going to tell you is hard to believe. I think I've been hearing your thoughts."

He frowned, "You've what?"

"Heard your thoughts. And you aren't the only one. I think I heard Wendy earlier today, and last night, when that woman was on me, I saw something. A vision, or a memory, or something. She was in pain and I think…I think someone was assaulting her."

"Hannah," he said, shaking his head, clearly at a loss. "Are you feeling all right? You were burning up this morning."

Images flashed through his mind, and in turn, appeared in mine. Corrupted wounds, the woman's jagged teeth, and the image of me thrashing in a pool of sweat. He thought I was delirious with infection.

I ripped the bandage from my arm and shoved the mostly healed wound into his face. "Look!" I said. "I'm not feverish. I'm not hallucinating this."

Jacob's mouth hung open, all the gears in his head grinding to a halt. "I never said – "

"Goddammit, listen to me! I can hear it, all right? I can hear what you're thinking."

He looked at me, then down at Wendy. I hadn't meant to tell him about the odd experiences, not yet, not until I had figured it out, but the cat had slipped the bag. Everything seemed like it was spinning now, as if all of reality revolved on a single pin, spinning faster and faster until it seemed everyone and everything would fly off into the void if he chose not to believe me. His thoughts hit me, washed over me. I felt his doubt, his fear that I had gone mad same as the woman on the road, his fear at war with the trust he had always placed in me.

I heard his response forming in his head a second before he said it. "Ok, prove it."

Then, he thought at me, one word emblazoned across his mind.

"Rabbit," I said.

Jacob blinked. "Ok," he said slowly, "do that again."

He thought of other words and I fired them back, one after the other. "Love, Rock, Wendy, Blood, Echo City, Lights, Sex."

Growing paler by the moment, he shook his head, placed Wendy on the cushion between us, and turned to face me fully.

He thought again, this time not in words but images, and I named them, the words flying from my lips as fast as they came. "Echo City Park, our first kiss under the overpass, the red-handled screwdriver you lost in the move, the night you put your father in the hospital." And on it went, naming images and feelings and ideas until they trickled to a stop, and the only sound coming from his mind was the hollow wind of numb shock.

"Holy shit," he finally said. Then he repeated it, a mantra to welcome the impossible.

I slid from the couch and knelt in front of him, taking his hand in mine. "Jacob," I whispered. "Something is happening. I don't know what, and I don't know why, but this is all connected somehow. The intruder, the woman on the road, The Light, even Astra. I think maybe she triggered something when she drugged me. I'm scared, I can't figure this out alone, and I need you to believe me. Please."

He sucked in a breath, then let it out slow. "I'll try. I can't promise, but I'll try."

The doubt was still there, a hard nugget that sat heavily in the center of his mind. But it was smaller now, and quieter, smothered under fear and, I realized, love. Love most of all.

5
INTERLUDE

Hypnotic Regression Therapy Session #4
Subject: Hannah Riley
Administered by: Dr. James Lorenz

Dr. Lorenz: Can you hear me, Hannah?
Hannah: Yes, Doctor.
Dr. Lorenz: Do you know where I am going to ask you to take us?
Hannah: You want to know about Wendy's birth.
Dr. Lorenz: That's right. Do you think you can take us back there?
Hannah: I can try. My memory of that day is a little fuzzy.
Dr. Lorenz: Let me worry about that. Take a deep breath, hold it, now let it out. Close your eyes. In this place, all memory is available to you. Take a deep breath, and as you do sink down into yourself. With each breath you're going to get more relaxed, until your entire body fades away...

The truck leapt when it hit another pothole, launching me three inches off the seat just as another contraction hit. I leaned forward, gripping the headrests of the front seats, and let out a scream. "If you hit another bump I'll fucking kill you!" I shouted at Jacob who, pale faced, was doing his best to keep the truck on the narrow dirt road we had been on for what felt like days.

Another pothole jolted the truck and I groaned in frustration, the muscles in my lower back slowly twisting and cramping, the pain radiating down my thighs and up into my neck. This was too soon; we were supposed to have another month. Jacob and I had been in the backcountry of northern Wisconsin, chasing a rumor of old farmhouses the state would practically give away to anyone who promised to fix them up. The rumors had turned out to be bullshit, and what few homes we had found in our price range were little more than crumbling shacks, the available apartments not much better. We were back in our motel room, arguing about what to do next, when my water broke.

It took ten minutes with the spotty internet connection to find the closest hospital (nearly sixty miles away) and we had to take back roads, many of which had been flooded by the recent rain, forcing us to make time-consuming detours. I spent every moment of the ride flinging every insult I could muster at Jacob, the truck, Wendy, and myself for being so stupid as to end up in this situation.

By the time we got to the hospital, three hours had passed and I was ready to commit a homicide. St. Bart's was a rundown hospital that had been built in the early 70s to service the local rural community, and never updated since. Three small, piss-colored buildings sat nestled on the shores of one of Wisconsin's fabled lakes which, with the dark clouds choking out the moon above, looked like a black pit that threatened to consume the structures whole. I groaned as Jacob burned rubber into the parking lot and hit the speed bump at the patient drop off hard enough to launch me out of my seat again.

"Sorry!" he said immediately, already climbing out. "Sorry, just hold on, one second, I'll – "

I didn't hear whatever he said next as another contraction hit and sent white light lancing through my vision. I gripped my watermelon belly and gritted my teeth, eyes squeezed shut so hard they ached. Then the door was open, and Jacob was lifting me out, helping me into a wheelchair pushed by two grey-haired nurses who looked jaundiced under the parking lot's yellow lights.

Next, a rush through the halls, a room that was old but clean, a bed, words flying around me as Jacob demanded they get a doctor in here to deliver this baby, as nurses stripped me bare and wrapped me again in a paper-thin robe. All the while, the pain dominated me, held me in a vice so tight I could barely breathe. It felt like I was splitting in two, as if the sword of God was sawing into me. It shouldn't hurt this much, not yet. It had only been a few hours.

Jacob screamed at someone to get me painkillers, his face red in rage and panic.

"Too late for that I'm afraid," the doctor, a short, balding man, said as he tucked his head under the hem of my robe. "This baby is coming, right now."

My eyes flew wide and I scanned the room, searching for Jacob, or maybe the hidden camera crew that would prove this was all a joke. Another contraction put an end to that fantasy, and I screamed through my teeth. I couldn't do this; not yet, not ever. The baby was going to kill me, and the moment I let that thought in, I couldn't shake the image of some grotesque, warped child ripping its way up and out of my belly with claws and hooves and a head full of quills instead of hair. I screamed again, and suddenly Jacob was there, placing his hand in mine, his mouth inches from my ear.

"I'm right here, Rabbit. And I'm not going anywhere. We can do this, all right? We can – "

"Does this look like a WE activity!?" I screamed as another wave of crippling pain washed over me.

He recoiled, startled, mouth opening and closing like a fish. "Uh, should I leave?"

I grabbed him by the arm and squeezed, "Don't you fucking dare."

And then the pain came again, swelled, and did not abate, the only sound my screams echoing down the halls of the empty hospital. Time boiled away to moments, single breaths for air in an ocean of agony. I felt my thoughts growing fuzzy, felt something inside me cracking. Then came the order to push, and my vision went white.

In that whiteness, I saw something strange: a small iron padlock that felt both alien and intimately familiar. It looked old, its surface pitted with rust. I watched it buckle, and then snap, and suddenly I could see everything. I saw myself. Me, sweating and screaming on the hospital bed, Jacob white as a sheet and thinking he was about to lose me. Then further out. The nurse stealing a nap in the break room down the hall; the suicidal thoughts of the security guard on the fourth floor; the nighttime frivolities of the fish in the lake beyond. Then, wider still. I saw plains, mountains and rivers, as if a map of the whole world was written across the inside of my skull and, at the center of it all, a rounded mountain top, covered in scraggly pine and ancient cabins.

Then, eyes. First the blue ones, dozens of pairs glowing in the dark behind my eyelids, looking at me, into me. Then a pair of black ones opened at their center, dark and wet like spilt oil.

'There you are.' The words echoed in my mind. *'We've been looking for you.'*

Another wave of pain washed over me, and I was back in the hospital room, lying in a pool of my own sweat as the doctor pulled Wendy from between my legs. At first, she didn't move, and for one heart-arresting moment I thought she was dead. But then I saw her head turn, and her lungs fill for the first time to unleash a warbling wail, announcing her arrival to an unprepared world.

"This little lady was in a hurry," the doctor said, smiling.

I must have passed out, because the next thing I knew, she was clean, wrapped tightly in a yellow blanket, and resting comfortably in my arms. I smiled down at her, unable to believe something so beautiful could have come from us. I reached out and found Jacob at my side, took his hand and squeezed it.

"Look what we did," I whispered, voice hoarse.

Jacob scooted forward and looked down at Wendy, tickling the edge of her nose with one finger. "She's beautiful, babe." Then, looking at me, "Are you OK?"

Was I? I was sore, a deep body pain that thrummed down my back, hips and thighs. But I was alive, and clearer headed than I thought I'd be. I squeezed his hand again. "As fine as a bumblebee that shit out a bowling ball," I said, and he laughed. I tried to laugh as well, but my throat felt like it was on fire from all the screaming, so all I managed was a weak chortle.

We sat like that for a time, hand in hand, cooing and marveling at the miracle we had created.

Dr. Lorenz: Let's back up a little. The vision you had, can you tell us any more about that?

Hannah: I'm...I don't think so. It's all still so fuzzy.

Dr. Lorenz: And you are sure you could not recall that incident prior to this session?

Hannah: No. I remembered the pain, and waking up, but that was... that was new. What does it mean?

Dr. Lorenz: ...

Hannah: James? What does it mean?

Dr. Lorenz: I haven't the faintest idea.

6
STAR CHASER

1 - Jacob

The morning after the revelation of Hannah's abilities, I found myself awake an hour early and drifting from room to room, peering out the windows into the pre-dawn gloom. I wasn't sure what I was looking for. The intruders? The Light? If I had to pick, I hoped for the former. People I could deal with, people had bones to break, but The Light? I didn't have a clue how to handle that.

I tried to recall the thing I had seen hovering over the road, but the memory was slippery, my mind constantly jumping to other thoughts, other images, as if in a desperate bid not to acknowledge what I'd seen. It had been round, and too bright to look at directly. Then it was gone, like someone had simply flicked off a switch up in heaven. No sound, no anything, just The Light and an intense 'watched' feeling that had made my neck hairs stand on end.

Eventually, I found myself drifting towards the living room, towards Hannah's laptop. Soon enough, I was staring at the Google homepage, fingers hovering over the keyboard, heart skipping as I typed each letter. I tried 'UFOs' and spent the better part of an hour reading through articles, old forums, and websites with star field backgrounds. Some of what I read was compelling: the Pentagon leaks, a pyramid-shaped craft in Brazil, the Phoenix Lights. But for every compelling video I found, there were a hundred grainy cell phone videos of specks of light dancing around in the sky with some excitable but anonymous voice screaming about aliens.

Next, I tried 'Balls of Light,' then 'Telepathy' and 'Signs of Schizophrenia.' For a hot second, I thought I had solved the case when I stumbled upon ball lightning. Supposedly the phenomenon was an as yet unexplained scientific process, by which balls of excited plasma seem to spontaneously form and zip about before either vanishing or exploding. I even found another cell phone video tracking a ball of crackling electricity dancing over railroad tracks.

I began to compile it all, pulling up quotes and videos and studies, lining up tabs in my browser like a wall meant to protect my frail reality from the strangeness beyond. But as dawn finally broke, ushering in a grey, cloudy day, I sat back and realized I had accomplished exactly nothing. The Light hadn't been ball lightning. It was too big, it didn't crackle or pop, and it didn't explode. It just hung there over the road like the biggest spotlight in the universe. And it had been watching us, hadn't it? I wasn't sure why I knew that, but I did. I might have been willing to ignore even that and gone on pretending it was a shared hallucination brought on by stress. However, even if I could accept that the light we'd seen was a natural phenomenon, I couldn't do the same for Hannah's newfound abilities.

Did I believe my own wife had constructed an elaborate ruse for no other purpose than to terrify me? I didn't see it. Hannah was many things, but she wasn't a liar.

Which left me stuck. On one hand, believe my wife and open my entire world up to forces I couldn't possibly understand? On the other hand, I could...what? Have her committed? Live in denial while the bonds of my marriage slowly dissolved?

My head was spinning. There was just too much to consider, too fast. I needed to get moving. I had a job to get to, bills to pay, a child to feed, and reality would not wait for me to grapple with its stranger elements. I closed the browser and tried my best to push it all to the back of my head as I made for the shower. Once I was clean and dressed, I went to the bedroom to bid Hannah goodbye, same as I did every morning. I leaned down over her sleeping form, brushed ink black hair from her forehead, and kissed her there. Then, operating on some need to confirm that the night before hadn't been a dream, I aimed three words at her.

'I love you' I thought, forming each word in my mind, imagining them flying to her like arrows.

She smiled, murmured in her sleep, "I love you, too."

I kept my cool as I walked the house one more time, checked all the locks, got into my truck, and left. It wasn't until I was halfway to town that I finally screamed — fear, frustration, and confusion unleashed in one unexpected bellow. I pulled over, head hurting, heart aching. I needed to come to grips with this, and fast, because it was happening. No matter how much I wished it wasn't, my life had spun uncontrollably into uncharted country and, if I wanted to keep my family safe, I needed to pull myself together.

I took a deep breath, then another. The choice, I told myself, was an easy one. Face the impossible, or let Hannah face it alone. Put like that, there was no choice at all. So why did I feel like throwing up? I drove to town, white-knuckling the steering wheel the entire way.

That was the day I met Carl Newland.

As soon as I got to Astrological, I was swept up in work. A trio of shitheads had come in, wanting matching tattoos of a naked pinup wrapped from the waist down in a confederate flag. Tracy wasn't having any of that, her hands on her hips as she stood toe to toe with six hundred pounds of pissed off testosterone, explaining in no uncertain terms that, "I don't do hate symbols and I don't do the flags of cowards. You can drive your ass all the way down to Gainsburg if you want something like that."

For a brief moment, I thought I would have to get involved when the leader of the trio, a beanpole of a man with a woolly beard, stepped closer to Tracy, looming over her. Tracy smiled up at him.

"Please, sweetheart. I've been blasted with water cannons and clubbed by cops. You keep looking at me like that, and I'll twist your bitty balls off."

Beanpole's friends laughed and, no longer feeling part of a united front, he sheepishly led his friends out the front, only to come back a minute later, head hung.

"I suppose an American flag will do us just fine," he said sheepishly.

Tracy smiled, all teeth, "Sure thing, hon."

I started to set out my inks, mind flashing through the hundred different pinups I had done before. Tracy appeared at my side, nudging me with an elbow. "I'll take these lugs. I got a special client coming in. Promised him he could get some free ink."

"You sure?" I asked, looking over her head towards the three men. "I can take care of them."

She waved me off. "No. I want to see them squirm. Besides, you're a better artist than me, and if you tell anyone I said that, I'll tattoo a dong on that big ass head of yours."

While she set to work on the first of the three, I killed time sketching for the other two. One wanted a blonde, country bombshell kind of deal, the other a Native princess with come-fuck-me eyes. That last part he was insistent about, repeating it five or six times as I adjusted and re-adjusted the sketch.

Just as I was finishing up, the front door swung open again.

My first impression of Carl was that he looked like a born victim. Round faced, eyes bright with enthusiasm, no more than 5'5", with matchstick limbs and a fluff of dark brown curls atop his head. He was dressed in cargo shorts, a t-shirt with a grey alien flashing the peace sign, and a weathered backpack that looked close to bursting.

"Carl!" Tracy called, looking up from her first victim. She put the needle gun down, stepped around the counter and, to my shock, swept him up into a tight hug. She even smiled in a way that was almost loving.

"Jacob," she said, "this is Carl. He's my son. I told him you were good at this, so treat my boy right."

I held out my hand to him, which he took, his hand vanishing into mine. "Nice to meet ya," he said, craning his head back to meet my eyes.

"Ditto," I said. "Tracy said you want to get a piece done? Have you ever done this before?"

He shook his head. "Nah. First time under the needle. Not going to lie, I'm kinda bad about pain. Kept me away until now."

"No worries," I said, wondering how a granite bitch like Tracy could have birthed this soft-boiled man. "I've tattooed plenty of people with sensitive skin. What were you looking to get?"

He reached into his pocket and pulled out a crumpled piece of paper which he tried to smooth out on the counter. On it was a crude sketch of a classic flying saucer, silver, its tractor beam on and focused on a stick figure. He tapped the stick figure. "I was hoping this could be Bigfoot. Or maybe Mothman. Just the silhouette though, like he's being abducted."

I forced a smile, swallowed to try to get rid of the sudden dryness in my mouth. "Shouldn't be a problem," I said in a croak. "I'll go and pull a few references."

I went to the computer and began to Google random images of Sasquatch and Mothman, eyeing Carl the whole time and trying to figure out if this was some kind of joke. I hadn't told anyone about what we had seen over the road, not even Quinn and Hanson had gotten that part of the story.

I printed a few options, went over them with Carl and he settled on one of the Sasquatch. I led him to my chair, wiped down his upper arm, and prepared to begin. Just as I was picking up the needle gun, he went pale, eyes flicking from it to me and back again. "Just be straight with me, how much is this going to hurt?"

As if on cue, Tracy's victim let out a low squeak of pain as her needle hit a nerve. Carl looked like he might puke.

"Don't worry," I said. "Upper arm is a good spot to start, plenty of meat. It's going to feel like a really intense scratch. If you're squeamish, don't look at it. Find something else to put your mind on. Give it thirty seconds, and you won't notice the pain as much. You start getting too sore, just say the word and we take a break."

He nodded, swallowed, and sank deeper into the chair. "OK, Doc. Do your thing."

The moment my needle touched his skin he yelped, his back going ramrod straight. To his credit, though, he didn't tell me to stop and, bit by bit, relaxed again as the tattoo needle buzzed in his ear.

"You're new," he said after a few minutes, a thin sheen of sweat already broken out on his forehead. "Didn't think Mom would ever get around to hiring someone."

"Newish," I said. "Wife and I moved here a few months ago. You live in town?"

He snorted, "No, thank Christ. I live in Michigan, going to MSU for my doctorate."

I started with the Sasquatch, outlining the big ape's famous mid-step pose in black. "What brings you back?" I asked, not really caring to know. It was just the usual banter to pass the hours a client spent in the chair.

Carl looked up at me and studied my face for a moment. "Well," he said sheepishly, nodding to his arm, "UFOs, actually."

My heart skipped.

"You OK, man?" Carl asked, eyes now wide with concern. "You look like you're about to hurl?"

I gave him a tight nod, swallowed down the bile stinging the back of my throat. "Yeah," I said, "just been a hell of a week." I put on my most reassuring smile and got back to work. "So," I said, hoping to sound casual, "you actually believe in all this stuff? UFOs, Bigfoot?"

He nodded. "Hell, yes I do. If the Sasquatch doesn't exist now, it sure as hell did in the recent past. The Patterson film proves that. No way anyone could have a suit that realistic in the 60's. That said, I've never seen one myself. Aliens are my main jam."

"And you saw one of those?" I asked.

"Yeah," he said, as if confirming that he had seen something no more strange than a passing bird. "Up at the dark sky park outside Petoskey. Guy I was seeing took me up there. I was a total skeptic till then but man, once you see one, it's like it reorders your whole universe. I've been capitol O obsessed ever since. You ever see one?"

"No," I said immediately, "I guess I'm still a skeptic."

He shrugged, "Hey, we need those, too. Keeps the cranks like me from running off without our pants. Living here though, you might want to look up sometime. This whole area is under a flap right now."

"What the hell is a flap?" I asked.

"It's a wave of UFO sightings. That's what we call them, when like a whole area suddenly lights up. Point Pleasant in the 50s, Denver in the 70s, big ass one in Belgium not too long ago."

"And now here?" I asked, not thinking, just responding.

"And now here," he parroted. "I've been seeing chatter on the web. Sky is lighting up all over the Bible belt. So, I figured it was about time to visit Mom and see if I couldn't catch something while I was here." He glanced at Tracy then, dropping his voice to a conspiratorial whisper, continued, "She saw one, too. She doesn't like talking about it, but my Dad was there and he told me all about it."

"Your father is a liar," Tracy said, not looking up from her own work, bloodhound ears apparently cued in on our conversation.

Carl's smile tightened. "They aren't on the best of terms."

"Hard to be on any terms with a sellout," she muttered, her current victim now squirming in his seat while his buddies looked on, increasingly pale.

Carl rolled his eyes. "You know, if you're interested, I have a couple cool videos I could show you. Still haven't caught anything on film around here, but I've got a good feeling. Seems like half the town has seen something in the past few weeks."

"Nah," I said, not feeling the need to tell him that Tracy had, in fact, told me about her strange satellite sighting. "I'll keep my feet on the ground for now."

He shrugged. "Probably smart. Got to tell you, being the UFO guy doesn't make you very popular."

"I'm sure that the aliens will love you," I said dryly.

"I'll ready my anus for probing," he said.

We both laughed, and the hard knot of anxiety eased off my stomach. Our conversation continued, leaving UFOs behind for idle talk about Victor's Point, his college classes, and the messy love triangle he was in back home until eventually even that died away and he just sat, eyes closed, occasionally wincing as hours ticked by. My mind drifted; the familiar movements driving out all the rage, confusion and fear that I'd woken with that morning.

Tracy finished off her second victim just as I was putting the finishing touches on Carl. She walked over, her brow furrowed first in confusion, then awe. "Holy shit, Riley," she said, placing a hand on my shoulder. "I knew you were good, but holy shit."

Carl opened his eyes, craned his head to look down. His mouth hung open, uttering a small squeak of surprise.

I looked up at her, brow furrowed. "It's pretty basic artwork, I don't know if…" I looked down at the tattoo. My head swam, my stomach dropped to my feet, and the whole world seemed to shift an inch to the left.

There was the Sasquatch silhouette, and the classic UFO tractor beam, just as Carl had asked. But where the silver flying saucer should have been, I had instead tattooed a luminous ball. The light that poured off it looked like solar flares, almost liquid, a few waves breaking over the Sasquatch's massive shoulders as it pulled him skyward.

Carl looked at me, then down at the tattoo. "This is perfect," he said, voice small. Then, looking at me, voice shaking, he asked, "You saw it, didn't you?"

My eyes didn't wander from the tattoo. The colors were confusing. The object was white, but hidden among the strands of luminescence, I could see flashes of other colors. Greens, blues, reds, purples, and other, stranger colors that seemed to slip past the edges of my vision, as if moving. It was beautiful and it was impossible, likely the best piece I'd ever done. And the longer I looked at it, the more untethered I felt, as if any moment the roof would tear away, and I would be sucked up into the night sky.

"Saw what?" Tracy asked, looking between us.

I forced my eyes up to meet Carl's and gave him a half-hearted shrug. "I guess I should see those videos you were talking about."

2

Half an hour later, we were at Ernie's Diner. A few patrons lined the counter barstools, but most of the booths were empty, and we took the one farthest from any prying ears. Tacy had opted to stay behind, insisting that she wanted nothing to do with "space men."

That was fine by me. The fewer people who knew how deep in the shit I was, the better.

Carl booted up his laptop and, once two mugs of coffee sat steaming before us, opened up a note-taking program and looked at me. "OK," he said, then he repeated it, taking steadying breaths as he went. "Before I show you anything, I think you should tell me what you saw." I must have looked apprehensive, because he continued, "It's important, and I promise nobody else has to know anything about what you tell me. I can use a fake name in my notes."

"Why do you need to know?" I asked, voice firm, trying not to betray how off-kilter I still felt.

"Because I need to establish credibility. If I show you a bunch of videos, talk your head off about UFOs, it might lead you to some conclusions about the phenomenon that you wouldn't have reached otherwise, get me? We need to make sure I don't taint your eyewitness account."

"You could say that's already happened. You told me there was a UFO flap happening around here, right? Wouldn't that lead me to assume the light I saw was an alien or something?"

"UFO means unidentified flying object," he said pointedly, "not necessarily aliens."

"What the hell else could they be?"

He opened his mouth, then paused, drumming his fingers on the table edge. "I think," he said slowly, "that you best tell me your experience first. We can get into all of that later. Do you mind if I record this?"

He produced a small audio recorder and sat it on the table between us. I eyed the device, internally debating leaving or maybe smashing the damn thing to pieces. Then I glanced at Carl's arm, the artwork warped beneath a transparent bandage, but still visible. I needed answers, and Carl might at least provide a direction.

"No names," I said firmly. "I have a family to think of."

Carl smiled. "No names," he promised. He clicked on the recorder and cleared his voice. When he spoke, his voice had lowered an octave and taken on a firm, no-nonsense tone that was undercut by his boyish face, like a kid playing Humphrey Bogart. "This is Carl Newland, investigator #345 of TRUFON, sitting with a resident of Victor's Point who has reported an anomalous encounter. The time is 3:15 pm, date is July 2, 2022. Subject has requested that his personal identity be concealed, and will be referred to as 'Harry' for this conversation. Hello, Harry."

"Uh, hello," I said. "TRUFON?"

"Trans-Regional UFO Network," he explained. "It's uh, like a club for this sort of stuff. Don't worry about it. Just start at the beginning. Where did you see the object?"

"That isn't the beginning."

"Ok," he said, eyebrow arched, "so start wherever you like."

I took a deep breath, and then I told him almost everything: the incident with the intruders, the odd footprints, and the seemingly miraculous speed at which they ran. I told him about the woman in the road, and the confrontation that ended when the ball of light appeared over our heads. I purposely excluded any details about Hannah and her new abilities, reasoning that it was *our* secret, and that telling Carl would only further complicate what was becoming a total shit show. More than that, I'd be damned if I would let Carl, or anyone else, treat her like a science experiment.

When I was done, Carl sat, idly stroking his chin, eyes hazy and distant. "And you haven't seen it since?" he asked.

I shook my head. "No. Not yet, anyway. It was so strange the way it disappeared – it wasn't like it flew away at all. It just sort of vanished."

Carl sucked in a breath, then steepled his fingers on the table before him. "I understand. I am going to ask you some questions now and I need you to be honest and bear with me, because some of these are going to sound pretty weird. For starters, have you noticed any lost time?"

"Not that I'm aware of. Not unless you count putting that tattoo on your arm."

He nodded, made a note on his laptop. "And what did you have for breakfast on the morning you saw the object?"

"Seriously? What the hell does that have to do with anything?"

"I know it's crazy, but just try not to think about the questions too much. I like to do a lot of statistical analyses of contactees. I promise I'll explain it all later."

I sighed and leaned back. "I think I probably skipped breakfast. Slice of toast at the most."

He typed on his laptop. "OK. And did you notice any particular smells when you saw the anomaly?" And so it went, the better part of an hour spent with Carl throwing increasingly bizarre questions my way. I did my best to answer, the whole time conscious of every person who entered the diner and the odd looks the waitress gave us whenever she returned to fill our coffee, her bright blue eyes sneaking suspicious glances at us as she moved about her business.

When Carl had completed his list, he pushed the laptop away, rubbing his eyes.

"That it?" I asked.

"For now," Carl said with a nod, taking a large gulp of his lukewarm coffee. I waited a beat and, when Carl said nothing else, I leaned forward.

"So, you going to tell me what the hell is happening to my life?"

Carl laughed, "Man, I wish I knew."

"The thing about the Phenomenon that you need to understand is that we still don't really know what it is," Carl explained. We had abandoned Ernie's, driven off by the incoming dinner crowd. Carl hadn't wanted to go back to Astrological, citing that his mother hated when he went on about his little green men, so we took a drive, heading out into the dirt roads and farmsteads that surrounded the southern half of town. "The extraterrestrial theory is the current status quo."

"But you don't believe that?"

He shrugged. "I don't know what I believe, and any investigator worth their salt should tell you the same. Don't get me wrong, I would love it if they were aliens. I grew up on *Star Trek* and *Babylon Five*, man, and that's the dream —*X-Files*, government cover-ups, physical crash sights and alien autopsies."

The world outside the truck was dappled in golden sunlight, playing off the rows of corn, soy, and wheat that blanketed the world beneath the hills like a patchwork quilt. In an hour or two, the sun would begin to set and I would need to get home. After what she'd told me, I was growing increasingly uncomfortable leaving Hannah to face the night alone.

"OK," I said slowly, taking another random turn. "And if they aren't aliens?"

He sucked in a breath. "Well, that's where shit gets super weird. Some people believe in the UltraTerrestrial theory. Basically, it posits that UFOs don't come from other planets, but other dimensions. Maybe they exist at a higher level of the electromagnetic wavelength that we cannot see until they drop to our level, or maybe they even come from some other realm. John Keel was the paranormal investigator who popularized the term. He thought the UltraTerrestrials were a construct of our consciousness."

"So a hallucination?"

"Sort of, in that they happen more in your mind than in reality. See, go back far enough with your research and you'll discover all kinds of old folklore about fairy abductions, trickster gods, witches on brooms, most of which included stories of lights in the sky, abduction events, and other hallmarks we now associate with aliens. He thought that all of those were expressions of the same basic Phenomenon, their form dictated by what we here in the physical reality could accept within our framework of understanding. Go back to Puritan times, people saw a light in the sky and thought, hey, that's a witch flying around with a lantern. And so, the Phenomenon makes itself look just like a withered old hag on a broom. In ancient Ireland, those same lights are seen as fairy lights. To some Native American tribes, a thunderbird. Around the 1950s, at the onset of the technological era..."

"They become flying machines," I finished.

He nodded. "That's why nobody can get a clear photo or video. And that's why so much other weird shit seems to happen around UFOs. If you look at the statistics, there is almost always a huge spike in Bigfoot sightings, poltergeist activity and other paranormal phenomenon in the time leading up to and after a UFO Flap. Which implies that they are all either related, or different expressions of the same underlying force. The problem is, most members of the paranormal community don't talk to each other. Bigfoot hunters go running after their guy, UFO hunters go chasing the lights, and neither stop to figure out why the two are both happening in the same stretch of woods. The Phenomenon lets us chase it, lets us try to understand, but never lets us arrive at hard proof."

I chewed on his words, feeling a bit like a drowning man. Did people actually believe this stuff? Then again, who was I to say they were wrong, given what I'd seen? "So," I said, careful to keep the incredulity from my voice, "they're like shape-shifting tricksters or something, right?"

He gave a big shrug and blew a raspberry. "Who the fuck knows? Some researchers think that. They could be some other form of life, or they could be something we collectively make up somehow. Like, enough people believe in witches, witches show up. Get me?"

My head was starting to hurt. "Not really," I admitted. "But I think I have a general idea."

He laughed. "I've been researching the Phenomenon since I was a kid, and a general idea is as close as I've ever gotten. And for the record, UltraTerrestrials are only one theory, and one with holes. Like the physical evidence sometimes left behind. There are tons of stories of burnt circles in the ground, pieces of ships, even whole alien bodies supposedly taken from crafts to an air force base in Ohio. Assuming those stories are real, the Phenomenon can't be entirely illusionary. What's more, you have the fact that tons of ancient art and carvings from around the world show what look an awful lot like flying saucers in the background, way before we as a species would have had the technological framework for the Phenomenon to become a flying machine."

Carl was getting excited, talking as much with his hands as his mouth. "Then you have the theory that aliens are time travelers, here on vacation to Earth's distant past. Some people think they are secret craft of the One World Government, built by Nazis in the final days of WWII. Fuck, I met a woman who swore they were angels of the lord, here to guide us towards salvation. And maybe all of that is horseshit! Maybe the Phenomenon is something so strange and enigmatic that we'll never understand it. Maybe all of it is true at once, and our skies are an inter-dimensional superhighway of a thousand species and etheric entities. The point is, nobody knows, and anyone who tells you they know for sure has either lost themselves to the rabbit hole, or they are trying to get you to buy some bullshit."

"Great," I said. "What do I DO about it?"

"Do?" he looked at me, his exuberance bleeding away.

"These things, whatever they are, are fucking with our lives. My wife is terrified; fuck, I'm terrified. Someone broke into our home and, if the sheriff is right, they might be after my kid. Not to mention the horror show that happened last night. My wife thinks that light is somehow connected. So, what the hell do I do about it?"

We both fell silent, eyes forward, watching the pristine countryside slide past. I turned the car again, this time north, toward the hills and the molar-shaped mountains that lined the horizon. The silence stretched on, the only sound the soft pings of gravel ricocheting off the bottom of the truck and our breath.

"I know a guy who might be able to help," Carl finally said. "He's a professor in Nashville. Does some interesting work with cases like yours." He looked down, eyes shadowed, and said softly, "To tell you the truth, he likely won't know any better than me. I don't think anyone does."

"So, we're fucked? You talk my ear off for two hours and that's your conclusion?"

He winced. "No," he said firmly. "What I'm saying is that we don't know. But if I were in your shoes, I would prepare for anything. If it is connected, the entities who came to your house might be hallucinatory manifestations. Which means they can't harm you unless you let them. If they are physical, then boarding your windows might help, new locks on the door, anything to make it harder for them to do what they do. That, and be prepared to take them on. I read a story about a guy in Moscow who supposedly fought several Grey aliens off when they came for his brother, so it might be possible."

"And if it isn't? Or if they're something I can't hit?"

Carl opened his mouth, then closed it, then shrugged. "I'll make some calls. I know people who have been researching this stuff for decades. They might have some ideas."

I wanted to punch him. More because it would make me feel good than for anything he had done. I gripped the wheel and started to turn back towards town. "Remember our deal. No names. Last thing I need is an army of UFO nuts crawling all over my life."

Carl flashed another sheepish grin. "Don't worry. We UFO nuts are a covetous breed. This will be our secret."

3 - Hannah

I was awakened by a telephone ringing and reached for my cell on the nightstand before I remembered that I had left it on silent, as I usually did. Sitting up and blinking sleep from my eyes, I realized the sound was coming from somewhere towards the front of the house. I slid from the bed and crept out into the hall, pausing at the nursery door just long enough to confirm that Wendy was still unconscious in her crib, then onwards towards the ringing.

It was the kitchen phone, an old, corded unit left behind by the previous resident. I didn't even think the thing was functional as we certainly weren't paying the bill. I picked up the handset and tentatively brought it to my ear.

"Hello, Riley residence."

The only sound on the other end was a dry, swishing sound, like wind blown over the receiver.

"Hello?" I repeated.

The dry swishing sound continued, followed by an odd series of clicks, sounding almost mechanical.

Gooseflesh crept down my arms and I found myself turning my back to the wall, watching the kitchen windows. "I think you have the wrong number."

Another couple of clicks, and then the line went dead. I stared at the handset, confusion mingling with an inexplicable dread. It was just a bad connection, I reasoned, or a squirrel playing on the telephone lines. That was a thing, right?

Pushing the strange call to the back of my mind, I decided that since I was already up, I might as well use the time. I showered, lingering in the hot water until it turned cold, trying to figure out how to fill the day while staring at the same four walls as I had for months. If only we had another car, I might have woken Wendy and gone to town, reasoning that some adult human interaction would do me good. Another car was a nice pipe dream, but we could barely afford to keep the roof over our heads as it was.

I stepped out of the shower, teeth chattering and skin scrubbed pink. Just as I reached for a shirt, the phone in the kitchen started ringing again. Wrapped in a towel, I returned to the kitchen. The moment I reached for the phone, that odd dread returned, along with that intense watched feeling. I lifted the handset off the cradle and pressed it to my ear, this time not speaking, just listening.

More swishing, and then a long series of excited clicks, followed by a sound I couldn't name. It was almost animal-like, a high warbling chittering as if someone had stuck a chipmunk in a helium-filled box.

"Who is this?" I asked, but the sound only intensified.

I set the handset back down on the cradle and almost immediately it began to ring again.

I should have left right then. Or called Jacob on the cell. Yet as I moved to do just those things, I found myself reaching for the phone again, pressing it to my ear.

No sound this time save for the gentle pulses of someone's muted breath over the receiver. "Who are you?" I demanded. "Are you the person who tried to break into our house?"

On the other end of the line, someone let out a slow breath, then disconnected.

I stood there for several minutes, staring at the phone in my hand, trying to convince myself that it really *had been* a squirrel. After the last week, my nerves were frayed. Likely I had only thought I'd heard someone breathing, tried to make sense of random electronic noise created by a faulty telephone line or something. Yet I couldn't bring myself to put the handset back into the cradle, for fear that it would begin ringing again, and the next time I picked it up, a voice would greet me on the other end.

Instead, I laid the handset down on the table and unplugged it from the base. I told myself that it was only the sensible thing to do; that surely someone would need to pay the bill if calls kept coming through; and that someone was not going to be us. I hurried back down the hall, checked on Wendy, then threw on a pair of jeans and a t-shirt. If I couldn't go to town, I could at least try to find Astra. I'd head only a few miles farther up the road and see if I could spot her commune. She had biked to our house. Wherever she had come from couldn't be *that* far away, could it?

I wished I could just call her, invite her over, then grill her over tea. But she had never left a number on either of her enigmatic notes, something that I was growing more confident had been intentional. I remembered what I thought I'd heard her 'say' in my head. She was me, just a few years down the road. Did that mean she had the same abilities I did? If so, her appearance at my garden gate seemed less like a chance encounter and more like a planned introduction. Who knew, maybe there was a whole community of psychics up in those hills, meditating for world peace, when not playing terrifying pranks on local families.

I strapped the half-sleeping Wendy into her stroller and we ventured out into the sun-dappled front yard, then up the inclined road to the hills.

I kept my gaze up as we walked: on the sky, on the distant mountain peaks, and the rounded top of Mount Olympus. In time, my thoughts drifted to The Light, and the bizarre dreams I had been having. Only, were they dreams? The shadowy entity I had seen stretched across my living room wall had felt terrifyingly real. I'd felt its presence in my head same as I'd felt Astra's. Its mind was vast and dark and without remorse. Whatever it was, The Light didn't seem to like it very much. But then, could I trust The Light?

If only I had Astra's number, I could try asking her. Even if I didn't yet trust her, she had to know more than I did. Suddenly it hit me and I came to a stop. She had said to call her, that I knew how, but left no number. What if she hadn't been talking about calling her on the phone at all?

I turned, looked down the road the way I had come, then back up, finding the long stretch of dusty road empty in both directions. I was at least a mile from the house – hopefully this was close enough. I took a deep breath, closed my eyes, and touched that strange little part of my mind that had recently woken up.

Astra. I sent the thought out to the world, picturing her in my head and holding her image there. *Is this what you meant when you said I should call you? I need to talk. I need answers. Are you out there?*

I kept my eyes closed, head tilted up towards the sun, waiting for a response. Minutes ticked by, the only sound the distant cry of a hawk and the gentle swishing of wind through pine needles. Just as I'd given up expecting a response, I lowered my head and suddenly heard something else – a car engine, rocketing up behind me.

Adrenaline flooded my body as I spun, shoving the stroller and sending it rolling towards the side of the road as a rusted yellow pickup truck blasted through the spot where we had been standing moments before, kicking up a great cloud of dust in its wake. I stood, watching it go in stunned silence, and wondering how I hadn't heard it approaching until it was almost too late. I heard Wendy begin to cry and I turned to find the stroller had tipped over on its side, leaving her half spilled out onto the grass. I ran to her, cooing and fussing as I struggled to right the stroller and get her strapped back in.

"I'm sorry, sweetie," I whispered, trying to put my own hammering heart at ease as much as I was comforting her as I righted the stroller. "It's all right, we're all right. See, no boo boos."

Bad man.

The thought didn't come with a voice. Wendy didn't have one yet. Nevertheless, her meaning was clear. I had a sudden understanding that went beyond words.

I paused and looked at her. "Was that you, sweetie?"

Wendy continued to cry, flailing her little fists against the sides of the stroller. *Bad man. No sleep. Bad man hurt.*

I turned back to look in the direction the truck had gone. Had the driver been trying to hit us? There was a full fifty yards of straight road behind us, enough distance that they should have seen us, should have had plenty of time to slow down, yet they hadn't. Looking at the tire tracks, I could see that they hadn't even tried to swerve.

I looked at Wendy, her tear-filled eyes looking like drowned sapphires. Blue, just like mine, just like Astra's. Then it hit me.

Wendy? I thought, tentatively reaching out to touch her mind.

Her crying immediately stopped and she regarded me with wide, sparkling, eyes. *Momma,* the thought came, again expressed not in words but an understanding. It wasn't pulled from her head, like it felt with Jacob, but sent and received. She was like me. This thing, this power, was genetic.

My head swam, and the world spun. I had never known my real parents. What if they were like this, too? What if there was a whole network of blue-eyed telepaths out in the world?

My fingers shook as I stood and pushed the stroller back out into the road, intent on getting home as fast as I could, locking the doors, and waiting for Jacob, when a flash of yellow caught my eye.

It was Astra, walking slowly towards me through the pines that ran alongside the road, her bare feet scarcely disturbing the bed of needles beneath her. She was wearing a luminous yellow sun dress, her long straight hair pushed back over her shoulders.

"You rang?" she called as she came to a stop, standing just inside the shade of the tree line.

I looked back up the road, heart hammering in my throat. "I wasn't sure if you...if you could hear me?"

She giggled, a sly grin on her face. "Of course I could hear you, with that big brain of yours. You blasted the message across half the damn mountain. I told Grandpa you would call." She practically preened.

I glanced back up the road, an intense feeling of being observed creeping up my neck. This wasn't right. Where had Astra come from? As far as I knew it was just empty woods in all directions for miles, and she was on foot. How had she gotten here so fast? However, no matter how badly I wanted to turn Wendy's stroller south and run for home, my feet remained planted on the hard-packed dirt of the road. I had called out to Astra. I couldn't turn back now.

"What are we?" I asked bluntly.

Astra shook her head. "We shouldn't talk about this here. Why don't you come with me? My cabin isn't very far. We can sit down, talk over some tea."

And give her another chance to drug me, I thought. I shook my head. "No. Right here, right now. If you really want to be my friend, I want answers. What are we?"

Astra blew out her cheeks and let the breath out slowly, leaning casually against a tree. "That's a complicated question. Star children, sons and daughters of the cosmos, the next phase of human evolution. Gifted is what I'd call it, though there are degrees. My brother and I are good. You though, you're great. And that little princess there," she said, gesturing to Wendy, "is a goddamn Titan. Unfiltered, raw, like you. Just missing someone to show you the ropes."

I glanced down at Wendy who stared, as if transfixed, at Astra, her little hands balled into tight fists.

"How many of us are there?" I asked.

She shrugged. "Who knows? More and less than you'd think. A few thousand, worldwide, I'd guess. We run in families. Around here though, there are not that many – a little over a dozen. Less if you exclude the chaff."

"Chaff?"

"Like I said, the gift comes in levels. Most of us can't do much more than read a word or two out of someone's head. Heck, we've got a couple who can't even do that. The ability seems to weaken with each generation. Half of us were even starting to wonder if the gift might be dying out altogether, but then, there you were." Her smile broadened, a faint twinkle in her eye. "The prodigal daughter, come home."

My stomach flipped. "What? You can't mean that!"

"You were adopted, right?"

"No. I mean, yes, but ..."

"Why did you choose to move to Victor's Point?" she asked.

I paused, opened my mouth to give the answer I knew: we had been searching for a home on a budget and had stumbled across the little red house on Strawberry Road. But that wasn't right, was it? Where had the money come for the down payment? By then, we had only a few dollars to our names, certainly not enough to purchase a house. Yet the more I picked at the memory, the more indistinct it became, like unraveling a moth-eaten sweater.

"I don't know," I admitted, the churning in my stomach slowly evolving into full blown nausea. "What the hell is happening to me?"

Astra shook her head, still smiling, "And you don't remember being here before? Living up on the mountain? Grandpa?"

An image flashed in my head, a mobile hanging above my crib, a crude decoration made from rough sticks and shards of glittery silver metal hung on strings. Then, it was gone. "I – I don't know. I don't think so."

She sighed and stepped out onto the road with me, reached out and took one of my shaking hands in hers. "Stop trying so hard. Your mind is powerful, with a capital P. Who knows what you've locked away in there without even realizing it? There are walls within walls in your mind. We'll take them down, together. I can show you how to harness your power, control it. Grandpa can help show you, he trained all of us."

"Who is he?" I whispered.

She shook her head, tugging at my hands. "That's a hard question to answer. But he's a friend, I promise. Come with me, meet him."

I stared down at her hands, remembering the way her delicate fingers had held the joint as she held it out to me. "You drugged me," I said.

"I did," she admitted, without a shred of guilt in her voice. "I wanted to be sure it was you. You were so blocked up, so blind to who you really were. I knew you needed a good shake to get the rust off, get all those little gears turning again. It was only ever to help, I promise." She squeezed my hand. "My whole life I've dreamed you would come home. We were always meant to be sisters, to grow up together. Now we have that chance. Let me teach you, let me show you why you never need to be afraid again."

I stared at the ground between us, at the sight of my hand clasped in hers, while her honeyed words seeped into the cracks in my mind. Wasn't this what I wanted? I went out today looking for Astra in the vague hope of finding answers and low and behold, they appeared. So why did I feel like an insect slowly tangling itself in a spider's web?

"And if I say no?" I asked, voice small.

"Don't say no," she replied. "This is your chance, Hannah, babe. Now that Grandpa has your scent, he won't lose you again. Just say yes, please, say yes."

I almost did. I felt her hands tug at mine, leading me into the woods and toward whatever future awaited me farther up the mountain. Then I looked up at her face, and the whole world screeched to a stop.

Her eyes were large – too large, each the size of a baseball and sparkling with unnatural light. Her teeth had also changed, becoming narrow and sharp, a mouth full of ivory needles glinting dully in the sunlight. I ripped my hand away, heart slamming inside my throat.

"Stay away from me!"

Astra turned, her inhuman face warping with hurt. "Wait," she said, holding one hand up in an attempt to cover her face. "This is part of what we need to talk about!"

I backed away, pushing Wendy's stroller behind me. "What are you!?"

"The same as you," she said, panic stricken. "I'm human, mostly, I just have some defects. My concentration slipped, that's all." Before my eyes she sucked in a deep breath, and then her old face was back, like flipping a light switch. "See? I'm still me. I just want to help you, please don't go!"

It was too late. Panic had seized me and all I could see when I looked at her were those teeth, curved and razor sharp, made for shredding meat. I opened my mouth to respond, maybe to threaten her, but the only sound that came out was a muted scream. I spun, grabbed Wendy from her stroller and bolted down the road toward home, my heart hammering louder than my sneakers slapping the road. I was sure I could hear her running after me, her bare feet a whisper on the dirt and her clawed fingertips inches from the nape of my neck.

I was several hundred yards down the road by the time I realized that no one was following me. I slowed to a stop, fresh sweat running down my back. I could still see Astra in the distance, standing right where I'd left her, a pale-yellow dot in the sun.

I'm sorry, she said in my mind. *Please come back. I'll keep my face on, I promise. Please, I just want to help.*

And she did. I could feel the emotion behind each and every word as if they were my own. Astra's heart was breaking. But beneath her compassion and her pain, I felt something else. Fear. For me or herself I couldn't tell.

Just leave us alone, I thought back as hard as I could.

He won't let me. Things are going to get worse.

Then, she was gone. I felt the connection break and watched as she slid into the distant tree line.

I turned on my heels and ran the rest of the way home.

4 - Jacob

There was a crowd blocking the road north of town. Carl spotted them first, leaning forward over the dashboard.

"What the heck are they doing?"

Half a dozen cars and trucks were parked across the road and a dozen or so people had gathered, heads craned back to stare at the sky. Carl followed their stares and then gasped, slapping me on the shoulder, chattering excitedly. "Stop the car, stop the car, stop the fucking car!"

I pulled the truck over to the side of the road and Carl leapt out, already fighting to free a camera from his bag and sprinting dead on toward the milling crowd. I saw it, too, the moment I stepped out of the truck.

A light. No, I thought. *The* Light. The same one I had seen in the sky only a few days prior. It hung five hundred yards or so above the road, pulsing softly in the twilight sky, liquid light pooling from it in tentacular waves. It was the size of a car or maybe even larger, it was hard to tell. Its surface rippled like water.

I froze, staring up at it, heart pounding. It was an impossibility, one my mind refused to accept. It had to be an airplane, or a helicopter with a search light, but where was the noise? Where was the wind from all those spinning rotors? The night was still, the only sound the murmurs of the amazed townspeople, looking as equally frozen as I. Only Carl seemed immune, scrambling from place to place to record The Light from every possible angle, a wild fever in his eyes.

"Sure are pretty, aren't they?"

I turned to find a familiar face at my side.

Mr. Friend's gaze was locked on The Light, its shine reflecting in his eyes, making them look almost black with luminous white pupils. It was then I noticed his red pickup, parked in the middle of the mass of vehicles.

I looked at him, then back up at The Light. "Yeah," I said, bitterly, "beautiful. What the hell do you think it is? Aliens?"

He laughed, though there was little mirth in the sound. "Lord, I wish it were so simple. No, what we got right there is a whole different animal."

"You know what this thing is?" I asked.

He wet his lips. "Yes and no. If you're asking if it came from space, I don't believe it did. I think it's been here a long, long time. Whatever it is, it is not a friend. Made the mistake of thinking it was, once upon a time."

I blinked, dropping my voice to a whisper. "You've dealt with this before, haven't you?"

Friend turned to face me, his smile gone, lips drawn into a thin white line. "In another life."

"What happened? What did it do?"

"Well…" he said, trailing off, running his tongue over his lips and hooking his thumbs into his pants pockets. "That's a long story, an old story. I don't like telling it much. Suffice it to say the experience wasn't pleasant. It took my family from me."

Immediately, I thought of Hannah and Wendy, still alone at home. At least I hoped they were. I was late coming home, and Hannah hadn't called as she usually did. What if it was too late? What if, while I farted around *not* believing, this light had swooped into our home and taken the only people that meant a damn to me?

"This isn't the first time I've seen it," I admitted. "A few nights ago, Hannah and I found an injured woman in the road. She attacked us, then that thing showed up," I said, jabbing an accusatory finger at the sky.

Friend fixed a measured stare on me. There was something in those dark eyes that I didn't like, a melancholy that seemed to run down to the core of the man. "So, it picked you this time."

"What do we do?" I asked, immediately feeling a flush of shame creeping up my neck at how small my voice sounded. My whole life I had been the guy who made problems go away, yet here I was, practically begging an elderly man for help.

He stared at me another moment, then shook his head. "Nothing. Now, I know that isn't what you want to hear, but in my experience, it's your best bet. Don't chase The Light, don't try to understand it, just keep out of its sight and hope to high hell the damn thing gets bored and finds someone else to play with. Oh, and I'd avoid that new friend of yours as well," he said, nodding towards Carl who was currently climbing atop someone's sedan for a better shot. "Those nut jobs tend to stir everything up," Friend said. "Too concerned with 'can I' to think about 'should I.' It never ends well."

He was right, none of this was what I wanted to hear. "So that's it? Hope it goes away?"

"Well," he said, "that and keep an eye on that wife of yours. She's…open, in a way not many are. I know that sounds like a load of bull pucky, but it's the truth. I knew it the second I stepped foot on your porch, could feel her inside. And it will be able to feel her, too. It'll try to get its claws into her and make her see things that aren't there and do things she doesn't want to do."

"Like what?" I asked.

"Hurt people," he said simply. "Sometimes, the people they love." In a flash, I understood he was talking about Wendy and me.

"Is that what happened with you? Did it make your wife – "

"No," he said, cutting me off. "But I've seen it happen."

I looked back to The Light, a hard ball of frustration forming in my throat. "We can't just ignore it. I think it was trying to get into our house a few nights ago."

"Then you have to deal with it, alone," he said. "The more your wife gets involved, the more you're going to expose her, and the worse it's going to get. You seem like a good man, Jacob, but you need to keep her in the dark on this one. Keep her away from The Light, no matter what."

"I can't do that," I said. "I've never been able to keep anything from Hannah." Besides, I thought, chances are she'd pluck the truth from my head anyway.

Friend looked back towards The Light. "Then get ready for one hell of a fight. Don't trust it, don't let her trust it. That thing up there will spin all sorts of silvery lies to get its way. And should the time come that you need a place to retreat to, have Hannah give me a call. I like you both, Jacob. I want only good things for you and yours."

I blinked in confusion. Friend had never given me his number, and I was fairly sure he hadn't even met Hannah. "We'll need your number."

Friend laughed and shook his head. "Not the kind of call I meant. Ask Hannah. She'll be able to tell you." Then he pointed skyward. "Looks like the show is ending."

Above us, The Light had begun to faintly pulse and swirl in the sky, carving a spiral pattern in the darkness. As it did, it grew smaller, the waves of liquid light that poured off it seemed to evaporate away, leaving a hard nugget of light too intense to stare at directly. Then it was gone.

I turned back to Friend confused by his statement about Hannah, only to find he'd vanished as well. His truck was gone as well, leaving an empty space in the middle of a clustered nest of cars. How the hell had he driven out of that? I craned my neck to see over the crowd, searching the road for taillights and finding none.

Before I could even begin to process the bizarre conversation, or Friend's equally bizarre disappearance, Carl broke from the crowd and jogged over to me, eyes wild with excitement.

"Did you see that!?" he demanded, already working to remove the memory card from his camera with trembling fingers. "I got it all! Minutes of footage, at least, and up close. This is huge, this is the kind of shit that goes viral. Can you believe it? It's just like the light you tattooed on me!?"

"Yeah," I said, "I saw it. I've got to get home."

Carl looked at me as if I had just suggested we cannibalize a toddler. "Are you fucking nuts? I've got to get these people to go on record," he said, gesturing behind him to the already dissipating crowd. "I have to get their raw reactions, before they have a chance to clam up."

"Good luck with that," I said. "I'm going home."

He looked at me, enthusiasm bleeding into concern. At that point, perhaps sensing that talking about it was the last thing I wanted to do, he shrugged. "Suit yourself, man. I'll swing by the shop tomorrow."

Then he was gone, jogging back towards the other witnesses. I got into my truck, started the engine, and maneuvered it along the side of the road and around the other cars. Within a minute, I had left them all behind and the only light to see was the wash of my headlights.

5

When I got home, the first thing I heard was the telephone ringing in the kitchen. I found Hannah sitting at the table, her head sunk between her hands, eyes glossy and staring sightlessly forward. On the wall, the phone's cradle continued to ring. The handset had been detached and now sat on the table before her, its cord coiled around it like the tail of a snake.

"Are you going to get that?" I asked, hovering in the doorway.

She jerked as if startled, eyes wild as she scanned the room until she found me and let out a breath. "It's been doing that for hours," she said. "I thought it couldn't ring without the handset attached."

"It shouldn't," I said. "Thing is probably broken." I'd been meaning to take the phone down for months, but whoever had installed it had glued it to the wall. I was still trying to figure out how to detach it without tearing a hole in the drywall.

"It was doing it this morning, too," she said. "I thought I heard someone on the other end." There was something in her tone that I didn't like, the same careful tone she used whenever she had to break news that she knew I wouldn't like.

I frowned at the phone, already reaching for the handset. "Probably just a faulty line. We never turned the service on."

"Wait, there's more. I went for a walk today, I thought I'd – "

"One second," I said, not wanting to hear whatever news she had to share, not wanting to add another layer of weirdness to the science fiction movie that my life was becoming. "Just let me take a look at this."

"Jacob," she said, voice still soft and pregnant with whatever shoe she was about to drop. "Please sit down? I went for a walk with Wendy, I thought I'd try to find Astra's home, maybe ask her some questions but – "

"Wait," I insisted, plugging the handset back into the cradle, then pressing it to my ear.

No sound on the other side, just soft pulses of static. I hung the handset back up, the ringing stopped. "There," I said, "all better. Now, what were you trying to tell me?"

The phone began to ring again. Hannah and I traded a long look.

"Don't," she said, but I had already picked up the handset and pressed it to my ear.

"Hello?" I said. "Who is this?"

The only response was more static on the other end, and a soft swishing noise that might have been breathing. I stared down at the phone, then gently set it back into its cradle. "Like I said, broken." The moment the word left my lips, the phone began to ring again and I found myself picking it up, a spark of rage blooming in my chest.

"Who the fuck is this!?" I demanded.

"Have you figured it out yet?" a voice on the other end said. The connection was bad, the voice soft and unfamiliar. I couldn't even put my finger on the gender or age through the shifting waves of static.

Hannah covered her mouth with her hand, eyes wide and locked on mine. "Figured what out?" I asked, voice firm.

There was an odd sound, almost like a laugh, but somehow insectile, like the rhythmic clapping of massive mandibles. "She's lost her mind. She's going to hurt the baaaabbbbeeee." The final word stretched out into electronic, mechanical screech.

I looked at Hannah, then dropped the phone, a muted scream locking my throat. The kitchen was inexplicably covered in blood, thick clots of it stuck to the walls, counters, and floor. Hannah was also soaked up to the elbows, old blood splattered over her face. The worst of it was near the sink, where a tiny corpse lay draped over the rim. It was Wendy, her tiny head shoved into the drain and fed to the garbage disposal. I then noticed the other form lying on the ground and with a start, realized it was me. I was lying crumpled against the counter, a jagged hole where my face had been, the shotgun I'd bought lying beside me.

I shot myself, I realized. I must have come home, found Wendy like this and shot myself. It made a kind of sense. Maybe this whole thing with The Light and telepathy was just a dream, the final thoughts racing out of the skylight I'd put into my own skull. I stumbled forward and lifted the shotgun, still warm to the touch.

"Jacob! Jacob, baby, wake up!"

I turned the shotgun over in my hands, ignoring the insistent voice screaming in my ear. It's over, I thought, leave me alone. I'm already dead. Then a slap landed hard across my jaw and suddenly the blood was gone. I was standing in the middle of the kitchen, the loaded shotgun in my hand, its barrel pointed up towards my chin. Hannah stood before me, eyes wide in terror, both hands tightly gripping the gun in an attempt to keep the business end away from my face.

I looked at her, then down at the gun, and realized what I had been about to do. Hannah pulled the shotgun from my hands and I stumbled back against the wall, a cold sweat crawling across my skin.

"Where did – how did that get in here?"

Hannah set the shotgun down on the table and stepped in front of it, hands held up before her as if trying to tame a wild animal. "You went and got it," she said slowly. "You put down the phone, left the kitchen, and came back in here with it. I was talking to you and you wouldn't respond."

I took a deep, steadying breath, forcing my eyes to meet hers. "Someone was on the phone; they said something and then – " And then what? I'd seen the blood. I'd smelled it, the rich scent of old pennies and the first sweet notes of rot. It hadn't been real, couldn't have been, but what about the gun? I looked at Hannah, then past her, my fear and confusion suddenly igniting into hot rage.

Someone was standing outside the kitchen window, hood drawn over their head, one gloved hand pressed against the glass.

"Get away from us!" I bellowed, startling Hannah until her eyes followed mine and she let out a sound somewhere between a gasp and a scream.

Adrenaline flooded my body and I sprinted down the hall, bursting out the front door, intent to leap upon whomever I found there and rip them limb from bloody limb.

Only there was nobody to maim. The area in front of the kitchen window was empty, as was the rest of the front yard. I spun, scanning the shadows, ears trained for the sound of feet fleeing into the woods. I heard nothing but crickets and the whisper of wind through pine needles.

I screamed, not out of fear, or even anger, but frustration. "Come back here!" I shouted. "Stop running and face me, you little fuck!" Yet with each word I screamed, I felt smaller – nothing more than a helpless minnow awaiting the mercy of sharks.

Hannah appeared in the doorway, holding a butcher's knife at her side. "Did you see what direction they went?"

I looked at her and tried to respond but before I could, the phone began to ring again inside.

"Leave it," Hannah said, eyes wide, their whites almost glowing in the dark. "Please, just – "

"No," I said. No to all of this. I pushed past her, back down towards the kitchen. I lifted the handset off the cradle and then screamed into the mouthpiece. "Leave us alone! Whoever you are, you can't always run. I'll get my hands on you and I'll rip your fucking head off, do you hear me!?"

I should have hung up right then but I found myself pausing, phone held inches from my ear, waiting for a reply. When one came, it was my own voice talking back to me. "Who is this?" the other me said. "Whoever you are, leave us alone!"

"Very funny asshole," I shouted, and, to my shock, so did he, mirroring my words a half a beat after I'd said them, like an echo. "Who are you!?" I shouted only for him to echo me again. "Leave us alone. We are armed!"

All was silent for a moment. Then, my voice again, the tone grief stricken and shaking, "I had to do it. She was coming at me with a knife, she was going to hurt the baby. Oh God, oh Hannah, I'm so sorry."

In a flash I saw another image – me standing above Hannah, plunging a knife into her chest over and over again. I slammed the handset back into the cradle, then ripped the whole damn thing out of the wall and smashed the hard plastic casing down onto the kitchen tile.

I stood there a moment, breathing hard, feeling like I might puke at any moment.

"Jacob?" Hannah tentatively called from the doorway. "What's wrong, what did you hear?"

I didn't reply, couldn't force the words out of my throat. It was all too much: the lights, the conversation with Friend, now this. I heard Hannah ask again, then felt her hands on my back.

"Talk to me. What's going on in that thick head of yours?" she asked tenderly. When I failed to reply yet again, I felt something stir inside my own head.

I could *feel* her looking inside me, her gentle fingers rifling through my thoughts as if they were files in a cabinet. I jumped and pushed her away, sending her stumbling against the table.

"Jesus Christ, don't do that!" I said. "Fuck, Hannah, can't I take a moment!?"

She looked immediately sheepish, holding her hands up in surrender. "I just needed to make sure you weren't about to try to blow your goddamn head off again, all right?"

"It's not all right!" I shouted. "None of this is fucking all right! I can't handle this weird-ass shit, Hannah. I can't do aliens, weird fucking lights, and psychic powers; I just can't. I wish I was strong enough to deal with all of it but I'm not, so fuck me if I need a moment!"

"You said you'd try," she said, tone hard, eyes wet. "You said you would try to believe me. I know you meant it, I could feel it."

"Well maybe this is me trying!" I shot back. "Maybe this is the best I can do. Maybe I'm just a big fucking moron who can't figure any of this shit out. Is that what you want to hear!?"

"This isn't exactly a picnic for me, either!" she shouted, matching my volume. "You go away to work and I sit here all day just stewing in this nightmare, waiting for something to happen. Meanwhile I have this *thing* inside me that I don't understand and the only person who can explain it to me is some shark-mouthed monster. We're both lost, we're both confused and scared."

My head was spinning, the sounds of our argument bouncing off the walls in the confined kitchen, ensnaring us in a web of barbed words. I felt the sudden, powerful urge to leave. If I ran, I could be at the door before she could stop me. Get in the truck, hit the freeway, and not stop until the sun came up over some distant ocean. I would vanish into the world, become an addict and die forgotten. Become "that bastard" that Hannah and Wendy spoke about for years to come, while living with some nice guy named Greg who worked in insurance, had a college degree, and no knuckle scars.

Hannah rushed me, grabbed me by the shirt and pulled me down towards her with surprising strength. "Don't you even think about it," she said, furious tears finally slipping past her eyelids and carving rivers down the sides of her face. "You promised me you'd never leave, you son of a bitch!"

I stared at her, my rage fading away, leaving nothing but suffocating guilt in its place. Where had those thoughts come from? Were they, like my other nightmarish thoughts, just projected by whoever had been outside the window? Or did I actually have a deep-seated desire to free Hannah of the burden of my existence? I wasn't sure which option scared me more.

"What is happening to us?" I whispered. "How is any of this possible?"

"I don't know," she said, not releasing my shirt. "But it's happening, so it must be possible. Whatever happens, all I know is I need you—your *family* needs you."

On the floor, the smashed phone began to ring again, the sound warped beneath shattered plastic and wires. We both stared at it, neither saying a word.

"Some things happened today," I finally said, voice hoarse. "I met a guy who says he might be able to help us. And I saw The Light again."

She tore her eyes away from the broken phone. "Something happened to me, too. It's kind of hard to explain."

I looked down into her eyes, Friend's words echoing in my head. What if this was a mistake? What if, by involving Hannah, I was handing her over to The Light and whatever the hell it wanted? But I knew my Rabbit, the fiery girl who marched into the bad part of town at midnight to save her idiot boyfriend from himself. She would be involved no matter what I did. I took a deep breath. I may not trust The Light, or this psychic stuff, but I trusted her.

"Then show me," I said, tapping the side of my head.

She stared at me for a moment before comprehension dawned in her eyes. "Are you sure?" she asked. "I'm not sure I know how. We can go sit down, talk it through. You don't have to …"

I took her hand in mine, then pressed it flush against the side of my head. "Just do it. Like ripping off a band-aid, right? If I've got a psychic wife, I need to get used to it." I gave her a smile I hoped was reassuring.

Hannah sucked in a breath, then nodded and closed her eyes.

At first, there was nothing. Then suddenly, everything –information flowed into my mind as if from some secret spring. Hannah's morning spent tormented by phone calls, her walk into the hills, meeting Astra. When I reached the memory of how the woman's face had changed into a ghoulish, predatory monstrosity, I gasped and clutched Hannah closer to me. I was receiving more than just her memory; it was her actual experience, as if I had lived those moments, too. I could still remember the burn in my legs as I ran home, Wendy clutched to my breast, and raw terror flooding my veins. Then she showed me her dreams, the infection in her hand, Astra's medicine, The Light – days of experience packed into a moment, leaving me gasping.

Slowly, the stream of information dried to a trickle. "Ok," Hannah whispered, voice gentle in my ear. "Now show me."

Unsure what to do, I thought about my day, starting with the moment I left her that morning, through giving Carl his tattoo, all the way up to seeing The Light. I stopped short before the conversation with Friend, unsure if showing her that part of it would put her in more danger.

She frowned. "Show me," she said.

"It was just a conversation with that old man I told you about."

"Show me," she said, softly but firmly. So I did, opening that last door in my mind. The memory played out behind my eyelids, and then slid forward. To the phone calls, the vision of murder and suicide, and finally our argument.

When it was done, she slid her hand off my face and stepped back, her expression pensive and thoughtful.

On the floor, the broken phone continued to ring.

"Well?" I asked.

She looked at me, at the phone, then down at her own hands. "I think that there is a reason Astra tried to lead me away, and Friend tried to get you to lie to me," she said. "I think they are connected, somehow."

"How could you possibly know that?" I asked. "Friend seems like a good guy; he was just worried about us."

She considered this, gnawing at the edge of her lower lip. "Maybe," she finally said. "But my gut tells me otherwise. That thing he said, about having me call him, it's exactly what she told me to do. I think he's part of the same group. She said there were more who could do what I do."

Hannah thought of Astra's warning as she was running away, and I heard it loud and clear. Astra had said that she would leave us be, but *he* wouldn't. Who was *he*? Friend?

I slumped against the fridge and closed my eyes. A moment later, I felt Hannah lift my arm and wrap it around herself, pressing against me.

"Do you trust me?" she asked into my chest.

"Yes," I said immediately. "But I don't trust myself. Hannah, I didn't choose to go and get the gun out of the closet. They could have made me...they almost..."

She squeezed me tighter, "I know. So, if we can't trust ourselves, we trust each other. We can't let them win. Whoever these people are, I think they want us apart. I don't know why, and I don't know *what* they are, but the only thing I do know is we will only figure this out together."

Put like that, my final resistance crumbled. On one hand, I could accept that my wife had gone insane, that we both had. And if that was true, we had a matching pair of his-and-her-straitjackets in our future. On the other hand, if we were both sane, it could only mean that someone or some *thing* was out to get us, with abilities we couldn't possibly predict, and motives that remained a mystery. Seemed to me, if I wanted to keep my family safe, I didn't have the luxury of believing my insanity theory.

"Ok," I said, nodding slowly. "What do we do first?"

I carried the still ringing phone outside, set it atop a stump, and then hacked at it with the wood axe until it finally stopped ringing. Then, as if to banish the suicidal vision it had induced, I doused it in lighter fluid and burned it into a melted puddle of warped plastic and exposed wiring.

Next, we drove together up the road to where Hannah had abandoned Wendy's stroller. We found it sitting upright on the shoulder, untouched save for a spot of bird crap on the handlebar. Inside was a crude stick doll, the same type that Astra had previously left for Wendy. This one had a yellow ribbon tied around its neck that anchored a small slip of paper.

Unfolding the note, Hannah held it up to the thin moonlight. It was short, only three words.

You should run.

7

INTERLUDE

Hypnotic Regression Therapy Session #5
Subject: Jacob Riley
Administered by: Dr. James Lorenz

Dr. Lorenz: All right, Jacob, you're all the way at the bottom now. Can you hear me?
Jacob: Yes.
Dr. Lorenz: Good. We're going to review more of your memories. I'd like to talk about what brought you to Victor's Point.
Jacob: We decided at random. We were driving through the area and Hannah saw the house. She liked it enough to want to take a look. We're going to flip it and move to a big city.
Dr. Lorenz: Yes, you've said as much. I want to inspect that a little more closely, is that OK?
Jacob: I don't want to.
Dr. Lorenz: Are you sure?
Hannah Riley: Jacob, please?
Jacob: ...fine.
Dr. Lorenz: Please tell us about the days leading up to your arrival in Victor's Point.
Jacob: It was a Wednesday.

◆ ◆ ◆

We were leaving Detroit, heading southeast, into the Appalachians. I had hoped to draw on one of Doug's old contacts in Detroit to get a job as a bouncer, but as it turned out, Doug's guy was doing a stint in Jackson County Prison for stabbing a prostitute. Hannah had found some work online, writing captions for streaming services, but the pay was meager, at best. By my count, we had only two hundred dollars to our name, half a tank of gas, and no prospects.

Hannah was in the passenger seat, her feet up on the edge of her window, thumbing through a Robin Cook thriller she had picked up at a used bookstore in Chicago, while Wendy snoozed in her garage sale car seat in the back, both unaware of the argument I was having inside my own head. I was debating leaving them.

At first, the months on the run had been euphoric. Just the two of us, out in the world, with no obligations, no structure. Just an open field on which our love could grow. We got married in a Vegas chapel, swore eternal love under the neon lights that poured off the strip. We laid on lumpy beds in seedy motels and I stroked her belly, whispering sweet promises to our growing child I knew I couldn't hope to keep.

The unforgiving roadblock of reality was approaching fast and we were on a collision course. We were nearly at the point where we'd be stranded with no gas, no food, and no money. Even a doctor's visit for Hannah would be beyond our reach. And when we hit that blockade, she would realize what a huge mistake she had made. It would be better to let her off the ride before we crashed.

I'd spend another day or two driving, all the while angling back towards Echo City. I wouldn't give her warning. We'd arrive at her parents' house in the middle of the night, I'd give her nothing but cold words, then kick her back into the life we had fled. She would be heartbroken, but safe, fed, and alive. Alive to raise Wendy free of my baggage, at the very least.

As for me, I figured best-case scenario I would go back to drugs before long and, I suspected, an early grave. At the time, that seemed like an all-right sort of thing.

As it turned out, I never got the chance to follow through. We were driving through Bible Belt country, billboards alternating between promises of Christ's love and advertisements for strip clubs with names like 'Crusin' Charlie's Chubby Chasers.' We were somewhere in Kentucky, headed east, when my bladder drove us off the freeway in search of a bathroom, and soon enough we found ourselves creeping along in a line of traffic leading into the town of Carver's Mill. Unlike most of the dying coal towns we had been passing through, Carver's Mill was practically bursting with activity. We had arrived the same day as their annual Founder's Fest.

The main road through town had been blocked off to make room for a handful of midway games and carnival rides, and the smell of the town barbeque competition in the nearby park filled the air with the tang of charred pork, which set my stomach howling.

Giggling at the sound, Hannah poked me in the belly. "Looks like fun. Want to stop? We could use a night off the road."

I almost refused, reasoning that if we rationed our little remaining cash, I could have at least another few days with her, but then I thought, what the hell? It didn't matter if I left her in a day or a week, it would break both our hearts just the same. At least this way we could end on a sweet note.

"Sure," I said, joining the long line of cars waiting for parking.

She squeezed my hand. "Don't look so glum about it."

I forced a smile, and gave her hand a return squeeze, promising myself right then and there that, for this night at least, I would do everything right. I would love her and make whatever eternal promises she needed to make her smile.

Pushing Wendy before us, we ate barbeque, watched a puppet show, shared a bag of cotton candy, and sat watching dusk sweep over the mountains from our vantage at the very top of the Ferris wheel. She leaned against my shoulder, arms wrapped around Wendy in her lap, a look of wonder and delight on her face.

"What about here?" she asked, voice small against the wind that gently rocked our gondola.

"What do you mean?" I asked, shifting to look at her. "To live?"

"Place seems as good as anywhere else. We can't raise Wendy in the cab of the truck forever. I know money is tight, but maybe we can find a way to make it work?"

She looked up at me then, naked hope in her eyes. I ran a thumb over her chin, wondering how long she would hate me after I left. Most likely, forever. Wendy would forget me soon enough, but Hannah? My girl could hold a grudge. I leaned down and kissed her on the forehead. "Ok," I said. "We'll take a look around in the morning and see if we can find something affordable."

And, I thought, once we had been denied at every place in town, maybe then she would understand how fucked we were. But not tonight. I pulled her closer as we watched the first stars emerge from the purple twilight.

We got a room at the cheapest place in town, a dingy twenty-unit motel with a rusted sign that still boasted "Color TVs In Every Room!" The entire place stunk of age, too many coats of paint, rotting wood, and mildew. However, it was cleaner than our usual stops and there was nobody doing meth in the parking lot. As far as we were concerned, that made it a five-star experience.

After Wendy had been fed and put down to nap, Hannah and I made love. The entire time, I never let my eyes leave her, tracing the delicate curves of her body and the fine structure of her face, as if to sear it into my mind. I wanted to make sure that, no matter how far I went from her, I would never forget that smile, those hands on my shoulders, or the hungry embrace of her body. I told her I loved her, and she responded with a stun-gun kiss that left me breathless.

Afterwards, I lay on my back, watching the thin light from the parking lot throw creeping shadows across the ceiling. In a rare moment of peace, Wendy and Hannah were both asleep, the former in a half-broken travel crib we had salvaged from the dumpster behind a Babies 'R' Us. Within that brief serenity, doubt assailed me. Could I really do it? Leave Hannah, leave Wendy? We had been together so long I hardly knew who I was without her. Jacob and Hannah, the Moose and the Rabbit, the rich girl and the criminal delinquent. We were an illogical yet unbreakable pair, and had been since the day I pulled her from that community pool.

I was sure she would survive without me. She was smarter than me, for one, and she also had a life to go back to. Family, old friends, even a college degree she could finish up. Being a single mother would be hard, but I knew my

Hannah. She could do it. She *would* do it. Yet every thought of the coming dawn filled me with a deeper and deeper dread.

I was still sifting these thoughts through my head when I noticed the shadows on the ceiling begin to change. I tensely followed their movement to the window. Someone was walking by outside – two someones. I could see them silhouetted against the closed drapes. I strained my ears and heard muffled whispers, followed by the sound of someone trying the door handle to our room. I sat up, reasoning that they were likely just drunk partyers back from the fair, but then I heard the tell-tale sound of a credit card being wiggled into the gap between the door and the jam. Someone was trying to break in.

I rose so fast I nearly threw Hannah off the bed, stepping towards the door, realizing I was still naked. Behind me, Hannah raised her head and mumbled in confusion. There was no time to explain, or even to find pants, as the door handle was already turning. I pressed myself into the shadows against the wall as the door swung open.

Two men stepped inside, both dressed in light jackets and jeans. One was a thick-set man, with a nose like mine, mushed from being broken one too many times, and narrow, rat-like eyes. The other, conversely, could have been a model with a classic action hero jaw line, thick black hair, and luminous blue eyes.

"There's our girl," the handsome one said just as Hannah managed to fully sit up, her eyes widening as she realized what was happening, her lungs filling as she prepared to scream.

The larger one took a step towards her, and I burst from my hiding spot, sweeping him into a tight hug and carrying him all the way to the far wall where we smashed against the dresser.

"Holy fuck!" the handsome one shouted. He laughed like a chortling hyena, "You keep that big ol' bear busy, Bruce. I'll take care of the little lad –"

He never got out the last word as Hannah snatched up the alarm clock and sent it whizzing at his head, clipping him across the temple.

Meanwhile, I had suddenly found myself in a grapple, Bruce and I grunting as our weights shifted and hands fought for purchase on each other's bodies. He pulled at fistfuls of my body hair, unable to get purchase, while I hooked my fingers into the front of his shirt and spun him, sending the bigger man stumbling back towards the handsome one, who was too busy dodging the Mormon Bible that had been aimed at his face to see the collision headed his way. They knocked heads as they collided, sending both crashing to the ground. Then I was on them, straddling Bruce across the chest and raining haymaker blows down on his face, snapping his cheekbone with the second blow and cracking an eye socket with the third, the only sound in my head the inferno roar of rage.

Hannah screamed my name, but I couldn't hear it, couldn't see beyond the face in front of me and the rhythmic collision of flesh on flesh. That is until a gunshot broke the spell. I fell off the bigger man, feeling suddenly winded, as if I had been punched in the gut.

I looked down and saw a jagged hole in my chest and dark blood flowing in a steady stream down my belly. I looked up to see the handsome one, risen to a shooter's knee, a smoking pistol held before him in a two-handed grip.

Hannah screamed and hurled herself onto the shooter, her knee slamming hard into his mouth and splitting his lip. I tried to rise to help her, tried to summon the familiar rage that had seen me through dozens of bloody fights. Where it had once been there was only pain and a distant, hazy feeling that was creeping over my body. I couldn't feel my hands, or my feet, and my thoughts had grown thin, and slow.

Hannah kicked and scratched at the man, while in the corner, Wendy woke and started to scream. I watched, unable to help as the handsome man managed to stagger to his feet and punch–Hannah directly in the mouth. She hit the ground, spitting blood, her eyes wide, half-mad with anger and fear. She tried to rise, muttering venomous curses under her breath, when he grabbed her and slammed her back down onto the ground.

"Whoa, she is a feisty one. But don't you worry, Daddy has your medicine." Hannah thrashed, trying to bite his fingers as he pressed them against her forehead. In the gloom of the motel room, his blue eyes seemed to flash. Hannah's eyes rolled back, her entire body going suddenly boneless beneath her attacker. Then, he rose.

"No hard feelings, Hoss," he said to me, leering down as I tried and failed to stand, every breath feeling like it was pushed through broken glass. "You've done a real fine job keeping her safe. Moving around like you did, it was a real bitch tracking her down." He leaned down and scooped her limp body into his arms. "But don't you worry, she's in good hands now."

"Fuck you," I managed to wheeze while trying to rise, but collapsed on the carpet. I was going to die. The thought came without emotion, a simple understanding which sucked the last bit of fight from me.

The handsome man laughed again. "God, I do like you. It's a damn shame, you would have made a great breeder. He turned his attention to the other man, who was in the process of slowly dragging himself to his feet, his face already livid with growing bruises. "Speaking of which, go and get the brat."

The larger man nodded and started towards Wendy's crib, stepping over me as he went, her cries reaching a fever pitch as the stranger clumsily scooped her up, holding her away from his body as if she were diseased. I wanted to scream for him to get his fucking hands off my child, but when I tried to draw in a breath, nothing came. I wasn't dying, I was dead and my brain just hadn't caught up to the fact that my blood was no longer flowing. Darkness edged in on my vision, and my heart gave one last stuttering beat.

Suddenly, trumpets.

A sudden blast of noise washed over us from above, a thundering bellow like the braying of God's hounds. Light poured in through the windows and, in that brilliant moment, I watched the handsome man's face contort with naked terror. The light enveloped me.

All at once, Hannah, Wendy and I were in the truck, driving down a dirt road.

I slammed on the brakes, the truck kicking up a plume of dust as it skidded to a stop.

Hannah bolted upright in the passenger seat, as if waking from a nap. "Wha – what happened? Did we hit something?"

I sat there for a moment, breathing heavily, one hand pressed to my chest. How had we gotten here? I had been shot, I was dying, but my chest was whole. Who were those men? And what had hap …happened to…

"No, we didn't hit …" I stopped, looking into the rearview mirror, for what I couldn't say. My thoughts were jumbled and confused. We were attacked, right? But by whom? When? And how had we gotten away? How was I even alive? The more I reached for answers, the fewer I found, the memory slipping away into some dark box inside myself that I could not open. "Thought I saw something in the road, I guess," I finally said.

Hannah looked at me, and for a moment I saw a remnant of fear in her eyes, then it too bled away. "Scared the hell out of me," she said, touching a hand to her chest. "You want me to take over driving? You look pretty tired."

"And you look like you recently squeezed a watermelon out of your belly," I said. "I'll be fine, you just relax."

We followed an old service road through the hills that cut down from the northwest into the unfamiliar town of Victor's Point. Within twenty minutes, we were rumbling along Strawberry Lane, the red house looming in the windshield. A 'Victor's Realty' sign hung in the yard, right next to another sign, this one yellow, reading 'No Credit Required. Steal of a deal.'

"Hey, that one's for sale. Want to take a look?"

"How could we afford it?" I asked.

She paused, looking momentarily lost, then shrugged. "We can use the money my grandmother left me. Remember? That was the plan? Looks like a fixer-upper, too, just like we talked about."

I blinked, then it clicked. That's right, how could I have forgotten? Hannah's grandmother had left her twenty thousand dollars, which we had wisely not touched during our months of wandering. It was enough for a down payment, enough to start a new life. It was a miracle we had managed to keep it untouched for so long. God knows, we could have used it. My brain stalled on that thought for a moment, like a sleeve caught on a loose nail. Something was wrong with that, I knew it. Something was missing.

"Can we take a look?" Hannah asked, a big smile creeping over her face.

"I don't know," I said, still perturbed. "We don't even really know where we are."

"Come on," she said. "We can worry about the neighborhood after. Besides, I feel like I've been in this car for days."

I smiled back at her. This was the plan, the one we had always had, far as I could tell. So why not?

"All right," I said, pulling the truck over to the side of the road. "Just a quick look."

Hannah beamed. "Hell yeah. I've got a good feeling about this place."

Dr. Lorenz: And you were uninjured when you came to?
Jacob: Yes.
Dr. Lorenz: And you had no recollection of this event until now?
Jacob: No.
Dr. Lorenz: And the money. Did it really come from –
Jacob: I don't know. I don't think so. If we had had that kind of cash on hand, we would have used it.
Dr. Lorenz: My… that's… wow. Do you recognize either of your attackers? Have you seen them since?
Jacob: The one who shot me, he's a cop in town. Officer Hanson.

8
PSYCHIC RADIO

1 – Hannah

"Seek and find," The Light repeated as the dream began to fade.

"What!?" I shouted back. "Seek and find what?"

"Seek understanding," it said, as it had the last three nights.

"I don't know where to start!"

I bolted upright in bed, the sheet pooling around my waist, cold sweat running down my back. I caught my breath and grumbled in frustration.

"Still no luck?" Jacob asked from his new guard post, an old beat-up easy chair set beside the bed so he could watch me sleep. It had been three days since the incident with the phone. That night we had sat down and laid out what we knew, compared it against our avenues of investigation, and found them limited.

Talking to Sheriff Quinn seemed presumptuous, especially as we had no proof of our claims. If I was right and Astra was somehow connected to all this, then she was logically the person to talk to, but we also didn't know *what* she was. I wasn't too fond of the idea of another sit down with the shark-mouthed woman. We tried instead to find out *about* her, to no avail. Jacob had asked around town to find that no one knew her—or anyone matching her description. What's more, there was no record of anyone by that first name ever living in the area according to the tax records at the city office. His new friend Carl had helped with that last part, spending two straight days poring over ledgers in the cramped file room behind the combined sheriff/mayor's office.

That left us stewing and back at square one, our only possible lead being the dreams and The Light, neither of which seemed inclined to give a straight answer. All the while, we waited for the next horror to invade our lives.

"The Light just keeps telling me to seek and find. Told me to seek understanding, but didn't tell me how or where to look. It's like arguing with a fortune cookie."

Jacob nodded and leaned forward, rubbing his temples. Neither of us had slept much in days. If the constant fear of attack wasn't enough, Wendy had been an absolute nightmare the entire time, howling at all hours, only quieting to eat or sleep in fitful bursts. I scooted across the bed and ran my hand along his back, kneading the hard muscles beneath his neck.

"Anything happen while I was asleep?" I asked. It was five in the morning, the world outside just starting to turn gray with the coming day.

He nodded. "Maybe nothing. Thought I saw some lights out in the woods

104

a few hours ago, moving too fast to be flashlights. Vanished just as quick though – might have been fireflies or something."

"Might have," I said, though neither of us believed it.

Jacob nodded, a look of consternation on his face. "I've been thinking," he said. "About our situation."

"Any conclusions?" I asked, wiping the last of the sleep from my eyes.

"We need help," he said flatly, sounding like he'd rather be chewing glass. We had already discussed the topic several times in the past few days or, more accurately, I played devil's advocate while Jacob discussed it. He didn't want to bring others in, fearing both ridicule and getting someone else involved in what was clearly a dangerous situation. On the other hand, it was becoming increasingly apparent that neither of us had a clue how to actually deal with any of this.

"OK," I said. "Do you want to bring Carl to the house?"

Jacob sighed and nodded. "Yes. I've already told him everything that's happened, so I figure there won't be much harm in letting him in the rest of the way. He also said he has a professor friend with interest in stuff like this. We might be able to get him out here. I also want to talk to Quinn about the psycho who attacked us on the road, see if he ever figured out who she was."

Mention of the mad woman sent a pang of phantom pain through my hand. "Astra called her a breeder, remember? Whoever she was, she had been with whoever Astra's people are."

"I'll talk to him today," Jacob said.

"Or," I corrected, "I can talk to Quinn. You get Carl to call his professor friend and see if he knows anyone else we can pull in."

A stab of cold fear sank into my gut – not my own emotion, but Jacob's. He was worried about me outside the relative safety of the house, with its locked doors and loaded shotgun. "Don't worry," I said, not wanting to remind him that the same loaded gun had nearly taken his head off less than a week prior. "I'll be careful. Besides, where am I more at risk? In here, alone? Or out in town surrounded by witnesses?"

"It's too dangerous. At least wait till I can come along and protect you. Just let me talk to Tracy and we can go tomor – "

I silenced him with a quick kiss on the corner of his mouth. "I can't just keep sitting here waiting for something bad to happen. It will be all right. Trust me?"

He looked at me. He was pale, dark circles rimming his eyes. Even his beard seemed somehow more brittle, but his eyes were the same, bright and attentive, all his focus mine alone. I felt him waver, then surrender. "OK," he said. "But keep your phone on you at all times."

I laughed. "A phone? I'm bringing a sword."

As it turned out, we didn't own a sword, so I settled on a can of Mace tucked into the bottom of my purse. We rode to town in silence, both nursing cups of strong coffee, Wendy bundled up in her car seat behind us.

Gazing through the windshield, I studied the expanse of the big blue sky, red rock, and dense vegetation that crept over the sides of the road as if to swallow it. Back in Echo City, everything was boxy buildings, streetlights and manicured lawns. Here, it seemed the real world had bucked its yoke, and all man could do was carve out little hamlets of survival amidst the chaos of nature. The Appalachians may lack the majesty and scope of the Rockies, but I'd be damned if they didn't have an ethereal kind of beauty of their own, one earned through age. They had been ancient when dinosaurs first walked the earth. Older than the first fish that flopped out of the ocean and figured out how to draw breath on dry land. Older than bones. I wondered what these hills had seen in the last five hundred million years. If they, too, gazed up into the stars and watched lights dance around in the sky.

We parked the truck behind Astrological and parted ways there, Jacob marching with shoulders slumped off to another day at the office. Meanwhile I unfolded Wendy's stroller and, once she was securely strapped in, set off for the sheriff's office. It was a Saturday, and the streets were as close to bustling as Victor's Point ever got. A few old men stood in a half circle in front of Red's Hardware; a couple kids chased each other in the shadow of the movie theater's marquee.

Only then did I admit to myself that learning something about the crazy woman who attacked us had only been half the reason I wanted to come to town today. I needed to see if my abilities stopped at Jacob and Astra. While I was still dubious about the ethics of uninvited telepathy, it was a fact that my newly talented brain was the biggest clue we had to unraveling what was going on. I needed to understand it, control it if I could. To do that, I needed to test its limits.

I tried first on a couple of older men milling around outside the post office, giving them both a sunny smile. They smiled back, one waved to Wendy, but their minds remained black boxes to me. I moved on, tried the next group I passed, then the next, each time failing to glean so much as a thought, growing more and more frustrated with each failure.

Ahead, two young boys were chasing each other with squirt guns just a few yards from where two dozen of Victor's Point's denizens milled about the town's finest, and only, ice cream parlor. Cream King had been built in the 50s and only sparsely maintained since. Its originally white paint peeled from the sides of the structure, and the massive ice cream cone on its roof was so faded it looked like a dollop of whipped cream. I slowed as I reached the crowd, flicking my gaze from face to face.

Maybe it wasn't a muscle as much as it was a question of familiarity? When I read Jacob's mind it was effortless, like walking through a door that had been laid open for me. Why should I assume that would be the case with strangers?

Maybe instead of walking through the door, I needed to force my way in.

I pulled out my phone and pretended to tap at it while I scanned the crowd until I picked out an elderly woman who was pecking at a soft serve cone with the timidity of a bird. I tried to reach into her mind and, when I got nothing, pushed harder, imagined my thoughts in the shape of a battering ram, slamming against her castle doors. After a moment I could feel it, a hard wall pressing back against me, refusing me. I gritted my teeth and pushed. The woman suddenly froze, her eyes growing wide and her hands trembling as a single drop of bright red blood flowed from her nose.

I recoiled, my phone clattering from my hands and drawing glances from the crowd. The elderly woman blinked, as if coming out of a particularly intense dream. I watched as she laughed it off, dabbing the blood from her face with a napkin. It seemed forcing my way in might be possible, but if the woman's reaction was any indication, it wasn't what Astra did. Astra's telepathy felt more fluid, sneakier.

Be like mist. The thought sprang to mind in what I recognized as the voice of The Light.

"I sure hope you know what you're talking about," I whispered back. I took a deep breath, then imagined my mind moving forward, formless, a rolling mist spread out among the crowd, creeping beneath their mental doorways like the vampires of old black-and-white films.

Bits of thought began to flow in, snippets of words, pulses of quick emotion. The joy of a child getting to eat their father's maraschino cherry, the frustration of a woman wrangling six kids, the exhaustion of the Cream King workers. Then, full thoughts began to flow in, one by one. James Cabbit, a young guy in his twenties with a deep farmer's tan and a love for chewing tobacco, was thinking about how many more months he would need to work to save up enough for an engagement ring for his girlfriend Victoria. She sat across from him, wondering how much longer until he figured out she was going to leave for college in a few months, and leave their relationship while she was at it.

Millie Redmont, a plump woman with a full head of curly hair, was thinking about how to tell her kids that their hamster had died. And Howard Franklin Ross, an elderly man sitting alone with a bowl of chocolate soft serve, was thinking about all the family he had buried in the town graveyard and how badly he wanted to join them.

A wild smile broke across my face. It was working. All around me, the secret plans and frustrations of the entire crowd sang out a tune only I could hear. It was a thrill – I felt like a live wire, a conduit for some great and powerful force that was both within and beyond me.

"Jesus Christ, she is filling out nice, ain't she?" A single clear thought cut through the noise. I turned, found its source. A man stood ten feet away, leaning in the shadow of a maple tree and languidly licking a vanilla soft serve cone. He was older, mid-fifties at least, with a full head of salt and pepper hair. He had his eyes focused intently on the girl working the front counter. She was pretty, with

long blond hair and dark brown eyes, but young. Terribly young, no older than thirteen or fourteen.

"Come on baby, bend over, show me a little skin," the man said, but didn't say. The words were only in my head, his lips remaining sealed as his hungry eyes crawled over the girl. *"Someone has got to fuck her eventually, right? Might as well be me. I'd treat her so nice. Make her like it. Fuck, I want to see that mouth wrapped around my —"*

I gagged, images rushing to my mind. I saw the man waiting under that tree all day, watched him counting the minutes as the sun sank below the horizon. Watched him approach her as she left for the day, offering her dinner, drinks, and all the adult attention he thought she wanted. And if she refused? Well, then, he would show her exactly why she ought to listen to her elders. He would do it, too, I could see the black hungry thing at the center of him. Not today or tomorrow, but soon enough. Before the year was out. Before anyone else could come along and pluck the little cherry he thought of every day while masturbating in the shower.

Before I knew what was happening, I was walking straight at the man, Wendy's stroller pushed before me like a war chariot. The man spotted me when I was only a few feet away and turned, eyes widening with surprise.

"Uh, can I help you miss?" he asked, voice bright and friendly, a soft flush on his cheeks. I stopped short. Looking into his eyes, I realized I knew all about him. His name was Frank Reddington. He had two sons, both of which he believed were dumber than stone and which brought him no small amount of shame. He blamed his wife, who'd coddled them. Filled their heads with so much softness that soft was all they could become. He dreamed of the day, long gone yet soon to come again he was sure, when men could be men and take what they desired. And beneath that, at the black root of the man, I saw an ice fishing shack and a withered old man named Hank.

"Shame on you, Frank," I said, barely contained fury coloring my voice.

He blinked, startled. "I'm sorry, miss, do I know you?"

"No, but I know you," I snarled, surprised at the chill I heard in my own voice. I stepped around Wendy's stroller and right up to him. He was a head taller than me, and while his face held kindhearted befuddlement, anger had already started to bloom inside him, a small spark of flame in the dark. I lowered my voice to a harsh whisper. "You go anywhere near that girl or any other child and I'll make sure you spend the rest of your life jerking it in a prison cell, do you understand?"

"I wasn't doing nothing…" He stopped and sputtered. In his head, I could see that he just wanted to shut me up, clamp a hand over my mouth and drag me to his truck and 'put my mouth to better use.'

I smiled viciously, showing as many teeth as I could. "Is rape all you're good for, Frank? Old Hank would be so proud of you. You're finally a big boy."

The moment the name of his childhood rapist left my mouth, Frank's face turned ashen and he seemed to shrink. "How did you…who the hell are you lady?"

"I'm a big fucking problem for you," I said, making sure to whisper so as not to be heard by neighboring tables. "Go home. Take care of your family. Get some therapy. And if I so much as see you glance at another little girl, I'm going to spread your dirty laundry from here to Maine."

His eyes flicked towards the girl at the counter, then back to me, holding his ice cream cone before him and looking a bit like an oversized toddler, lost at the fair. "How do you know all this?"

"Because I'm an Angel of the Lord, Frank," I said. "And I'm in a smiting mood."

He looked at me, then down at the ice cream cone that had begun to melt over his hand. For a moment, I thought he was about to hit me. He wanted to, the urge rising up from the chthonic pit inside his soul, but shame won out. "Crazy bitch," he muttered, dropping the cone and marching sullenly away.

A strange slurry of emotions washed over me as I watched him go. There was pride, a great swell of it. I had saved a girl a lifetime of trauma and, if my feelings were right, had kept him from indulging his fantasies for at least the next couple of years. But beneath that, something rancid squirmed in my heart. In one moment, I had unearthed the secret Frank Reddington wanted hidden more than anything. I had ripped it from his mind and laid it out like a cut of meat on the butcher's block. I didn't need to imagine the feelings of violation, I could feel his, radiating from his mind. It didn't bother me that I had shamed a potential rapist, what bothered me was how much I had *enjoyed* it.

"Who the hell is she?" I heard someone nearby say.

"She's pretty."

"She's strange looking."

"So she's the one married to that big ol' bull at the tattoo shop."

I turned to see none of these words had been spoken. People still ate their ice cream, pointedly looking anywhere but at me.

"Last thing we need is another troublemaker in town," an old man thought while spooning strawberry soft serve into his mouth.

"What the hell did she say to Frank?" thought another. Then more, a chorus of voices rising up, the flood gates blown wide open. Thoughts crashed over each other, pulsing over my mind, not one sound but hundreds, overlapping and building on each other into a cacophonous scream.

I pressed my hands to my ears but of course it did nothing to drown out the voices. It was too much! A lance of hot pain spiked through my head and my vision doubled.

"Stop it!" I shouted, drawing the bewildered stares of the townsfolk.

"Freak – Very strange – Drugs –Shame – Baby –" Their thoughts were no longer separate, just an unending stream of psychic noise. I fled, grabbing Wendy's stroller and pushing her quickly up the street, the thought explosion not leaving me until I rounded the corner out of sight.

2

I found a quiet spot in the covered doorway of a defunct tailor shop where I stopped, back pressed against the smudged glass door, breathing deep until my heart slowed its hummingbird beat. Once I was sure I wasn't about to suffer a fatal stroke, I sucked in a deep breath and let it out slow, Wendy looking up at me with her big blue eyes.

"Mommy OK?" The message popped into my head.

"Mommy is OK," I whispered, choking back the urge to cry. Wendy stared at me, uncomprehending; so instead, I thought it at her.

"Mommy is OK. Wendy is OK. Everything is good," I thought through each word slowly and, to my amazement, Wendy began to smile.

"Good," the thought came back, as Wendy clutched my ring finger and shook it. *"Good, Mommy safe."*

I took a steadying breath and did my best to wipe the sweat off my face. The psychic storm had left me with a lingering headache and a deep desire to lay down. What had all that noise been about? It was like a radio tuned into every station at once. Had Wendy also been able to hear it? I thought not, otherwise she would have been screaming. Maybe, I thought, I just stretched too far, tried to touch too many minds at once. Not for the first time in the past few days, I longed to find Astra, if just to have someone to explain all this to me. However, such thoughts always led to the image of her needle-like teeth glinting in the summer sun. Whatever she was, I wasn't sure I could trust her, which meant I needed to figure this out, and fast, which meant getting on with the business I'd come to town for. I straightened my back, took another deep breath to compose myself, and then pushed back out onto the street.

The city offices were housed in a small red brick building that had been the town's firehouse before the new station was built. The side was covered in an old mural showing a firefighter wrapped in an American flag, the words 'Victor's Point Firefighters' emblazoned in white above it, the paint chipped and fading after decades of sun and rain.

Jaw clenched in what I hoped resembled steely determination, I pushed through the front doors. I had only been here once, when we had closed on the house, and it was much the same as I remembered. The entire first floor of the station had been partitioned off into sections with cubicles, the old fire pole the only visible evidence of the building's former purpose. A large oak desk sat near the front, behind which sat a bored looking girl in a 'Victor's Point Miners' hoodie.

"Help you?" she asked as I approached. Her gaze flicked down to Wendy. "Oh my god, your baby is adorable."

I smiled graciously. "Isn't she just? She knows it too."

The girl cooed at Wendy, waggling a finger at her. Then, clearing her throat, asked, "Something I can help you with?"

"Is Sheriff Quinn in? I was hoping to talk to him about a problem he helped us with a few nights ago."

"Sheriff is out on a call," she said apologetically. "But Hanson is scheduled for duty soon. I'm sure if you stick around he will – "

As if summoned, Deputy Hanson strode in through the front doors behind me, already dressed in his brown deputy uniform, a bag of bagels in hand.

"Speak of the devil," the girl said.

Hanson smiled at her with a mouth full of pearly teeth. "Hey now, let's not give me more credit than I'm due. Don't need to offend Old Scratch. Got your fix." He reached into the bag and pulled out a bagel laden with salt and handed it to the girl. Then, seeming to notice me for the first time, nodded curtly. "Mrs. Riley."

"We were just talking about you," the girl said as she tore into her breakfast.

"Good things, I hope," he said, flashing her another smile, making her blush.

I cleared my throat. "Deputy, I was hoping to talk to you about the woman who attacked my husband and me. I was hoping you might have found out something about her?"

Hanson ran a hand through his wavy black hair and gestured deeper into the station. "Why don't we talk at my desk?"

He led the way. Deputy Hanson's cubicle was decidedly spartan, little more than a cheap computer, a contact lens case, and a jar of pens on his desk. The only personal item I could see was a small, framed photo, hanging on the cubicle wall. In the image, a motley assortment of children stood in a line in a wooded area. Behind them stood a man dressed in a thick flannel shirt and bright red suspenders, a cottony brown beard hanging beneath his smiling mouth.

"Camp Olympus," Hanson said when he saw me looking. "Used to be a program for problem youth. Send them up into the mountains for a few weeks, learn the merits of manual labor and nature, and yadda yadda."

"Did it work?" I asked, noticing the dark-haired boy down in front, obviously Hanson as a child.

"Well I'm a cop now, so, could have turned out worse. Place shut down about twenty years ago, when they put in the Juvenile Hall over in Gainsburg. Now, about the woman?"

I stared at the photo a moment longer, an odd sense of familiarity itching the back of my mind. I tore my eyes away and sat up straighter. "Yes. I was wondering if you had identified her."

He shook his head, "We put the word out to the neighboring communities, but thus far, nobody has been reported missing. Our guess is she lived in one of the communes up in the hills. Folk like that don't tend to register themselves with the government, if they can help it."

"Do you know where any of them are?" I asked and, when he gave me an odd look, I quickly added, "We were hoping to find her people. Let them know what happened to her."

He clicked his tongue. "Sure, that would be the right Christian thing to do, but that's our job. Mrs. Riley, may I ask a personal question?"

"Sure."

"Why the heck do you care? Forgive me if I'm missing something, but from the sounds of it, that lady was ten kinds of crazy in a bag fit for five. You aren't angling to get revenge or something foolhardy like that, are you?"

"No," I said immediately, thinking up a quick lie. "I'm a mother and, based off what she was babbling, I'm guessing she was, too. I'm worried about her kids. Can't stop thinking about them, if I'm being honest."

"Well, I'm sad to say I don't think your kindness would be returned if the shoe was on the other foot," he said apologetically. "Like I said, the lady was certifiable. Anything she said can be put down to that. Besides, you saw the wounds on her body. Wherever she came from before showing up on that road was not exactly a jolly place. I'd hate for anything like that to happen to you." He leaned across the desk, his expression softening, emerald-green eyes shining in a way I was sure made all the women in town swoon. "Are you sure we've never met before you folks moved here? I can't shake the feeling that we know each other from somewhere."

"I'm sorry, no I – " I paused, studying his face. There was something there, another twinge of familiarity. "Maybe? Though I can't imagine where we would have met."

"Well, I never forget a beautiful face," he said, letting his eyes wander down my neck.

To my own surprise I felt a twinge of arousal in my stomach, fluttering up into a full blush. I leaned back and took a breath. "Sorry," I said, trying to look anywhere but at his eyes. What the hell was happening here? "I think you've got me confused with someone else."

His eyes lingered a moment longer, and the feeling of arousal intensified, a heat pulsing in my core. He shrugged and leaned back. "Maybe so," he said, the feeling leaving as suddenly as it had arrived. "While I've got you here, there is another matter we were hoping to speak with you about, privately. It concerns your husband."

"What about Jacob?"

"I'm not saying he's done anything wrong," Hanson continued. "But Quinn's kid got messed up pretty bad in a fist fight a few weeks back, kid named Danny. Jacob already settled the matter with Quinn, so there won't be any charges. But let's face it, Jacob's a big guy and he didn't get those scars on his hands playing bridge. People around town are worried he's going to hurt someone. They say he's antisocial. Now in my mind a man has every right to be as big a prick as he desires, but most often violent men end up taking it out on their family. We just want to make sure you and Wendy feel safe."

Acid boiled in my throat. "Jacob would never hurt us," I said firmly. "He's done nothing but try to protect us. My husband's past is the past."

"But he does have a past?" Hanson asked, a small smirk twitching at the corners of his lips.

"Don't we all?" I responded, careful to keep my tone neutral.

Hanson held up his hands. "Hey, no argument here. If you feel safe, then I feel better. If that ever changes, please know you can come to us." His voice was all honey, but there was something wrong about his eyes. A steeliness. An intent. I nearly reached out to his mind right then, but didn't even try for fear of enduring another psychic storm.

"I appreciate it. You can be sure that Jacob is not the threat. Someone is messing with us, Deputy. I intend to find out who."

"We all want the same thing. Believe me, we haven't forgotten about you up there. We're doing everything we can to make sure we catch these guys the next time they come snooping around, I can promise you that." He glanced at his watch and winced. "Now, if you don't mind, I need to be somewhere." He stood and offered his hand, "It's been a pleasure, Mrs. Riley."

I rose with him and shook his hand. "I take it I'm not going to get the location of any mountain communes, am I?"

He laughed. "You're like a dog with a bone – we have that in common. I'm sorry, Mrs. Riley, I can't just let you go running off up there and get yourself killed by some yokel with a rifle. As you should know by now, folks in those hills can be dangerous. Just trust us," he said, giving my hand a reassuring squeeze before releasing it. "We're on the case. We'll find whoever it is that's been harassing you, I promise."

I smiled back and thanked him, although I felt anything but reassured. Something was wrong, I had missed something. I wracked my brain as he led me and Wendy out of his cubicle and back to the front of the office.

"It's good to see you around town for a change," he said. "Don't be a stranger."

I smiled, told him I wouldn't, then watched him head back to his desk.

"Don't like," Wendy thought. I looked down at her, frowning. Her eyes were locked on Hanson as he wound his way back through the building, her gaze laser-focused. *"Bad. Don't Like. Fake eyes."*

Fake eyes? I looked up and spotted Hanson standing near the back of the room, talking to another deputy. I thought about the photo on his wall, and the contact case I had seen on his desk, and it all clicked together. The bearded man had been Mr. Friend, younger, less grey, but it was him. And that strange attraction I'd felt had been odd... could Hanson be one of them? He had been so kind the night the mad woman had attacked us. He had been in our house, even. I had to be sure.

"Oh fuck it," I whispered. Then, I reached out and touched his mind.

A sudden scream filled my head, like the tearing of sheet metal, so loud I gasped. Hanson whipped around, one hand pressed to his own head, eyes scanning the room until they settled on me. The sound intensified, and I felt as if a stone had lodged itself in my throat. I couldn't breathe, could barely see, the sharp tang of bile scorching the back of my throat.

A thought boomed in my head. *"You figured it out, huh?"*

Hanson narrowed his eyes and started towards me, his country boy good looks hardened into something strange and unnatural looking, like a leering plastic mask.

I tried to turn, but my legs remained locked, his fingers dancing through my mind, pulling strings as if I were a puppet. To my horror I felt my body begin to move on its own, to walk towards him.

He was close, maneuvering around the fire pole. I screamed internally, thrashed and kicked, but to no avail. He was closer, ten feet, hand outstretched towards me.

That was when Wendy screamed, a discordant howl that I heard not only with my ears but inside my mind. By the looks of it, so did Hanson. He stopped cold, his smile vanishing into a snarl of pain. He dropped to his knees, hands clasped over his ears. All over the station, people were turning to look as Hanson flopped on the ground.

"Get away from me!" he shouted as the front desk girl knelt to help him as he struggled to his knees.

I found my legs were my own again. I spun, shoved the front door open and spilled out into the street. I needed to get to Astrological, needed to get Jacob and get the hell out of this town. I started to run, but the stroller wheels kept catching on cracks in the sidewalk. I was only half a block away when I heard Hanson crash out onto the street behind me. I risked a glance back to see him stumbling like a drunk after me, his knees shaking but face warped with hideous rage.

The stroller hit another crack, began to tip, and I let it. I scooped Wendy from her seat and ran full out, clutching her tight to my chest.

"Stop her!" Hanson was bellowing, his shambling gait moving up into a jog, and then a sprint.

Across the street, two young men were emerging from the hardware store and upon hearing Hanson's shouts, turned their eyes to me. All over the street, people were looking at us now, a few already moving towards me, their venomous thoughts bombarding me.

"Bet she stole that baby."

"She's one of those freaks."

"What the hell did she do to Hanson?"

I needed to get off the street, hide. I sprinted to the end of the block and then turned, heading down a side street into the abandoned western side of town. Crumbling houses, weed-choked lawns, and cracked streets stretched out all around me. I turned at random, running at a suicidal pace, my breath scorching the back of my throat.

I risked another glance behind me to see Hanson and the two men from the hardware store were still in pursuit. The two strangers were leading the way, their eyes glazed with an odd, dreamy, contentment. Hanson was in their heads. I could almost see it, like psychic threads connecting him to them.

Terror drove out all rational thought. I ran blind, legs aching, lungs burning, my heartbeat pulsing in my own head like a drum. I plunged past rotting homes and a sagging church, its pointed steeple crumbling in on itself. I didn't see the couple standing around the corner until I crashed into them. It was a man and a woman, standing in the middle of my path, arms wide to receive me as I tried to stop, couldn't, and stumbled forward into them. Before I knew what was happening, strong hands ripped Wendy from my grip, and another pair shoved me hard. I spun, then crashed to the ground.

The couple looked down at me, both smiling pleasantly. The man was tall, with close-cropped black hair and wearing a faded yellow smiley-face tee. The woman was dressed in a pale blue waitress uniform, the sort worn at Ernie's Diner. Her brown hair was pulled up into a bun and her nametag glinted in the sunlight as she pulled Wendy to her breast. To my shock, Wendy wasn't screaming anymore. In fact, she was asleep and looking peaceful as the woman held two fingers to the baby's head. I looked from Wendy to the woman to the man.

Their eyes were blue. Pale, sparkling blue. Just like mine.

3

At the sight of the woman clutching Wendy, something inside me came alive: a predatory, vicious beast. I sprang to my feet and threw myself at her, fingers curled into killing claws, before rough arms seized me from behind. Hanson and his puppets had caught up, the two glassy-eyed kids from the hardware store hugging me from the sides, their arms encircling me like a cage.

Screaming, I managed to slam my head into one my captor's noses, hard enough to crunch bone, but the man didn't seem to notice. He just kept holding me as blood poured down his face, his expression distant and wistful.

"Let me go you bastards!" I screamed, and inside me something else screamed back. Some massive force rushing up from a dark pit at the bottom of my mind. It was gargantuan, a volcano exploding from placid earth to scorch the skies. I desperately reached for it and felt a surge of power coursing through my body, every cell inside me coming alive after decades of sleep.

Then Hanson punched me in the face.

I sagged in his puppets' arms, suddenly very dizzy, the sense of enormous power gone, leaving me with nothing but the taste of blood and a ringing in my ears.

"Hot damn," Hanson said, smiling ear to ear. "Astra said you had some fight in you, but no need to go nuclear. Shit, Lacie, you are a little tiger momma, ain't ya?"

I tried to respond, maybe to scream a choice insult or two, but all the words in my head had become clunky, jagged things too unwieldy to get from my brain to my mouth.

"Oh, I like you. You're just what the family needs, someone with fire to liven up these sad bastards," he said, hooking a thumb toward the blue-eyed couple. "Lacie, meet Indrid and Mildred. I suppose you could call them your cousins, but around here, ain't we all? Good thing they heard me call or we'd have had to chase your ass all day."

"We need to get off the street," Mildred said. "I can't keep the little one down forever. She's fighting me."

Hanson nodded and scanned both sides of the empty street, confirming that we were alone. "Take them in there," he said, nodding to a ramshackle cottage with a sagging porch and bright yellow pair of testicles spray painted on the front window.

"We should take them to Grandfather," the man, Indrid, said, leveling a cold glare at Hanson. "He said – "

"I know what he said," Hanson snapped, staring right back at the larger man who, to my surprise, shrank back a step. "But I have some curiosities I need to settle before Grandpa gets his."

Mildred shook her head. "But he said to –"

Whatever complaint she was about to make died when Hanson turned his gaze on her. She swallowed, face pale as she silently turned and started towards the house. The next thing I knew, I was being dragged, the yawning dark mouth of the house looming larger and larger until it swallowed us all.

Hanson had his puppets hold me down on the floor while he handcuffed me to the old iron grill bolted to the front of a blackened fireplace. At his instruction, they searched me and handed my phone to Hanson, who promptly smashed it under his boot. Then, he dismissed them.

"You two boys get going, or your daddy will have your hide. And remember, this didn't happen." They nodded, still placid as cows as they turned and marched back out the front door. I watched them go until they vanished through the doorway, leaving me alone with the three blue-eyed lunatics.

"Did anyone on the street see you chasing her?" Mildred asked.

"A few," Hanson said, his eyes trailing over me, that same disarming country boy grin on his face. "Don't worry. Bruce already pinged me and he's scrubbing memories as we speak."

He crouched down in front of me, studying my face. "You know, you look just like your mama. Not the hair, that's from your daddy, but that face. Man oh man, when I was a kid, I had such a crush on your Ma. I think I must have kept Kleenex in business just thinking of her." He reached out and cupped the side of my face despite my efforts to flinch away. "You know, once upon a time, we were supposed to end up together. Truth be told, I always thought your daddy drowned you in a river somewhere. Didn't think he had it in him to put a lock on your head strong enough to hide you from us, but that little wimp surprised us all. Too bad little Wendy there shredded the lock on her way out. One thing I can't figure out though – how the hell did you end up here?"

I swallowed and tried to crane my head away from his touch. "You're insane," I managed to say. "I'm not – "

He slapped me across the mouth and I tasted blood. "Tsk tsk. No lies," he warned. "After what happened in Carver's Mill, we thought you'd go to ground. Consider our surprise when we came home to find you had beaten us back here, and your hubby was all healed up from what should have been a fatal chest wound. I am mighty curious as to how both of those things happened. So, how did you do it?"

I blinked at him, trying and failing to think through the crippling fog inside my head. "I don't know what you're talking about. My husband and I were searching for a place to settle down, we came across a house here that we could afford and – "

He slapped me again, this time harder, bouncing my head painfully off the iron grate at my back. "I said no lies. You know what, let's make this simple." He reached down to his belt and slid his service revolver from its holster. Then, he pressed the barrel against my right kneecap. "You tell me what I want to know, and you get to walk out that door with us. Lie to me, I'll deliver you to Grandpa in a wheelchair."

117

"Brandon," Mildred hissed, a veneer of nervous sweat on her face. "That isn't what he wants. You're going to get us into trouble."

"Oh, no! You hear that, Lacie? We're going to get in trouble," Hanson chortled.

Indrid stepped forward, hands curled into fists. "We have our orders."

"And good orders they are, soldier boy," Hanson said, still facing me. "But you take one more step closer and I'll make you skull fuck Mildred until her head comes off. Like I said, Grandpa will get his. Now," he slid back the hammer of his gun and met my eyes, "let's see if we can jog your memory."

I looked up at Indrid and Mildred, desperate for any help I could get, but they both shrank back, eyes averted.

"Why did you come to Victor's Point?" Hanson asked.

"I swear I'm telling you the truth," I whispered urgently. "I don't know a place called Carver's Mill. I've never met you before and I don't know what you're talking about!"

Hanson grunted, eyes not leaving mine. "And The Light? How did you get it to save you? How do you control it?"

"I don't," I said. "The first time I saw it was here, in Victor's Point. The night the woman attacked us and we – "

A sudden gunshot stopped me cold. I braced for the pain, but it never came. He'd aimed an inch to the left of my knee, leaving a smoking hole in the hardwood. "Answer me," he hissed through his teeth. "Are you planning to come after us? Is *it*? What do you know about it?"

"I don't know anything!" I shouted. "I don't know what the fuck is going on, or why you people are harassing us. We just bought a house, that's all!"

He growled, then rose and marched towards Mildred, grabbed Wendy by the shirt and ripped her from Mildred's arms. Then, he pressed the gun against my daughter's sleeping head.

"How about this, then. You keep clinging to your lies while I redecorate around here."

"You wouldn't," Mildred said.

"Oh yes I would," Hanson shot back. "Why worry about one little golden egg, when we got the goose right there." He turned back to me, speaking in a low, mocking tone. "Think real hard now Lacie. You're going to tell me everything you know about The Light, real slow, so even Indrid can understand."

I pulled against my restraints, a single note of pure panic ringing through my head. Frantically I scanned the room, looking for a weapon or a way out, but finding only dust and spots of black mold growing up the walls. We were going to die here; Wendy and I left to rot in some forgotten hovel. The realization crushed me into the floor.

"This is ridiculous," Indrid interjected. "Brandon, stop dicking around and just rip what you want out of her head."

"The Light touched her, idiot. I ain't going in there. I won't have to, because she's going to tell us the truth now, aren't you, Lacie?" Anger, contempt, arousal, all radiated off him in brutal pulses of emotion. And something else, something I could only just pick up in the sweat on his upper lip and the soft tremor in his hand. Was that fear?

"All right, I'll tell you! Just put her down. Please!" I begged. "The first time I saw The Light was the day Astra visited me – the day she drugged me. I had a dream. It told me not to be afraid then…," I paused, seizing on that thought. The Light told me to not be afraid. I still didn't trust it, but it had never hurt us. What if it had been protecting us? And what if I could call it, the same as I had Astra?

"And then?" Hanson said, gesturing with his gun, "I'm getting real fucking tired of pregnant pauses here."

"I'm sorry," I said, hastily slapping together a suicidal plan. "It's just confusing. The Light, it comes and it talks to me in my dreams. It tells me to seek something, but it won't say what or why. Truth be told, I'm so goddamn scared all the time, and nobody will tell us what the hell is going on. Please, I'm not lying to you, I swear. Please, don't hurt Wendy." As I spoke, I summoned up all the pain and fear inside me, dove into it, wallowed in it. I gathered all of that up, and I sent it crashing out from me in waves.

"And your husband?" Hanson pressed, leaning forward, eyes alight, drinking in my misery like liquor. "Has it spoken to him?"

"No!" I cried, then began to blubber, my rush of words lost in a tangle of choked sobs and half breaths, while inside I kept a small island of calm inside my turbulent mind. I focused on The Light and imagined a pulsing beacon stretching from the top of my head into the sky.

Hanson didn't seem to notice what I was doing. He had a cruel little grin on his face and a growing erection in his pants.

"Hanson," Mildred whispered, her eyes widening in alarm.

"Shut it," he hissed.

"Jacob's just trying to keep us safe!" I shouted, pushing out more fear, more sorrow, anything to keep his attention fixed on me and me alone.

Hanson laughed and gestured to the ruins around us. "Well, he's done a real bang-up job of that. Don't worry, I'll chew him out for you just as soon as we're done here."

"Hanson, she's up to something," Mildred continued.

I kept my eyes locked on Hanson, one half of my mind bombarding him with terror, the other half still reaching, silently screaming for The Light. Hanson spun, pointed the gun at Mildred and snarled, "Will you just shut the fuck up for once? I'm trying to enjoy this!"

"Hanson, *look* at her!" Indrid barked.

That finally seemed to break the spell. Hanson turned, peered back at me, then recoiled. "What the hell are you doing!?" he screamed.

I squeezed my eyes shut and pushed as hard as I could, summoning up that monstrous force inside me and sending it burning across the heavens as a single, desperate, plea: *Help! Please, help us!*

Suddenly, everything seemed to move very slowly. Hanson shoved Wendy back into Mildred's arms as he stepped towards me, smile morphing into a terrified scowl. Indrid looked out the window, eyes widening in shock. Mildred screamed.

Light exploded through the broken windowpanes of the house. Not waves this time, but spears of it punching through the holes in the crumbling walls. The ground shook, and the entire house pitched like a boat on rough water. I pressed my eyes into my shoulder and screamed as stinging heat blasted across the skin of my exposed arms and face. I couldn't see and could barely hear over the roar of the thing. Somewhere a door was slamming open and Hanson was shouting. Mildred's scream turned into a shriek and then a broken, almost mournful whine. And then, all was quiet.

I lifted my head. The room was the same as it had been, save for still smoking scorch marks on the edges of the windowpanes. The front door was open, Hanson's warped, half-melted pistol left lying in the doorway. A pile of broken stone lay where Mildred had been standing moments ago. No sign of any of them. And, I realized, mouth going dry, no sign of Wendy.

Panicked, I pulled against the handcuffs and was rewarded with a snap of the chain. The cuffs had somehow become rusted and brittle, crumbling off my wrists with little more than a tug. I crawled to the pile of stones, desperately peering into every dark corner for sign of my little girl.

I began to push through the pile of salt white rock, until I felt my hands brush a cold, hard face. It was Mildred's. I saw stone fingers, a bit of a knee and her nametag frozen to a chunk of her torso. No blood, no burns, just the final moment of pained shock on her petrified face.

"Wendy!" I called, a pit opening inside me. I called her name louder, then screamed it; the only response was the dry hiss of wind through the halls of that broken house.

I sat on the curb outside the house, wishing I was dead. My skin hurt, the flesh of my arms and face was bright red and stung like a bad sunburn every time the wind blew. My mind, meanwhile, orbited Wendy. Was she dead? I didn't find any trace of a stone infant in the ruins of Mildred. And what about Indrid and Hanson? There had been no trace of them. They must have run. If Wendy wasn't dead, it could only mean one thing: they had taken her. Why hadn't The Light just fried them, too? Why had it let them get away with my baby? Stomach churning, I doubled over, half sobbing, half gagging as I vomited my breakfast onto the street.

I needed to get up, get moving, try to save my child, but I stayed glued where I sat, staring sightlessly forward, a sinking hopelessness swallowing me. What could we do? We couldn't go to the cops. Anyone in town could be either one of them or one of their puppets, like the two goons Hanson had used to run me down. I felt the sudden urge to cry, to curl up and wait for the elements to strip the flesh from my bones until I became just another bleached wreckage among the ruined houses around me.

Suddenly, I thought of Jacob, a sudden intuition bubbling up from the dark corners of my mind. Hanson was still out there, and I got the feeling he wouldn't be bothering with his 'good guy deputy' routine now that I knew what he was. He would go after Jacob, try to take him out. I needed to get back to town, needed to warn him.

That's when I felt it, a sudden shrill note of alarm and pain pulsing across my psychic radio, coming from Main Street. It was Jacob, something was happening to Jacob.

I rose to my feet, took two shaky, stumbling steps, then broke into a run.

4 – Jacob

Carl about pissed himself with joy when I told him he could call his professor friend in.

"You won't regret this," he said, already sweeping aside candy wrappers and empty energy drink cans to reach his keyboard. "He's on sabbatical right now, but I have his private email. He'll make time for this, I know it."

We were standing in the Astrological break room which had been slowly transformed into a den of strangeness. A poster hung on the wall of a UFO sucking a hapless victim into the sky above the caption 'The TRUTH is HERE'. Every other chair in the room was filled with stacks of books and reams of print outs, several of which advertised themselves as the definitive record of 'The Phenomenon' or 'The Visitors'.

"Sure hope he does. He's not going to write about us, right?" Last thing we needed was to end up the starring case study in one of these books. If the rest of the UFO community was anything like Carl, I'd be chasing them off my porch until I'd gone gray and saggy.

Carl didn't take his eyes from the screen as he opened up his email and began composing a quick message. "He might. He is working on his first book about the topic now, so he might want to include you guys. If you're worried about exposure, he can put you down under fake names. You'd be shocked how many contactees request that."

"I really wouldn't," I said dryly, already trying not to regret giving Carl the go ahead. The word contactees irked me. Was that what we really were now? A few months ago we were newlyweds, first-time parents quietly working hard to come out from the shadow of our past. Now we were an oddity, our entire lives boiled down to a single experience that we didn't ask for. I watched Carl finish out his email and hit send.

"This guy is legit, right?" I asked.

Carl nodded, swiveling his chair to face me. "As legit as you can get. Dr. Lorenz came up through John Hopkins as a clinical psychiatrist. He didn't even get into the Phenomenon until about ten years ago when he had a patient come forward claiming she'd been abducted. Way he puts it, he spent six months trying his hardest to find a conventional answer for what she was experiencing, and the Phenomenon fucked with him every step of the way."

"How so?"

"Phone calls from unlisted numbers, black cars following him, the usual *Men in Black* kind of stuff. Eventually, he said that he just ran out of conventional explanations and that kicked him hard down the rabbit hole. He's been trying to legitimize the field ever since."

"And how do you know he isn't just delusional?"

Carl shrugged. "I don't. Just like I don't know if you are, and you don't know if I am. But you saw The Light, man. Sort of like a walnut calling a cashew a nut, right?"

A chime on the computer drew Carl's attention back to the screen, where a new email had just arrived. He opened it, then smiled.

"He's coming."

"That was fast."

"Are you kidding? He's been researching this stuff for years, talked to hundreds of contactees, but always after the fact, never while the Phenomenon was going on. He wouldn't pass this up. This is like Christmas, Halloween and all those saints' days rolled into one."

My expression darkened. "Glad you're having so much fun."

Carl glanced up and frowned. "Hey, I didn't mean it like that. This is just exciting stuff, world-changing stuff. If we can prove the visitations are real, definitively, scientifically, it will throw the door on a whole new age of discovery wide open. We can change the paradigm for the entire species."

"Yeah, well just remember that while you're trying to change the para-whatever, it's my family who's suffering. I'm not signing up to turn us into lab rats. I want what is happening to stop."

"Well," Carl said with a heavy sigh, "I can't promise that. What I can say is that we will never figure out how to stop it until we understand it. I know this is frustrating but please, trust us."

Before I could answer, Tracy called from the front, "Jacob, got one for you. Get your ass up here."

I left Carl to his work and walked back out to the main room to see someone was already sitting in my chair, a heavily muscled kid wearing a Taco Cat tank top and basketball shorts; it was Danny Quinn. Tracy stood beside him, hands on her hips, face puckered as if she'd tasted something sour.

"Jacob," she said, waving me over. "Mr. Quinn here requested you by name."

I approached cautiously, staring at Danny. He still had the lingering remains of a bruise around his right eye from our last encounter. Although, unlike then, his gaze was focused. He extended a fist to greet me. "Hey man," he said, "Nice to meet you. It's Jacob, right?"

I returned his fist bump, trying to keep the surprise off my face. "You don't remember meeting me before?"

Danny smiled. "No, but my Dad told me," he said sheepishly. "I was totally shit-faced that night. Heard I took a swing at you?"

"Yeah," I said sternly, "You also said some things about my family that I didn't appreciate."

He winced. "Sorry, dude. Like my Dad says, I got shit for brains. I'll make sure not to go picking any fights with you again, though. Face feels like someone took a shovel to it. No hard feelings?"

I stared down at him, wary, thinking of the shadowy figure I had seen him talking to just before our altercation, and the strange look that had come over his eyes when he threatened to kill Hannah and Wendy. The old Jacob would have told him to go fuck himself, but he was a customer, and this was my job, so I swallowed my unease and pasted on a smile that I hoped wasn't menacing.

"Sure, no hard feelings. What kind of work were you looking to get done?"

He clapped an enthusiastic hand to his bicep. "Right here. I want to get one of those cool ripped skin tattoos, you know, the ones that make it look like you got a hole ripped in ya? Only inside I want it to have like, sick-ass robot parts. Like the Terminator."

"How big were you thinking?"

"Whole upper arm, my dude."

I let out a low whistle. "You sure?" I asked, doing a quick scan of his body, noting the distinct lack of any other tattoos. "That's going to run you a couple grand. Three or four sessions, each one four hours or so."

Danny shrugged, "I got the cash, and I got the time. Fuck my shit up."

I got to work selecting pots of ink and prepping his arm, all the while trying to figure out if he was acting normally or not. The Danny I had first seen in Ernie's diner had seemed like a volatile little shit. The second time, he had acted like a total loon. So where was this cool bro attitude coming from? Was this how Danny was normally? As I didn't really know him, it was impossible to say.

I set to work on him, using a couple photos from his phone as reference and free-handing it from there. It took a minute, but soon enough I lost myself again to the buzzing of the needle. We talked; or rather, Danny did, with the occasional grunt from me to help him along. He prattled about his exercise routine, the supplements he used, and the body-building competition in Nashville he wanted to attend. Soon enough, his words drifted together and became part of the ambient noise. Hours slipped by without my notice until I realized I had a growing knot in the base of my back and a mounting tension headache.

I pulled the needle gun back. "Let's take five," I said. "I need to shake a few kinks out."

Danny stared into the nearby wall mirror, flexing his bicep and tilting it from side to side. "Yeah, no problem," he said, distracted. "This is going to look fucking sick when it's done."

I stood, stretching. I was thinking I'd run down the street and pick up something highly caffeinated from the corner store, when movement on the street outside caught my eye. To my surprise, I saw a familiar face standing on the sidewalk outside, facing the shop window.

It was Deputy Hanson. He looked like he had just run a 10k through hell, his uniform rumpled and singed black in a few spots. His hair was plastered to his scalp with sweat, his face bright red with what looked like a nasty sunburn. At first I thought he was staring at me, a look of intense focus on his face.

Danny let out a gasp, then a moan. I turned to see his entire body going rigid, back arching up out of the chair with such force I thought he would snap his spine. His eyes rolled back to white, his mouth hung open in a wheezing, silent scream.

I took a step back and looked back to the window just in time to see Hanson look right back at me. He smiled, winked at me, then turned and continued up the sidewalk, moving out of sight. Meanwhile Danny began to twist and shake, his entire body one undulating muscle.

"Oh shit," Tracy shouted, noticing the commotion. "He's having a seizure! Hold him down, hold him down!"

Reality snapped back into place. I grabbed Danny by the shoulders and tried to force him back down into the chair, but it was like pressing up against stone. Tracy took hold of his head and Danny suddenly relaxed, slumping down into the chair. He closed his eyes and, when he opened them again, he had a soft, dreamy expression on his face.

"Danny?" Tracy said, her hands still holding his head. "You all right, buddy? If you swallow your tongue in my shop, I'll whip you blue."

"No worries," he whispered in a harsh rasp. "I'm good, I'm good. Just a muscle spasm."

"That was one serious fucking muscle spasm," Tracy said. "You need me to call your father?"

Meanwhile I found myself backing away. There was something wrong here. The look in Danny's eyes was the same as the night I'd encountered him behind the shop.

Tracy slowly released Danny's head and helped him to his feet, where he swayed like a drunkard.

"There you go," she said. "Just walk a little, loosen everything up."

"Walk a little," Danny parroted, a childlike smile on his face. "Loosen it up, gotcha. Get *real* loose. Loosey goosey," then he giggled. "I'm sorry, I'm going to make a big mess now."

"Uh huh," Tracy said, eyebrow arched. "If you feel like you're going to shit yourself, the bathroom is in the back, just don't – "

It happened fast. One moment Danny was standing there, looking like he'd just stayed through last call at the Mad Hatter's Tea Party, then suddenly my tattoo gun was in his hand. Tracy screamed as he plunged the buzzing needle into the flesh above her right breast. She fell away, tried to shield herself, but tripped. Then he was on her, stabbing the needle at her face.

I grabbed him by the back of the shirt, hoisted him, and threw him clear across the shop floor. Danny thrashed when he hit the ground, howling like a wild animal, the blood-matted tattoo gun now shattered on the floor beside him. He sprang to his feet and then he was on me, raining haymaker blows across my shoulders, chest, and jaw. The flare of pain and stench of blood brought the adrenaline. My vision sharpened, fists tightened, and then I was swinging back.

There was nothing pretty about the fight, just two big guys hammering each other over and over in the face until I managed to grab hold of his wrist. I moved around him, wrenched his arm behind his back.

"Calm down!" I tried to say, but he didn't give me the chance. With his free hand he swung wildly behind him, catching me across the temple with a lucky backhand. I released him and stumbled away, vision momentarily blurred. He came at me again, and the next thing I knew I was airborne.

He'd picked me up and tossed me, sending me crashing through the break room door, revealing a startled Carl, just now beginning to pull his headphones off. In a flash Danny was on me again, straddling my chest, pinning my arms to my sides. Then he was beating me to death, his fists connecting with my face one after the other, each time coming back with more blood on his knuckles.

Carl leapt atop Danny, wrapping his scarecrow limbs around the larger man's neck. Danny stood, carrying Carl on his back, wildly spinning from side to side in an attempt to dislodge his passenger. Finally, he managed to get his hand around Carl's arm and, with a harsh pop, wrenched it free. Carl collapsed to the ground, screaming, clutching a clearly broken arm to his chest. Danny was right on him, kicking viciously at Carl's ribs.

I scrambled to my feet and tackled him, the two of us slamming hard enough into one of the old barber chairs to snap two of the bolts holding to the floor. I punched, kicked, grabbed fistfuls of meat and twisted, but no matter what I did, Danny didn't seem to notice, let alone slow down. He flipped me over again. Desperate, I managed to palm his face and shove my thumb into his right eye. I felt something pop as hot blood ran down my hand.

Inconceivably, Danny just kept smiling down at me while wrapping his hands around my throat. "Sorry my dude," he said. "But you're in the way. No hard feelings?"

His thumb pressed my windpipe shut. I flailed against him with my free hand and felt his ribs snap beneath my knuckles, but I might as well have been beating on a corpse for all he reacted. Darkness edged in on my vision. I thought of Hannah and Wendy, tried to hold them in my mind as long as I could.

Then, air. Danny's grip released and I sucked in a lungful, which came back out in a series of hacking coughs. Above me, Danny was struggling against Carl and Tracy, each of them wrapped around one of his arms and trying to wrench him off me. I rose to a sitting position, grabbed him by his shirt and, together, we managed to force him onto his back. Then I was on top of him, raining blows across his face and throat, a roaring scream ripping through me. No serenity, no peace, just blood, bone, and the collision of flesh upon flesh singing the oldest song in the human language.

Eventually I realized he wasn't moving anymore. I released him and stumbled to my feet. I became aware of the room around me again. Tracy was screaming, holding a wad of gauze pads to the hole in her chest. Carl was in the break room, fumbling to pull his phone out with one arm hanging limp and useless at his side.

And Danny was very still.

5 – Hannah

Sherriff Quinn beat me to Astrological by seconds. I whipped around the corner onto Main just as his brown cruiser came to a screeching halt outside the shop. The Sheriff leapt out, his eyes wild and furious, one hand already on the butt of his pistol. For a moment I thought he was here for me, another puppet sent by Hanson to finish me off, but the sheriff's eyes slid right over me as if I weren't there. Instead, he ran into the shop.

Even from across the street, I could hear the cry that escaped the sheriff's mouth as soon as he got inside. Something had happened here while I was gone, I realized, a sudden dread turning my blood cold. What if Hanson had sent someone for Jacob?

No! He had already taken Wendy – he couldn't take Jacob, too. Unable to stop myself, I ran across the street and looked in the shop window. Jacob was leaning against the far wall, his face swollen and bleeding in a few spots where the skin had split. His hands, which dangled in front of him and were coated in blood. On the floor laid a mangled human shape that the sheriff was kneeling over, his face pale and hands shaking as he checked for a pulse.

I let out a breath I hadn't realized I was holding; Jacob was alive. Distantly I could hear more sirens approaching, and a small crowd had already begun to gather at the sight of the sheriff's car making such an abrupt entrance. I wanted to run inside, wrap my arms around Jacob and never let go, but discretion won out in the end. Hanson could easily be in one of those approaching cars, and God knew how many more like him were living among the people of Victor's Point. I slipped into the narrow alley between Astrological and the neighboring building and found my way to the rear parking lot.

I found our truck and was relieved to find it unlocked. Once inside, I curled up in the passenger's seat, knees pressed to my chest, eyes on Astrological's backdoor. I tried not to think for fear of a panic attack. About Hanson, about the pain radiating from the spot where he'd hit me. About Wendy, or Jacob, or the enormous mess we had found ourselves in.

I failed, of course.

I watched as the town's two ambulances pulled into the lot and four EMTs jumped out. Twenty minutes later, a pair of them emerged carrying someone on a stretcher. Not Jacob. Whoever it was looked like they'd been mauled by a bear, their face a swollen ruin of broken bones, a wad of bloody gauze pressed to their right eye socket. The first ambulance peeled out, likely heading thirty miles north to the regional field hospital in Gainsburg. The second followed shortly after, with a pissed off looking Tracy and a kid I didn't recognize, likely Carl, inside.

Finally, the back door swung open again and Jacob stepped out. He looked exhausted, and his shirt was smeared with blood, but he wasn't handcuffed. He walked stiff-legged to the truck, his eyes fixed on his phone, a look of concern on his face. As he reached to open the driver's side door he finally looked up, saw me, and jumped, startled. I watched his eyes travel over my face, watched his nostrils flare as his eyes found the bruise on my cheek and the split in my lower lip where Hanson had punched me.

He opened the door and got inside, not saying a word as he started the engine and then sat, eyes forward, hands resting on the wheel.

"What happened?" he asked.

"You first," I whispered.

He wet his cracked lips with the edge of his tongue. "The sheriff's kid, Danny. He came into the shop to get some work done. Everything was fine, then all of a sudden he went –fuck, I don't even know. Feral. Stabbed Tracy with a needle gun and tried his best to kill me."

"Oh, god," I said, thinking back to Hanson's offer to 'chew Jacob out.'

"It was the damndest thing," he continued. "Like he wasn't really there anymore. I don't even think he was feeling pain." He glanced at me again before his eyes slid to the back seat, where Wendy's car seat sat empty. "Where is Wendy?"

I opened my mouth, but no sound came out. My vision flattened, my heart started to race, and I felt cold sweat bead on my forehead. "I – she was –" I stuttered and started to hyperventilate. How could I tell him that I had taken our little girl into the world and I'd lost her, let her be taken by psychopathic telepaths to who knows where. I felt sick, was sure I was about to vomit again, when Jacob's calloused hands enveloped mine.

"Show me," he said.

"But I …"

"Show me," he repeated, voice soft but firm. "Like you did before."

I focused on the feeling of his hand against mine, let it be the anchor that kept me grounded. I took a deep, shaky breath and opened our minds once again.

Twenty minutes later, Jacob guided the truck onto Strawberry Lane, his face stony. He hadn't said a word, but inside, I knew, a storm was raging. I could feel it pulsing off him – fury, fear, and pain, all mixing into a toxic slurry.

Neither of us needed to say it to understand what had happened. After The Light showed up, Hanson tried to get rid of Jacob. Maybe to destabilize me, maybe as vengeance for Mildred, or maybe just because I'd pissed him off.

"I think Hanson was working on Danny for a while," Jacob finally said. "I think that's who I saw talking to him out behind the shop."

"Maybe that was why he didn't feel any pain?" I suggested. I could see it. The puppets Hanson had taken control over when chasing me had seemed to be in an almost dreamlike state. However, Danny had been conscious and alert. Was it some sort of psychic conditioning, like the way a sleeper agent could be triggered in a spy movie? It wasn't just the blue-eyed people we needed to watch out for, then. Chances were the whole town could have been similarly conditioned.

"There's more," he said cautiously. "That photo you saw in Hanson's cubicle, all those kids lined up?"

I looked up. In all the chaos I had nearly forgotten the photo. "Yeah? What about it?"

"The adult in the picture? I know him. That's Gaylord Friend, the guy who helped me rebuild our porch railing."

"I thought the same thing. Are you sure?"

"He's older now, but it's definitely him."

I thought back to the fleeting images of Mr. Friend I had seen inside Jacob's mind. His eyes weren't blue, but then what if he wasn't one of the telepaths? What if he was their caretaker or something else entirely? I sank lower into my seat. "What are we going to do?" I whispered.

"They have our girl," he said.

"They also have potentially the whole town on their side. And we still don't even really know what they are. We don't know what I am! What can we do? How could we possibly…"

"Hannah," he said, looking me in the eye. "They have our girl." There was something familiar in his voice, a hard edge I hadn't heard in over a year – not since leaving Echo City. His quiet words promised violence, broken teeth, and torn flesh.

My first impulse was to calm him, talk him down, and force him to contemplate a non-violent option as I had done a hundred times before. Only this time, I felt the rage, too. Beneath the fear, beneath the loss and the pain, a hot coal of anger burned. I reached out, took his hand, and gave it a squeeze. I set my eyes forward, jaw locked.

Somewhere out there, something had our little girl.

And that meant *war*.

9

INTERLUDE

Astra

Brandon came home in a foul mood. I felt the rage billowing off him a full ten minutes before his cruiser rumbled up the gravel road into camp. I sent Trevor away, letting him leave out the window so he didn't need to risk going out the front, where he might run into his father's boot. I watched him go, scurrying on four mismatched limbs across the short yard and into the tree line beyond, where the other children waited in the branches above.

Our cabin was the second largest in the camp and had been a dorm for the two adult counselors who would have worked here right up until the camp's closure in '73. Even so, it was little more than two closet-sized bedrooms, and a larger living area that included a kitchen and dining table. I moved from the bedroom and perched on the time-weathered edge of the table, facing the front door. Outside I heard his cruiser come to a stop and his car door slam a moment before the cabin door was thrown open.

He looked like hell. Uniform rumpled, hair plastered to his scalp with sweat, and the skin on his face and hands colored a deep red as if he'd tried to bob for apples in a deep fryer.

"That bad, huh?" I asked, one eyebrow arched.

He stepped inside and slammed the door closed. "Not a fucking word," he snarled as he stalked past me towards the bedroom, throwing off his clothes as he went.

I drifted after him, pausing in the doorway and watching as he stripped out of his sweat-stained uniform and set to work grabbing another from the old, chipped dresser.

"You going to tell me what happened, or will I need to pull it from your head?"

He whirled to face me, and for a moment I was sure he was about to hit me. I presented my cheek, daring him. He had hit me before, once beating me so badly I'd pissed blood. And every time it happened, Grandfather banished him to sleeping in the general barracks with the rest of the failures. Two days, three at most, and he would come crawling back, usually with flowers.

This time, however, he stayed his hand, instead slapping a palm down on the dresser. "It was a fucking disaster. Lacie showed up at the station, asking about the breeder that got away. Don't know how, but she figured me out. Had to chase her halfway across town before we got her, but then the crazy cunt went and called that fucking thing." He gestured to the sky while visions of white light played over the surface thoughts of his mind.

My stomach fluttered, and gooseflesh sprouted over my arms. "What did it do?"

He laughed bitterly. "What do you think? It killed Mildred and took the brat with it. Indrid and I barely got out with our skin intact."

I turned, eyes wide, not sure I'd heard him correctly. "What do you mean it took her?"

"What do you think I mean? It fucking took her." He said, pulling a fresh shirt on. "Lifted the baby right out of Mildred's arms while it was killing her. Same thing it did to Grandpa's people."

"And she called it?" I asked, my mind already racing. I had already failed to lure Hannah home with kindness, and that was when she had barely begun to touch her power. Now she was able to call down The Light?

"Well, I sure as fuck didn't!" he snapped back, fumbling to fasten his belt. "Now if you're done playing twenty goddamn questions, get in the car and come with me to town. We need to grab the bitch and put a bullet in that husband of hers, before Grandfather finds out and – "

"Before I find out what, exactly?" Grandfather called from the other room.

We both tensed, staring wide-eyed at each other before pasting on practiced smiles and turning towards the main room. Grandfather was sitting in the old rocking chair in the corner that had been empty only moments ago, still dressed in rubber waders. He was wearing his human mask, a red-cheeked old man with a Santa Claus beard and jolly old laugh to match.

"Hey, Gramps," Brandon said, voice strained. "We – uh, didn't hear you come in."

"Because I didn't want you to," he said genially. "Indrid called a little bit ago, had a heck of a story to tell me. So, I thought I'd swing on by and see if I can't help you kids out of this mess you got yourselves into." He stood, grabbing a small, red cooler from the ground at his feet. "Damn shame, too, because the fish were biting like snapping turtles today. Wash your hands, both of you. Help me clean these boys up and I'll make us some lunch."

"No, that's all right," Brandon said, stumbling. "We've got this handled. You don't have to –"

"Man wasn't asking," I whispered, then went to do as we were told. Brandon joined me a moment later, glaring at me out of the corner of his eye as we soaped and lathered at the kitchen sink. We then set to work gutting and descaling the three bass Grandfather had caught. The smell of their briny innards filled the cabin.

Brandon side-eyed Grandfather as we worked, pulsing waves of panic radiating from him across psychic radio.

"Really though," he tried, halfway through gutting his fish, "we have this handled. There was no need for Indrid to go and ruin your day at the river. We can..."

"No talking," Grandfather said. "We can yammer on once we have a meal to share."

Brandon looked like he was about to be sick, and I made sure to avoid his gaze. Grandfather was leaving him out on a line to dangle, which usually meant he was in a special kind of trouble. And I, for one, had no intention of getting sucked into my brother's punishment.

Once the fish were cleaned, Grandfather found a pan and began to cook them over the old propane stove, while Brandon and I silently watched from the table. Brandon nervously bounced his knees then fiddled with a fork, trying to look anywhere but at Grandfather. Good, I thought, let him squirm. Would serve him right for all the nights he crawled into my bed and woke me up with his dick.

Finally, Grandfather turned and sat plates down in front of us, laden with vegetables and a fish fillet. He then sat and carefully laid a napkin across his lap before picking up his knife and fork.

"Well, what the heck are you two waiting for? Dig in."

Brandon and I exchanged another glance, then tentatively picked up our forks and began to eat. The fish was good – it always was when Grandfather made it, though Brandon could barely do more than push his around the plate, eyes downcast like a sullen teenager.

Mercifully, Grandfather didn't let him dangle much longer. He set down his knife and fork, his meal only half eaten. "I've always found difficult talks are best done with some food in the belly. Don't you agree?"

"Yes, Grandfather," we replied in unison.

He looked between us, expression somewhere between wistful pride and bemused indifference. "I've always loved you two the most, you know that. Which is why it's a damn shame that both of you are such massive embarrassments."

I looked up as if I'd been struck, my face growing hot. "Me? Grandpa, I wasn't even there! Brandon is the one who – "

"Silence," Grandfather pronounced. My jaw snapped shut, and my throat closed of its own accord. "Don't think I've forgotten that you couldn't even keep that piranha face of yours hidden from an untrained child. Really now, Astra, you are better than that." He stared a moment longer, long enough for my vision to start going dark at the edges. When he finally let me breathe again, I nearly fell out of the chair, gasping.

"And you," he turned his attention to Brandon. "I don't even know what to say to you. I'm just so goddamn disappointed, son. What did I tell you? If you get Lacie alone, bring her to me first. Not after you terrorize her. Not after you lose the baby. But first. And don't think I didn't notice you lurking outside her windows like a schoolboy with a hardon."

Brandon looked like he might cry, or scream, I couldn't be sure. "I was just trying to impress you!" he blubbered. "I wanted to — "

"You wanted to be the big man," Grandfather said, his tone inviting no argument. "You wanted to be the one to take down the big old light in the sky, is that it?"

Brandon looked at me, then around the room, as if to find a window he might leap out of. When no exit manifested, he hung his head and the words slipped out of him. "Yeah. You're always talking about The Light, and after what it did to you, I just...I just wanted to make you proud. Get vengeance for our family."

Grandfather raised an eyebrow. "For our family? By my count, all you did was drive Lacie further from us, and you got my dear sweet Millie killed. And what about the mess with the Quinn boy?"

Brandon looked up, startled, and Grandfather's smile widened.

"That's right, I heard about that, too. Sending a puppet in to try and murder poor Jacob," he shook his head. "That was messy. It was unprofessional. And worst of all, it was wasteful. Jacob could be an asset to this family; lord knows we could use another strong breeder. Did you even think of that?"

"No- I mean, I did but he's in the way! Lacie will never come to us as long as he's around. We should isolate her, make *us* her best option."

"Uh-huh," Grandpa said. "Murdering her hubby would be the fastest way to forge familial bonds, is that it? I know you were never blessed with an abundance of brains, but that is dense, even for you."

"What do you want me to say?" Brandon asked, sounding more like the child I remembered than he had in years.

"Well, an apology would be a good start."

Brandon sucked in a breath and met Grandfather's eyes. "I'm sorry. I should have listened to your orders. Mildred's death is on me, I own that. I was just trying to impress you, to prove I can lead this family. I know I fucked up and I can do better, please believe me."

Grandfather sat back, his eyes fixed on Brandon's. Then, to my surprise, he shrugged. "There now, was that so hard? Remember what I taught you. Always be honest with a telepath, they'll know the truth anyway. Do you feel better now? Unburdened?"

"Yes, Grandfather," Brandon said, hope creeping into his eyes. "Please, just give me another chance to make this right. I'll capture them both. And I'll figure out how to get the baby back."

"You'll have another chance," Grandfather said, ponderously scratching his beard, "but from here on I think we're going to have to do this the hard way. First, I'm going to need something from each of you." He turned to me. "Astra, I want you to gather up a group of cousins to hit the Riley house. None of the children, but anyone who can pass for human and won't be missed too much if things go south. And as for you," he nodded to Brandon, "pick up that knife you got there."

Brandon hesitated, then picked up the serrated steak knife "OK?"

"Good," Grandfather said. "Now, I'm going to need you to go ahead and shove that thing right through your hand. Left hand, mind you, I don't need you crippled."

Before Brandon could utter a single word of alarm, his body obeyed, his left hand slapping flat on the table while his other raised to stab. I felt power pulse off him as he tried to resist, freezing mid-thrust. His face reddened and a vein protruded from his neck.

"Grandfather," he said through gritted teeth. "Please! I apologized."

Grandfather smiled peacefully. His eyes turned black and glossy, then grew like oil until they encompassed half of his increasingly oblong head. He leaned forward, tenting his long, tapered fingers on the table before him.

You did apologize, Grandfather broadcast into our minds, so loudly it hurt. *Now take your punishment, we have work to do.*

Brandon held out a moment longer, then with a scream, surrendered to the compulsion. He drove the knife into his hand, through it, into the hardwood of the table beneath. He doubled over, moaning softly.

Grandfather stood to his full, seven-foot, height. He circled behind Brandon's chair and took him by the shoulders. *That's a good boy,* he said, smoothing the hair on Brandon's head with large, three fingered hands. *That's my special boy.*

10

THE WAY TO WEIRD MOUNTAIN

1 – Jacob

Carl arrived at the house early the next morning, his impenetrable enthusiasm seemingly muted by the events at Astrological the day before. His arm was now in a cast, the right side of his face near black where it had smacked against the floor. He greeted me at the door with a halfhearted wave and introduced me to the man standing behind him. "This is Professor John Lorenz."

Professor John Lorenz was a tall, gaunt man with a bald head, narrow face and pinched expression as if he'd bitten into a lime. Standing in the middle of our overgrown front walkway in his polo shirt and chinos, he looked as though he'd been abducted straight from a golf course and dropped unceremoniously on our lawn.

When Carl waved him up, he approached with a polite smile and an outstretched hand. "Carl here tells me you have quiet the remarkable story."

I took his hand. "Remarkable is one word. Fucking nightmare might be a better description."

His smile tightened, his eyes flicking from my battered face to my equally battered knuckles, "Yes, I've heard that, too. May we come in?"

I agreed and shuffled everyone inside where Hannah was standing before a hissing coffee pot, dark bags under her eyes. Neither of us had slept much the night before, spending the long night pacing the house together, waiting either for an attack that never came, or news that Wendy's body had been found mangled along some roadside. The fact that Astra had implied they wanted Wendy alive wasn't much of a balm either.

"This is Carl's friend," I said.

Hannah smiled wanly. "Hannah Riley," she said, offering her hand. "Thank you for coming."

The professor's expression softened in compassion, and he took Hannah's hand. "It's my pleasure, Mrs. Riley."

"Nice to meet you," Carl added, offering his own hand. Hannah blinked, confused, then laughed and took his hand.

"Sorry, Carl. I've seen so much of you in Jacob's head, I almost forgot we haven't actually met."

Carl's eyes widened and he glanced at the professor. "So it's true? You're a telepath?"

Lorenz cleared his throat. "I think we should wait to ask questions like that until we're keeping a record, don't you?"

Carl gave one of his sheepish grins and hung his head. "Right, sorry."

We waited until the coffee was done. Then, once everyone had settled at the kitchen table with steaming mugs before them, Lorenz produced a digital audio recorder and a notebook, laying them out before him like a surgeon's tools.

"Before you tell me anything," he said, his reedy voice nearly a whisper. "I don't know what Carl has told you about me, but I want to make sure everyone understands why I am here, and what I am doing. My background is in clinical psychology, specifically abnormal psychology, a path which led me to some techniques that the established psychiatric community believes are hokum and snake oil. I have used these techniques to help many contactees better understand their situation. Before I get into what exactly those techniques are, we need to establish a baseline, unclouded by any expectations of what you think I want to hear. Carl has told me some of what you have experienced, but I would like to hear it from the two of you, in as much detail is possible. Would that be all right?"

Hannah and I exchanged a glance.

Can we trust him? Hannah asked in my mind.

Fuck if I know, I thought back, *but do we really have a choice here? Grasping at this straw is just as good as any other.*

She considered this, then shrugged and nodded.

I cleared my throat, "To be honest with you, Professor, we're up shit creek without a paddle here. We need information and if you can provide it, great. The faster the better."

Lorenz smiled, a surprisingly warm expression on his otherwise withered face. "*Well,* be assured that I intend to do everything I can to help. Do either of you mind if I record our conversation?"

We didn't, and he hit the record button. "Now, please start at the beginning. No detail is too small. I need you tell me everything."

"Tall order, Professor," Hannah said, taking a sip from her coffee.

Lorenz shrugged and tapped his pen on the blank page of his notebook. "I have the time."

In all, it took five hours, during which Lorenz hardly said a word save for asking a few clarifying questions, or to ask us to repeat something. He seemed particularly interested in Hannah's dreams, asking her to repeat them four or five times before we were done. By the time we were finished, the kitchen had begun to smell of sweat – too many bodies in too small a space. Lorenz had undone the top two buttons of his polo and begun to smoke with our permission, sucking down Parliaments with mechanical efficiency, using one of our chipped bowls as an ash tray. He made one final note, then set his pen down and let out a long breath.

"Well?" Hannah ventured. "What do you think?"

Lorenz leaned back in his chair. "I think it's one heck of a story. I'd like to get a look at those footprints, if they are still there, and I'd still like to interview you both again, preferably separately to ensure there's no cross contamination."

I bristled, a headache having crept its way up my back and into the base of my skull. "Contamination? You think we're lying?"

Lorenz shook his head, tone placating, "Not at all, but I've talked to plenty of honest people whose minds have played tricks on them. You must understand, I've been interviewing folks like you for the better part of thirty years. I've been to the Roswell crash site, Zamora, Rendlesham Forest. I've talked to all those guys, watched the interviews. To be frank, Mr. Riley, this story is incredible, a little too incredible. I can't say if I believe it happened as you described or not, but I can say that you seem to be genuine in your accounts and that means more to me than you might think. If there is evidence to find, I want to help you. Maybe get your story out."

"Get our story – " I glared at Carl, who was doing a credible impression of a slug, slipping lower in his chair and threatening to ooze down to the floor. "We aren't interested in sharing our story. We're interested in getting our daughter back. Carl said you might be able to help make sense of this! I'm not going to put my family on YouTube to be picked apart by vultures!"

"Mr. Riley," Lorenz continued softly, "I understand you and your wife have been through an incredibly trying ordeal. And if there is some sort of clue that can help you get your daughter back, I intend to help you find it. If I do write about this case, it will be years from now and only with your express blessing, I assure you. For right now, we simply need to focus on the events you have experienced and do what we can to verify your stories. We need to document other witnesses, police records, anything we can find."

"Look," I grumbled, "we appreciate it. But this isn't a scientific study. This is a fight. God knows how many of these things are out there right now, and they are *not* friendly. We don't have time to collect evidence, we need to start punching back."

Lorenz spread his hands before him. "I can only help if you'll let me. I must warn you that this process is slow. The Phenomenon is complex. Perhaps you should consider leaving town? Our first concern should be getting your family away from these people who have been harassing you."

"They have our daughter!" I roared, standing up and slapping the table. "This was a fucking mistake. We appreciate you coming, but if you don't have something useful to tell us right now, you can fuck right off back to where you came from."

"Jacob –" Carl began before I cut him off with a glare. Wendy was out there and as far as I could see, all we had done was waste a day on this lunacy.

"Very well," Lorenz said. "I won't impose if I am not wanted, but please, I urge you to reconsider. If even half of what you have told me is true, then this is one of the most remarkable contact events I have ever recorded. I could spend years analyzing just what you told me this afternoon."

I was preparing to yell him out the door when Hannah suddenly stood. "I'm sorry, Professor, but we don't have that kind of time." Without warning she reached out and touched a finger to the side of Lorenz's head.

"What are you…" Lorenz moaned as his eyes slid back into his skull. "*Oh, oh my,*" he whispered, mouth hanging agape, entire body rigid as if electrified.

Carl scooted back from the table, looking wild eyed between Hannah and Lorenz. "What the fuck is happening!?"

"She's talking to me," Lorenz said softly, a dreamy smile on his face. "She's actually talking to me."

Hannah gently retracted her hand, and Lorenz's body relaxed. He closed his eyes and when he opened them again, they were wet, focused entirely on Hannah. "Thank you," he whispered. "That was… thank you."

"You're welcome," she said. "Now, how can you help us, John?"

He took a deep breath, looked down at his notes, and then over to where Carl still sat, wide eyed and terribly pale. "Carl and I will need to collect some materials. You both have likely experienced missing time, chiefly surrounding your arrival in Victor's Point. I have had some success in the past helping contactees recover their memories from these periods using hypno-regression therapy. I'd like to start there. If there are any clues to be had, they may already be in your head."

"What exactly does this process entail?" I asked.

"We can discuss that later tonight. For now, I have preparations to make. Carl, I'm going to need you to get your hands on some *research* materials." He stood with a sudden urgency that made him seem a decade younger. He held out his hand.

"I will be back at seven this evening, sharp. I know you likely want to get out there and search for your daughter, but I implore you to stay home today. Try and maintain a peaceful and reflective mood, it will help you when we perform the procedure tonight. Can you do that?"

I burned at the suggestion, wanting nothing more than to drive to town, find the first fucker with blue eyes, and bash their head against a wall until they got to talking.

Thankfully, cooler heads prevailed. Hannah placed a hand on my shoulder. "We'll be here."

The professor was nothing if not punctual. He arrived at seven on the dot, a milk crate loaded with recording equipment balanced in his hands. He was somber, but there was an undeniable energy in his posture, like a man preparing to leap out of an airplane. Hannah directed him to the living room while I busied myself helping Carl finish unloading his jeep.

I found him struggling with a large black duffle bag, one strap caught on the edge of his cast as he tried to loop it up over his shoulder. In his efforts to dislodge it, he had somehow gotten the other strap looped around his neck and was now fighting against both the weight of the bag and the tangle he found himself in.

"Need help?" I asked as I approached.

He glanced up. "All I can get."

I managed to extract him from his predicament then slung the bag over my shoulder with a grunt. Damn thing had to weigh over a hundred pounds. "What the heck has he got in this thing?"

Carl shrugged. "No clue. The professor is nothing if not prepared."

I cast an eye towards the house. During our long wait for the professor's return, Hannah and I had worked to secure the house. Hannah put screws into each windowsill to jam them shut, and I had managed to scrape together enough scrap wood to build rudimentary cross beams over the front and back doors. I'd wanted to nail wood over the windows as well, but we didn't have nearly enough materials for that. Going to town for more felt less like a pleasant Sunday drive and more like a mission into enemy territory.

The whole time we worked, I wondered if we were making a mistake. Lorenz had promised to keep our confidence, but what was a promise? Hannah trusted him, as whatever she had seen in his head had apparently convinced her, but I didn't have the luxury of an inside view.

"He's actually going to help us, right?" I asked, watching as Carl worked to pull a black plastic case from his jeep.

Carl paused, glanced up at me. "He'll try," he said earnestly. "The professor got into this stuff to help people. If he can, he will."

"And can he?" I asked.

Carl shrugged. "A few days ago I would have said yes, but given what I've seen… I mean if these blue-eyed people really turned that Danny guy loose on us, then I don't know. I don't know if anyone can help. But he's going to try, and I'm going to try, and we're just going to have to hope that is good enough."

He began walking toward the house. I stopped him with a hand on his shoulder. "Wait," I said, lowering to a whisper. "Just tell me one thing. Why are *you* helping?"

He raised an eyebrow. "Are you kidding? This is one of the most spectacular events I've – "

"Did that feel spectacular?" I cut him off, gesturing to his cast. "You know the stakes. They sent Danny to kill me. There's no guarantee they won't add your head to the chopping block as well. So before you go in there, before we do this, I need to know why this is so important to you."

Carl looked at me, the house, and then the night sky above. "Because of the mystery, man," he said, pointing skyward. "All my damn life I've been waiting on something miraculous to happen. My letter to Hogwarts, my induction to the Jedi, my chance to see there is more out there than 401ks and shopping malls. I know this situation is ugly, and I know that this isn't a game. But as horrifying as all this is, it's also what I've been looking for my entire life. But, more importantly, I couldn't walk away right now and live with myself. There is an innocent child out there who can't defend herself, and who is somehow caught up in all this. If there is anything I can do to help rectify that, I will."

Despite my misgivings, I felt a surge of affection for the smaller man. "Thank you," I said. "Whatever happens, I'll know you tried."

Carl smiled. "Hey, what are friends for?"

2

The professor set up in the living room, a large bank of computer monitors and a sound board taking up the entirety of our coffee table. He also produced several scientific looking devices whose purpose I could only guess at, positioning them at the four corners of the room. By the time he was done, our living room had been transformed into an ad hoc laboratory.

I made sure that the crossbeams were in place over the doors, each window thoroughly jammed, and that the wood axe was in reach, right beside the coffee table. Only then did I allow myself to be guided to the couch where I sat next to Hannah, the two of us nervously fidgeting in our seats like unruly kids waiting outside the principal's office.

"The process is simple enough," Lorenz explained, sitting behind his wall of computer monitors and balanced atop a folding stool he had pulled from his duffle bag. "I'm going to guide each of you through a hypnotic session, during which I'll ask you to recall an event or series of events. It's key that you relax. You need to trust me, and trust the process. Despite what you may have seen on television, you will not be in a full hypnotic state. Think of this more like an intensive, guided meditation. Do you understand?"

"Does this stuff actually work?" I asked, unable to keep the incredulity from my voice. Hannah nudged me in the side with her elbow. "I mean, is it real?"

Lorenz shrugged. "Real is just results written down. Hopefully, the answers we need have just been locked away in your memories by the Phenomenon. We need to find the key that lets you open that door. Would either of you like to volunteer to go first?"

"I'll go first," I said.

Hannah raised an eyebrow at me. "Are you sure, I can – "

"It's fine," I said, giving her hand a reassuring squeeze. It stood to reason that whatever had been messing around with our minds wouldn't like us tampering with their work. If there was any danger, I wanted it to find me long before it could get anywhere close to Hannah. "So, how do we start?"

Lorenz nodded to Carl, who went to the wall switch and dimmed the lights.

"All right," Lorenz said, "first I'm going to need you to get comfortable. Lie down. Try to relax."

I snorted out a halfhearted laugh. "Fat chance of that."

"Just try your best," he said, clacking softly on his keyboard. A moment later he produced a pair of headphones and passed them to Hannah. "Place these on his head. Jacob, these headphones produce a tone which some believe aid in this sort of work. Some people call it Hemi-Sync. Don't try to actively listen, just keep focusing on relaxation."

I let Hannah slide the bulky headphones over my ears, savoring the small kiss she placed on my forehead as she did. Then I let myself sink into the couch as the odd tone began playing. It wasn't music – there were no notes, no words. Just a single, unending, hum.

Lorenz's voice cut in through the headphones. "We're going to try focusing on our breathing now. Count to four on each inhale, four on each exhale. In through the nose, out through the mouth. That's it."

Despite my earlier misgivings, his words combined with the strange tone were beginning to worm their way into my ears, sweeping through my mind like bath water. I *was* tired. Exhausted, in fact. I breathed, my earlier thoughts and doubts dying silent deaths until I wasn't thinking anything at all.

"I'm going to begin counting down now," Lorenz said softly through my earphones. "We're going to start at the beginning. Ten, focus on your breathing. Nine, you are sinking into the couch. Eight, you are sinking deeper. Seven, the light is fading away."

"And then?" Dr. Lorenz asked as my vision of our last night in Echo City began to fade. "You moved around a lot? Stayed mostly in motels, is that right?"

"Yes," I said automatically, voice hoarse as if I'd been screaming.

"And then you ended up here?" he asked.

"Yes."

"Why?" The question hurt my brain to consider. Where was I? What was I doing? Moments ago I had been in my truck, fleeing Echo City with Hannah at my side, and two corpses in our wake.

"Jacob," Lorenz's voice pressed, "why did you come to Victor's Point?" The question gnawed at me, dragging me back out of the dark hole of memory into which I'd fallen. Why *had* we come? We stumbled on the house, that was right, but at the same time somehow wrong.

"Jacob?" Lorenz asked again, and suddenly my eyes were open and I found myself upright, blinking reality back into my eyes. I was in the living room, sitting in the easy chair. Hannah was beside me, perched on the edge of her seat, eyes wide with concern. Carl and the professor had taken up side-by-side posts on the other side of the computer monitors. Carl looked like he was going to be sick, the professor almost thrilled.

"How long was I out?" I asked, my thoughts cottony and indistinct.

"That session was close to forty-five minutes," Lorenz reported. "An exceptional first try, Jacob. Truly."

"Did we learn anything?" I asked.

Lorenz shrugged apologetically. "We learned some things, but I think we are still missing a few key pieces here. Namely, I am most interested in two questions. First of all, I want to know why you two chose Victor's Point as the spot to settle."

"We told you," I said. "We stumbled upon the house and cashed in on Hannah's inheritance. We wanted to flip the place so we would have enough to move to Portland or Seattle or something."

"Yes, your inheritance," Lorenz looked at his notes. "Twenty thousand dollars, right?"

Hannah and I exchanged a glance and nodded.

Lorenz sighed and looked at each of us pointedly. "Well, I may not be a real estate agent, but it seems to me that if your goal was to live in either of those cities, twenty thousand dollars is more than enough to get an apartment – maybe even a down payment on a house if you're lucky. With that in mind, the question is, again, why you chose to settle here?"

"We liked the house," Hannah said, sounding as if she only half believed it herself, her brow furrowed in thought. "When we found it, it felt like fate. We figured this town is as good as anywhere else."

Part of me wanted to agree with her. Our grand plan to fix up the house and move had been part of our story for so long I could no longer remember which of us had come up with it.

"All of that may be true," Lorenz said, still addressing Hannah. "However, think through this rationally. You are a young couple with a newborn, looking to set down roots for your future. You really want to live in Seattle or Portland, yet you buy a house in a town that lacks any discernable form of industry and, by all appearances, is in the process of dying. Does that sound like a logical decision?"

Hannah locked eyes with me, her confusion and fear mirroring my own. "No," I finally said. "It doesn't."

"And your other question?" Hannah asked.

"That would be the matter of Hannah's parents," Lorenz said offhandedly, his eyes already scanning the pages of notes he had taken during my first session.

"Because they're part of this," Hannah confirmed, turning to face Lorenz. "Astra and Hanson clearly think I'm from the area, that I'm the same as them. And so do you, right?"

"Gold star to the lady in the front row," Lorenz said. "We need to determine the source of your abilities. It could inform the next questions we ask."

Nodding in agreement, Hannah sucked in a breath and looked back at Lorenz. "So, what do we do now?"

"Normally, we take a week off to analyze the session, to ensure the patient reaches a level of emotional stability and is able to properly contextualize the experience." I started to make a face, preparing to object on the basis that we didn't have a week, but Lorenz cut me off with an outstretched palm. "That said," he continued, "given the extenuating circumstances, I think it best if we power on as much as we can tonight. Repeated sessions can have an intense psychological strain on the patient, so we can only proceed if both of you are willing."

Hannah answered for us, standing immediately and heading for the kitchen. "I'm putting on the coffee, then it's my turn next."

◆ ◆ ◆

The first fingers of dawn poked through our blinds just as Hannah was coming out of her most recent session. We had done twelve in total, six each, leaving us both feeling raw and frayed down to our bones. Of the dozen sessions, nine hadn't yielded anything of value and had focused on events we had already told Lorenz about: the encounter with the mad woman on the road, Hannah's psychic storm at the ice cream stand, and Danny's attack on me.

The remaining three sessions, however, painted a bleak picture. A frenzied escape from Victor's Point when Hannah was still a baby. The breaking of a psychic barrier when Wendy was born. The attack at the motel and our inexplicable appearance on the road into Victor's Point.

"So we were lured here?" I asked slowly, rubbing the spot on my chest where Hanson had apparently shot me during our encounter in Carver's Mill. A wound that had somehow been healed without even the faintest scar.

"Abducted seems more appropriate," Hannah said, her voice hoarse, head sunk between her hands with a few strands of frizzy hair poking out between her fingers.

"Yeah, but by who?" Carl asked. He had taken over the easy chair beside the couch and spent the majority of the night dutifully clacking away at his keyboard. "From the sound of it, The Light saved you guys after you were ambushed at the motel. I'm guessing it's the one who healed Jacob."

"And delivered us right into the home turf of the guy who shot me," I said. "Seems to me like the damn thing served us up on a silver platter."

"It is perplexing," Lorenz said, standing near one of the living room windows, watching as the sky brightened in the east. "Given what Officer Hanson told Hannah, I don't think we can assume that they are in collusion with The Light. In fact, I think there is more evidence that it, whatever it may be, is opposed to these...let's call them non-people."

"So why bring us here?" I asked. "Why not talk to us and tell us what's going on?"

Lorenz shrugged, "I think the argument could be made that it has. Hannah's dreams could be the key to understanding The Light. I'm also very interested in the references to these non-people keeping 'breeders' around."

Hannah frowned. "I've been thinking about that, too. Astra was interested in getting me to follow her home, but she called Wendy a titan. Said she was special. What if... what if they have been trying to create more kids like her?"

"Like the breeding programs," Carl said. Then, perhaps noticing the utter lack of comprehension on our faces, he hurried to explain. "It's one of the theories out there about aliens. Contactees, especially abduction victims, report being impregnated with alien hybrid children. Some say they're even brought back onto the ships later to meet their kids. The story goes that the Greys are a clone race, and with each generation their DNA degraded a little more until eventually they couldn't produce viable progeny. Supposedly they plan to fix that by using us to spice up the gene pool."

"You can't really believe that?" I asked.

"Why not?" Hannah said, nudging me in the side. "It fits what we've been seeing to a point."

"I'm inclined to agree," Lorenz said somberly. "Given your fragmented memories of your birth parents, I believe I have the beginning framework for a theory." He turned towards the room, a dark silhouette against the morning sun streaming in through the window.

"Might as well lay it on us, Professor," I said.

Lorenz paused a moment longer, then cleared his throat. "Carl is correct. There is a small but statistically significant segment of abduction victims who report being made to take part in an ongoing breeding and hybridization process. While I do doubt the validity of many of such claims, I have never been able to totally disprove them and, more importantly, I have encountered a case or two that I might classify as truly extraordinary. However, there are some key differences between those experiences and what we are seeing here."

He began to pace, showing none of the exhaustion that was currently crushing Hannah and me into the couch cushions. "For one, we can find no indication that Hannah was taken by a ship, nor did we uncover any traumatic memories of the impregnation process. Furthermore, the involvement of this mysterious light, and the relatively localized nature of the non-people, leads me to believe that we are dealing with something a bit more unique. I believe that what we are looking at here is potential evidence that the hybrid program succeeded beyond their first generation."

He let his words marinate in the open air while we stole glances at each other.

"Think about it," Lorenz continued, "these non-people seem quite concerned with getting Hannah and Wendy into their fold. The one known as Astra even helped heal her from injury, correct?" Hannah nodded. "What if these people are the genuine offspring of an alien and a human? They abduct human breeders to keep the population strong, perhaps even seeking out those already on the psychic spectrum. Then selectively breeding them to try and promote these abilities."

"What about Mr. Friend?" I asked. "He's clearly involved, but he doesn't have the same eyes as the rest of them. Is he a breeder too?"

"Maybe he's the alien," Hannah countered.

Lorenz shrugged. "Or perhaps he's an earlier hybrid, looking to perfect his second generation. Or, he could be none of those things; perhaps something we've not considered, or even paranormal. Without genetic testing, we can't be sure of anything." He looked pointedly at Hannah and asked, "What if this town is the base of operations for the program? Perhaps a program that your parents chose to escape, your father being a member of the group and your mother brought in to breed."

I shook my head. "That doesn't make any sense, though. I've met Friend, talked to him, and he seemed pretty human to me. If they wanted Hannah, and if there are as many of these things as we think there are, why haven't they come and beat down our door? Their behavior doesn't make any sense."

Lorenz, however, only nodded more excitedly. "Which is why this is so interesting. Something truly strange is happening here. The way I see it, there are two possible paths for us. One, we need to locate this Mr. Friend and, if possible, the location where the rest of them are living. And two, we need to locate The Light, perhaps have Hannah try to initiate contact with it again."

With a snort, Hannah shook her head. "Fat chance. I've been trying to get that thing to talk to me for weeks. It doesn't seem to be the helpful sort."

"Uhhh, professor?" Carl said, though Lorenz either didn't hear him or ignored him.

"That's why I believe we may need to do some real out of the box thinking. Your abilities began to manifest after you first encountered The Light, yes? The day that Astra drugged you?"

Hannah nodded.

Carl stood. "Professor?"

"There have been some very interesting studies regarding DMT and, while this is hardly a scientific view, some even think it allows us to perceive higher levels of reality. I believe that if we can induce such a state again, it may allow you to make more substantive contact. I – "

"Professor!?" Carl shouted, his entire body rigid, eyes wide.

"Yes, Carl?" Lorenz said, snapping out of his reverie and following Carl's gaze towards the window. He stiffened, mouth falling slack. "Jacob, what was that you said about them coming to beat down your door?"

I looked, cold dread blooming fresh in my gut. There, standing in the first rays of the rising sun, half a dozen people stood in a line across our backyard, barely visible in the shade from the trees. Their eyes were all blue, so bright they nearly glowed, and large. Too large for a human face, each eye the size of a closed fist. At their center stood Astra, the wind swirling her floral sundress around her ankles, golden blond hair piled high and tied back. She saw us notice her and then, walking with the grim determination of a headsman marching to the cutting block, she approached, not stopping until she was inches from the window, breath fogging the glass with each exhale.

Up close she looked even more inhuman, the strange immensity of her eyes seemed to draw us into their drowning fathoms. Lorenz began to scramble for a camera, while Hannah stood and took a protective step in front of me.

"Go away, Astra," she said, loud enough to be heard through the window.

Astra tilted her head. When she responded it was not with words, but with a look, focusing her immense gaze on Hannah. Hannah's body went rigid, while the professor raised his camera and began snapping photo after photo of the creature beyond the glass.

"Hannah?" I asked.

Her face twitched, then morphed into terror.

"No!" Hannah whispered. "Everyone run!"

3 – Hannah

It doesn't need to be this way. I don't want to hurt anyone, Hannah. I want us to be sisters. We are blood. Astra's silky thoughts slid into my mind before I could think to block them. Images flashed before my eyes. Astra smiling and joking with me in the garden, sharing her joint, Astra caring for Wendy, tending to my hand: a parade of friendship and affection meant to blot out all the horrors we had seen. *I've only ever tried to help.*

Go away, Astra, I thought back, forcefully. *I don't need a sister, and I don't need whatever fucked up family you come from.* To punctuate my point, I sent the image of the woman we had encountered on the road and the crude stitching across her gore-slicked belly.

Sadness lanced through Astra's thoughts, a deep, cold emotion that seemed to run to her core. *You don't understand anything. You aren't like them, Hannah. You don't see it yet, but you will. Their lives are small things, ruled by pettiness and pain. To take part in what we are is the greatest gift we could ever hope to give them. You will understand. He's going to take care of you, and Wendy. He'd never let anyone hurt you.*

More images flashed in my mind. I saw myself sitting amidst a group of blue-eyed people before a roaring fire pit. This version of Hannah was smiling, her entire body relaxed, pale eyes sparkling with merriment. Wendy was sitting on her lap, an unrestrained smile on her face that seemed to brighten the darkness at the edges of the firelight. I could almost taste the sticky sugar of toasted marshmallows, smell the deep earthy pines that surrounded the camp.

"We're happy here," a familiar voice said. I lowered my gaze to find that the other Hannah was looking at me, her voice clear over the roar of the fire and the booming laughter of the blue-eyed non-people. "You could be happy here. Wendy, too. You just need to trust them."

Wonderful feelings began to surge over me in an awesome wave. Joy, peace, contentment, a sense of bliss that radiated down into my bones. I gasped, my entire body feeling as if it was turning to liquid. *'I don't – I don't want this,'* I thought. *'You aren't real, this isn't – '*

"It could be," the other Hannah said firmly, suddenly and inexplicably standing before me. The laughter cut out just as abruptly, the entire circle of blue eyes now staring silently at me. "This future exists. All you need to do is walk to it. This is better for us." A figure rose up behind her, a man with a Santa Claus beard and a merry twinkle in his eye.

"Trust her, Lacie," he said. "We are family."

Another wave of bliss scattered my thoughts like gnats. What was I doing? Where was I? Moments ago I had been alarmed, terrified even, but now all I wanted was to sink down onto the fire- warmed dirt beside the pit and let the laughter of my siblings wash the stains of a forgotten life off my skin.

"What about Jacob?" I asked weakly.

"Don't worry," the other Hannah cooed. "We don't want to hurt anyone. Go to them. Join with them, and Jacob won't be harmed. Nobody will. You just need to tell us now – where is Wendy?"

I glanced up at the other me, the bliss still singing its impossible lullaby through every cell in my body. Just as I felt my final resistance begin to crumble, a clear thought blasted its way into my mind from somewhere beyond the house.

'Momma! Astra, bad!'

I blinked and suddenly the woman in front of me wasn't me at all. Long strands of blond hair snuck out from beneath her raven black hairline as if she wore a wig, and her face was much longer and narrower than mine. Making a snap decision, I reached out, pressed my hands to her chest, and shoved with everything I had. There was an immense lightning bolt of pain that started in the center of my head and raced down every limb, a bright flash of light. The vision was gone and I found myself staring out the window of our living room.

Astra met my gaze, her face contorted with hurt. *Fine,* she thought at me, *I wanted this to be wonderful, but you're ruining it! You and your little girl are ruining everything! And now, you've gone and gotten these good people killed.*

Outside, a man broke from the line and started approaching the house. It was Indrid, pulsing waves of righteous rage billowing off him, his surface thoughts all of Mildred and vengeance. In his hands, he carried a black, military-style rifle.

"No!" I shouted. "Everyone run!"

The window exploded under a hail of bullets.

The first shot shattered the glass, the second blew a fist-sized hole through one of Lorenz's computer monitors. Carl leapt onto the ground, dragging Lorenz with him, while Jacob wrapped his arms around me and pulled out of the line of fire. Something hot splashed on my face and for a moment I was sure I had been hit. When another drop stuck my forehead I looked up. A bullet or bit of debris had clipped Jacob's ear lobe and sheared the bottom half-inch.

Shots pounded into the house, splintering the window frame and tearing cottony holes in the couch. Somewhere nearby, Lorenz was crying out in pain and Carl was screaming. Jacob, however, remained still through it all, his breath coming in even measures, his eyes never leaving the shattered window, the wood axe somehow already in his hands.

Another flurry of shots lit up the room, then silence, just the pained groans of the professor coming from his hiding place behind the couch. As we watched, positioned flat against the wall beside the window, the barrel of Indrid's gun poked through the opening. Next came the hand holding it, then a leg as Indrid began to crawl inside—only for his clothing to catch on shards of glass.

Jacob narrowed his eyes, his body stiffening, rage and fear pounding through his head. And beneath it, something else. A monster that roared murderous intent. It was the old Jacob, the bad Jacob with split knuckles and blood-slicked teeth. In my mind's eye I could see him, pacing in his cage, a ravenous beast desperate for release, for ruin.

Around the front of the house someone was slamming against the front door, another against the back. There was nowhere to run.

I stood on my tiptoes, kissed him on the cheek, and sent a thought into his mind.

Get them.

Jacob looked at me, then slowly pushed me behind him. In front of us, Indrid had managed to kick the remaining glass out of the window frame and was now climbing through, the gun held up and ready as he swept the room. He spotted Jacob and fired, but the shot went wide. By then, the axe was in motion.

The blade took Indrid at the knee, sliced through muscle, tendon, and bone, sending a spray of blood up the wall. Indrid fell, shrieking, his jaw distended unnaturally into an inhuman scream. He raised the gun to fire again. Without thought, I leapt on Indrid, wrapped my whole body around his arm and pinned it, along with his rifle, to the ground. Indrid thrashed like a wild animal, snarling and spitting, his free hand slamming into my ribs until Jacob managed to get a boot on his chest.

"Wait!" Indrid screamed.

With a ferocious roar, Jacob brought the axe down onto Indrid's head, splitting his skull open like an overripe watermelon. The smell of dirty pennies filled the air, and Indrid's body twitched madly beneath me as it caught up to the reality of its execution.

I stared down at him, momentarily transfixed by his one remaining eye that stared hatefully at me and his split lips turned down into a permanent scowl. Before my eyes, his body started changing, the flesh rippling and twisting as if a sea of worms writhed just beneath the surface. His skin turned a mottled grey and his blue eye began to darken at the edges and turn black.

The next thing I knew, Jacob's hand was on my back, urging me to my feet and shoving me ahead of him down the hall amidst the cacophony of fists hammering on doors, and Carl's panicked shouting. The sound of breaking glass came from the master bedroom a moment before a woman appeared in the doorway to block us, her arms sliced up and bleeding from crawling through broken glass. She was dressed like a soccer mom, complete with capri pants and a cardigan, and she held a polished skinning knife in her hand.

She ran at us, needle-like teeth bared, hissing. Jacob swung the axe around, but the blade caught on the ceiling, the hallway too narrow for a proper swing. She was closing in, slashing the knife in the air before her. I ran at her, dodging under a sweep of her knife and pressing a palm to her forehead.

I thought of razor blades, barbed wire, electric shocks, poison, and bullets. Then, I shoved them into her mind as hard as I could, imagining a storm of steel slicing ribbons through her grey matter. The woman's body went rigid, her eyes rolled back into her head, and she unleashed a scream that Jacob cut off with a savage punch to her neck.

Back in the living room, Carl's shouts took on a desperate quality.

"No, no, get away! Get away! No!"

Jacob and I exchanged a glance. "Go," he said, pointing towards the bedroom. "Get to the truck. I'll try to get those two and meet you out front."

"Like fucking hell!?" I shouted back at him.

Jacob didn't give me a chance to argue further. He placed a hand on my back, shoved me into the bedroom, and then he was gone, back down the hall towards Carl.

"You asshole!" I shouted back at him, though more out of fear than anger. Resisting the urge to chase after him, I jumped over the woman writhing on the floor and sprinted into the bedroom.

Trying to avoid the shards of glass that littered the floor beneath, I scrambled through the now broken window and hit the ground running. While the battle inside the house raged on with a series of screams and house shaking crashes, the areas to the rear and side of the house were clear. I slowed as I approached the front yard, peeking around the corner of the house. Only one of the blue-eyed people was visible, a bulky man in a black tank top, arms covered in swirling tribal tattoos. He was standing in the doorway to the house, his whole attention seemingly focused on the battle inside where, I presumed, the rest of them were currently engaged with Jacob. I needed to clear them a path, distract the non-people long enough for everyone else to get out. Scanning the street, I spotted Jacob's truck and an idea struck me – an awfully dangerous one.

I slipped around the tattooed man and ran to the truck, hurling myself into the driver's seat and flipping down the sun visor to retrieve the spare key. Eyes locked on the front of the house, I brought the engine to life, slammed the gear into reverse, and angled the car directly at the tattooed man's back, intent to slam the truck right through him.

I went to shift into drive, but my hand froze the moment it touched the gear stick. I stared down at it, confusion giving away to dread as I felt the muscles in my hand lock up and turn rigid.

"You can't run from this, baby girl," Astra said from her hiding place in the back seat. I tried to reach for the door handle, but my whole body was locking up. This was nothing like when Hanson tried to puppet me. The control was absolute, every muscle in my body pulled taut by psychic strings.

"Astra," I wheezed, "just leave us alone. Please."

"I'm sorry, Lacie-Bear," Astra said, stroking the hair on the back of my head. "Isn't my call to make."

A shadow fell across me as someone stepped up to the driver's side window. It was Mr. Friend. He gestured for me to roll down the window and to my horror, my hand moved to comply, working the manual crank.

"Hello, Lacie," Friend said. "How about you scooch on over and let Grandpa drive?"

Again my body obeyed, sliding over along the bench seat. Friend opened the door and got inside, running his fingers over the wheel. It was then that it clicked. The psychic hold wasn't coming from Astra, it was coming from him. I could almost see the strings, like gauzy spider's webbing stretching from his mind to mine.

"Let me go," I whispered.

"I am sorry," Friend said, a forlorn note of sadness humming off him via psychic radio. "I was hoping we could avoid all this ugliness. But I'm afraid powers beyond both of us have made that impossible. Please understand, we're your family. I already lost Wendy, I can't lose you, too."

"I already have a family," I said through a rapidly constricting throat. Something loud crashed inside the house, and someone who might have been Carl was shrieking in pain. I summoned up every bit of willpower I had and threw it against his hold, but I might as well have been kicking steel for all the good it did me.

"No," Friend coached. "You *had* a family. But you let that filthy thing take Wendy. As for the big ol' lug, well," he sucked in a ponderous breath, scratching his beard, "I am fond of Jacob. I was hoping we could spare him. But maybe Brandon was right. He's already killed Indrid. Maybe that bull is just more trouble than he's worth. I need to think of the whole herd, you understand?"

I tried to speak, but he'd already taken my breath from me. *Please*, I thought at Friend, *Don't hurt him.*

He smiled sadly and patted me on the knee. "I'm afraid he's already gone and made that decision for me. I'll tell you what though. If he comes out on top in there, I might just let him give me a few more grandbabies." Then, glancing behind me toward Astra, "Dear one, Lacie looks mighty tired, don't she? Why don't you help her out?"

"Just relax, Big Sis is going to take good care of you," Astra whispered. She pressed one hand to my forehead to hold it in place, and pressed a sweet smelling rag to my mouth with the other. I tried not to breathe, tried to turn my head away, but soon enough the burning in my lungs became too great and I gasped.

My limbs turned to jelly and my vision darkened. I stared at the house, sent a thought of love toward Jacob, then Wendy, then one last thought up towards The Light.

Please, I begged, *help them.*

If there was an answer I never heard it. Darkness swallowed me whole.

4 – Jacob

Murder isn't anything like what they show in the movies, where death can come with a single bloodless stab to the belly. In reality, people fought to live until their bodies were coming apart at the seams. At least, that's what happened with the non-people I found assaulting Carl and Lorenz in the living room. I burst in to find a man in a mechanic's coverall trying to drag Lorenz out from behind the couch. Nearby, Carl was doing his best to save himself, using his laptop as an impromptu shield to block knife strikes from a pot-bellied man in a NASCAR shirt. None of them noticed me until I was upon them. After that, all I can remember is swinging the axe, screaming, and the dark spray of warm arterial blood soaking through my shirt.

Next thing I knew I was standing above the corpse of NASCAR man with my arms burning, still mechanically swinging the axe down into his dead flesh over and over again, spreading bits of bone and viscera around the living room like birthday confetti.

"Jacob," Carl said, his voice sounding distant, as if coming down a long hallway. "It's over, they're dead. You can put the axe down now, buddy."

I looked down at the weapon in my hand, shocked by the thick layer of gore that caked the blade. Then I looked past that to the corpses on the floor. Counting Indrid, I had just murdered four of these non-people. At some point, soccer mom had broken free from whatever Hannah had done to her and tried to save her friends. I had no memory of killing her, nor did I know how her skinning knife ended up embedded in the muscle of my shoulder. Her dead eyes stared accusingly up at me, already blackening just like Indrid's had. Her chest was a concave ruin of broken ribs and exposed heart muscle. I dropped the axe and slumped down onto the couch, feeling sick.

Nearby, Carl was helping the professor sit up against the back of the couch. The professor had caught one of Indrid's bullets in his right hand, blowing the tops of three of his fingers to mist. Carl had been slashed across the chest and belly with a knife of some kind, though the wounds looked shallow. We needed the first aid kit Hannah kept in the kitchen. Someone ought to get that, I thought. Hannah would, she was always better at that stuff than I was and… Hannah. Where was Hannah?

I had heard an engine start during the fight, hadn't I? With a hard knot of dread forming in my gut, I ran to the front door and burst out onto the porch, eyes scanning the empty drive where our truck had been moments ago. I continued out onto the road, scanning in either direction, but the only thing coming up the road was the approaching line of sunlight as it snuck over the rim of the mountains.

I called her name, then I screamed it, turning in circles. Only the cicadas greeted me, the final notes of their evening song dying under the morning light.

My Rabbit was gone.

Back inside, I helped Carl wrap the professor's hand, then applied bandages to the wounds on his chest and stomach. "Going to leave some badass scars, right?" he joked, looking pale enough to pass out. "And just think, I can say I got them fighting aliens."

I could only grunt in response. These things, be they The Light or the blue-eyed bastards, had taken everything from me. Wendy had disappeared, and now Hannah was out there with them. God knows what they had planned for her. When I was done helping Carl and Lorenz patch themselves up, I retreated silently to the bathroom where I did my best to scrub the gore from my body. Then, I grabbed a trash bag and fished out the bits of skin and hair that had been too big to go down the drain. Finally, I bandaged the stab wound on my shoulder.

Once done, I returned to the living room. Seeing the carnage with fresh eyes, I felt a surge of acidic nausea creep up my throat. How had it all gone so wrong? This little red house on Strawberry Lane was supposed to be our launching point to a life free of bloodshed and violence. Instead it had become a slaughterhouse. I needed to move the bodies somewhere, clean up the blood, fix the window and the bullet holes. I needed to make it right so that when Hannah came home, she wouldn't see it like this and … and what? Hannah wasn't coming home, not under her own power at any rate.

I moved to the kitchen where Carl had seated the professor at the table. The older man's eyes were glazed, staring blankly into the middle distance.

"Everyone alive?" I asked tersely.

"In here, yeah," Carl said. "Professor is a little out of it at the moment, but don't worry about –"

"They took her, didn't they?" Lorenz asked, his voice barely a whisper.

Carl looked at the professor, comprehension dawning on his face. "Oh, shit."

"Yeah," I said. "I think they did. And I need go find her, and Wendy. Right now."

Carl sputtered, "But, that's fucking crazy, man! Who knows how many more of those things are out there, and you don't even know where to start looking."

"I know they live somewhere up in the hills. That's a start."

Carl stood, looking unsteady on his feet despite the fire in his voice. "That's bullshit! Those hills go on for miles, you can't just expect to find them by yourself, with nothing else to go on. We need the Army, the Air Force, fuck, we need Seal Team Six. We can't just head out – "

"You're not heading out," Lorenz cut him off gently. "You aren't going with him, Carl. Neither am I. Neither of us are in any condition to stage a rescue."

"We can't just let him go alone!" Carl shouted back, nearly hysterical. I couldn't say I blamed the kid, given the night we'd had.

"I can't just sit here while they have her. If there is even a chance that I can find her, I have to try," I said.

The professor nodded. "I assumed as much. You said that the sheriff's deputy is one of those things, yes?"

"Yeah, Hanson," I said, thinking of the first night he had come to the house, looking every bit the hero cop from a movie.

"What about the sheriff himself?" Lorenz asked.

"No clue. If I had to guess, I'd say he's not one of them. He doesn't have the eyes. He seemed just as freaked out as we were when this all started."

Lorenz considered this for a moment, then looked to Carl. "Well, I think he's about as close to a cavalry as we can expect to find around here. Carl, head into town and find the sheriff. Get him up here. Lie if you have to. Just don't let him bring that deputy, are we clear?"

Carl wavered, looking between us. "Yeah, I guess, but what about you? Your fingers are gone, man."

"And I won't die this second. Please, Carl, go. I have my own task to see to."

Carl looked between us again, then, muttering curses under his breath, he made his way to the front door on wobbly legs. Lorenz gestured for me to be silent until we heard Carl's jeep start up and rumble away.

"Now," Lorenz said, "before you go searching the mountains, I have an idea. We should ask The Light for help."

"I would love to, Doc," I said dryly, "but the thing didn't leave a business card. How the hell do you expect me to – "

"Drugs," he said simply. "We give you the same dose of DMT that we were going to give Hannah. It allowed her to make her first contact with The Light. It's possible it will allow you to do the same."

"But I'm not," I faltered, gesturing towards my head, "you know, gifted. I can't do what she does, so there is no reason to think that thing will even talk to me."

"Don't be so sure. My records are full of everyday people, just like you, who made contact with anomalous intelligences after a controlled dose. Some of the entities described during the DMT experience sound very much like this cosmic firefly of yours."

I considered it, then shook my head. "We don't have time for that. They have my family, John."

"You won't find them any faster randomly wandering around in the hills," he wet his pale, bloodless lips. "Jacob, I've spent my entire career looking to help people that nobody else would give the time of day to. Please, believe me, I want to reunite you with your wife and get to the bottom of this almost as badly as you do. Just give me an hour. Try the drug. Worst case scenario we will be no better off than we are now, and I'll saddle up and go hunting with you, ruined hand and all."

I weighed my options, decided I didn't like either. I stared out the open doorway of the kitchen to where four bodies lay cooling in my living room. Fuck the deep end, we were ten miles out to sea with only sharks for company.

Only thing left to do was swim.

"One hour," I said.

Lorenz gave me a terse, apologetic smile, "More or less."

5

Just as Hannah had, I rode out the trip on the couch. I had assumed that I would be drinking some strange fluid or shooting up a radioactive cocktail. The reality was a small glass bottle of yellowish powder and a pack of Parliament cigarettes. Pulling the cellophane from the pack, he used a box cutter to split one of the cigarettes down the middle. Moving with the care of a surgeon, he extracted the tobacco and mixed it with some of the powder, then rolled the concoction into a rough looking joint. I stared at it, wondering if I was making a mistake, if we were wasting precious seconds while Friend tore Hannah to bits. Lorenz gave me a light off a dented gold Zippo and within a few minutes I wasn't worried about anything anymore.

The first cigarette I had had in three years tasted like burning mothballs and caused me to hack so bad I nearly vomited. I choked it down, sucking in deep draw after draw, waiting for reality to fall apart around me.

"That's it," Lorenz said, his face swelling before my eyes. "Just take a deep breath and relax. I'm going to guide you as best I can." Lorenz's face was now the size of a car, each eye a tumbling sphere of black stone. The floor rocked, the world outside glowed with neon light. I squeezed my eyes shut, laid back, and thought of Hannah.

"Focus on your objective," I heard Lorenz say, his voice echoing as if from some distant mountain top. "The Light is...it's here, Jacob...I can see it, I ...
"

I lost the rest of what he said, sound turning to color then to sensation. I became untethered, as if that loadstone at the center of my being had been stolen away. Colors bent and melted together into a spilled-ink tapestry of pulsating shapes and forms, each humming with its own strange music that was more than sound. It was taste, and smells, and a buzzing sensation that crept through my skin and nestled into the marrow of my bones. I was nowhere. I was nobody. I was a mote of thought in a sea of unfiltered perception.

"Focus, Jacob," I heard someone say. "What do you want to see?"

"Light," I said without words, the thought springing forth from my mind. I watched as thin lines of white gossamer thread drifted from my eyes, my mouth, swirled in front of me, growing brighter, fueled by some invisible reaction, like the birth of a star. The world of shapes had faded, and all I could see was a single brilliant point of light hovering in a darkness that had consumed the universe.

It felt immense, an intelligence older than thought, older than time. I croaked out a single word: "Help."

The Light vanished. I found myself standing under the boughs of a pine tree. Needles crunched underfoot, and I could smell the sticky sweetness of the tree's sap. I was on a natural rise in the landscape, the ground before me dropped away sharply into a steep slope which leveled out some fifty feet below, in what appeared to be a small mountain hollow. In the dead center of it sat a cluster of cabins. Silver smoke drifted above the buildings from what looked like a number of cook fires and, if I squinted, I could just make out people moving about the grounds.

"Is this where they come from?" I asked aloud, unsure who or what I was talking to. "Is this where they took her?"

"She isn't there yet, but soon." The voice, a very real voice, came from directly behind me. I turned, and what I saw there stunned me into slack jawed silence.

The woman was in her early twenties, with shoulder length red hair. She had Hannah's face, her eyes, her hands, and her neck. She had my nose, my brow, my smile. She was wearing ratty jeans and a black Megadeth t-shirt. My t-shirt, I realized, noticing a familiar bleach stain on its hem. Although, the decal was badly faded, as if the shirt had aged decades since I'd last worn it. I looked carefully at her face, then it clicked.

"Wendy?" I whispered.

She smiled at me and stepped to my side. "Yes. Maybe. Someday. Who I could become, anyway."

I gaped at her. "How are you here? Friend's people – "

"The Light," she said. "It took me before they could. I've been here since then."

"But you're…last time I checked, you were still in diapers."

She rolled her eyes, still grinning. "Time isn't fixed around here. Past, present, future, it's all the same to The Light. It needed someone to talk to you, so it asked me to grow up for a little. It's fine, Dad, promise. Nothing is permanent."

This was too fucking weird. I reached out, touched her shoulder, and felt hard bone and toned muscle beneath the sleeve of her shirt. The wind blew, carrying the scent of the forest, and the morning sun felt warm on my skin. This was real. Not reality as I knew it, but real all the same.

I looked back down at the cabins, a tremor in my voice. "What are they going to do to her?"

Wendy's face darkened. "They aren't going to kill her, if that's what you're worried about. Friend wants to make her *want* to stay and be part of the family. He'll treat her well, at first. Worse, the longer she resists, and she *will* resist. But they won't kill her. Friend has been looking for her, for me, for a long time now."

"But why? Why Hannah, why you? Who, or what, the hell is Friend?"

She turned to me, blue eyes sparkling like lake ice in the sun. "That's a long story, but we have the time. Follow me."

She turned and started to walk deeper into the trees, up the sloped earth towards the still distant peak of the mountain.

"I know this is going to be hard for you to understand," she continued as I moved to follow. "Some of it is strange, and some was never meant to be explained with words. I'll do my best. Friend is…" she trailed off, edge of her tongue caught between her teeth, searching for the right word, "a Visitor."

"An alien?"

"Sort of," she said with a casual shrug. "How you would understand it, I think that's close enough. He's a different lifeform that came from somewhere else, somewhere out there in the dark," she gestured upwards.

"So Lorenz was right? He's running some sort of breeding program?"

Wendy chuckled dryly. "Yes, though calling it a program is a little generous. Others like him exist, and they have programs. But Friend? He's alone. He had people once, but he lost them when he crashed here. He's been stranded ever since."

She was walking at a fast clip, and I found myself hustling to keep up, my brain racing along with my legs. "Ok, but why the breeders? Why our family?"

"Because we're not broken, and he needs us to win the war he thinks he's fighting. Half his kids lack any kind of power, and the other half are mules, if you catch my drift."

I blinked. "You mean they're sterile?"

She nodded. "Yeah. Or worse, gave birth to little monsters."

"But what about you, or your mother? You're not monsters, and…" The words died on my lips as I finally made the connection. "Hannah had you."

"And my Grandpa had her. A genetic line strong enough to carry his power," she said. "Grandpa was one of Friend's favorite children until Grandma came along. She wasn't part of the family, she was a breeder they took off the side of the road. But, one thing led to another, and they fell head over heels for each other. Friend was furious, right up until he saw Mom and realized what he had on his hands. You know the rest of the story."

I did – I'd heard most of it from Hannah's own lips during the hypno-regression sessions. "What about The Light? What the hell is that thing?"

"A God? A spirit? Another thinking aspect of reality? Carl would have called it an Ultraterrestrial, though I don't think the name really matters when you get right down to it. No more questions," she said softly, gesturing up the path ahead of us to where light was shining between the trunks of the trees. "You'll see soon enough."

We came upon a forest clearing through which a small creek ran, its waters running silver under the intense gaze of the light that hovered above it. It was massive, the size of a house, maybe bigger. And so bright it would have made the sun seem like a light bulb.

"It's another visitor," Wendy whispered, "one not like Friend. I think it came from somewhere closer, maybe Earth, or another version of Earth. Somewhere to the side. I don't know if it's always been with humanity, or if it showed up just to stop Friend, but it is here to help us, as much as it can."

"Why though? Why does it care?" I asked, surprised to hear how timid I sounded. It was like standing in the presence of some ancient God, the power rippling off it immediately understood in the depths of my animal brain.

Wendy shrugged. "Because it does. Though, if you're asking my opinion…" she trailed off, staring into the white light, a look of childish rapture on her face. "I think it has always been with us. Maybe it's part of our universal unconscious, or maybe it made humanity, or maybe it's just a tourist who took a liking to the locals. Whatever it is, it's here."

I should have felt excitement. Finally, a chance for answers, a chance to put an end to this nightmare. Now, staring at The Light, a cold sliver of rational doubt wormed its way into my chest. "How do you know we can trust it? It took you; it played games with Hannah's brain. Hell, it delivered us right into their hands."

"It can't always communicate in ways we understand, and it can't interfere as much as it'd like. Otherwise, it wouldn't have had to bring you and mom to Victor's Point. I won't pretend to understand it, but I think it's done everything it could to this point," she said calmly. "Why not go and meet it? It's why you're here. We'll have plenty of time to catch up over the next couple decades."

I looked at her, then forward toward the entity. "So, I will see you again? Your mother and I, we come out of this all right?"

Wendy reached out and wrapped her arms around me in a fierce hug. "The future is real, but it is not set. Who I am right now, in this moment, might never exist in your time. You need to make it happen, Dad. The Light is keeping me safe. Right now, you need to save Mom."

"I love you, kiddo," I said.

She flashed my own smile back at me. She started pushing me, and I obeyed. With each step, the light took on a viscous quality until I felt like I was wading through thick, warm syrup. Another step, I felt it pushing through the pores of my skin. Another, and I could feel liquid warmth seeping into my bones. And another, a spike of bliss shot through my brain until I stood beneath it, trembling.

An image came to mind – a red door. The red door of our red house on Strawberry Lane. A knock came from the other side, it was asking me to open it.

"Please," I whispered, imagining that door swinging wide. "Help us."

The Light crashed over me, lanced through me. My mind ripped free of its moorings and fluttered in the wind like pages from a tattered book. Suddenly, I was thirteen years old and pulling Hannah from the pool. I was fourteen, huddled from the rain beneath a freeway overpass, and stealing my first kiss with the love of my life. I was twenty-two and beating Adam Letchie, I was six and being kicked by my father. I changed, grew older, then younger, moments flying by on an invisible gale. I would have screamed if I had a voice, but I had no throat, no mouth with which to speak.

Then, a single image appeared before me: a single, dried yellow leaf.

The leaf twirled through the air toward me, then slid into my skin as if it were a ghost. Images flashed before my eyes, but not just images.

Understanding. I felt as if my mind was stretched across the stars, all points in existence laid bare before me. Time stretched, became malleable, and for one brilliant moment I knew all there was to know.

Then, without warning, I was awake, lying on the couch in a pool of sweat. Lorenz stood at the nearby window, a handheld video camera in his good hand, his wounded one wrapped in a ball of bloody gauze and seemingly forgotten in his excitement.

"Jacob, you're awake!" he said breathlessly. "It was the most incredible thing. The Light, it came right over the house. I must have half an hour of footage. This is remarkable, truly remarkable! Did you make contact?"

I laid there a moment, feeling something akin to shock. My throat felt like I had been guzzling hot sand and my bones ached. I croaked and a moment later Lorenz appeared at my side, pushing a water bottle into my hand. The water inside was lukewarm but it was wet, and it drowned the rasp in my throat.

"What did you see?" Lorenz asked as I drank. "Any images? Words of any kind?"

"I saw Wendy," I croaked. "And a leaf, and I think it showed me something but … " I tried to grasp at the memories, at that sense of cosmic knowledge that had momentarily stretched me to the corners of the cosmos. "It's hard to describe."

Lorenz frowned. "Take a breath. Contact aside, you're coming down from a massively powerful hallucinogenic. Your mind will need time to recover."

"Don't have that," I said, a powerful urge coming over me. I needed to get out into the world to go searching for Hannah, and I had to do it now. "Any word from Carl?"

Lorenz nodded. "He's still tracking Sheriff Quinn down. He'll be here as soon as he can, and then we can all go looking together. Safety in numbers."

I nodded, staring wide eyed around the room as if seeing it all for the first time. The image of the leaf came to mind. I wasn't sure what it meant, but I knew it was important. Was it a message, or maybe a warning?

A guide.

The thought slipped into my head in Wendy's adult voice. Then, following some strange intuition I could not name, I looked out the window to the backyard.

Hannah's garden sat undisturbed, protected in a cage of boards and chicken wire. And there, stuck in the wire mesh-was a leaf. *The* leaf.

Before I knew what I was doing, I stood and lurched to the window, stepping over Indrid's corpse, now covered in old sheets. Something about that almost struck me as funny. Here I was, having axe murdered four people, and about to investigate a dried leaf because my adult daughter from the future told me to. And the strangest part was, it no longer felt strange to me. For once, I knew exactly what I needed to do.

"I have to go," I said, eyes locked on the leaf.

"Go where?" Lorenz asked. "Jacob, you're still hurt. We all are. I know you're concerned about Hannah, but we have to play this smart. We can't – "

"I wasn't asking, Professor," I said, moving to the hall closet where I retrieved the shotgun I had bought and shoved a fistful of shells into my pocket.

"Jacob! Jacob, you need to sit down. You will need time to process what you just – Jacob!?"

He followed me down the hall and out into the yard. With each step closer to the leaf, a strange sort of humming started reverberating through my bones. I plucked the leaf from the mesh and turned back to see Lorenz standing unsteadily before me, as if to block my way.

"Please, Jacob," he said, looking dreadfully pale in the full light of day. "Let us help you."

"Wait for Carl and Quinn," I said calmly. "I need to go it alone for a bit. It's all right. I think…I think this is supposed to happen."

I released the leaf just as a breeze rolled through the yard. It danced in the air, just as it had in the vision. Then it twirled and flew off toward the woods.

And I followed.

11

ABDUCTIONS

1 – Hannah

Pain roused me from the deep black of a chemical sleep. My throat felt raw, and my lips burned with traces of whatever Astra had soaked the rag in. The intense pain came again, a sharp stabbing that lanced up my legs and directly into my brain. I tried to burrow deeper into my own mind to escape it, to fall back into a black nothing where despair couldn't find me, but the pain was insistent and eventually my eyes were forced open.

I was sitting on the floor in a small, ramshackle room. The walls were rough wooden boards, same as the door, the lone window single-paned so old the glass looked like it was moments from toppling from its rotten frame. My wrists were bound with coiled metal wire anchored to a rusted pipe sticking out of the wall. There was no furniture at all, just a bit of splintery debris lying in a heap in the corner.

That, and one little boy. He was sitting on the ground in front of me, one of my feet held delicately in his lap. He wasn't human, at least not entirely. The boy's skin had a thin, sallow quality to it, like old, yellowed tissue paper, revealing root-like patterns of veins pulsing softly beneath. He was bald, his cranium as enlarged as his eyes, each the size of a baseball and sparkling like sapphires.

He looked up at me and saw me notice him. Then he smiled, revealing two rows of needle-like teeth. He held something up in the hand. It was a long sewing needle, the top half of which was slick with blood.

"What are you – " I started to ask when he jabbed the needle into the bottom of my heel again, the tip scraping off bone and sending another surge of pain up my leg. I screamed and tried to pull my foot away, but his grip tightened, and he stabbed again, this time driving the point into the arch of my foot.

I kicked, managing to catch him under the chin with my free foot. The boy's head snapped backwards, and he fell away, letting out a sound not unlike a mewling infant. The boy scurried away, moving rapidly on all fours in a bizarre, herky-jerky motion until he pressed himself against the far wall, hugging his knees and staring at me with wide, wet eyes.

Before I could even begin to process what had just happened, the door swung open. Upon seeing the figure silhouetted in its frame, a man of titanic height, I felt a momentary surge of relief.

"Jacob," I whispered, "How did you find me? How long have I – "

163

"Afraid not, darlin'," the figure said. As it stepped closer and came into focus, the silhouette seemed to shorten and thicken. Mr. Friend stepped into view, his thumbs hooked under the red bands of his suspenders, a grandfatherly smile splitting his cottony beard. His eyes were black, though, like pools of glossy oil.

"Get away from me, you bastard," I croaked, pulling fruitlessly at my restraints.

Friend approached, then looked at my foot and winced. "Now, now, there's no need for the theatrics," he said as he knelt and with one calloused hand, snatched my foot and held it firmly. "I know what you must think. With all you have been through, none of us blame you for hating us, Lacie." With great care he grabbed the needle the boy had left halfway submerged in my foot and slid it free. "Forgive me, you prefer Hannah now, right?"

I bit my tongue so as not to scream.

"That will take some getting used to, but I suppose it will do. I did prefer Lacie, though, if I'm being honest. It was the name your daddy picked, before he lost his damn mind over that breeder."

"You mean my mother?" I snapped. If only I had my hands, I could rake my nails against those hideous black eyes.

Friend shook his head. "She was a spirited one, I'll give her that. Seems like she passed some of that onto you. That's good. It will serve you. I know you disapprove of how we have conducted ourselves, but you'll come around. You've been living among the cows for so long you think you're one of them, it's only natural. Give it time."

"My father didn't," I said flatly.

"Kids," he said with a heavy shrug, "never turn out the way you want them to. And the grandchildren they gave me, well," he gestured to the boy who still sat cowering behind him, "don't even get me started on those failures. But your Daddy? He was something else. Hell, I used to think he would lead this family someday. When he left, it about broke my heart in two. Hardest thing I ever had to do was kill him. It felt like I was murdering my golden child. The day we felt Wendy coming into the world was the happiest I'd been in years."

Wendy. Her name ran through me like lightning. "Where is she?"

Friend looked at me, one eyebrow arched in confusion. "Darlin', you were there. The Light killed her."

"No!" I said immediately. "Hanson must have grabbed her. There wasn't any…she wasn't in the pile of stones, she – "

"The Light killed her," he repeated slowly. "Go on, reach out, try to feel her out there. I'll wait."

I wanted to tell him to fuck off, but only a little less than I wanted to prove him a liar. I closed my eyes, reached out, pulsing Wendy's name over psychic radio, just as I'd done with The Light. Only this time, I felt no great swell of power and the only response I got was the dreadful quiet of my own mind. Tears pricked the corners of my eyes, and I opened them, staring hatefully up at Friend. "I don't believe you," I said, my heart breaking in my chest. "You've done something to her. Hidden her."

He laughed, a full-bellied chuckle. "Sweetie, if I had that kind of power, I wouldn't need her or you. Afraid even I'm not strong enough to snuff out a spark that bright. No, sadly little Wendy has gone and crossed that great rainbow bridge to the sky. But don't you worry. We have plenty of handsome young men here. We'll try again and you'll make a dozen Wendys for me."

Would that be my life from now on? Chained to a wall, used as a breeding sow by psychopathic telepaths? I pulled against my restraints, summoning up every bit of vitriol I had left. "I'm not giving you a thing!"

He reached out and cupped my face, forcing my eyes to meet his. "Hannah, darlin', look around you. It's over. We got you. That husband of yours and those poor folks you got helping you are going to be dead within the hour, if they aren't already. This is your life now. You can live it here, tied to the wall in a shack, or you can live it out there, surrounded by your brothers and sisters — your family."

"My husband is coming for me," I said, forcing hollow conviction into my voice. "And when he gets me out of these shackles, the first thing I'm going to do is rip your fucking throat out."

"That's simply not going to happen. I'll tell you what is, though," he said, his rumbling voice still warm as soft bread, at war with the indifferent malice in those black eyes. "You're going to stay in here for a week, maybe two. Long enough for the reality of your situation to set in. Then will come the sorrow, and the screaming and the moaning. But eventually, you're going to ask me to untie you. Maybe you'll play a game, try to get us to trust you enough to give you an opportunity to run, but even if you do, you'll soon realize there is no place you can run to. And in a month or so, you'll start getting used to the family. You'll find some small moments of joy to keep you sane and before long you'll forget what it was you were trying to escape in the first place. In a year, you'll be pregnant with another perfect grandchild. I'd bet the farm on that."

Hatred like napalm burned through me. I clutched it, fed it, anything to avoid feeling the black hopelessness that was congealing in my chest. I wanted to see him writhe, I wanted to boil his blood until those black eyes of his popped. I did as I'd done to Hanson, focused the rage into a barrage of cutting thoughts and sent them barreling at Friend. He winced, then flicked his finger.

A suffocating hand closed over my mind, abruptly silencing my thoughts. He smiled. "There's that spirit I was talking about," he said, both with his lips and in my mind, his psychic voice booming like dictation from God. He stood and wiped his palms on the legs of his pants. "You're going to come around, *Lacie*. It's in your blood. And when you do, your family will be right here waiting for you." He glanced at the boy who still sat cowering in the corner, one hand pressed to the ugly bruise forming on the side of his face.

"You come with me, boy," Friend said, holding out his hand. "Let your Auntie get some rest."

Moving tentatively, like an abused dog, the boy detached from the wall and marched sullenly to Friend's side. I managed not to scream until the door was closed and I could no longer hear his retreating footsteps on the gravel path outside.

2 – Jacob

All was as it should be. It was my only thought as I followed the twirling leaf through the front yard, across the road, and into the woods. With each step, I couldn't shake the feeling that I had been put onto a human conveyer belt. I had now entered a space where the only option was to go forward, no matter horrors what may lie at the end of the path.

I nearly lost the leaf twice; once when I slipped wading through a shin-deep river, and again when I got tangled in a thorny bush. Both times the leaf was waiting for me on the other side like a loyal dog, twirling in the air at head level, as if teasing me for my lack of grace.

After an hour, I came to a long dirt road I didn't recognize. It was overgrown at the sides, though not abandoned. There were fresh tire marks in the hard-packed earth. The leaf moved out into the road and started drifting slowly up its center, twirling impatiently. I wiped the sweat from my brow and turned to follow, when a sound caught my ear and I paused. It was a car, coming up the road behind me, and fast.

My first thought was that it was probably just a local out cruising the back roads or maybe a bunch of kids looking for a quiet spot to get fucked up, but the standing hair on the back of my neck suggested otherwise. Sparing one more glance at the leaf, I stepped back off the road and quietly slid into the shade of a dense copse of trees. Peering between two branches, I watched as a Victor's Point sheriff's cruiser came roaring into view, moving at a breakneck pace, leaving a cloud of dust in its wake.

I caught sight of the driver: Hanson, fresh from eating a pile of babies, or whatever the hell he did when not accosting my family. I watched it pass, breathing a sigh of relief as the taillights vanished around the next curve in the road. I waited until the sound of the engine died off, then stepped back out. The leaf was still there, floating high above me.

"Yeah, I'm coming," I muttered, jogging to catch up. Ears perked, I kept to the side of the road, close enough that I could dart into the tree line should another car approach.

It wasn't long after when the road began to incline upwards, the elevation slowly increasing. By the time I reached where the road became a series of crude switchbacks carved into the side of the mountain my lungs were burning, and I had a nasty hitch in my side. The mountain road was old and badly maintained, its edges uneven where sections of the road itself had broken free and fallen. There was an old wooden sign beside the road, barely visible beneath a shell of thorny thistle. The leaf fluttered to the sign and twirled around it. I followed and used a nearby stick to push aside the accumulated plant matter.

Welcome to the Mount Olympus Boy Scout Retreat, the sign read in faded red paint. Beneath that, someone had used yellow spray paint to add *'We Shoot On Sight.'*

The leaf twirled and suddenly shot straight up into the sky. I looked up, stupefied, as the leaf spun far above me, now little more than a speck against the blue sky. Did that mean this was the place? Hannah was somewhere up the mountain?

I hoisted the shotgun onto my shoulder and prepared for a climb. The sound of a dry click and the feeling of cold metal pressed behind my ear stopped me in my tracks.

"Easy now, Hoss," Officer Brandon Hanson said into my ear. "How about you drop the toy and get on your knees. Now." Before I could even think to disobey, my entire body cramped painfully and did exactly as he commanded. I watched in numb horror as my hand tossed the gun away. My body turned and dropped to its knees.

Hanson was right there, his uniform streaked with mud and covered in small thorny burrs as if he'd been running through the woods. His left hand was wrapped in gauze streaked with dried blood. The gun he held in his right hand was a *Dirty Harry* special, a .44 Magnum, and the business end was pointed right at my forehead. "Hanson," I said, wheezing through my constricted throat. "Where did you stash your car?"

He nodded up the hill. "Drove it up the first couple switchbacks. Thought I might have sensed you back on the road. Doubled back to make sure."

"Smart," I said.

He shrugged. "I do have my moments."

"And you thought you'd come down here and take me out on your own?" I said, forcing as much false confidence into my voice as I could. I needed to get him angry, or talking, or just delay him long enough to figure out how to break the hold he had on my mind. "Didn't work out so well for your friends back at the house."

Hanson grinned, then dropped to an eye-level crouch. "You think you really did something, don't you?" he whispered. "You killed off a couple of no-power half-wits and suddenly think you're ready to take on a god?"

"Thought I might try," I said voice even despite the titanic battle happening inside me. I strained against his hold, a low fury building to inferno inside my gut, but my body had become a cage without a door.

"You thought wrong," Hanson said calmly. Then, to my surprise, he slid his gun back into its holster and stood. "Get up. We've got a long walk back to the car."

My body did as bid as if hoisted on invisible puppet strings. "Not going to just pop me in the road?" I asked.

He frowned, waving his bandaged hand in the air before me. "Oh no, you son of a bitch. You have caused me enough trouble. Grandpa will get his crack at you, just like he wants. Besides, I'm a real ten-year plan kind of guy, and I can't have that little lady of yours peeking in my dome and seeing your face turn to confetti. Might sully our relationship."

Flames blasted against the bars of my cage. "Ship has sailed on that, you motherfucker. She hates you."

Hanson smiled, though his eyes remained hard. "For now, sure. But eventually all that rage will burn out, once she can't remember your face no more. When she gets lonely, I'll be there for her to cry on. I'll hold her close and make her feel safe, and when the time is right, I'm going to fuck her brains out. I mean really fuck her, a real righteous pounding. I'm going to do everything to that girl, and when I'm done that uppity little cunt is going to thank me. Who the fuck knows, maybe I'll even marry her. Pop out a couple more grandkids for the old man." He leaned in close, his breath cold against my ear. "Or maybe I'll just rape the bitch to death and leave her husk on the side of the road for the coyotes."

My vision flattened, the world falling away save for his face, his voice, his words, while the monster deep inside me howled for blood. I strained, then groaned, each effort sending another lance of agony through my cramping body, but it was working. I could wiggle my fingers, just a little. I summoned up my rage, my hate, everything inside me that wanted to rip and rend, and used it. I snapped my head forward, slamming it hard into Hanson's face. Hanson shouted, stumbled, then fell onto his ass, blood pouring from a broken nose.

His hold lessened, just a little, but enough for me to curl my hands into fists and take a step towards him. I grabbed him by the collar of his shirt and punched him in the mouth, splitting his lip and sending a spurt of blood down his chin. I raised my fist again with the intent to bash his skull in when something sharp pressed into my belly. My legs fell out from under me, twitching madly. The prongs of Hanson's Taser Gun were hooked into my skin a few inches above my navel.

The next thing I knew, Hanson was on his feet, face beet red and screaming. "You stupid fuck! You stupid breeder fuck!" Each word was punctuated by a hard kick to my ribs.

He knelt over me as I felt the psychic strings take hold again, pinning me to the ground. He raised his fist and brought it down on my face, my neck, my stomach, and groin, howling like an animal. I lost count of the blows as I felt my mouth fill up with blood and at least a couple of teeth.

He didn't stop until a thick sheen of sweat coated his face and his breath came in ragged gasps. "Oh no," he said, breathless. "Don't you die on me yet, you stupid fucking breeder. I'm not done punishing you."

He stood, then snapped his fingers. "Get up!"

My body moved to obey, despite the screaming pain that seemed to radiate from my very bones.

"Good doggie," he said, a vicious smirk on his face. "Now, march. We got a long ass climb to the car, and I ain't carrying you."

I wanted to tell him to fuck off or, better yet, tell him I would rip his arms out of their sockets, but the fight had gone out of me and my body had other ideas. With the mechanical efficiency of a tin soldier, I turned about face and began to hike up the long switchback road to Mount Olympus.

3 – Hannah

My arm was caked in dried blood from the wrist down, a consequence of the twenty minutes I spent pulling against the wire that bound me to the wall. Rather than break, it had cut into my skin. With the slick blood lubricating my hand, I had dared to hope that I might actually be able to slip out of this mess; but in the end, the wire won and all I got for my efforts was an increasingly deep gash in my wrist. I sat now in a puddle of red, staring empty eyed at the far wall, trying and failing not to believe that it was really all over: Jacob, Wendy, our little house, our plans for our perfect future. All of it was as good as smoke now, drifting and fading away on a killing wind.

For the sixth time in the last hour, I closed my eyes and tried to reach for Jacob, but I couldn't find him, or Wendy, or even The Light. My world, which days ago had been widening by the moment, had suddenly shrunk down to this barren room. I couldn't sense anything, couldn't touch the minds of the people I heard walking by outside. It had to be due to Friend's psychic manacle, so much like the one my father supposedly put on me the last time I was here.

I might have sat like that all night, silently hoping the cuts in my wrist would prove fatal, but as the light outside shifted towards the plum of evening, I heard someone approaching on the gravel path. I held my breath and listened as someone fiddled with what sounded like a padlock on the outside of the door. Despite myself, I couldn't help but hope, to imagine that door being thrown wide to reveal Jacob, Wendy, and fuck it, the whole US Army out there with tanks and flamethrowers and enough grenades to reduce Friend to a wet stain on the ground.

As the door cracked open and a head of blond hair poked through, I let that small hope wither on its vine.

"Hello, Astra," I said.

Astra stepped the rest of the way into the room, a metal bucket in one hand, a covered plate in the other, which she set down long enough to bolt the door. She had shed whatever strange illusionary disguise they wore to hide their nature, and she regarded me with sparkling, fist-sized eyes. "Brought you dinner," she said, collecting the plate and bucket. "You're in luck. Brother Jasper caught us a couple of wild turkeys to celebrate our family being together again."

I watched her with open suspicion as she crossed the room and set the plate down where I could reach it. I tried to ignore the savory smell that soon filled the room. I hadn't eaten since dinner the night before, and that had been a couple slices of cold pizza crammed down between hypnotic sessions. My stomach growled at the scent of warm meat.

"It's not poisoned, if that's what you're thinking," Astra said, setting the bucket down.

"Can't you tell what I'm thinking?"

She folded into a cross-legged position a few feet in front of me, just beyond kicking range, but close enough for me to see the momentary pang of guilt in her eyes. "I can, yes, but I won't. Not unless you give me permission."

"You didn't need it the last few times," I snapped. Anger was good. It helped burn away the fog in my head. I was beginning to understand why Jacob had such a hard time letting it go.

She knelt beside me and reached for my bound wrists. I flinched. "I'm trying to help," she said, nodding towards my bloodied wrists. "I don't want you to get an infection. Please?"

She didn't wait for a reply. Astra reached up and carefully worked to unwind the wire from around my wrists which, numbed from hours held above my head, flopped into my lap like dead fish.

Then, Astra reached into the bucket and pulled out a frayed rag, soaked in warm water, which she used to begin carefully cleaning my cuts. "Those last times, I didn't want to deceive you," she said softly. "I wanted to enlighten you – show you that you were so much more than you ever thought possible. But then you saw my real face, and Grandfather...well he has his own way of doing things." She shook her head. "I'm sorry. For any fear or pain I had a hand in. But you're here now; we can start over and be the sisters we were always supposed to be."

"And what? I don't get a say in this? What about what I want? What about my husband, my daughter, my whole fucking life, huh?"

"That was a lie, though. All of it. You never belonged out there. It's hard to understand but, to us, being alone like you were is an unspeakable hell. The more you explore your gift, the more you'll understand. We are all connected. We never have to feel alone, or afraid, or cast out. The family is always there for me, like it will be for you. Those humans, they could never really understand you. If only we could have protected Wendy, too."

"Protect her from what!?" I snapped. "You people talk and talk, but you never actually say anything. What is The Light? What is Friend? What are we?"

Astra looked back towards the door, then at me, her jaw shifting side to side as she ran some silent calculation. When she finally spoke, her voice had taken on a hard, grave tone. "Do you *really* want to know?"

I opened my mouth to say yes, or maybe to scream it, but something in her face gave me pause. Apprehension, fear. Suddenly the Astra who had whispered in my ear from the backseat of my car was gone and in her place was a frail woman with haunted eyes.

"Yes," I said.

She turned her attention to my wrists. Working quickly, she produced a glass jar from her skirt pocket and then pulled out two long strips of linen soaked in something sticky that she wrapped around my wrists. Then she wrapped those in more strips of dry fabric, tying each off with a small knot. "Too tight?" she asked.

I shook my head and she stood, holding out a hand to me. "Let's go. You can eat when we get back."

My heart skipped. Was she letting me go? I tentatively took her hand and let her guide me up onto my feet, stumbling the first few steps with my pins-and-needles legs. She led me to the door, removed the lock and threw it wide—letting in a gust of night air that smelled of campfire, meat, and the sticky sweetness of the pines. The world beyond the door revealed itself to be a shallow hollow, positioned near the peak of whatever mountain we were on. Beyond the door, a long gravel path stretched out, leading farther uphill towards a distant cluster of cabins.

"You aren't afraid that I'll run?"

She shrugged and led me away from the path, around the back of my prison where another gravel path led down the slope. "Where would you go? We own the town. Besides, you'd never make it down the mountain in the dark. Do me a favor though, and don't try. Grandfather would skin me alive if you got eaten by a bear or something."

I got the feeling that Astra was not exaggerating in the least, yet even as she spoke, I found myself staring down the slope of the mountain. Trees lined the southern edge of the hollow like a fence. Beyond those, the distant lights of Victor's Point shone against the evening gloom. So close, just a half hour by car, maybe less. Somewhere down there, Jacob must be looking for me. It took everything in me not to try screaming for him.

"Hurry up," Astra called from ahead of me. "Everyone is at dinner right now, but they won't be for long."

"Where are we going?" I asked.

Astra sucked in a breath, her massive eyes flicking upwards towards the sky. "We're going to where this started."

"What does that mean?"

She gave me a wan smile, "Fewer questions, more listening. I don't know everything, just what Grandfather told me."

The path ahead of us split, one path leading toward a large wooden building positioned at the very edge of the camp, the other leading toward a distant rocky outcropping. She chose the latter path.

"What's that?" I asked, pointing to the structure.

Astra followed my finger, then shook her head. "That's just where we keep the breeders," she said dismissively. She increased her pace, her words barely audible over the crunch of gravel at our feet. "Friend came here a long time ago, and he wasn't alone."

"Came here from where?"

She shrugged, gestured upwards at the blanket of stars that was just beginning to show through the last dying light of day. "Somewhere out there. Somewhere far. There were twelve of them at first, Grandfather's family. Friend was the youngest of them when they crashed."

"Crashed?" I asked. "Like Roswell? Like a UFO?"

"Yeah," she said dreamily, "something like that. He lost some of them that day. Others to the germs. And the rest to The Light."

That stopped me cold. "The Light? You mean it killed some of them?"

"Friend and his family, they first wanted to integrate with humans. Marry, have children, make a new home for themselves here, but the kids…" she trailed off, eyes cast down at the ground in front of her feet.

"Like Trevor?" I asked.

She looked at me as if slapped, "Yes, like Trevor."

She turned and continued forward at a brisk pace, the path rounding towards our destination. The rocky outcropping that I had spotted from the distance revealed itself to be the top lip of a cave set into the slope of the mountain with massive stones piled up at its sides and along its top, making the entrance a perfect, unnatural circle.

"They were determined to keep trying," Astra continued, voice shaky. "Then one of them made a mistake. There was a woman among the locals who was spirit touched and supposedly communed with their gods. Friend's people thought that she might be able to bear viable offspring, but her father wouldn't allow the union. They tried to bribe him by giving him gifts, but he was adamant. So … "

"They took her, didn't they?" I asked, eyeing the cave as we approached, the entrance yawning wide as though it was the dark mouth of the mountain.

"Yes. Took her, bred her. They thought that her connection to her gods was just a primitive understanding of telepathic abilities, but they were wrong." She stopped at the cave entrance, swaying with the wind as if she were no more substantial than a cloud. She turned and looked at me, her eyes questioning. "Do you understand?"

I wasn't sure if I came to the conclusion on my own or if she slid the idea into my head, but a sudden insight flashed across my mind. "The Light," I said. "The Light was their god?"

"Yes. Well, maybe. The Light is…something else. Grandfather thinks it's another visitor, one who somehow moved beyond a physical body, or maybe it never had one to begin with. To tell the truth, I don't think he really understands it any better than you humans do. Whatever it is, it has been here longer than us, maybe even longer than the humans. One thing we do know: it did not take kindly to us abducting one of its favorite pets."

Astra paused at the cave entrance to retrieve a lantern left hanging from a small, rusted hook embedded in the nearby rocks. She coaxed it to life, then continued forward, the light making phantoms dance up the smooth, glass-like walls of the cave. The cavity beyond appeared to be a large domed room, not carved in any sort of natural manner but molded from the earth as if shaped from putty. I spotted several areas where it looked like hallways had once branched off the central chamber, each long collapsed and filled with broken rock. Astra led me toward one such pile.

"I found this when I was a little girl," she said, as before my eyes, Astra slipped into the rock pile and vanished as if she'd turned into a ghost and passed right through. I stood stock still, eyes wide and stunned, when Astra's voice came from somewhere beyond the rock pile. "Come on, keep up."

I approached, noticing the thin light of the lantern streaming through narrow windows in the rock. One of them was large enough for me to crabwalk through, the placement of the stones rendering the passage invisible from the front and impassable for anyone as large Friend or Jacob.

"Think thin thoughts," Astra advised from the other side as I wedged myself into the opening. It wasn't until I was halfway through that I realized how monumentally stupid I was being. Here I was, free and unwatched. I could have sprinted out of the cave and vanished into the tree line before Astra could have squeezed back through. Part of me insisted it was because I knew Astra was right – I'd never survive a night out alone on the mountain. But another part of me, the new part that touched minds and spoke with living lights, knew better. I wasn't running because I needed to see whatever it was she was about to show me; to scratch an itch for truth that had been tormenting me since the moment this nightmare began.

When I emerged out the other side, Astra was standing there waiting, the light from the swinging lantern making a leering skull of her face. I looked past her into the chamber beyond. It was smaller than the first one, but more fantastic. The walls in here were some kind of metal, smooth all the way around with no sign of rivets or panels. In the center stood a strange mechanism consisting of a silvery plinth on which sat a five-foot tall, murky purple crystal. Four metal bowls were attached to the plinth on each side, all empty. It had the air of a dead thing, something that was once vital but now had nothing in its future but rot. Then I noticed the figures standing in the shadows beyond it.

Astra had obviously been waiting for me to see them, and when I did, I gasped and unconsciously pressed myself back against the rocks behind me. She smiled and held the light up so I could clearly see them. There were six figures, huddled together against the far wall, their massive glassy eyes wide open in their final moments of pain and terror. Their bodies were strange and elongated, like people fed into a taffy machine, with each arm ending in three eight-inch-long fingers. They appeared to be petrified, just as Mildred had been.

"Friend couldn't dislodge them without breaking them to pieces, so he buried the whole ship. This was the punishment handed down by The Light," she said. "Like Lot's Wife, only swap the salt for granite."

"Don't tell me you think it's an angel?" I whispered, trying and failing to fully wrap my head around the bizarre scene before me.

"Angel, alien, god, does the word really matter?"

Tentatively, I detached from the wall and approached the stone figures to study their faces more clearly. They were strange, yes, but there was something in their expressions that felt almost human. Pain, suffering, and love was apparent. Yes, love most of all. I could see it in the way they clung to each other, in the desperation wrought in vivid detail across their faces. One in particular stood at the front, arms splayed wide as if to shield his family from the coming end.

"He was alone for so long," Astra whispered in the dark behind me. "Long enough for anyone to go mad. All he wanted was a family, a place he could belong on this stupid rock." Suddenly I was aware of her arms wrapping around me, one palm pressed firmly against my belly. "We can give that to him, or rather you can. We've all tried and we failed; but your father, you, Wendy—I don't know why or how, but your bloodline is the key. All he wants is grandchildren. All that talk about ruling the world is just hot air. Give him what he wants, and we'll never have to leave this mountain. Nobody else has to get hurt."

Her honeyed words sank into my brain like a heady narcotic and, for a moment, it almost didn't seem so bad. Wendy was gone, Jacob likely dead. What did I have left if I walked off this mountain? An empty house? My garden? Even the dream of some distant city life now seemed a chimera. I stared into the stony eyes of the nearest figure and sighed. "I don't want this," I whispered. "I want to go home."

Astra tightened her grip into a vice-like hug. "Lacie, sweetie, you are home."

I almost gave up right then, almost sank to my knees and sobbed because, on some level, I wanted this nightmare to end, and that hurt most of all. There was serenity in surrender.

Before I could speak, Astra suddenly pulled away, turning back toward the rock pile we had slipped through, her head cocked to the side and a sharp tension in her posture.

"What's going on?" I asked.

"I'm not sure," she said, a small tremor shaking her voice. "Brandon is home. He's happy." Without another word, she snatched up my hand and led me forcefully from the cave and back up the gravel path. I expected her to lock me up again, but as we drew closer to the small shack that served as my prison, she instead ushered me onwards toward the cabins.

"Won't they be mad you let me go?" I asked.

Astra didn't reply, her lips drawn into a thin white line.

4 – Jacob

When we reached the cruiser, Hanson snapped his fingers and turned my consciousness off like a light. The next thing I was aware of, I was somewhere dark that stank of rot.

I opened my eyes, at first unable to make out anything more than moving shadows. My left eye was swollen nearly shut, and my right crusted over. I was now naked, sitting on a hard, splintery floor. I wiped at my eyes, peeling dried blood away like chipped paint until I could see.

I was in a cage made from old, pitted iron bars. One of many from the looks of it; at least a dozen more were set against the wall opposite me. Most were empty, but not all; at least six other prisoners on that side alone. Directly across from me a young girl sat naked, hugging her knees, her skin streaked with old blood and dirt. Her eyes stared sightlessly forward, empty of even the slightest bit of humanity, like a doll. Beside her, a man I'd initially thought was a corpse lay against the door of his cage, his skin stretched over bare ribs and joints swollen from God knows how long in a space no bigger than a dog kennel. Then I saw his chest rise on a ragged breath, spittle flecking his scraggly beard on the exhale. None of the cages were tall enough to stand in, forcing everyone to sit curled against themselves.

In the middle of the room, between the two banks of cages, a pregnant girl was writhing atop an old wooden table. She was human by the looks of it, no older than sixteen. Her skin was pale, covered in a veneer of sweat, and her eyes wide in wild desperation. She pulled at the thick leather straps that connected her arms to the legs of the table, her feet likewise immobilized in the vice-like grip of two grim faced men who stood to either side of her. Between her legs stood a woman with a deformed jawbone that gave her an enormous, hook-toothed, underbite. Some of the teeth were so long they had curved out of her mouth and back towards her face; the longest of which had grown into her cheek and then through it, the tip emerging just behind her ear.

The girl let out a pained shriek that was muffled by the cloth gag shoved into her mouth. She convulsed, and the air grew thick with the smell of dirty pennies.

The tusked woman shook her head. "She going to die."

"What about the child?" one of the men, a dark-haired youth with one human eye, and one softball sized eye, asked.

The girl begged with her eyes, straining, pleading, her words unintelligible but her desperation clear.

Her captors ignored her cries, all their eyes set on whatever was happening between her legs. She needed help. Now fully awake, I turned and pressed my feet against the bars of the cage, and pushed as hard as I could. Metal groaned softly, but the door held firm.

"Hey! Hey!!," I croaked, voice too hoarse to shout. "Leave her alone! I'll kill you – I'll rip your fucking heads off!"

I might as well have been screaming into a hole in the ground for all the good it did; none of them even raised their eyes to look my way. The girl's screams hit a fever pitch, her back arched into an unnatural horseshoe. Blood poured from between her legs, running down the legs of the table and pooling at the tusked woman's feet. She screamed, an awful, gut-wrenching sound. Then, very suddenly, the girl went limp. She lay twitching, her cries so soft they sounded like the cooing of a dove.

The tusked woman stepped back, held the girl's baby up to the light. As soon as I saw it, bile surged up my throat. It was an abomination, an undulating mass of exposed muscle tissue, patches of black hair, and barbed, bloody quills. It had no head or arms, yet there was an eye – a single exposed eyeball on the side of its body, rolling in its socket.

"Will it live?" one of the men asked.

The tusked woman held the squirming thing up to the thin light of the electric lanterns that hung from hooks on either side of the room. She turned it over, then shook her head. "It dead soon," she said dismissively. She handed the mass off to one of the men and said, "Kill it."

The man, a human-looking adult with salt in his beard, nonchalantly took the creature and hurled it at the floor in front of my cage. Its body split open like an overripe melon, leaking a mixture of sickly yellow puss and black blood. Yet, it didn't die. It screamed, an awful, shrill note like the warbling of feedback from a stereo. I clapped my hands over my ears and pushed myself as far away from it as I could. The screeching ended abruptly when the man brought his boot down on the dying creature, crushing its lone eyeball into purple jelly.

"What about the girl?" the youth with the mismatched eyes asked.

The girl was growing paler by the moment, her thighs and legs caked with blood and chunks of tissue torn free from her body as the thing was pulled from her.

The tusked woman shook her head. "She's done. Give her to the children."

Before I could so much as scream, the bearded man drew a knife from his belt and slid it across the girl's throat. Her eyes flew open and a gurgling gasp escaped her as blood flooded her open windpipe. She gagged and convulsed, shook violently, and finally, fell still.

Then I was screaming, threatening, kicking against the cage doors, weaving a tapestry of profanity, yet they kept ignoring me. I watched, powerless, as they dragged the dying girl off the table and set her down on the other side of the room, near what looked like an old cellar door. They threw the corpse of the thing she'd borne atop her.

The three talked among themselves as they filed out, though I didn't hear a word of it. My eyes were locked on the dead girl, her empty gaze staring right at me. For the first time since waking, the reality of my situation hit me. The people in these cages were the breeders, human stock to liven up Friend's genetic pool. I was now just a part of the inventory. Had The Light led me right into a trap?

I needed to get my wits about me, find a way out, and find Hannah before anything else happened. I tested the cage door again and, when it would not yield, called out to the other captives. "Hey, any of you know where they keep the keys to these cages?"

One of the others, the man with the spittle-caked beard, looked up, and tilted his head in confusion.

"Keys," I repeated, miming the motion of opening a lock.

He blinked, then nodded and pointed with one shaky finger. There, on the far wall, a set of old iron keys hung from a peg. It was too far – no way for any of us to reach them. I needed something else, something I could pick the lock with. I scanned the ground surrounding my cage and spotted it. One of the black quills from the newborn creature had broken off and was now stuck into the warped floorboards a few feet in front of my cage door.

I reached through the bars and found I could just barely touch the top of the quill with my fingertips. Gently, I began to rock it back and forth, trying to dislodge it from the floor, when one of the other captives sucked in a breath.

"Stop," a woman's voice hissed from somewhere to my right. "They'll hear you."

I looked up and noticed that the other captives within my limited view had all scooted to the backs of their cages, hugging their legs tightly to their bodies. A moment later, I heard the creak of old wood as the cellar door lifted.

The children that crawled up from the darkened hole were all wrong. Too many limbs or too few, twisted bulbous heads, hooked claws. No two were alike, but each horrible in its own way, a nightmare parade of twisted flesh and clattering teeth, chittering at each other like squirrels.

The largest of them was a boy with a matchstick body and a pumpkin head. His eyes were huge, great glimmering blue saucers that crowded half of his oversized face. The boy sniffed at the corpses and then let out a sound like the yipping of a puppy. Suddenly, the mass of children surged over the corpses, ripping away handfuls of steaming flesh with hooked talons. Others, those without hands, dove in mouth first, snapping through bones and chewing the girl's fingers off with razorblade teeth. Even the newborn creature was on the menu, snatched by two of the smaller children and dragged away where they wrestled for it like dogs, each with a mouthful of puss-slick flesh clenched in their teeth.

My stomach rioted and vomit threatened as I redoubled my efforts to get the quill, wiggling it back and forth until it dislodged and clattered to the floor. I tried to grab at it, and ended up only pushing it another inch away.

"Stop it!" one of the other captives hissed. "Stop it, she sees you, stop!"

I looked up and my breath left me when I saw what was perched atop the table. It was a young girl, or I thought she was female, based on the half-head of long blond hair that ran in gore-matted clumps down her back. The other half of her head collapsed inward like a rotten apple, the skin brown and paper thin, revealing pulsing veins of dark blood beneath the surface. Her arms dangled before her, elongated and seemingly boneless. At their ends, her fingers likewise stretched out, pooling in neat piles in front of her like unspooled ribbon. She smiled at me, then clacked her teeth hungrily.

I redoubled my efforts, scrambling for the quill, my entire body pressed painfully against the bars of my cage, all the while watching the girl slide off the table and begin to crawl towards me; her tentacular limbs whipped and slapped the ground in front of her. I brushed the top of the quill with my fingertips but failed to get hold. She was close, now only feet away.

With a shout I slammed myself against the bars, stretched my arm out as far as it would go, and wrapped my fingers around the quill just as the girl lunged. I snatched my arm back, narrowly avoiding her snapping teeth, then pressed myself to the back of the cage.

The girl screeched and thrashed, slapping the ground around her before hurling herself at the cage door. She reached through the bars, her elongated fingers whipping painfully across my legs, drawing thin lines of blood. I kicked at her, but there was no room to get enough force behind it. She snatched my foot, all ten of her fingers coiled around it. She pulled, dragging me a full inch, trying to force my foot through the narrow bars. Her grip was impossible – coiled bands as strong as iron cutting off blood flow and crushing the bones in my foot.

The quill, I thought desperately! It was still clutched in my hand. Holding it like a dagger, I shoved the sharpened point into her wrist, then her fingers. She cried, but didn't release her hold; in fact, she seemed to grow stronger. She forced my toes through the bars, then leaned in to bite them off.

I pulled the quill free, then slammed it through the bars into her one good eye with a wet squelch. The girl screeched, released me, and fell back, flopping around on the ground in a wild tantrum. Then, whimpering, she rolled up on all fours and scurried past the other children and back down into the dark hole of the cellar, taking the quill with her.

I pulled myself into a tight ball against the back wall of the cage, a deep tremor running through the core of me. The other children were still eating. The pregnant girl had been reduced to a wet pile of meat, her face an exposed skull that one boy was splitting open with the rapt joy of a kid on Christmas.

I watched as the boy brought the first handful of wet brain matter to his lips, listened to the smack of his lips and the clack of his teeth.

I closed my eyes, covered my ears, and swallowed my screams.

5 – Hannah

We slowed as we neared the cabins, peering between the moss-coated structures to the flickering bonfire that sat at the center of the camp. Over a dozen of Friend's blue-eyed grandchildren stood at the edges of the light, half looking elated, half exhausted, as they watched Officer Brandon Hanson preening like a prize-winning turkey.

He stood close to the fire, still dressed in his rumpled deputy's uniform, splattered with mud and flecks of blood. His face was visibly battered: nose crooked, lips split and dried blood crusted around the edges of his nostrils. Friend stood before him, thumbs hooked through the bands of his suspenders, smiling proudly. Astra led us closer, keeping to the shadows of a nearby cabin the whole time, until we were close enough to hear what Hanson was saying.

"… he was a big guy, but had a tiny brain," he boasted, smiling ear to ear. "Moment I saw him, there wasn't much he could do. Got the guy to basically beg me to beat him down, so of course I obliged!" He displayed his hands, not so subtly showing off the fresh tears and scrapes that lined his knuckles. "I beat that boy black and blue for what he did to our brothers and sisters, then marched him right here, just like you wanted, Grandpa. Guy didn't even get a chance to fight back."

Was he talking about Jacob? I looked at Astra, then back to Friend, sorely wishing I could peek into their minds, but Friend's lock was still firm. No matter how much I stared at the back of her head, Astra's thoughts remained barred to me.

"Uh-huh," Friend said. "And I'm sure you broke that nose at the gym?" Hanson froze, his eyes widening in obvious fear that vanished the moment Friend clapped him on the shoulder and laughed. "You did good, boy," Friend said. Then, to the rest of his grandchildren, he proclaimed, "Let this be a lesson to all of you. I can be cruel at times, but it's only because I know what each and every one of you is truly capable of, and I want you to be better. Yesterday, Hanson was a failure in my eyes. Today? He brought home the prize-winning hog."

"What are we going to do with him?" someone, a young woman in a Cream King uniform, asked.

"He killed Indrid," one added.

"And Bill, and Sampson, and Judy," called another.

They *were* talking about Jacob, he was here! I turned, scanning the cabins I could make out around me, searching for some sign of where they had put him. Around the fire, everyone was talking at once, the names of their fallen intermingled with calls for Jacob's head. Just as the clamor was reaching its peak, movement in the tree line caught my eye.

At first, I thought it was just wind stirring branches, but then I caught the flash of a pale face peeking out. I squinted, then saw it again, a familiar face among the trees. It was Sheriff Quinn, his Yosemite Sam mustache recognizable even in the gloom, and he wasn't alone. At least one other person moved through the darkness with him, heading away from the cabins and towards the shack where I had been imprisoned. But Jacob wasn't down there, he was-

Astra's words from earlier flashed across my mind. The dark structure I had spotted while she had led me to Friend's cave, the breeding pen. That had to be where they were keeping him. A surge of hope bloomed within me – the cavalry was here! If I could only get away from Astra, I could join them, free Jacob, then get the hell off this mountain. I eyed Astra, prepared to make my move, when Friend's booming voice silenced the bickering masses.

"Quiet!" he bellowed, hands raised for attention. "Quiet down now, children. The fate of dear Mr. Riley is my decision and my decision alone, do we understand?" When he received demure nods in return, he lowered his hands to thoughtfully strok his beard. "There is no denying Jacob's crimes against our family. But you don't throw out a slab of Grade 'A' Beef on a whim. So here's the deal. Ladies, if you want a crack at him, tonight is your night."

He then turned to Hanson, a ghost of a smile touching his lips, "And in the morning, Hanson gets to blow his damn head off."

Hanson's smile could have curdled milk. Meanwhile, I was fighting to silence the scream building inside my throat. I needed to move, and now, but Friend was already turning back toward the crowd, shooing them away. "Go on, enjoy yourselves," he said, "the night is only so long, and I expect to see some ox-blooded grandchildren in nine months."

Several of the women in the group tittered, and a few had already turned to get a head start towards the breeders' shack. If they got there too fast, they would find Quinn before he could release Jacob. I needed to buy time, but how? I was supposed to be tied to a wall right now. I could try to talk to them, but how long would it be until Friend ripped my mind open and saw the deception?

My only idea was a bad one, but it was all I had. I backed up, took two running steps to build momentum, and shoved Astra as hard as I could. She was caught off balance and stumbled, then tripped, falling out into the ring of firelight, her head bouncing off the hardened ground. I waited a beat, long enough for a few of the others to look up, to notice me, then I was running.

"What the hell are y'all doing!? Get her!" I heard Hanson scream. I spared only a single look back. Hanson was chasing me, and most of the others were moving to follow. But not Astra. She sat upright on the ground, a narrow gash on her forehead leaking blood down her face and over the needle peaks of her teeth.

Her voice slid into my thoughts; the tone full of hurt. *Please, don't do this, please.*

I ignored her, focused entirely on putting down first one step, then the next, sprinting full out under the light of a cold moon.

12

THE LIGHT BETWEEN US

1 – Jacob

Most of the children had gone back below by the time Sheriff Montgomery Quinn and Carl Newland opened the door to the breeding pen. What few remained were the smallest, wretches with mangled limbs, too weak to have gotten any good meat. They gnawed on shattered bits of bone and licked dark blood from between the cracks in the floorboards, hungrily snorting like hogs.

When I first heard the door open, I made myself small, dreading whatever nightmare had just walked inside. When Carl's face appeared at my cage door, I was sure that I had finally cracked, and was now full-on hallucinating.

"Wow," he said, "you look like shit."

"Don't feel much better," I said, surprised to hear how hollow my voice sounded. "Are you real?"

Carl smiled sadly. "Real as the shit in my pants. The sheriff led us up an old logging road. A leaf led us the rest of the way."

Sheriff Quinn appeared beside Carl and handed him the keys off the wall, all the while never taking his eyes off the remaining children or his hand off the butt of the revolver on his belt. "Get him out of there," Quinn said. "We need to be off this mountain before they notice us."

Carl did as asked, trying two keys before he found the right one. My entire body felt like one giant cramp after hours in the tight confines of the cage. Just the act of crawling out and standing brought tears to my eyes. "We need to find Hannah first," I said.

Quinn glanced at me, looking about twenty years older than he had when we met only weeks ago. "Mr. Riley, we have no idea where your wife is. Right now, my main concern is getting the hell away from the things that live on this mountain."

I blinked. "You knew about them, didn't you?"

"No," Quinn said. He glanced at the children and visibly shuddered. "All right, maybe I knew something was amiss. But not this. Nothing like this."

"I'm guessing they messed with his head, too. I had to practically force him into the car before he'd even look at the mountain," Carl whispered, reappearing at my side with a bundle of clothes in hand. The same clothes I had been wearing when Hanson grabbed me, fished from a bin of prisoner castoffs in the corner.

I quickly hurried to put them on. I wanted to be angry at Quinn, wanted to scream at him for not giving us more warning than he had, but I had nothing in me for him. Right now, Hannah was still out there and we were surrounded by monstrous telepaths. He had just handed me a chance to help her; my complaints could wait.

"We're finding Hannah," I said firmly. "I'm not leaving her on this mountain."

Quinn grimaced. "Jacob, you don't know what you're talking about. She could be anywhere out there, and that's assuming they didn't kill her already. Smart move is to – "

"She's running!" Carl interjected, standing at the lone, dirty window. I rushed to join him, squinting to make out the dark figures who raced by a few hundred yards from the building. I caught sight of her face in the moonlight. It was Hannah, no doubt about it, with a whole hoard of pissed off looking non-people on her heels.

I spun, scanned the room, and spotted my shotgun resting against the far corner, a quick plan forming in my head. "Carl, take the keys. Open the rest of the cages," I said, lifting the shotgun. Still loaded, and the extra shells were still in my pocket.

Carl moved to obey but was blocked by Quinn, "What the hell do you two think you're doing!?" he hissed through clenched teeth. "There have to be over a dozen of those things out there. We need to leave, now, while we can."

"I'd rather split your goddamn skull than leave her out there alone," I said, surprised to find I meant it. I'd murder him in cold blood if it meant another night, another kiss, another moment with my Rabbit.

Carl looked between us, then set his shoulders and looked at Quinn. "Sorry, Sheriff. I'm with the big guy. We've come this far – we can't leave her."

"Fuck her, don't leave us!" someone in one of the cages shouted.

Quinn looked between us, then out the window. "Fine! But nobody else. We won't get a group this large off the mountain alive."

"No," I said, eyeing the cages. "Everyone is getting out of here tonight, one way the other."

"Scatter!" Carl shouted. The thirteen other captives, half mad with fear and desperation, did just that. Running on cramp-hobbled legs, they teetered out into the night, gaining strength with each step. They spread out the moment they were through the door, some heading for the trees, others across the field, and even a few poor souls running towards Friend's cabins in their confusion.

The response was almost immediate: distant shouts filling the night, cries of fear and rage, and the ringing of a sonorous bell somewhere near Friend's cabins. All across the hollow, the dark shapes of the breeders darted about, soon joined by blue-eyed pursuers who had broken off from the pack chasing Hannah, creating a smokescreen of shadowy bodies and confusion.

"Stay close," I said, then we were running right into the bedlam we had created. Screams punctured the night, some ending in shrill notes of mortal terror. The grass was slick and a cloud shifted in front of the moon, plunging us into darkness. We made our way south toward a distant rocky outcropping, and then around it to the spot where we had last seen Hannah running.

We were halfway there when we met resistance, two figures springing out from behind a copse of pine trees. One, a portly man in a red hunter's flannel, tackled Carl to the ground. I spun and raised the shotgun, but the other, a smaller woman, leapt onto my back and snared her arms tight around my throat. The gun clattered from my hand as I struggled to pry her fingernails away from my windpipe.

Quinn drew his revolver and put two rounds directly into the portly man's back. He turned and pointed the gun at the girl, but he had no clear shot. She clawed at my eyes, shrieking in my ear until something swung inches from my face and she fell with a thud. Carl stood above her, shotgun in hand. There was a massive dent in her forehead where he had hit her with the stock. He swung again, one armed, and the girl's face collapsed inward.

"Did I...?" Carl looked like he was about to be sick. "Did I kill – I didn't – " he mumbled.

I grabbed him by the shoulders, spun him and shoved him forward. "Move!"

Then we were running again, more pursuers heading our way, drawn by the gunshots.

I scanned the ground in front of us, frantic, my mind repeating the same words over and over, Hannah, Hannah, where is Hannah!? We were nearing the rocky outcropping, the entrance to a small cave just coming into view, when suddenly, there she was.

Hannah darted around the rocks, her face slick with sweat, her arms covered in caked blood and bandages. I wanted to run to her, to embrace her, but then saw the half dozen blue-eyed non-people round the corner after her, their eyes so bright they glowed.

"Run!" Hannah screamed.

I raised the shotgun and fired both shells at the pursuers blindly. One of them fell, screaming, but the rest were still coming, and then we were all running. I fumbled for the shells in my pocket, drew two out, then stumbled and dropped them.

"We have to get off the mountain!" Hannah shouted.

"How!?" Carl shouted back.

"Make for the tree line!" she responded.

I reached for more shells, but I was going to be too slow. They were right behind us. A loud crack split the air, and the flare of a muzzle flash left white dots dancing in my vision. Then came another, and another. It was Quinn, stopped dead a few feet in front of me and firing back at our pursuers.

"Go!" he shouted between gunshots. "Go, go, go!"

None of us argued, sprinting past him as our pursuers scattered to avoid the barrage. I spared one glance back, when the gunshots stopped, to see Quinn frantically jamming a speed loader into his gun, two dead non-people at his feet and four more closing in. He tossed the speed loader and raised the gun, yet he didn't fire.

I slowed, then stopped, confused. Quinn's entire body was trembling. A moment later I saw why, as Hanson rounded into view, smiling like he'd just won the lottery.

"Is that you Quinn? Ain't this a small world," he called, mirroring Quinn's pose, one hand outstretched and curled as if holding a gun. He turned his hand around, and Quinn's body followed suit, pressing the barrel of his gun up into his own stomach. "Sorry to say, I don't have time to chitchat. But it was nice of you to drop in."

Quinn let out a single scream and began firing, shredding his own gut and blowing great bloody holes out his back. At that point, Hannah's hands were on my back, pulling me, urging me to move.

All around us, the entire hollow had descended into chaos: dozens of shadowy figures dashing about in the gloom; the sounds of distant struggle and the smell of gun smoke on the wind created a disorienting cacophony. It was Hannah who kept us on track and led us right toward the distant tree line near a small shack. We were nearly there when I spotted shadows sliding out from their hiding places among the branches. It was the children, their faces still crusted with the blood of the girl they had eaten. We skidded to a stop, scanning for a way out.

Blue-eyed people behind us, cannibal monster children ahead – we were surrounded. I hastily reloaded the shotgun, prepared to die fighting, when Hannah pulled me again, this time toward the shack.

We spilled through the building's lone doorway. The room was bare, nothing but splintery boards and a single window. I slammed the door shut and threw myself against it only a breath before I felt someone slam into the other side. Across the room, Carl went to the window then stumbled back. Outside the dark glass, the little girl with the boneless arms was peering in, the quill still jutting from her mangled eye.

"The gun! The shells are in my pocket!" I shouted. It lay at my feet, dropped in my rush to block the door. Hannah ran to my side, snatched it up, and retrieved a small handful of shells from my pocket. On the other side of the room, glass shattered and the girl's tentacle limbs began to snake inside while Carl, shrieking, clumsily swung at them with his cast.

Hannah had never fired a gun before. I wasn't sure she'd ever touched one, but when she raised it, there was a cold fury in her eyes and when she fired, her aim was true. She blew the little girl's head off in a spray of bone and blood. No sooner had she dropped when more appeared, clawing at each other to get through the window first. All the while, the door bucked and groaned against my back.

Hannah focused on the window, pouring slug after slug through the opening and reloading with mechanical efficiency, but it would never be enough. Outside the shack walls, I heard more and more of Friend's children arrive, the sound of axes against the shack wall joining the chaotic din. Maybe, I thought desperately, I could buy them some time. Throw the door open and leap upon them, take as many as I could down while Hannah and Carl ran. Before I could move to do so, the pressure on the door suddenly vanished.

I had only a moment to release a confused breath before a sharp crack sounded outside and hot pain lanced through my body. I looked down, surprised to see a red, wet spot growing across my belly. Hannah turned, saw me, and screamed.

The pressure at the door returned and this time there wasn't enough strength in my legs to hold it shut. I stumbled, a cold feeling sweeping up my body. There was a neat gunshot hole in the door, now splattered with my blood. The door opened and they started to rush inside, one woman near the front of the hoard brandishing a hatchet and moving towards me for the kill when something collided with her jaw and propelled shattered, bloodied teeth across the room.

It was Hannah, swinging the shotgun like a war hammer in wide, warding sweeps. I stared up at her, dumbstruck. Here we were, at the lowest circle of hell, and my Rabbit, my warrior bride, was still right there fighting for a lost cause like me.

Carl was at the window, screaming and trying to beat the invading children back with his backpack. On the other side of the room, more and more blue-eyed people rushed through the door. Maybe if we had more guns, or fuck, maybe if I had listened to Carl and gotten the Army... but the cold was spreading across my body and I had no more time for maybes.

Wheezing, I grabbed the hatchet the woman had dropped and struggled to my feet. If they wanted to hurt Hannah, they would pay for it, pound for pound. I reached for my rage, that old familiar weapon. My chest grew hot, vision flattened, and blood washed through my thoughts.

"I love you," I said.

Hannah looked at me, eyes wide. "Jacob, what are you – JACOB!?"

I bellowed and charged the doorway.

The moment I slammed into the people crowding the door, the world became a blur of motion and violence. I swung the hatchet, ripped ears and gouged eyes, snapped necks and shattered eye sockets. I was stabbed, punched, kicked, but I barely felt it, barely felt anything other than the blood hot on my skin, fueled by some manic engine of fury inside of me, singing the song I'd been born for. I managed to fight my way outside when I spotted Hanson moving through the crowd, pistol in hand, likely the same one I'd been shot with. My vision narrowed, a scream rose to my lips, and I ran at him.

Hanson grinned lazily, then held out his hand. I felt the strings of his psychic control hook into my body, twisting my muscles, demanding obedience, but this time my rage was greater. I shoved through the pain, watched the smug confidence on Hanson's face bleed into surprise, and then terror as I crashed into him and took him to the ground. Pinning his arms to his sides with my knees, I rained fists like stones over his face, cracking bone and tearing skin. I grabbed a fistful of his hair, ready to twist his head clean off his shoulders.

"I'm sorry," a soft, feminine voice whispered in my ear as a hand lightly touched the back of my head. "I can't let you kill him. I'm so sorry."

Like sinking into a dense fog, I suddenly wasn't sure where I was, or what I was doing. My body relaxed, the only sensation I felt was the blood pouring softly from my stomach and the deep exhaustion in my bones. I released Hanson and stood, unsure why I had even been angry in the first place.

Then it came to me. I knew what I was doing here. I had to go get my girl.

I turned, the hands not leaving me, now pressed softly against my back, guiding me toward the shack. We waded through the crowd of blue-eyed people who had filed in and surrounded Hannah and Carl.

"Jacob?" she said, her eyes growing wide as I approached her.

Somewhere deep inside me, a beast raged against its cage, demanding I open my eyes, demanding I think, but all my thoughts were unwieldy things and no matter how hard I tried, I couldn't wrap my head around them. It was better not to think, a voice inside me insisted, better to let this nightmare end as it must.

I approached Hannah, thought I'd like to embrace her. I was just as surprised as she when my hands rose and wrapped around her throat.

2 – Hannah

Jacob was killing me. I struggled against his grip, clawed at his hands, but he was still so terribly strong. He laid me on the ground, almost gently, his eyes dull and empty, face filled with a strange sort of serenity.

"I'm sorry," Astra said from behind him, her hands softly resting on his shoulders. "It's better this way. Grandfather would have never let you leave." She stepped around him, knelt beside me, and pressed a cool hand against the side of my face. I stared hatefully up at her, through the dark dots dancing in my vision. "You'll come around," she cooed, stroking my hair. "Once you wake up, he'll be dead, and we'll be like sisters. You'll see. Just give it a year or two. I promise, I'll make sure nobody ever hurts you again."

I tried to lash out at her with my mind, but Friend's psychic manacle remained firm. Desperate, I punched at Jacob, kicked, but he didn't even seem to register it. Just as the dark started to swallow me whole, Friend stepped into view above us, still smiling like the Coca-Cola Santa Claus.

"That's enough, Astra. Don't go murdering the blue-ribbon girl."

Immediately Jacob's hands retracted from my neck, and I gasped, then gagged, each cough sending a fresh lance of pain through my bruised throat. Jacob didn't release me entirely, though, instead he pinned my shoulders down, every bit of his body weight stapling me to the floor.

"Jacob," I wheezed, sobbing, "please, it's me. You have to – "

"Jacob ain't home right now," Friend said as he crouched down and rapped a knuckle against the side of Jacob's head. "Astra is a real maestro, ain't she? Too bad that womb of hers is more corrupted than a New York sewage drain, or we might have been able to avoid all this nonsense in the first place."

"Let him go," I wheezed. "I'll do whatever you want, just let him live, please, I'm begging you!"

Friend's eyes hardened. "When are you going to get it through your head? Your life was never yours, and he was dead the second you two met. You're property, and the sooner you understand that, the sooner we are going to start getting along." He grabbed my face and stroked my stinging cheek with his thumb. "Though it was mighty kind of him to come after you the way he did. Saved me a hunt."

"What do you want us to do about the runt?" Another voice, Hanson's, asked. He emerged from the group of onlookers, dragging a dazed Carl by the leg, bleeding from a fresh gash on his temple.

Friend leaned back on his haunches, looked from Hanson, to Carl, to me. Staring me in the eyes he shrugged. "Kill him."

"No!" I tried to shout, the sound coming out as a croak. At the edges of my vision, I saw Hanson slide a large revolver off his belt. "He's not part of this! He just wanted to help, please!"

Friend held a hand up, and Hanson paused, the hammer already drawn back, barrel pointed down at Carl. "Why should I show mercy, Lacie? These people on this godforsaken rock will never understand real love, or family. I used to think, maybe, someday, we could live among them. Be part of them, accepted and cherished. But you can barely stand yourselves, let alone us." He shook his head. "For our family to survive, all these damn savages got to go."

Hanson smiled. "Any last words, kid?"

Carl blinked, eyes swimming with fear, yet when he spoke he managed to keep his voice from shaking. "I hope your kiddies choke on me you son of a-"

The gunshot sounded like an explosion in the confined space of the cabin, blowing a fist-sized hole through Carl's stomach. He gasped as blood poured from his mouth. Pressing hands against the mess of raw flesh his belly had become, he whimpered. Then, Hanson cocked the hammer back again and shot him square in the chest. Carl's body seized, then fell still without another sound.

I stared at Carl's body, mouth open. "He was just trying to help us," I whispered, as if that would somehow bring him back to life.

Friend nodded, "Yeah, he was. And look where that got him. Hanson, bring that cannon over here," he said, slapping Jacob on the shoulder. "Time to put this Bull Moose down."

Panic cut a path through the shock and I watched as Hanson, grinning ear to ear, approached, and held his gun out to Friend, grip first. I craned my neck to look Astra in the eye. "Help us!" I begged. "If you really want us to be sisters, then don't let this happen!"

Astra smiled sadly. "This is for the best. He's right, they'll never accept us. You belong with your family, with me."

Friend took the pistol from Hanson, testing its weight in his grip. "You know, I never did like guns. Too crude, too brutal, like the humans. But after three or four centuries on this rock, I'm starting to come around. There is just something so satisfying about putting a hole in someone."

I watched as he lifted the gun, pressed the barrel against the side of Jacob's head. I reached for my power, pulled, begged, but it wouldn't come. I stared into Jacob's glassy eyes, trying to memorize every angle of his face. "I love you," I whispered.

Something shifted in his eyes, a moment of recognition, a soft twitch of his lips. "I lo-"

I barely heard the gunshot, just felt it, as Jacob's entire body jerked and hot blood splashed across my face. He remained upright a moment longer, his eyes still locked onto mine, but the man behind them was already gone. He crumpled to the floor, a twitching hand outstretched toward me as if in one last bid to hold my hand.

Then I was screaming and thrashing, an animalistic shriek tearing through my battered throat. It couldn't be true, this wasn't happening – and yet, the cold reality lay beside me.

Astra stroked my hair as Friend broke the momentary silence, his voice again soft and grandfatherly. "This was always going to happen," he whispered. "He was never meant to live."

I couldn't breathe. I tried to fight, to reach for his eyes and scratch them out, but other hands were holding me down. I turned my head and looked to Jacob.

"Please," I begged, "please, don't be dead, please, please – "

A boot appeared in my vision. Hanson, standing above me, Jacob's shotgun in his hands. He reloaded it, aimed, and fired twice, blowing what was left of Jacob's face off in a shower of brain and shattered bone.

"I dunno," he said, "seems pretty dead to me."

I stared up at him, uncomprehending, every thought wrapped in chains of shock and grief.

"Kill me," I whispered.

Friend cupped my cheek, drew my face to stare up into his. Before my eyes, he was changing, the pudgy face and scratchy cotton beard sinking away into a hard, narrow chin and a domed head. His skin darkened, as if rotting, until it took on a rubbery grey texture. His eyes were the worst though: massive, wrap-around tear drops the color of crude oil.

Not yet, Friend's thoughts pounded into my head. *Not until you've given me some proper children.*

Staring into those hateful black eyes, seeing my own terrified face reflected there, something inside me began to stir. Not the fear I expected, or the rage. Without knowing why, I thought of Wendy, taken from us. I thought of Jacob, dead at my side. A chasm of grief a mile wide cracked open across the bedrock of my soul, and from it something rose.

Friend's eyes widened; he stood and began to back away.

Everyone out! He commanded over psychic radio. They released me and began to flee, but too slowly.

Friend's mental lock groaned, then shattered. A rumbling shook the cabin as a white light began to fill it. Not from outside, but from *within,* pouring from my eyes and mouth and ears as if I'd swallowed the sun. The non-people writhed, clutching their heads, blood flowing freely from their noses. I thought about Jacob and me, holding hands as we drove through the countryside. I thought about putting Wendy to bed, and making love, and all the futures we had dreamed that now lay dashed on the floor beside me. I thought about the freeway overpass where we'd shared our first kiss, the chill of rainwater slick on our lips, and something bright warming us from within.

Hanson appeared above me, hands on my throat, squeezing. "Stop it! Stop it you fucking whore!" He screamed as blood poured from between his needle teeth. I reached up, cupped his face as I had done to Jacob's a thousand, thousand, times. Only this was not Jacob, and the love in my heart changed, sharpened into a blade. White light burst from my fingertips. The flesh of his face blackened, then peeled away, and for a moment a leering skull hung above me, shrieking as his eyes boiled from their sockets. Then I pushed outwards, the light swelling to a blinding maelstrom.

There was a great booming sound, and a dozen voices rising in one shrill note of unified panic. The roof cracked, the walls buckled, and the shack exploded.

3

I sat up and surveyed the wreckage. The cabin had been blown to splinters; the debris field stretched a hundred yards in all directions. The remains of Friend's children lay around me in heaps of bleached bones, some with mummified skin still stretched over them. Were any of them Friend himself? I couldn't be sure. I stared at each body and then, when I had nowhere else to look, I turned to Jacob.

Her light hadn't touched him or Carl, though part of me wished it had. The sight of the ruined hole where Jacob's face had been nearly broke the last thread of sanity from which I hung. Hands shaking, I cleared the rubble off of him and covered his shattered face with the singed remains of someone's shirt.

"I'm sorry," I whispered, pressing my lips to the spot where his forehead had been. "I wasn't fast enough, I couldn't stop –" my voice broke and a screaming sob ripped out of me. I wanted to die, to burrow beneath the stones beside Jacob and wait for the worms to pick my bones clean. I thrashed, throwing stones at nobody, anything to give voice to the howling emptiness inside me that demanded to speak. Frantic, I found a rock with a sharp edge and raised it high with the intent to smash it into my own head.

Stop! That single word crashed through my mind in an awesome wave. I looked up and found its source. The Light floated high in the sky above me, watching. *You must survive.*

I looked from The Light, to the rock, then back, surprised to find that a small ember of rage still burned in my chest. "You could have stopped this," I said. I stood, staring defiantly up at The Light. "We did everything you wanted. You led us by the nose right to their door, when you could have finished Friend years ago! You could have stopped him, so why!? Why us!? Why Jacob!?"

The Light pulsed, and a gentle wave of warm love crept over me, pushing at my thoughts, trying to calm me. I resisted it, rolled my shoulders as if to shrug it off. "No! You answer me right now, you son of a bitch!"

For you to become who you are, the thought came. An image flashed to my mind, a winding road stretching from this point onward over a dark, moonless road. *Your path is long. There is much for you to do.*

I laughed, a hysterical, bitter sound. "So that's it? This was all, what? Training for something else? Well, I don't want it. I want Jacob! You bring him back. You do it right now!"

I cannot.

"Then what good are you?!" I was growing dizzy, my breath coming in sharp gasps. "I can't do this alone. I can't keep walking forward without him – I – I can't – " I squeezed my eyes shut, stumbling, falling, each breath a sharp dagger in my lungs. My whole body felt hot and sore, my brain screaming in a thousand directions but returning to the same thought over and over again: Jacob was dead, he was dead, he was dead.

You are not alone. This time, the thought brought an image, a babbling infant with a shock of red hair on her head.

"Wendy?" I gasped, looking up. "She's alive? You know where she is?"

She is safe, for now.

"What does that mean? Are you threatening her!?"

The Intruder will never let her go. As long as he lives, she will be hunted.

"Friend?" I said, looking at the wreckage around me. "He's dead, he has to be."

Stop thinking. Feel.

I glared balefully at The Light, then reached out as it suggested. I felt Friend almost immediately. His rage and his pain pulsing loud as a rock concert over psychic radio, coming from the direction of the cave.

As long as he lives, The Light continued, *she will never be safe.*

"And what if I'm not strong enough?" I whispered. "Whatever I just did, I don't think I can do it again."

You are, and you will.

What choice did I really have? Legs shaking, I stood. Stood because Wendy was out there, and she needed me. Because the last vestige of my husband, of our life together, needed me. A simple fact that became the hard stone on which I stood. "Promise me," I said, "that I'll see him again."

From the one to the one, all things come in time.

I wasn't sure I understood, then I realized it didn't matter. It didn't change what I had to do. I searched through the rubble and discovered that all the guns had been warped by heat or broken in the blast. Instead, I found one of Hanson's rib bones, the tip sheared off into a sharp point.

Clutching it tight in a blood-crusted hand, I followed the pulsing of Friend's misery, The Light trailing me every step of the way.

I was halfway to the cave when I found Astra. The woman was lying in a heap at the base of a tree where she had collapsed after fleeing the cabin. The skin of her hands had burned away to blackened bone, a few toasted ligaments still somehow holding the fingers on. Trevor lay with his bulbous head on her lap, his eyes glossy in death and his limbs a smoking, twisted ruin.

As for Astra, shards of cabin walls and debris poked from her body in half a dozen spots, seeping glossy blood that shone in the moonlight. Her face was the worst of it, her nose gone, left eye punctured by a splinter and protruding halfway from her skull. She ought to have been dead with all of those injuries, but as I drew near, I watched her one remaining eye flicker towards me and focus.

I knelt beside her, feeling for her thoughts. There was pain and fear, yes, but these were distant things, echoing into a vast and growing darkness. "You're dying," I said, surprised to find I felt no joy in this revelation. She had drugged me, played games with my mind, and in the end, despite all her talk of sisterhood, she had controlled Jacob and delivered him to his murderers. Even so, there simply was no room left in me to hate her.

I suppose I deserved this, huh? she thought at me, the connection sputtering as her brain struggled to live another moment.

"Yes," I said without malice, "I suppose you do."

I thought that he would let Jacob live. I thought he would want to keep him as a breeder.

"No, you didn't," I said. "You knew exactly what would happen. This whole time, you knew Jacob was never part of the deal, from the first moment you saw me."

Astra considered this then, minutely, nodded. *I'm sorry,* she thought, and on some level, she meant it. *Friend, he has a way of* —

"Don't you dare," I said, gently wiping bloody strands of hair from her brow. "Don't explain it away. You did what you did."

Can you forgive me?

"Probably not, no."

To my surprise tears began to flow from her good eye. I wouldn't have thought she had enough moisture left in her to spare, yet there it was, carving a path through the soot and blood on her face. *Will you kill Grandfather?*

"Yes," I said.

Will you kill me?

"I already have." I leaned down and kissed her on the forehead as I felt the dying sparks of her final thoughts racing towards oblivion.

Goodbye. I wanted to love you.

"That would have been nice," I said. "Goodnight, sister."

I left her there, watching me with one luminous eye as I continued down the gravel path. I didn't look back, but I felt her go as a soft rush of wind that danced past me, trailing thin fingers of air over my skin before heading off to whatever came next.

I paused, eyed the rocky outcropping that concealed the cave, only fifty yards ahead now. Power was pooling there, a great sea of hatred and sorrow that seemed to suck in all light and give nothing back. It was a leviathan, whose lashing tentacles could cleave mountains and reduce cities to ash. Nevertheless, when I began to walk again, I felt no fear. I was tired, and filled with a grief I was sure would kill me, but not afraid.

I walked around the rocks and into the dark mouth of the earth.

4

The cave was different than it had been when Astra led me here only hours before. Deep cracks split the walls, and the path that had been blocked by fallen debris was now blown clear, as if by a bomb. As I approached, I felt stray bits of thought bleeding off Friend, exploding away from a fracturing mind like shrapnel.

Gone. Dead. Failure. Alone. Death. Alone. Girl. Hate. Murder.

Steeling myself, I walked down the passage and into the buried ship, following the flickering lantern light. Friend was there, wearing his true face. He stood beside the petrified remains of his family, one hand resting atop the head of the smallest.

He looked up as I entered. I expected him to assault my mind. Instead, the room twisted around me, the walls melting away, becoming trees and blue sky. In an instant, I could no longer see the cave or Friend. I found myself crouching in my garden at the little house on Strawberry Lane, my hands half submerged in rich, dark earth. A hawk circled high above, wind rustled through pine needles, and a squirrel chattered noisily at me from the trees.

There was a garden trowel in my hand and an odd plant rooted in the ground between my knees. The stem and leaves were pale blue and reflective, like silver. The flower at the top, or maybe it was a fruit, was the size of an egg and glowed with a soft yellow light.

"There isn't a name for it," a voice, soft and friendly, said. "Not in your tongue, anyway."

Mr. Friend, wearing his rosy-cheeked human mask, was leaning casually against the fencepost at the edge of my garden, just as Astra had the day we met.

Then, in the blink of an eye, he was kneeling at my side. He ran his calloused fingers over the smooth leaves of the plant. "They take a thousand years to grow. Once they're mature, they yield only a single fruit. I've only ever had one, but the taste is indescribable. Like eating sunshine. Gives you a real boost in the noggin, too," he said, rapping his knuckles against the side of his head. "If I had a field of them, I never would have had to bother you or your family. I would have had all I needed right here to turn my children into proper powerhouses."

"Too bad you didn't," I said. "Your kids might still be alive."

His smile didn't fade. He looked off into the middle distance, blue eyes twinkling. "Well, maybe that's for the best, right? Cut the chaff, leave behind the best of them all. Say, how about we make a go of it? Rebuild. Do it right this time."

It took me a moment to realize he was talking about me. "You can't honestly believe I'd ever trust you," I said.

"Now hold on," he said. "Before you go doing something foolish, I want you to think for a moment here. Jacob is dead, and I couldn't change that even if I wanted to, which I don't. He was a good breeder, good stock, but that was all he was. A lesser life form. But you, what you did in that cabin? You're a miracle, Hannah. Your mind is more powerful than anyone could have ever expected. Maybe it's because The Light chose you, or maybe you just won the genetic lottery, but you have been handed the keys to the whole damn world. There isn't anyone alive on this miserable rock who will be able to resist you. Just think, you could have a thousand Jacobs, and from them, a thousand Wendys ten times stronger than you or I could ever be. You could live wherever you wanted, do whatever you wanted."

"And I suppose you would be right there by my side, reaping the benefits?"

He frowned. "You misunderstand me. I'm cruel, yes, but I've been made that way. The Light is the enemy here. It stole my family and my future. And it delivered you and yours right into my hands. It could have warned you, prepared you, but it didn't. I might be a liar, but that thing? That thing doesn't even have a concept of truth or lies. We don't have to be its victims. You, you're strong enough. We could destroy it, if you were properly trained."

I tried to imagine it – killing The Light, putting an end to whatever destiny it had planned for me. Living as a queen with a thousand puppets all dancing to my strings, filling my bed with lovers and luxury and a profound emptiness.

"I'll do it," I said, "if you can bring Jacob back to me."

"Dammit, girl, ain't you been listening!? You don't need him! He was just meat, a fucking sperm donor. You have the keys to the cosmos at your fingertips and all you can think about is some ape who never amounted to squat."

"So, you won't do it?"

"I can't!" he shouted, irritation bleeding to rage. "What's done is done!"

I tightened my grip on the trowel, closed my eyes, and soaked in the last bit of illusionary sunlight. "Then I think, Mr. Friend, I think it's time we said our goodbyes." I stabbed the trowel into his stomach, and the false world shattered around me like porcelain, revealing the smooth walls of the ship. The trowel embedded in his stomach also changed; it became the rib bone I'd taken from Hanson's corpse.

Friend shot up and stumbled back, screaming, the sound both in my ears and my head. *You stupid fucking sow! I'm giving you everything! I'm giving you the whole damn world!*

I struggled to stand, each of his words sending lances of blinding pain through the center of my head. Gritting my teeth, I threw power right back at him, imagining a blistering column of flame enveloping him, fueled by the maniacal engine of hate that had churned to life inside me. Friend clutched his head, his knees shaking. Yet, he didn't drop. He took a shaky step forward, then another, gaining strength. I reached deeper, pushed harder, but something was blocking me, a psychic shield like steel that wrapped around his mind. Suddenly he was on me, his massive three-fingered hand enveloping my face.

Did you think it would be so easy!?

He lifted me and hurled me into the wall. Something snapped in my arm and pain whited out my vision and broke my focus.

Friend advanced, his narrow slit of a mouth turned down into a hideous scowl. *My species conquered the stars when yours were still monkeys. I was ancient before you were even a thought. I have seen thousands of worlds, realms you cannot imagine, and you thought you'd kill me with a rib bone!?*

He grabbed me by my head again and lifted me. I kicked, clawed at his hands with the one arm I could move, but he held firm, bringing my face within inches of his. *I've changed my mind, Lacie. I am going to kill you.*

He slammed me back into the wall, driving the air from my lungs. He did it again and dancing stars blasted across my vision. This was it, I thought. Soon he'd split my skull against the metal wall. I closed my eyes, ready for it all to end. I thought of Jacob, of running towards him, sinking into his arms. I thought of Wendy, alone in this sandpaper world that had ground me down to dust.

With the next slam, my head bounced off the steel and my vision flashed white. Then there was no more pain, no more anything. All around me was an endless white void, through which gossamer ribbons of bright light floated through the air like seaweed drifting on an unfelt current. There was no floor, no ceiling, no anything.

Am I dead? I asked.

Very nearly, but not yet, a young woman's voice responded. A vision appeared before me. She had my face, Jacob's crooked nose, and a shock of her father's bright red hair.

Wendy?

Wendy smiled. *You look like shit, Mom.*

Are you here to take me away? Is your father here?

Yes. But that doesn't matter right now. You need to fight.

I tried, I protested. *I did everything I could!*

She shook her head and took my hand. *Stop thinking like Dad. Rage, fury, vengeance: none of that was ever going to be enough to beat him.*

What am I supposed to do? I'm not strong enough to do this alone!

At that instant I heard another voice, deep and soothing, at my back. *Nobody ever said you needed to, Rabbit.*

Wendy took my hand. *Use what matters. Use what has always mattered.*

The ribbons pulsed brighter, swirled closer, and enveloped us as powerful arms wrapped around me from behind. I sank into a warmth without limit, a feeling I knew all too well, distilled from a thousand midnight kisses, changed diapers, inside jokes. I was hurting, yes, but in that hurt, there was something else, something old, and powerful, and perfect. Suddenly I was in the cave again, my face still clutched in the grip of Mr. Friend as he lifted me from the wall and prepared to deliver the final blow

I thought of Jacob, of Wendy, of that bright light of love between us. With a scream on my lips, I pushed that light into the world. It streamed from my eyes, my ears and my fingertips, swirling in the air around us. Friend hesitated.

What are you doing? He thought, unease stirring in his heart. *What is this?*
An act of love.

The ribbons of light curled around Friend, snaring his arms and wrenching them away from my face. I called for Jacob in my mind, and he came, stepping out from one of the ribbons as if it were a doorway, his entire body glowing and whole. With bearish arms, he grabbed Friend around the chest, pinning his arms to his sides. Friend thrashed and clawed at Jacob's arms, but his fingers went right through them as if they were water, leaving ripples in their wake.

Release me! Friend shrieked over psychic radio, terror rushing off him in nauseating waves.

I stepped forward and stared into the midnight-black eyes of Mr. Friend. I thought of all his mad plans and efforts, all the pain he inflicted in an insane quest to get what I had all along: a place to belong, a life to share, and love. Love most of all.

I thought of Wendy, and so she appeared, stepping out of the light beside me. Together, we placed our hands on Friend's shoulders.

You can't do this! I made you! I'm the only one who can show you your real power. I'm
—

No, we thought in unison. *This is real power.*

Together, we pushed, the light surging off all three of us, crashing into Friend, into the awesome immensity of his mind. He revolted, sending psychic assaults at us in rapid fire, each blow like the thunderbolt of a god yet entirely ineffectual, splintering against the light that encircled us.

Friend threw his head back and screamed. The sound echoed around the metal chamber, multiplying until it seemed all the souls in hell had come forth from his throat. I felt the moment his defenses fell, his mind sending out one last hateful pulse before the light poured in through his eyes.

Friend seized, his whole body going rigid, fingers curling inward like dead spiders. Then, with one last gasp, he turned to stone.

5

I swayed on my feet, then stumbled, legs buckling. I would have fallen if not for Jacob, who caught me and lowered me to the ground. He still glowed, the old scars on his face and hands wiped clean in death.

"Please don't go," I whispered, exhausted down to my fingernails.

He smiled sadly and kissed me on the forehead. "I'm OK, Rabbit. And so are you. I'll be waiting for you, when it's the right time."

I must have blacked out, because the next thing I knew I was sitting on the ground at the base of Friend's calcified body and Wendy, again an infant, was sleeping soundly in my lap. It took me an hour to drag my battered body out of the cave, up the gravel path and into one of the cabins, where I fell onto the first bed I found, curled around Wendy, and slipped into a pure, dreamless sleep.

When I woke I was initially confused, staring at the rough timbers of the cabin's ceiling. With a jolt, I remembered where I was and what had happened. My heart sank and it was as if Jacob had died all over again. Then the screaming came again, and the body wracking sobs that only stopped when my throat was hoarse and my eyes burned. That's when I smelled the mess in Wendy's diaper, saw the concern painted vividly across her blue eyes. Sore in every joint, I forced myself up.

I fashioned a sling out of an old bed sheet. I checked the pantry, and found it filled mostly with jars of preserves. I cleaned Wendy with a bucket of water drawn from an old well, then fed her apples mushed into a fine goo, working slowly around my broken arm. Carrying her on my hip, I dared to step outside to see the wreckage of the previous night. I couldn't bear to look to Jacob, so I saw to Carl first, dragging his corpse out from the debris. I pushed his eyes closed, and then I wrapped him in a blanket taken from one of the beds. I did the same for Quinn and the breeders who hadn't made it off the mountain. Just as the sun began to sink beneath the curve of the mountain, I finally went to Jacob.

There was very little left in the mangled corpse that looked like my husband, save for his hands. I took one and interlaced my fingers with his, trying to ignore the chill in his flesh. Tentatively, I reached for that piece of him that had lingered after death long enough to help me destroy Friend but found only a void where something had once been and since departed.

"I'll take care of Wendy," I said, hoping that somehow, somewhere, he could hear me. "I'll make sure she grows up just as strong as her Daddy. I'll make sure she knows you were a hero. And I'll…" I couldn't continue. I just wanted to tell him to get up, to scream at the injustice of it all. Jacob was supposed to be here, in my arms. We were supposed to move to some big city, put his past behind us, embrace our future. He was supposed to watch Wendy grow, intimidate her boyfriends, and become a tired old man. He was supposed to be mine and I his. Not in some distant place beyond death but here, now. As unfair as it was unchangeable. I stayed with him until Wendy began to cry and the coming night snuck a chill into my bones. Then I kissed each knuckle on his hand and told him I loved him one last time. I lingered a moment longer, waiting for a reply I knew wouldn't come.

Wendy and I stayed in Friend's camp for two more days. I buried Jacob, Carl, and Sherriff Quinn on a quiet patch of earth on the eastern slope, where they could see the sunrise. The rest of Friend's grandchildren I burned, piling them up in of the cabins before lighting the whole thing up. The stench of charred pork hung in the air for hours, until an afternoon thunderstorm washed it all down the mountain.

After that, I expected someone to have seen the smoke. I waited for them to arrive: cops, the forest service, or hell, more aliens. Instead, the figure that eventually limped into the camp, dehydrated and delirious, was Dr. Lorenz. He looked like he hadn't slept in days and was still wearing the same sweat-stained clothing I had last seen him in, now decorated with twigs and smears of dirt. He mumbled unintelligibly as I led him to a bed. After twelve hours of sleep and many tiny sips of water taken from a bowl, he eventually woke.

Upon seeing me at his bedside and noticing the bruises on my face and the thousand little wounds that covered my body, he frowned. "Is it over?"

I nodded.

He looked around the room. "What happened? Where are Jacob and Carl?" When I didn't reply he studied me, his eyes softening as he realized what my silence meant. "*Oh*," he whispered.

I spent another day with him and told him what had happened as best I could. In return, he told me his story. How he had come looking for us after Carl and Quinn didn't return, how he had stumbled from our house, weak from his wounds, and gotten lost trying to follow Jacob's trail. He spent two nights freezing in the forest until a leaf came along, spoke to his mind, and showed him the way. When we came to the end of our tales, we were sipping broth on the porch of Friend's cabin and watching the sky fade to darkness. I broached the difficult topic I had been dreading since the moment he stumbled into camp.

"We can't tell anyone," I said.

Lorenz's eyes widened and he sat up straighter. "Why? This story and what you went through? It's remarkable. Paradigm changing, even. Friend, The Light, it's a whole new world. People need to know."

"Who will believe it?"

"I have footage!" Lorenz said. "Back at your house, I filmed The Light. I have pictures, sensor data. It's a treasure trove! They'll believe, they'll have to."

I nodded. "All right, let's say they do. What happens then?"

His eyes lowered in thought. "Well, I imagine researchers will want to come here. See the cave, see the bodies. Likely some government types will get involved, they always do. And they…" He trailed off, coming to the same realization I had days before. "You and Wendy. They will want to confirm your abilities, test you. We'll be lucky if all three of us don't end up locked away in some government lab."

"And I can't let that happen," I said. "Jacob is gone. Wendy is all I have now and I won't let her become someone's experiment. Do you understand?"

"We can protect you," he said without conviction. "We'll go to the press first, break the story before anyone else has to know."

I shook my head. "Promise me. Promise me that this will remain our secret."

He studied my face as I watched a war wage behind his eyes. Finally, he hung his head. "Very well. I will keep your secret." At that moment, he meant it. I could feel it. The pain of surrendering the culmination of his dreams radiating off him. He wouldn't talk now, but in a year? In two? He wasn't that strong. I knew it, and maybe he did, too.

Still, I smiled graciously. "Thank you."

"What about Carl's mother? What do we tell her?"

"I'll tell Tracy, in as much detail as I can. Just leave it to me."

Looking a decade older than he had only a few days ago, he sighed deeply. "I understand."

That night, while the professor slept, I found a couple cans of kerosene in one of the supply sheds and spread it across the floor of each cabin, dumping extra in the breeder pen. In one of the largest cabins I found Astra's bed, a nest of comforters and well-loved pillows, all smelling of lilacs. There, on her bedside table, sat a pair of hand-knitted baby socks with Wendy's name stitched on the bottom. I took those, doused the rest. Doused the cars, too. Hanson's cruiser, Friend's truck, saving only Jacob's pickup, still parked alongside the other camp cars ever since my abduction.

Once the professor had woken and climbed into the passenger seat of the truck, I sparked the flame and watched it race like burning snakes through every doorway.

As the flames consumed Friend's village, I felt nothing. No joy, no triumph, just a soul sickness that ran to my core.

I sucked in a breath, clutched Wendy to my chest, and walked to the idling truck. As the tires crunched over gravel and we headed for the road that would take us down the mountain, I looked back only once. A column of black smoke stretched to the heavens, creating a thick black scar on the sky.

We went to the house on Strawberry Lane first, where the professor helped me pack a few bags. Every room contained memories; some bad, mostly good, and all painful. We buried Indrid and the others Jacob had killed in the garden, the last thing I'd ever plant there. Then, standing on the front porch, we said our goodbyes.

"If you ever need anything," the professor said, holding out his card, "please do call. I want you to know, this was never just academic for me. I wanted to help your family. I'm so sorry that I wasn't enough."

I smiled, took his card, then his hand. "You did all you could. Thank you, Professor. And I'm sorry."

He blinked, confused. "For what, dear?"

I reached into his mind. His body went rigid, and his eyes rolled back in their sockets. I found the memories of his visit to our house, the long night of hypnosis and coffee, The Light, his journey to the mountain, and wiped it all away. Next, I left him with something new: a memory of coming to visit his old friend Carl and finding him gone. And also of a harrowing late night encounter with a roadside mugger who had shot his fingers off and driven him into the woods where he hid, then spent days trying to find his way out.

When his eyes rolled back and he looked at me, it was with the confusion of a stranger. "OK, then. Sorry to bother you, miss. I'll – I'll be going. I suppose I should find a hospital?" He left without waiting for an answer and stumbled to his car like a drunkard, quickly vanishing up the road without another word.

Within five minutes, I was in Jacob's truck with Wendy sitting in her car seat behind me as I pointed us toward town and the larger world beyond. I would stop by Astrological to see Tracy on my way through Victor's Point and somehow explain what had happened to Carl. His mother deserved at least a version of the truth.

I looked back at the little house on Strawberry Lane as it vanished into the rear view and noticed the pulsing ball of white light that hovered in the sky above it.

We will meet again, The Light said in my mind, and again came the image of that long road stretched out before me into an uncertain darkness.

Yes, I thought, maybe I would walk that road. But not today, not now. Right now, I had a lot of mourning to do, a new home to find, and a daughter to raise.

Together, we turned toward the sun and let it guide our way.

ABOUT THE AUTHOR

Nick lives in Michigan with his wonderful wife, Kelsey, crazy dog, and two morally questionable cats. He is a graduate of the Central Michigan University's creative writing master's program, and his work has appeared in *1029, Tenemos,* and *F(r)iction* magazines. When not writing, working, or bothering his wife, he spends his days reading about UFOs and slipping slowly into madness.